CLARAH

THE CURSE OF BEGRUDGERY

BY SHEILA MUGHAL

THE PROPHESY OF TAMAR SERIES

BOOK 3 IN THE SERIES

2nd Edition

Published August 2017

AspirelNation

www.sheilamughal.com

Twitter - @LinesTamar   Facebook @ClarahBegrudgery

Sheila Mughal

Dedicated to some wonderful friends, readers & reviewers.

Apologies to any reviewers I have missed from this list, and/or incorrect spellings. If you can email me your name. I will be sure to add you to a later edition - Sheila_mughal_author@mail.com

With special thanks to: -

Peter Granville & wife - Lesley & Brian Norris – Susie Barker - Jayne Shufflebotham - Barbara Robinson - JR- Dori Thomas Peaple - Gillian Eckersley –Jill Bruce - Ann-Veronica Howitt - Julie Pugh - Sharmillah Gardner - Sandra Waterworth - Dr Donna Allison - Sandra Geraghty - Merilyn Selwyn - Mary Halliwell - Kay Ashton - Tommy Jackson - Dr John Turner -Colin Norris Jane Ansell - Annette B – Louise Beacock – M Pars Julie, Malcolm & Laura Walton, John-Paul Yates, Jean Donagain, Wendy Norris, Paul Fox, John & Karen Wright, Trevor Burtonwood, Jack Orchison…plus…

all the other readers whom I may or may not know personally, but whose encouragement & complements have not gone unnoticed.

Clarah

Acknowledgments

The Prophesy of Tamar…is a series of books that belong to the genre of science-fiction and fantasy. Welcome to my world of make-believe.

However, despite entering the realm of fiction, the various story lines, *(which are all interconnected)*, have been crafted from a modicum of historical fact. I have merely taken the creative liberty of bringing an old story into the 21st century, and sprinkling a liberal dose of imagination onto the existing mythology. I hope that a scattering of fairy dust on some of these ancient legends and theories, will shimmer brighter than layers of historical dust.

These are modern tales, not biblical extracts. The books refer to contemporary issues, beliefs and challenges we can all relate to in our modern-day world. Expect new, not antique.

Between the years of 1365 and 2034, a series of events tie a group of characters together in a most unusual way. The series delivers a definite beginning and then a mind-blowing outcome, but not necessarily in chronological order.

In true science-fiction style, the three books introduce a whole set of thought-provoking conspiracy theories.

Sheila Mughal

You will be taken on a journey

Expect to laugh and expect to cry. Some scenarios will come as a surprise, some as a shock and much of it will make you wonder, and yes- there is some humour.

Expect to read about aliens, demons, angels, ghosts, time-travel, love, hate, destiny, murder, birth, magic, science, gothic mansions, secret tunnels and all things paranormal.

Expect to ponder the origins of mankind, the concept of pre-defined fate and just about every distortion of universal laws.

Expect some international travel - my nomadic tales like to wander around the planet and I love to describe the native scenery in exquisite detail.

Expect to think and be prepared to come along for the ride. Some of the story lines are complex and some slow-burning, but your patience will be rewarded.

Expect to read between the lines – there are a multitude of concealed messages hidden within the words.

Expect the unexpected and you won't be disappointed.

Expect to be entertained – after all, escapism into a world of make-believe is why we watch films, listen to music and mostly…why we read.

The books are a series, and are best consumed as a whole. However, they convey three very different storylines and so can also stand alone on a bookshelf and be read independently. I hope you enjoy the journey…

New to the series?
Then read a brief about the other books.

"THE LINES OF TAMAR" - Tamar did exist, and in fact she is an ancestor of mine and many thousands of others. She turns up in Genesis 38, when she became somewhat of an infamous lady. She pretended to be a prostitute in order to become impregnated by a king. Daring…yes, but she wanted to ensure that her genes were passed forwards into the future and she was willing to do whatever it took. Read the book of Genesis if you want more specifics.

Tamar's belief in her own DNA was indeed verified, when one of her twin sons became the start of a lineage that could boast an impressive line of descent. Not wanting to name drop, but try King David, King Solomon, Mary, Joseph and Jesus. As families go, you can't get more noble or divine. It is widely believed that her other twin son (Zarah) and his family left the holy lands and set sail for Ireland. The legend of the red cord/red hand of Ulster and the ancient hieroglyphics at County Meath, all evidence the fact that people from the Holy Lands travelled to Western Europe. Indeed, many of the royal houses of Europe can trace their ancestry back to Zarah.

Sheila Mughal

The storyline within "The Lines of Tamar" mainly takes place during the years of 2013/14. It diverts away from the well-known male twins of Tamar, and instead tells a tale of Tamar's fictitious twin girls, Leda and Sheol. Their birth heralds a strange line of descent; female twins born throughout millennia and existing only to carry Tamar's unique genetic code into the future. They are a much-revered line of clones. But what was so special about Tamar's DNA? Why do angels try to protect it and demons attempt to destroy it? Why does a global cult endeavour to manipulate lives, travel continents and surrender their existence to protect this lineage of Tamar clones? What makes their chromosomes so unique and special? I promise that you will get to find out…

"THE UNBEKNOWN" – is a totally different storyline, but it is connected and many of the characters from book 1 make a welcome reappearance. Urban myth has it, that in 1793, four young boys became lost in a vast myriad of underground caverns and tunnels. They are known as Crank caves and these caves really do exist. They can be located near Rainford, England. This is a true story, in that the boys became disoriented and confused in the dark underground maze. Only one child escaped. The child's frightening tale of what he encountered in the deepest darkest pits of the earth became entrenched in local folklore. The cave entrances were deliberately sealed up. Some believed that this was not so much to keep inquisitive young explorers out, but rather to keep something in.

Centuries later; this strange subterranean world was exposed to the stark light of the 21st century. Moving forward to 2011 and the main character is a stage magician called Soul; a troubled young man who was born with a rare clairsentience ability. He can connect with energy from inanimate objects, and read into their past as easily as we could read a newspaper. However, he makes his living by being on stage and entertaining people with illusions & trickery, often suppressing his natural magical abilities. Soul is hired by a secretive group of investors to find out what is trapped deep inside Crank caverns. He then becomes pulled into the strange world of a lost civilization – beings who have been here for millennia. Some walk among us as humans, whilst others are buried underground. All these beings really desire, is to escape earth and return home. However, they need the help of someone who can connect with their energy. Soul happens to be that person. As such he is pushed unwillingly into a very strange rescue mission.

Sheila Mughal

"CLARAH – THE CURSE OF BEGRUDGERY"

Welcome to the third book in the series. The story line differs from its older paper siblings, yet for those of you who have read both books, it contains common threads, known places and familiar characters. Welcome back to the strange mansion known as Darwydden and the demonic foursome who strive to break through its invisible borders.

Clarah has an Irish tinker father, and a true-blood Romany mother. She lives with a Gypsy vitsa - a community that collectively travel the North Yorkshire circuit. Clarah is different from her female contemporaries. Often described affectionately as a feral kitten, she shuns their world of fake tans, false eyelashes and acrylic nails. Clarah had no need for superficial glamour. She is gutsy, out-spoken, feisty, yet humorous. Expect occasional comedy in this strange tale.

Set between 2014 to 2016, this is a modern-day story of prejudice, abuse, betrayal, jealousy, crime, murder, hauntings, superstition, witchcraft, alien worlds, creatures from the devic kingdom and stomach crunching bigotry.

This is also a tale about the concept of pre-determined destiny. Does such a thing exist, can it be changed, and if so, what are the consequences?

Six numbers on a lottery ticket change the lives of Clarah's Gypsy family, however their lives do not change for the betterment. As misfortune and tragedy beset them, they blame the evil eye of jealous onlookers and the curse of begrudgery. Fearing yet more unwanted consequences of their new fortune, the travellers leave the sanctuary of their close-knit vitsa, and settle amongst the gaje, *(the non-Gypsy community of settlers)*. However, things are not as they seem, being neither real or imaginary. Clarah finds herself in a strange realm of existence. Science fiction now kicks in with a hard-supernatural punch.

Caught in the limbo of a humdrum world, a single event changes the entire course of Clarah's life. This event alters her destiny to such a profound degree, that it also alters the course of humanity and worlds beyond worlds.

This story challenges the concept of time travel, causal loops and questions the theory of a predestination paradox. It quizzes the validity of the free will versus a fate set before birth. Are we really all bar coded for a preordained life?

What Clarah then becomes, will enter the realm of the super-extraordinary. Who Clarah then meets, enters the dominion of the super-impossible. What Clarah then does, is beyond the imagination. The question is – will Clarah ever return to just being Clarah, and if she does, at what cost?

To pour oil on water, she is also tangled up with the enigmatic prophesy of Tamar, so the decisions she makes are not just life changing, but history changing.

Sheila Mughal

Will the fuzzy laws of quantum physics give Clarah back to herself? It is a conundrum. She sleeps unaware of the clarion call.

Clarah

CHAPTER 1

Saturday July 12th 2014
THE GYPSY CAMP IN SCARBOROUGH

The air had a toxic smoky flavour. The lads had been burning damp logs and thrown both paraffin and plastics onto the offensive flames. The resulting alchemy covered the camp with a noxious cloud.

The travellers had pitched their vans on a rectangular strip of common land. Mick remembered that it had once served as a rugby pitch, back in the days when the locals cared about such things. Now overgrown with reeds and bog plants, it served no real purpose anymore. The Gypsies seemed to be doing no harm. They were simply using what the town's folk had made redundant. None the less, the clock was ticking and it wouldn't be long before someone accused them of breaching the peace. Freedom of the road was always a double-edged sword in the traveller world, and the police or bailiffs were only ever a heartbeat away.

Kane sat away from the younger boys. He crouched down; partially perched on an old tyre and sucking hard on his spliff. It was a full moon, and despite the smouldering air, a clear star-spangled sky provided a breath-taking canvas. Kane could see the shadows of the younger lads as they frolicked in the distance. He observed the macho rivalry of the youngster's through marijuana dazed eyes. Only a few years ago, he had been one of them. Fuelled by testosterone and the bravado of adolescence, they tussled for hierarchical dominance amongst their peers.

Kane laughed inwardly as he observed their antics. 'Bunch of bloody fuckin gorillas,' he mumbled to himself, spitting gum on the floor as though spitting out his contempt.

Kane wasn't as hard as the other lads. He lacked their muscular bulk and arrogant swagger. None the less, he had an inner strength that none could match, and a brain which was borderline genius. As such, the debauch behaviour and cheeky affronts of the traveller youths, failed to impress or shock him. Kane certainly wasn't a fist fighter. However, he was respected by his male contemporaries, because nobody could beat him at polka or backgammon. They could cheat as much as they liked, but only his father Mick was a match for young Kane. He was a king amongst gamblers, and try as they may, none of the scrappers could push him off that throne.

After chain smoking his way through too many illegal ciggies, Kane was in a fuzzy world of his own. A few shots of cheap Vodka only served to dull his brain even further.

To begin with the noises swam around in his head. The din was muffled, but as it became clearer he noticed that the laughter was now followed by screams - heart-rendering cries for help. He could tell by the tones of the voices, that the young lads were taunting someone.

It was dusk; that time of the day when objects morph into shadows, and when things once clear become dark and obscure. In the smoky haze, he could only make out distant silhouettes, but he knew something was happening. Without hearing the exact words, he could tell that they were teasing someone, and he guessed that their gibes would be brutal and cuttingly cruel. He had heard their bullying abuse many times before. They sniggered amongst themselves. They found it entertaining - whatever it was that they were doing.

Kane tried to ignore them. The lad wasn't a fighter. He wasn't a part of their callous world. Some deeper instinct told him to intervene, but he ignored it. He vindicated his actions with a slug of cheap cider, and he walked away. Whoever it was, would have to take care of themselves. This was the harsh reality of life, in an ecosystem that didn't take prisoners. He stumped out what was left of his roll-up and walked away. He walked and walked and he didn't look back, abandoning the screams and laughter with cold disregard.

Kane looked at all the lights in all the tiny windows. All he cared about was finding the caravan that belonged to him. Where was the van with the narcotics; the forbidden Horlicks to lull him into a chemically induced sleep? All that mattered was shutting out the sounds of screams and mocking laughter. But he knew. He knew that no matter what, he couldn't shut out the sounds from inside his head. The voice that was telling him that he shouldn't have walked away. Someone out there – someone in the distance, was a victim, and he had turned his back, leaving them to fight their own fight. Too late- he had already convinced himself that their destiny was not his responsibility. Such was the nature of life on the camp, and like a seasoned psychopath, he distanced himself from any emotion.

Kane then tripped up. It was like a karmic untying of his shoe laces. The light was dim and the common-land was full of tiny ponds. He fell headlong into a stinking boggy hole hidden in the earth. It was only shallow, yet it covered him with reeds and jellied tadpole spawn. He spluttered as he partially choked on the green algae tinted water. He pulled himself out of the mud, cursing as he wrenched his sodden body up the embankment. He knew the fall was his prikaza; *(Romany for bad fortune*), for deserting someone in trouble. His hands grabbed hold of some bull rushes and he heaved himself up with all his might. He was stoned; spaced out on booze and skunk. His hands were cold, wet and slippery. The bull-rushes did not want to cooperate with his rescue, and as though they had an intelligence of their own, they rejected his grasping fingers.

With hypothermia now threatening his consciousness, his befuddled mind started to play tricks. A slender female hand clasped at his wrist and started to pull him onto the bank. Looking upwards with gunk laden eyelashes, he could only make out a scarlet cloaked figure. In his hallucinatory state, he imagined this to be the ghost of a female pirate. Kane had never been a man of great instinct; but in his blood- this is what he felt. The stagnant aroma of skulduggery and rum, mixed with cheap perfume… enveloped his drowning body.

At that precise moment, he felt less like he was being rescued, and more that he was being pulled into hell; dragged into the pits of death by one who had come to collect him. Indeed, his redeemer was strong, and one with fingernails as long and as red as demonic talons.

***

Mick and Violet felt numb as they stared at the numbers in their new bank accounts. They should have both been ecstatic, elated, thrilled and maybe even euphoric…but Violet looked worried.

'My God Mick, how can we share this with the Vitsa? It will change everyone's life, and for some, it won't be for the better. There are those who will buy shiny new cars, and others that will drink and gamble it all away.'

'Like Kane, you mean.' Mick glanced over at his wife with a heavy look of disappointment etched on his face. He had never come to terms with the reality that his only son; a bright and articulate boy – had sunk to the depths he had. Violet ignored the comment.

She continued, 'it will divide us all; I know it will. We should leave it in the bank and take our time to decide. Tis a blessing in disguise Mick. It could bring upon the evil eye.'

Her husband Mick understood exactly what she was driving at.

'If we don't share it, what happens then Violet? We won't be liked. We won't be tolerated. Family and friends will turn against us. We will be out on our own in a world we don't understand. The gaje will never accept our kind. Our type sticks together, you know that love. Can we cope with being on the outside? Can we turn into settlers, because that's what all these big fat zeros' will buy us Violet?' A big house in the settler's world.'

Mick sighed as he looked around their cramped caravan. He raised his hands in the air and exclaimed, 'this is all we know. My God, this is a strange baxt to consider at our stage in life Violet.'

The couple were in the midst of an unusual debate. A numerical gift had created more questions than answers, and more problems than solutions. It was a nice problem to have, but right now it felt like a moral conundrum.

They each took it in turn to sigh and take a sip of tea.

'I need something stronger,' announced Mick as he rummaged in the cupboards for the whisky bottle. He didn't normally drink strong spirits, so this requirement was far from usual and so the bottle hard to find. Eventually he located it at the far back of the cupboard, hidden behind tins of beans and chicken soup.

Mick was a good man. He wasn't a full Roma like his wife, but Violet liked that about him. She had met him at the Appleby horse fair, and instantly fell in love with his Irish brogue and Celtic charm. Sure, she had married a hedgecrawler and for many years the clan condemned her for that, but she tolerated their name-calling and raised her four children the Roma way. However, she hadn't forgotten how the true bloods had treated her new tinker husband, and now that she had money – she saw no reason why she should share it with anyone other than her sister, mother and children.

Violet glanced out of the window to the neighbouring caravan, and looked pitifully upon her sister Mary. With painful arthritic hips, she struggled to make her legs lift high enough, to reach the steps to the van. Violet caught the grimace on her twisted face, as each movement brought searing pain.

She turned to her husband, 'money would make a difference to our Mary,' she announced. 'I could buy her new hips and posh private medical treatment. I could get her one of those devices that lift her up and down a staircase. She could live in a proper house with heating, so the dampness of winter doesn't chill her bones and turn her joints into blocks of ice. The money would change her life Mick.'

They looked at each other in silence. It was that knowing nonverbal communication; the psychic messages that long married couples often share.

Violet felt so sorry for her sister. God had not blessed her with children and her husband had died ten or so years ago in a road accident. Sure, she was happy enough living with their mother "Baba May" …but none the less – she was a woman alone in a man's world. Mary's body was racked with a disease that had ravaged her youth and contorted her limbs. Without her elderly mother as her nurse and carer, Mary would not have survived. The traveller life was hard enough on the young and able bodied, but it could be pure torture for the old and fragile. Poor Mary. Two words Violet had whispered to herself many a time.

Mick knocked back his second whisky and scratched his balding head. He was a tough man and a hard worker. He had worked since he was ten years old and never seen a day's unemployment or taken time off sick. He may have been illiterate, but he always earned and he earned well. He had laid tarmac, put up scaffolding, sold on doorsteps, repaired roofs and then eventually set up his own scrap metal business. Because of his work commitments, he wasn't able to roam too far from his yard. So, his family had formed a four-month route which took them in a small circuit around his enclosure. For Mick and his family, it was a challenge just being consistent. The local gaje would soon get to know their route and block off any field they had used before. It was hard living the traveller life. The only time Mick took a break from working, was when they visited the horse fair. The gypsies on the same circuit had all bonded with each other. Some were related and some weren't. Some were Irish, some Roma and many of mixed blood. None the less the vitsa were a tightly knit community. As far as Mick was concerned, he was more forgiving than his wife. In his eyes, the closeness they shared with each other as a community, made the decision all the harder.

'Anyway, 'continued Violet, 'our children all have nice new bank accounts now and they each have £500,000 deposited in them. That gives us £7.2 million to play around with Mick. Maybe we could give each family in the vitsa a couple of thousand to shut them up.'

Mick looked at his wife with disbelief and disdain. He couldn't understand why she was acting so mean.

He threw his hands up in the air and asked, 'why Violet? Why after all these years do you still hold a grudge against the way you were once treated for marrying a non-Roma? It was a long time ago…25 years or so. Can.t you just forgive? Some of their caravans are falling apart. We can afford to give them all more than just a few thousand each and you know we can. For Christ's sake woman, we have won more money than we will ever know how to spend in our lifetime. Its money that could help out our friends and cousins.'

Violet was not listening. The resentment she held against them had rooted itself too deep. As far as she was concerned, she had an elderly mother, a physically disabled sister, and a mentally disabled daughter – all of whom she felt responsible for. Not to mention a wayward alcoholic son, two other daughters and baby grandchildren. Her loyalty was for them and not for the community that had given her years of harassment.

'For now, let's watch some telly and go brain dead,' suggested Violet. She had grown tired of the money debate and didn't want to discuss the matter any further.

She continued, 'Clarah will be back soon and we should talk this over with her. She is part of this decision, and so is Kane, Katalyn, my sister Mary and Baba May. We will discuss what to do with the money as a family Mick.'

Mick stood up to replace the whisky bottle in the cupboard, agreeing with his wife.

'In that case, let me put this away. Better keep a clear head if we are debating how to spend a few million pounds.' He then moved over to the door adding, 'on the subject of our children, where is Nina. I haven't seen her since she went to the pond to catch frogs or tadpoles or whatever it is she thinks she is doing in that strange little head of hers.'

Nina was a peculiar girl. She was 20 years old, looked closer to 15, but inside her head probably had the intelligence of a 7-year-old. She was a pretty child with the purest of souls; one who was always smiling and singing. She lived in a world of imaginary friends and unheard voices. Voices which whispered secrets in her childlike ears. Sometimes the voices took over and changed her. Most of the vitsa were highly protective of Nina, but some could be cruel and would taunt her. Her father was constantly on his guard. Their world was a double-edged sword – brutal yet caring at the same time.

Mick glanced at his watch and began to look worried. 'It's getting dark Violet– I better go out and find where she is.'

As he opened the door, their barely conscious daughter fell into the caravan. Violet screamed out in shock. They both stood as though paralysed for a moment. Violet moaned out in horror.

'She yelled, 'my God, Nina – who has done this to you?'

The maternal cry of anguish could be heard around the campsite. They each pulled their daughters muddied body into the caravan. Their daughter had been stripped to the waist and her bare breast were covered with mud stained handprints. Her slim tummy bore the mark of one single footprint. The outside of the caravan door was also stained with Nina's bloody handprints, as her desperate plea to be let in had gone unheard. Her bashing at the door must have been too soft, knuckles weakened by her tortured frame. Her father didn't know what to say. They dragged her onto to the couch. His daughter's eyes flickered, but there was little life behind them. Blood poured from an open wound on her head. Cord marks were visible on her wrists, as though she had been tied up and hung by her arms.

Violet gagged as the vomit rose inside her throat. Trying hard not to throw up she exclaimed, 'my God Mick, her white skirt is stained with green phlegm. The monster who has done this to our child, has been spitting at her.'

Micks eyes welled with a mixture of tears and anger. 'Call for an ambulance,' he instructed his wife. 'No need to involve the police – I will find who has done this. Shame on them for picking on a vulnerable young girl. Shame on them, shame on them – the bastards.'

Maybe for the first time and the last time in his life, he cried. He turned to his wife and roared, 'make it quick Violet. Call the ambulance first, then find Kane, Katalyn, Clarah, Baba May; call everyone on this bloody fucked-up shitty camp site. Get them here. Get them now. I want answers.'

He wept as he spoke. His wife had never seen him shed tears before. The scene was horrific. Violet trembled as her young daughter gasped for breath. She grabbed her mobile phone and did as her husband instructed.

Her last words to her husband as he left the caravan being, 'don't do anything stupid Mick.' She knew her request would fall upon deaf ears. He banged the caravan door shut, and upon that action many fates had been sealed. Nothing would ever be the same again.

It started to rain. The camp site was muddy, messy, chaotic. Violet could smell the fear and anger in the damp air. The caravan window had misted up with the heavy breathing of anxiety. She wiped it clear to see where her husband was heading. His destination mattered not. She knew that nothing good would come of this evening. Just an hour earlier life had seemed to be full of promise, but now hope had been replaced by despair. Soggy, putrid, bloodstained despair.

CHAPTER 2

Wednesday 5th August 2015
BALI, INDONESIA & PURE ESCAPISM

Looking out at the infinity pool from his deckchair, it was hard to distinguish where the pool ended and the sea began. The water seemed to merge into one, with only the slightest ripple of a wave identifying the Indian ocean from its chlorinated partner. The most exquisite of purple sunsets cast its lilac palette upon the beach, whilst only the mauve silhouettes of palm trees interrupted the line of the lavender horizon.

Konnor Baratolli stretched out his youthful aching limbs, happy to have escaped the manual labour of his uncle Alan's sheep station. As he sipped upon a chilled tumbler of Singapore Sling, he silently hoped that the Mount Raung volcano would spew out more of its flight delaying ash. Whilst on his back-packing adventures around Asia, he had tried hard to forget USC and the beginning of the fall semester. He so longed to be like his older brother Asher, who had finished collage and could now wander the globe with wanton abandon. Law tutorials seemed some zillion miles away from this Indonesian slice of paradise. Konnor tried not to think about it. He closed his eyes and yawned, resigned to enjoy himself with what little of his summer vacation was left to enjoy.

Just as Konnor began to fall into a deep state of relaxation, his older brother collapsed alongside him.

Out of breath he gasped, 'man, I have just run up the steps from the beach. I must be one fuckin crazy psycho dude. You know where I am talking about don't you. They are carved into the limestone crevice next to the bridge. Shit they are steep.' Asher stopped talking whilst trying to catch his breath, lying flat out on the deck like a starfish.

Konnor sat up and looked over to his brother with bemusement, admiration and just a tiny smidgeon of jealousy.

'Why didn't you take the funicular,' he asked. 'That's a bloody steep cliff. I am surprised you attempted it bro.'

Of course, Konnor recognised that his brother was a fitness freak and would do anything to keep his well-honed body in peak physical condition. Asher was a younger version of his father Reed; with deep emerald eyes and mocha brown kiss curls, now clinging beguilingly to his sweaty forehead. His thick tresses framed his sand-kissed face like a Renaissance painting. He was quite the playboy; affluent, charismatic and almost too pretty for a lad. Charm oozed from every pore of his wilting muscular frame.

'Where's your girlfriend?' asked Asher, still out of breath and not overly concerned with the answer. He didn't really like Clarah. He was just being polite and Konnor knew it. Konnor didn't care what his brother thought. He had met the girl in Cambodia and she had been a good companion. Sure, she wasn't sophisticated and was a little rough around the edges, but Clarah was funny and she made him laugh. He liked the fact that she wasn't up her own backside, unlike the stuck-up valley girls back in LA. Yet as much as she cajoled him with her earthy humour, he recognised a deep sadness behind her eyes. Life had wounded her in some way, but he had known not to pry.

Konnor was nothing at all like his sibling. Sure, they had been born from the same loins, and indeed the younger boy had inherited his mother Julia's show-girl looks, with his feral blonde locks and surfer-dude smile. However, he was also warm, attentive and the family court jester. With far more advanced social skills than his older siblings, he was always the one who asked about everyone else, yet not one to ever talk about himself. With his soothing manner and imperceptible interview technique, Reed was sure that his youngest would make an excellent lawyer. So, following on from the demise of his music company, Reed went back to New York to start his homeless charity, and packed Konnor off to the Gould School of Law. It was a place now awaiting Konnor's reluctant return.

Asher pulled himself out of the pool following on from about 20 laps of the butterfly stroke. Dabbing his tanned frame down with a fluffy white hotel towel, he sat next to his brother, stealing a sip of his Singapore Sling. He then caught the attention of the waiter and shouted out for a Yogurt Soju.

'So, what's the deal with the girl when you fly home tomorrow?' he asked. Konnor hated the fact that Asher kept demeaning his companion by referring to her as some unnamed girl.

'Stop that,' Konnor responded. 'You know very well that her name is Clarah, and I was sort of hoping that you would keep an eye on her after I fly back.'

Asher nearly chocked on the Yogurt Soju which had just been deposited carefully into his hand.

'No way man. That girl is trouble. I am surprised you are too spellbound to see it,' he replied.

Feeling affronted Konnor sat up to face his brother and asked, 'what the hell do you mean by that. Why should Clarah be trouble?'

Asher looked at his younger sibling as though he was a toddler about to take his first roller-coaster ride. 'Seriously Kon? You mean you haven't figured out that there is something very strange about your new girlfriend. I mean, she talks, she dresses and she acts, like someone who has just been thrown out of a wild-west saloon bar and fallen into the garbage. Trailer trash and yet she has money and lots of it- more than you I can bet. She has travelled the world and stayed in all the best places. I mean… don't you find that a bit odd given that she….' Asher was about to be incredibly insulting, so he didn't finish his sentence. He simply shook his head in disbelief of his brother's naivety.

Konnor picked up the sentence, 'given that she was working in the stables at Uncle Alans farm in Queensland. Is that what you were about to say? Working Ash. She was working. She isn't afraid to earn money. She has worked, saved, backpacked and then worked some more – just as you and I have. Why are you making all of this sound so…criminal? What do you think she is? Some Columbian drug baron or a great train robber?'

'No, I am not saying that at all Kon, 'he replied. 'I am just saying that something doesn't fit. When we were all working out at the sheep station, a detective came to question Uncle Alan. It seems that Clarah has gone walkabout from home and her family want her back. Look, I know she is not a kid, but for whatever reason this girl has run away from something. Even you said that when you were in Cambodia, she was always looking over her shoulder. Always paranoid about being followed. Am I lying Konnor?'

The younger brother shrugged his shoulders. He knew Asher was telling the truth. He changed the subject.

'Hey, I had better go and pack. I will catch up with you later. I have booked a table over at the Pavilion tonight. 8pm, if you care to join us?'

Asher nodded, 'nope it's okay Bro. It's your last night with your girlfriend, so I am sure you guys will want to be alone. Don't forget the candlelight and roses. Where is she by the way?'

Konnor was already gathering his things to walk back to his room, 'oh, you mean Clarah. She has been over at the spa all afternoon. She booked a papaya enzyme wrapsutilize, whatever that is, along with a Javanese body scrub and some massage that involves putting volcanic stones on the chakras. Pampering Balinese style. Sounds great.'

'Hmm,' mumbled Asher. 'I bet those treatments don't come cheap.'

Konnor shot Asher a look of contempt. 'Stop it,' he commanded.

Ignoring his brother's sarcasm, Konnor turned to walk back through the hotels tropical gardens. He soon reached his thatched sea-view villa. Before walking inside, Konnor sat on the steps and took a moment to sit and think. Darkness had fallen, but his villa was awash with exotic golden light. Red Chinese lanterns swung in the trees and candles had been lit and placed carefully along the parameters of his decking. From somewhere in the distance he could hear traditional gamelan music and the eerie tones of bamboo flutes. He looked out at the Indian Ocean, watching the lights of the fishing boats as they bobbed up and down on the waves. Chimes jingled in a gentle breeze, and the aroma of patchouli incense wafted in his direction. This place truly was paradise and he would miss it. The surf, the talcum powder sand, the amazing coral that grew in warm turquoise waters. It had been a magical experience and one he would never forget. It was distraction he needed after the recent catastrophes in the Baratolli household.

His step-mother Eenayah came to his mind, and like a million times before he wondered where she was in the world, and if she would ever be found. Missing presumed dead; it didn't sound right. He couldn't allow his mind to go there.

He then thought about Clarah. Aside from her bleached blond braids, she had a look of Eenayah. Asher had even joked about their similarity, accusing Konnor of having some sort of repressed Oedipus complex. He shivered. He hadn't found the joke in any way amusing. Asher could be cruel sometimes, but he did have a point. The two women's facial features were strikingly similar. What did it matter? Tomorrow he was going home and he didn't know if he would ever see Clarah again. He had hoped so, but in his heart, he doubted it. Perhaps all this relationship had ever been was just some summer romance. Like all such flitting affairs, it had been built on a bedrock of sea, sand and escapism; just waiting for the stark light of rainy-day reality to wash the passion away. It wasn't what he wanted, but he knew that his world back at USC, *(University of Southern California),* was one that involved his snooty academic friends, and their well-connected parents. He suspected that his world was poles apart from Clarah's wind-swept Yorkshire. Backpacking had been a great social leveller. Dust, dehydration and squatting to take a dump, had made all of them equal…but away from that carefree nomadic existence- reality was a wakeup call.

As he sat on the steps, chin cupped in hands, deep in thought, Clarah watched him. She had been hiding behind a large Bougainvillea bush. As she quietly observed him, she knew what was going through his head. After all, her grandmother Baba May was a Romany witch and one cannot be the granddaughter of a witch, without inheriting some psychic abilities. However, Clarah recognised that on this occasion, it was more common sense and not so much telepathy that made her see the truth for what it was. The magical moment of escapism was ending, and perhaps now it was time for her think about heading home. She knew that something terrible had happened back in England. The head in the sand technique had been a welcome, but temporary panacea. Clarah had avoided the truth for too long – a year to be exact. She had paid to stay in her luxury hideaway until September, and despite her new wealth, she still couldn't walk away from something she had paid upfront for. A lottery win could take the girl out of the caravan, but never remove the caravan psyche from out of the girl. Her mind had been made up – a few more weeks in paradise and then she would also head for home. She wasn't sure where home was anymore – but she would find it. Baba May would reel her in as though she was hooked onto some psychic fishing line. Her grandmother had probably been watching her through some Romany crystal ball all along. She was sure of that.

She mentally said goodbye to Konnor and then perched herself on the steps next to him. She put a friendly arm around his shoulder. Just friendly – nothing more. In total silence, they both sat and watched the ships in the ocean as they passed each other by. The irony of the passing ships had not gone unnoticed.

CHAPTER 3

Thursday 24th September 2015
HOME AT LAST – WHITBY ENGLAND

Her eyes tried to open, but they were stuck shut. Where was she? It felt as though someone had plunged a Samurai sword into her temples, leaving her with the worst headache of her life. Everything she saw in her mind's eye, was a murky shade of stinking rotting mud-brown. Clarah had fallen into some weird out-of-body experience. Maybe just an illusion, but one which was as real as anything that could ever be deemed as real. This wasn't a joyous trip into another realm; this was like being stuck someplace between heaven and hell…but probably closer to hell.

The vivid image lacked the romanticism of cinnamon glades and hickory forests carpeted with pecan caramel. In contrast to the promise of a fairy-tale chocolate box, the vision penetrating Clarah's Gypsy third eye, evoked a sense of perpetual gloom.

The sludge-coloured mountain hosted a wraparound pathway, which although inclining upwards, never actually delivered its passengers to the mountains apex. Weary travellers carried heavy loads upon their backs, struggling to walk uphill, only to find themselves back at the place they started. Clarah was amongst them; draped in rags and walking through an eternity where no colour existed - aside from shades of a nasty shit coloured secretion. Heaving a weight for no reason; going nowhere…achieving nothing. Not an ounce of meaning in what was already meaningless! Neither fiery brimstone or clouds of angel dust pervaded this scenario. This was limbo in its most futile nothingness. She concluded that this was what limbo must be – aimless, purposeless, directionless, nothingness. Just going around and around and around.

She gasped, as sleep apnoea forced an almighty snore to escape from her tonsils. Slowly the nightmarish image dispersed. A white light illuminated her retina, as consciousness flowed back into her brain, and blood pelted through her veins.

'Where am I', she gasped. 'Thank God, it was just a bad dream,' she uttered. She was no longer on the mountain and the infinite path that led to nowhere.

Clarah' s thoughts were muddled. She became aware of forward movement. She was in a car. Not just a normal car, but a stretch Limo. She was being driven by a man in uniform. She voiced her thoughts out-loud.

'Who are you? Why am I here? Where am I?' One minute she was on an aeroplane flying through French airspace and now she was – where was she?

The uniformed man, who she now knew to be a chauffeur, responded in a formal tone.

'Miss Clarah, my name is Tobiah and I am your driver. Your family asked me to collect you. I have just picked you up from the airport. I am taking you to the family home in Whitby. You are back in England. You have nothing to worry about. You are very tired. I understand from the flight attendants that you may have taken too many sleeping pills. They are probably still in your system, so you should stop trying to fight it, and try to get more rest. We have a long journey ahead, but I will deliver you soon.'

With that, the driver closed the dividing window and deactivated his microphone. He wasn't going to tell her anything more anytime soon. Tobiah wasn't in the mood for conversation. He had made that quite clear. He had a dull monotone voice anyway and Clarah instantly disliked him. She rubbed her bewildered forehead and sat in silence. She had no memory – no recollection of anything beyond the last few days in Bali. Ouch, her brow was sore to the touch. Since her driver had evaded all attempts at conversation, she drifted back into a troubled sleep.

A few hours later, her eyes opened again. Her body ached and her ribs hurt as though they had been broken. Her head was still swimming in an ocean of medication. Perhaps the chauffeur had been right. Maybe she had overdosed on sleeping tablets. It was frustrating to forget recent events aside from being driven to Ngurah Rai International Airport, waking up over France and then whoosh – nothing aside from the brown mountain nightmare. How could she have not have remembered revelling in the delights of the first class pamper zone?

Clarah slowly began to realise that she had recalled her crazy dream with greater clarity than the entire flight home. For a moment, she shuddered at the memory of walking in circles on that brown nothingness dump. Perhaps her memory would come back to her… once this life sucking tiredness had vacated her body. My God; she had never felt as weary or as sick as this…ever.

She then glanced at her watch; proud that it wasn't actually a fake. The shimmering diamond encrusted dial confirmed that it was very early in the morning – too early! 4.09am to be precise. Still, the watch looked good, and contrasted well against her long-tanned arm. 4.09 – was that Indonesian time or had her watch auto-corrected itself. She didn't know, nor did she care. Tiredness prevented her from paying too much attention to detail.

Suddenly becoming aware that the bling may look a touch too authentic, she covered it with the sleeves of the cardigan her Baba May had knitted for her. No point in arousing suspicion and attracting too many questions. High bling with a low profile – that was the paradoxical reality of a Gypsy girl's life.

Like many of the Roma clan, Clarah was a superstitious young lady; forever mindful of the "evil eye". Although she had just turned 21, she had already experienced the consequences of envy and what Baba May referred to as begrudgery. It seemed such a pity that a time-piece of such beauty could insight resentment. Yet Clarah knew exactly what it represented in the world she had come from. She was no longer in that world, but it was never very far away. Perhaps she should remove the watch!

The feathered dawn chorus was in full orchestral mode, as the limo wheels grated along the gravel driveway to her parent's new home. "Driveway", the word resonated in her head. She had never lived anywhere which had an actual driveway before. Her former world was that of a caravan parked somewhere…anywhere. It could be a field, a lay-by, a hidden space below a motorway bypass. The driveway from her old world, was usually wasteland filled with empty beer bottles, potholes, used condoms and cigarette stubs. Sometimes the younger lads would shit outside their tow-hitch so it would stink out her bedroom. They would find this funny. She hated the Gypsy lads and the way they thought they could grab her any time they wanted. She was her own person – not a piece of meat to be taken. She had an ambition that didn't involve a life of domestic drudgery.

Many of the vitsa girls welcomed the notion of motherhood, wifehood and eternally keeping a caravan clean. However, this had never been Clarah's ambition. She didn't disrespect their cultural aspirations. If anything, she deeply wished she could adhere to their norm Yet try as she may - she simply couldn't. Clarah knew she was different...and always had been. Like a moth attracted to a deadly flame, diversity was a lethal attraction and one that she longed to explore.

As the limo made its way up to her new front door, Clarah took a long deep breath of relief, realising that she had been saved. Lady luck had given her the chance to escape the hardship of a traveller existence. A life which had been destined to resemble the brown mountain of limbo. A world of shifting sands; pitching on site after site, only to be evicted and then ending up back at the same place a few months later. Groundhog Day- around and around and around. She had enjoyed that film and yet- she had become it. Clarah was fully aware of her good fortune, and was determined not to waste a promising future. However, first, she had to apologise to her family and that wasn't going to be easy.

The chauffeur zapped down his electronic passenger barrier.

'You are home now Miss.'

He courteously opened her door, holding out a leather gloved hand to help her out. He then removed a single yet large, backpack from the trunk. Unlike the majority of his female clientele, she had travelled light; that had surprised him...and yet not. For a moment, she caught a glimpse of his chiselled face, and thought he looked familiar.

Tobiah turned around quickly and lowered his cap, possibly before she could further scan his features. Few words were exchanged other than, 'I am told that the front door has been left open for you ma'am?'

Clarah simply nodded. Yes, she knew. Of course, she knew. Gypsy doors were seldom locked.

"Home" – that was also an alien word. Home to her was usually a temporary stopover; that was until the police appeared with an eviction notice to move her and her kind along. All this seemed another life time away, and yet it was only last year.

Clarah shivered at the memory. She pulled her mind away from her past, and took time to drink in her present.

As they approached her new home, the early morning mist partially covered the building like a shroud. Almost in jest, the curdling clouds seemed to be playing peek-a-boo. Beneath the white haze, she could just about make out the outline of her new abode. From what she could see, it was huge. Huge in her eyes.

'My God', she thought, 'Da has really gone to town with this.'

She offered to pay the driver in cash, even negotiating an overly generous tip – but he refused.

'Your family have taken care of it Ma'am,' was all he said.

Tobiah stood outside the car and watched her as she tried to make sense of where she was – his eyes not once making contact with hers. He had a long thin face, and wore sunglasses that were intended to keep out more than just the light. Personality shades; that was what her Granny Baba May would call them. Baba May had her own "made up words" for all sorts of things. She was a smart old lady, in a quirky and witchery sort of way.

Clarah attempted to delicately manoeuvre her heels across the gravel in silence. She was exhausted from the long-haul flight, and the last thing she wanted to do was wake the tribe and create an impromptu family gathering. She would endeavour to find out where her allocated room was, and put her weary limbs to bed. She took one last look back at the limo. Too late- it had already gone. Strange…she hadn't noticed the sound of tyre on gravel. Most odd – the car had seemed to almost vaporise.

Clarah found the door open as expected and tiptoed quietly upstairs with the soft foot placements of a mouse. It was a queer feeling – as though she was a thief who had broken into somebody else's home. She vaguely remembered a text telling her where her room was, and hoped that her memory served her well. Top of the stairs, turn left and hers was the door at the end of a long corridor. With each gingerly placed step, the floorboards creaked. She stood motionless and held her breath. The house was silent; everybody was asleep – good! She concluded that she would make an awesome cat- burglar, accept that she didn't need to be. With a huge stash of green notes tucked away in her bank account, Clarah had no necessity to beg, borrow or steal – not anymore. Life would be different now. She was a Roma girl made good.

After what seemed like a very long walk, she located a thin rectangular room that framed the end of the house. Any doubt of room ownership had been removed, since her sister Nina had created a massive "welcome home" poster and blue-tacked it onto the door. It was cute. Nina had decorated it in butterflies and flowers, with a sun poking out from behind a cloud. It was the innocent "colouring in" one would expect from a child; not a 21-year-old. But then again, Nina was not of average intelligence for her age. She had a loving trusting purity which Clarah had desperately missed. She was massively overly protective of Nina. She let out a guilty sigh…feeling sorry that she had abandoned her childlike sister for such a long time. It was a sigh from the heart and a timbre stained with remorse. Yet she knew Nina would forgive her, because Nina wouldn't understand enough not to. She understood it took a certain amount of IQ to truly hate, and Nina did not possess that.

Indeed, Clarah was far more fearful about how her parents would react to her home-coming. It was a fear she would finally have to face. After all, they had gone to the expense of hiring a detective agency to travel the world to find her, so surely, they would expect some sort of explanation. Why had she run away? They would want answers. How could she possibly tell them what Katalyn had done, or what she had seen that night in Scarborough? Some things should not be spoken of.

Refocussing on her new bedroom, she simply had to laugh out loud. Never to be accused of the sin of subtlety, her family had attached balloons around the inside door frame and wardrobe. It made her smile. Despite all their crazy idiosyncratic wiles; she had missed them. My God, she had missed them. Missed them so badly. Why had she ever left them? She must have had suffered some sort of crazy mental break down …surely?

Whatever abomination happened to her sister in the woods, was diabolically awful. Clarah didn't want to remember. She didn't want to know the gruesome details. She dared not think of it anymore. Her brain had shut down as many memories as it could, yet some survived.

She turned and closed the bedroom door, once again taking in the runway size passageway leading to her room. She replayed the word "corridor" in her mind for a few moments. She had been given the room at the end of the corridor. Clarah had never been at the end of any corridor before…. ever. It seemed odd to find herself in bricks and mortar, having lived on wheels and in fibreglass for her entire life.

Prior to her parents spending a quarter of their fortune on a listed manor house, she had headed for the airport and all those faraway exotic places she could once only dream about. Sleeping on plane seats, in hotel rooms and bunked up in various tents in Cambodia or Australian outhouses, she had so far avoided the whole domicile scenario. Clarah had achieved what the clever rich kids of settlers normally did – she had taken a gap year. Her vitsa cousins didn't do gap years.

Now here she was in a house, with a delegated room that had 3 windows. A room with 3 windows all to itself. 'Dear Lord, 3 bloody windows,' she whispered to herself. The tiny caravan room she shared with her sister Nina, only had one tiny plastic skylight and a bit of a hole cut into the fibreglass. The contrast both amazed and confused her.

She went to draw the curtains across each window in turn. The rear bowed window faced the sea. The light outside was still dim and hazy, but as she opened it for air, she could hear the waves crashing on the rocks below. It was a nice sound, and strangely reassuring. She knew that she could fall asleep forever, listening to the sound of the sea singing its lullaby. She would leave the window open and let the salty breeze kiss her to sleep. The serenade of the waves would become her new comfort blanket.

Moving over to the side window, a horizon of freshly ploughed fields provided a quintessential rural vista. She imagined that on a sunny day, the view would unfold and present a cascade of golden barley bowing in the breeze. However, right now; in the dim light of dawn, she saw little but an empty void… yet she had a great imagination. Clarah had already sketched a mental image of how the fields would present themselves against the back drop of a clear blue sky.

Finally pulling shut the floral curtains at the front, she noted the silhouette of a church in the near distance. Beyond the church, was the village that the limo driver had driven her through. She couldn't remember the name of it – but she noted its size and remoteness. A post-office, a couple of shops, a pub, a village green and of course the church. A few rickety houses lined the cobbled High Street, but that was just about it. In its complete entirety, this secluded Yorkshire village with a name she couldn't even remember, housed less than 50 people…maybe even less than that. Brilliant! She had never had such a thing as neighbours before, so being semi-reclusive was much favoured. Travellers could never fully comprehend the whole neighbourhood thing, although they identified strongly with the inner circle of their own vitsa community.

So here she was at last. This was what a lottery win could buy.

The house seemed large, flawless and picture-perfect …yet somehow perplexing. Her Romany instinct sensed something menacing, but for now she couldn't quite define what was wrong. She touched the lilac floral wallpaper and addressed the house, 'you are just a bit too good to be true my new friend. Give me some time and I will discover your secrets.'

My God – she was talking to a house. Actually, she was talking to a wall. A lilac flowered wall at that. She was turning into Nina. The pills and the jetlag must surely be to blame. What the hell was wrong with her?

She reasoned that this was a giant step from all that was familiar to her, and despite the physical discomfort of her former life… ironically her former life was emotionally comforting. It was what she knew, and as flawed as it may have been - the perfection of the unknown presented the bigger challenge.

Finally collapsing on her queen-sized bed after the hottest and most welcome shower she had ever experienced, Clarah considered her new existence.

Had her parents made the right decision? It had all happened so quickly. They had abandoned their own Roma community, who in turn *(understandably)* had turned their backs on them. Cultural abandonment; hell that was a big deal. Some ancient vitsa rule had been broken and it was a fracture that could not be healed. Her family had slapped their kin folk and friends good and hard. Little wonder that they were now hidden away in a remote corner of Dracula's domain; crouching behind tall serpentine stone walls. She considered it paradoxical that those who once avoided walls, now used them as armour plating.

Could just a few numbers tilt the universe on its axis? She had remembered them by heart. They were low numbers because they all represented birthdays. They seemed to be an unlikely mix – 4,5,7,11,13,15 – just dates in a diary and nothing more. In numerical isolation, they held no power. But together on the right ticket and at the right time, they equated to £9.2million.

Could £9.2 million change a person's world so radically? What if the owners of the winning ticket just happened to be a family of Roma travellers living on shite wasteland? Hell yes- they were just that and it just had! But was it for the best?

Clarah tried to switch off her brain so she could sleep, but her cluttered thoughts were haunted by the consequences of the win and what it had meant to them.

There were two winning tickets with the same numbers. It seemed a strange coincidence. It was in all the newspapers, though neither owners of the tickets had made their win public. She recalled some journalist writing about how two families somewhere in the United Kingdom, could possibly share all the same birthdates and how statistically unlikely that would be. They were clutching at straws. Maybe the numbers were not birthdates, but a combo of car registration plates and telephone digits. Who knows why or how people pick lottery numbers? Had they not considered random selection? Pure chance! The tabloids had made too big a deal of it- suggesting that the same secret family had won twice. Such irresponsible journalism, had only made matters worse.

To add insult to injury, someone – God knows who or how, also tipped the papers off that a Gypsy family held one…or maybe both… of the winning tickets. From that moment on, nobody in the tightly-knit travelling community ever looked at one another in the same light again. Eyes looked upon the wearer of designer labels and posh watches with suspicion. Could the items be real or fake? Indeed, was the owner of the items real or fake? Who had just updated their caravan, bought a new car or gambled and drank as though money was no object or concern? Who would become a settler and mix with the gaje? Everybody watched everybody else. It wouldn't take long to figure things out. It never did. It never does.

She thanked God that her Dadro *(father)* had been made to share his winnings. If £9.2 million could cause such immense begrudgery, what would £18.4 million have done? It was for the best that half this amount was channelled elsewhere. As much as folk could guess, the other £9.2 million had become some other family's dream come true or living nightmare.

Clarah

Clarah looked down and raised her tanned leg so that her foot pointed to the ceiling. She felt happy. The leg that was once white and plump, was now thin and bronzed and that was exactly what every traveller girl sought- tone and tan. Normally this look was achieved by dieting and spray paint. As far as Clarah was concerned, her hike through the southern hemisphere was a natural, yet excruciating form of beautifying attainment. She was pleased that for once in her life, she wasn't fat. She tried to shut out the bullying slurs that had marred her teenage years. *"Clarah is plump, she lives in a dump, eats like a pig and dresses like a frump"*. If ever she needed to remember why she had ran away, maybe that childhood taunt was a suitable aide-mémoire.

She needed to sleep. She was thinking too much. She opened up her wardrobe; delighting at the thought that she no longer needed to live out of a backpack. She mentally scolded herself for still being awake, but everything seemed so new-so different. She was completely, totally, absolutely exhausted, yet a rush of jubilation stopped her from closing her eyes. A wardrobe – yet again another new experience.

She tucked herself up in her duvet. My God, the mattress was so comfortable. She sank into the soft white covers. Surely, she would drift into a deep sleep soon. She had to forget all about Denny and her past, and as for Konnor, he was surely just a summer fling.

This village, this house …it was well hidden. Her parents had done a good job in finding somewhere so reclusive. Somewhere far from the people they had abandoned – because that is how they would see it. They had insulted their own kind. They would not be forgiven, even though they had every justification to move away. She knew the vitsa wouldn't see it that way.

She lay back and listened to the sea as it lulled her into a deep and perfect sleep. All too soon her life would become a topsy-turvy whirlwind of noise. The family would want to hear all about her adventures in Asia and Australia. Maybe she would be scolded for losing touch with them all for so long – but then they would forgive her. Families do that- don't they? Yes-they would drink and laugh and forgive. She closed her heavy eyes. Sleep Clarah - time to enjoy the peace while it lasts. As yet, she had no idea that the peace, would last longer than she thought.

Eyes closed – she was out of it, in more ways than one. In more ways than she could possibly yet know. But the house knew. The house knew everything. The unseen was watching, listening…. plotting.

CHAPTER 4

Thursday 24th September 2015
LATER THAT MORNING

'Which key in which dammed effin lock', he cursed?

Kane's befuddled head deduced an eventual chance of success if he kept aiming his hand in the right direction. The reality was less eloquent than the mathematical probability. Kane's grubby fingers were struggling to make the connection, and his liquor soaked brain didn't help matters. He had quite forgotten that the doors were never locked.

Finally, he managed to push the door open; at the same time as his Grandmother also opened the door from the inside. He fell headlong into the hallway, unable to apply the brakes.

Cracking his head as he landed on the tiles, he cussed and blasphemed - using every swear word he had ever catalogued in his mere 18 years of life. His Grandmother pulled him to his feet and then whacked him good and hard across the face.

'You are a disgrace lad.' Yet again Kane's muddy body fell to the floor. Kane could do little else but shout out, 'Baba May stop. Leave me alone. For bugger's sake – why did you hit me? You mad bloody witch.'

His Grandmother looked down on him with utter contempt. His tee-shirt was sweaty and smeared with both old and new blood stains. His jeans had the aroma of stale urine and were caked in clay. He was a good-looking lad – dark skinned, with deep brown eyes and a strong face framed by dishevelled kiss curls. Had he not been such a drunkard he may have been quite a catch, but in his present state, he was the sort of wild stallion that the fairer sex avoided.

Baba May tutted to herself. 'Your sister has come back home from her travels,' she informed him. 'Do you really want her to see you like this?' No reply. Kane was snoring - still lying on the hard-cold tiles where he had fallen. He weighed more than she could carry. Baba May would be unable to move him. She took off his muddy boots, placed a pillow under his head and threw a blanket over his stinky crumpled body.

Forever the matriarchal leader of the household, she tidied up around him – mopping up the dirt he had walked in and cleaning up the blood tricking from his cut head. She despaired of him. Her Grandson coming back home in such a state, was not an unusual event. If anything, it was a regular occurrence.

The squeaking steps of the aging staircase caught the old lady's attention. On seeing her Granddaughters radiant lemon-fresh face, she couldn't help but gasp. With tears falling from her tired eyes she shouted out, 'Clarah! My sweet grandchild. It is so good to have you back. I didn't want to wake you. What time did you get home?' She rushed to hug her, almost squeezing the life from her ribs.

Clarah had forgotten how strong her Gran was, and tried to back off. For some reason, her ribs hurt – though she had no idea why this should be. Baba May held her shoulders and drank in the view of her favourite Grandchild. She caressed her hair.

'My God child, you look like Bo Derek.'

'Who?'

'10.'

'What?'

Clarah was confused?

'Oh, never you mind,' sighed Baba May. 'There was a film called "10" back in the 70's or 80's, and the actress who played in it – that would be Bo Derek…she had her hair braded; just like you. It suits you. Matches your tan. Dear Lord, you look like you have walked straight off a beach. You have lost so much weight. My goodness, I have never seen you look so skinny, but despite seeing your bones, you still look beautiful. I have missed you my child. You are too thin though. I need to fatten you up.'

It was every fat girls dream – being called "too thin". She smiled in silent appreciation.

Clarah touched her Grandmothers ruddy cheeks and chuckled. 'Yes, I had it braided on Sai Khao Beach. That's a place in Thailand. Imagine Bob Marley, dreadlocks and hippies smoking wacky tobaccy. Not that I ever touched that stuff.'

Her Grandmother sniggered, knowing that Clarah was trying to shock her. 'You are my beautiful girl,' she proclaimed as she tugged at her chin. Baba May always knew the right things to say. At that precise moment, Clarah wondered why she had ever run away. She had been so very selfish. How could she have deserted her dearest Granny?

The old woman took her Granddaughter's hand and led her into the kitchen.

'Once you have recovered from your jet lagging, I will show you around the house and gardens. It is so lovely here Clarah. It's quiet. We get no bother from anyone. We keep ourselves to ourselves… except for the times when your brother goes out, gets inebriated and sleeps it off in the cemetery. Take my advice child – don't mix with the gaje. They seem nice enough, but we should not become a part of them. They cannot be trusted…not yet. You just don't know. You cannot tell what beats in the hearts of strangers.'

Clarah was about to make herself comfortable at the large farm-kitchen style table, when her Grans words punched her with their content. She backtracked, 'Kane does what?' She almost screeched out the question.

'The boy is a drunken idiot,' responded Baba May. 'He takes a short cut back from the Red Lion through the church yard. One time he fell into a grave dug out for Mr Morrison's funeral. He is…I mean was... the local butcher. That idiot brother of yours, was just too sozzled to climb his way out. So, I guess he just spent the night in Mr Morrison's grave the day before the old man's funeral. It was shameful. We couldn't look his family in the face. I don't know how it can keep happening, because it's not like we have a death a week in this tiny village. This is such a small wee place. Yet, once a week…sometimes even twice a week, he comes back covered in clay. I don't know what to think Clarah. He must be too lazy or too drunk to make it home. I am ashamed of him. The boy sleeps with the dead.'

'Is he at home now?'

'Oh yes, he is here alright, but don't look at him child. He's still out for the count, and far from a pretty sight. I will clean him up for your later.'

Clarah held her head in her hands, not knowing who to feel sorry for the most, her alcoholic brother Kane, or her over-worked overly-burdened Gran. What a nightmare. She drank her tea and awaited the large plate of cheese and tomato dip Baba May would soon present before her. It was a simple dish, but nobody aside from her Gran seemed to make it. She had missed Baba May's simple home cooking.

'Where is Da,' she asked of her Gran? 'Your Dadra is gambling his money away in a Las Vegas casino my love. If he knew you were coming back, I am sure he would be here. You gave us such short notice child. I am sorry. I have let him know that his prodigy daughter has returned. So, I bet he will be catching the first flight back.'

Clarah had to laugh, 'I think you mean prodigal daughter Baba May.' Her grandmother shrugged indifferently. She had little interest in correct pronunciations. She owned the word – not the other way around. As far as she was concerned, without her mouth it would never have been spoken.

'What about my ma? Where is my ma?' Clarah looked confused. She sensed that her mother wasn't around. Baba May looked away, not wanting to expose her true thoughts.

'She comes and goes. She will be out shopping, or having her nails done, or having her face paralysed with some boxic injections. She is hardly at home these days. I think she lives at some spa place. Don't be shocked when you see her – she has changed Clarah. Money can change people you know, but your ma has really changed. Her face has been lifted up above her head, and her lips filled with fat they sucked from someone's bum. That woman is addicted to her looks. I don't get it, but it is as it is. My daughter is living a life that suits her- I guess. No idea who the woman is trying to impress.'

Clarah could tell that her grandmother was lying. Baba May averted her eyes to the stone floor, having added just a touch too much detail to her invented story. Clarah let it pass.

'What about Nina. Is she still…still disturbed? I presume she must be having some sort of expert help?'

Baba May simply shook her head. Maybe it was too early in the day, but she went to pour herself a shot of her hot brandy infused milk.

'Dear Jesus, poor Nina. She still thinks she is many different people. She is on medication, but nothing much changes. I think that those tablets concoctions are all kidology. Just a way for them chemist to make money from folk who don't know any better. They don't work.'

Clarah shrugged despairingly.

'I am sorry Baba May. Who does she think she is now?'

'For the moment, 'responded her Grandmother, 'she calls herself Anju. She claims to be a Hindi girl from some time long past.'

Clarah looked sad. 'Bloody hell no,' she gasped. 'Why could I not have a normal family? Has she done anything ridiculous yet? I am guessing we need to keep a low profile amongst the local gaje?'

'Low profile – our family – that's hilarious,' responded Baba May. 'Last month Nina, or should I say Anju. did set up a shrine beneath the "hole in the wall" outside Barclays bank. I guess it could have been embarrassing had anyone seen her. She made a mark on the cash machine with kum kum powder, lit joss sticks on the pavement and left it an offering of egg fried rice in gratitude for the money it gave us. It would have been funny had it not been so bloody crazy. Anyhow, I managed to clear it all away before anyone saw it – but, you know…it could have been awkward. We don't really want to attract any attention from the local folk. Poor Nina…well she isn't right in the head, is she?'

'Sorry I wasn't here to help out Baba May. I had… you know…problems of my own. Personal stuff. Things I can't tell you about. I feel terrible about the whole situation, but I simply had to get away. Hey, at least Nina seems to have recovered after the attack.' Clarah covered her face with her hands, feeling somewhat shamefaced.

She continued, 'I am so very sorry Baba May. I just couldn't deal with what happened to her. It was all too much…and well… other bad things happened that night. I caught Denny cheating on me. It was just weeks away from our wedding, so I just ran. I didn't know what I was doing. I am just not ready to talk about it yet. Is Nina okay by the way…I mean physically?'

Baba May didn't beat about the bush. 'They didn't rape her if that's what you meant.'

That wasn't exactly what Clarah intended to ask, but it was good information and nice to know… she supposed.

'Did they catch the lads who did it?'

Baba May seemed reluctant to answer.

'You really don't know anything do you Clarah? Eventually – yes,' came the blunt reply. It was obvious that Baba May didn't want to talk about the specific details any more than Clarah wanted to listen. It became something of a stunted conversation. Both women were holding the truth back from their lips in case it bit their tongue. Baba May loved her granddaughter, but deep inside she was boiling with Romany rage; incensed by Clarah's desertion at a time of family crisis. Cheating fiancé or not, in her grandmothers mind it was still a pitiful excuse.

After a few moments of woe, they each recalled Nina's worship of the bank cash machine and it seemed to lighten the mood. For a few minutes, they laughed hysterically. Baba May was happy to see her Granddaughter giggle like a child. She guessed that Clarah had been through more pain than she would yet dare admit to. Laughter began to feel strangely therapeutic.

Eventually the moment of hilarity died down, and Clarah got up to pour herself some water. On so doing, she noted the brown candle wax by the window. Brown; she had come to hate that wretched colour of late. She slowly turned to face her Grandmother.

'Baba May, are you still spell-casting?'

She knew that no normal person would have brown candles by way of a norm. Brown was a nothingness colour. Her Grandmother pursed her lips and focused on the carrots she was chopping for tonight's casserole. Clarah repeated the question. Baba May eventually responded, throwing a cold stare that could have frozen water.

'You know me to be a drabarni. That will never change. I was born with a 3rd eye – a sight that can see the unseen.'

Clarah grew impatient. 'That was not what I asked you. Do you still spell cast? Have you used sorcery to bring us all this money? Answer me truthfully Baba May.'

Her Grandmothers coyness gave Clarah the answer she required. Clarah bit her lip, so much so that her cold-sore started to bleed. She was annoyed.

'Baba May, you of all people, should know that such spells can backfire. If the money came as God's gift- then so be it, but if it was delivered by witchcraft it can bring upon a curse. You know these things, Baba May.'

Her Grandmother shrugged nonchalantly and replied, 'I guess you are referring to begrudgery and the evil eye of the jealous wanton.

'Aye, just that Baba May. It's true isn't it. Our people now begrudge us the wealth that we didn't share with them. We are all as guilty as one another. Maybe Katalyn was right about this all along. I hope that magic of yours can protect us from the fallout of all of this. Your powers had better be strong enough. What do we do? Live our lives walking in a pentacle of salt, or whatever it is that you witches hide inside to protect yourselves from crap you don't really understand.'

Baba May fired back at her.

'It works both ways child. Are you telling me that you don't hold a grudge against the vitsa kids? Those who teased you for being a bit on the plump side?'

Clarah simply shrugged. She was tired of being reminded of the past – that was why she had escaped. She didn't have to play this game if she didn't want to. She had walked away once before, and she could do it again. She was like the dog that had tasted blood. After the first bite, the second bite is always easier.

Nothing more was said. For several minutes, the two women sat in complete silence. Each mutely acknowledging that their family seemed to be far from normal, that their heritage was far from understood and that their new wealth was far from accepted. Each wondering, if recent events had been due to some curse of begrudgery. After all, had not Clarah's mother Violet held a 25-year grudge against the vitsa for not accepting her Irish tinker husband.

Clarah had also held a grudge against the vitsa kids for a life-time of bullying, and now she added Denny's infidelity to that list of resentment and bitterness.

With that deceit came the new loathing of her sister Katalyn; begrudging her for her sirenical beauty and the perfect body that had led Denny into her bed whilst husband Peter was out of town.

In return, the vitsa begrudged them of their new-found wealth. The bad kismet was like a cold metal spoon, heaping yet more bad luck into a cup of the most negative pungent karma. Clarah trembled inside as that vision hijacked her thoughts.

Thankfully the image left her mind as soon as Aunt Mary hobbled into the kitchen. Clarah looked at her aunt with both delight and pity. She could see that her hip was lopsided, and that each forced movement of her leg caused a spasm in her muscles and a rush of pain down her sciatic nerve. She dashed over to hug her. Clarah couldn't let go. She rested her head on her aunt's shoulder; listening to her heartbeat and inhaling the familiar lavender scent on her clothes. Mary was her favourite aunt; a kind gentle woman who had lived a tragic life. A random tear fell from Clarah's eye. In all of her travels, none of the exotic Dharmic incenses from a multitude of Buddhists or Hindi temples, could override Aunt Mary's lavender. She inhaled slowly and deeply.

Her aunt finally broke free and kissed her niece on the cheek.

'I have to sit my love. I struggle to stand for long.'

It wasn't long before a gentle scolding followed.

'It is a pure joy to see you again, but you shouldn't have left like you did. You know your Ma will tick you off when she sees you.'

'Yes, I know Aunty. I had my reasons though. When I am ready to tell you my story, we will all sit down as a family and I will explain everything. Now is not the time. I want to wait until my parents are here. Is that okay?'

Her aunt simply nodded in agreement, but Clarah noticed the look of disapproval on her face. Mary was a hard nut to crack and it would take many apologies to get back into her aunt's good book. Baba May broke the awkwardness of the moment.

'Clarah, you should go outside. We have stables and horses.'

Clarah

Clarah was grateful for the change in conversation, plus she could hardly contain her excitement.

'Really…we have horses? Are they Kane's? That boy so loves horses. When I was in Australia, I worked in the stables as a jillaroo. I am a dab hand at mucking out. I must go and check them out.'

Baba May knew she had said exactly the right thing at exactly the right time. She had successfully pulled Clarah away from the harsh words of her scolding aunt.

'The black stallion belongs to your brother. When he is sober, he is the best bare back rider I have ever seen. He is a natural. However, the white mare is yours. He hasn't named it yet. He was waiting for you to come back so you can give her a name. We have all waited for you for so long Clarah. Now go and meet your horse, and while you are out pick some Comfrey for your Aunt Mary so I can make her a poultice. Her legs are throbbing today.'

The young woman could hardly contain herself.

'Yes, for sure, I will bring back some Comfrey, but in the meantime, where are the stables Baba May? Point me in the right direction.'

Baba May moved to the patio doors of the kitchen and gestured towards the sea.

'There is a bridle trail over there. It runs along the coastal path. The stables are just behind the paddock. You cannot miss them. Have fun Clarah. The fresh sea air will bring the colour back to your cheeks, but hear me now - no bare back. You need to act like a settler. We are part of their community now. Saddle up and wear a hard hat. Blend in. You know what I am saying, don't you girl?'

Clarah knew exactly what her Grandmother meant.

She found the stables as directed. Waiting patiently and chewing on a concoction of hay and oats, were four handsome Shire horses, a black stallion and the most exquisite white mare. Clarah did as she was told. She saddled up and named her horse "Molly Malone", as in the old Irish song. After a 'getting to know you' canter, she rode the mare fast and fearless, as though she was riding on the wind. She rode without a care in the world. She didn't know what it was that her brain didn't want to remember – only that it was something best forgotten.

She rode to the sound of the seagulls and the rush of the waves, but mostly she heard the pounding of her own heart. A heart that was free. This was her new home now- everything and everyone else was just a yesterday away.

CHAPTER 5

Friday 25th September 2015
THE SHOCK OF SEEING NINA AGAIN

Surely it was every girls dream - riding a white horse, galloping upon white sand through white effervescent waves, and doing all of this beneath a turquoise sky peppered with fluffy white clouds. It was perfect, but perhaps a little too perfect.

Clarah had always craved a horse of her own, yet had never dare believe it could ever happen. Not only had her dream come true, but the entire seascape setting of a horse on a beach was almost too good to be true. For a few special moments of her young life, she actually felt emancipated. Unshackled and unfettered – both she and Molly Malone.

Free… she gagged on the word.

The travelling community boasted about their freedom; the wanton abandon of the open road. Yet she saw her place in their plan as anything but.

Looking back to her childhood, it was not what she would have described as being free. For her, it was judgement, discrimination, conditioning, presumption, accusation, hardship, sexism, racialism and a belonging to nowhere, yet everywhere. Many in her community did not share her feelings, but she owned her own feelings and this is what she felt. For once, she could think this out loud and admit it to herself. Clarah's life that was a heady cocktail of many flavours, yet within this mix, freedom was just a promised cherry on a stick. The avoidance of council tax could hardly be seen as so big a benefit that it equalled freedom. Not in her eyes.

She looked up at the white house on top of the cliff. It was her house. She had a house. She spun the thought around in her head, like bricks in a tumble drier. She had a house. Not just that, but a big house and now… a bonny white horse. She pulled on the reins and brought Molly to a standstill. She decided that sometimes, one has to hit the pause button and drink in the moment, and this was such a time.

Clarah breathed deep and inhaled the brackish air. She turned to face the wind coming off the sea so it brushed her face with saline droplets. It was the familiar breeze of late summer…warm and yet with the cooling promise of autumn. The leaves hadn't yet bronzed, but the chilled early mornings implied Halloween and Bonfire night were queuing up to replace the halcyon days of picnics and BBQ's.

She held her face up to the sun; drinking in the last warm rays of September. An Indian summer; wasn't that what folks called it? She closed her eyes. It was a wonderful precious moment of being lost in time, but it was a moment that couldn't last.

Clarah was in big trouble. The world hated her…aside from Baba May, who didn't know the meaning of hate. After all, wasn't she the one who had not just run away, but had cut all ties. Unlike ET – she had not phoned home. In fact, she had been to every remote beach, rain forest and mountain that didn't boast Wi-Fi and a phone signal. She had behaved rashly; like a troubled steed that had been spooked by a loud noise and had bolted. She had galloped away out of trouble and into trouble, and now the stable door had been firmly closed behind her. As much as she wanted to delay the inevitable, she now had to leave this glorious beach and face up to her mother.

She knew that her Ma was due back from somewhere sometime soon, or at least that was the lie she had been fed. Clarah would have done anything to avoid this confrontation. The torch light would be shone into her retina, followed by a painful inquisition. Nails would be torn from their nail beds and vertebra stretched on a rack. Questions would be asked. Why she had left so quickly? Why she had disappeared off the planet for so long? Why had she not even bothered to get in touch with her family in their moment of total despair? Why had she deserted her fiancé just weeks before their wedding …why?

Even without her Aunt Mary's icy stares, she knew she was the deserter; the one who went AWOL when the going got tough. Shit…she really didn't need reality to pop this beautiful seaside bubble – but it would be popped and the popping would happen very soon. With thoughts of her brain being zapped by pulsating high voltage, she set a track for home. Of course, she knew this wouldn't actually be the case, but that was how it felt. She had already endured the wrath of Aunt Mary. This was small fry compared to the meeting she anticipated with her mother.

Riding back up the bridal path, *(which Molly negotiated like an expert mountain goat),* she thought about Denny again. She had been engaged to marry him. What a joke that was? What a lucky escape? By Roma standards she was old for a single woman. By tradition, she should have been married and impregnated in her teens. Her own mother Violet, was 17 when she had been married, and her Granny Baba May was a mere 15.

She whispered a silent prayer of gratitude; grateful that she had not met the same fate. Thankful that she had seen Denny for what he really was, and that luck had exposed him as the two-timing despicable man he always had been. A man she once loved and a man who had deceived her.

She then saw Denny in her memory, the way he was that night with that girl. That girl- who was she kidding? It had been her own married older sister for heaven's sake. It hurt, but she was grateful to have seen the truth before he had tied her down with a manacle of fool's gold. She was driving herself insane by these thoughts.

'Got to stop thinking,' was the thought she thought to herself, and then scolded herself for yet having another thought about a thought.

Being 21 and thin and bronzed and rich and single was more than okay – it was good. The here and now was good. Sod the past! She would face her mother and tell her the truth. Perhaps now was the time for the grand expose? For a moment, she considered that maybe she was going insane…that maybe she was turning into Nina.

'Oh, that was such a cruel thought. Shut up mind; be gone ye stupid thoughts' she uttered to herself. She knew that she was driving herself crazy. Maybe she really had flipped over the precipice of sanity. Was this how it felt to go insane? She was falling off that brown murky mountain, but maybe the fall was better than trying to tread its path to nowhere.

***

As Molly and Clarah cantered through the extensive gardens of their new estate, she came across a random river. She hadn't known that a river flowed through the gardens, but then again, why should she? This was her first time outside. Clarah was exploring her new territory with a kitten-like curiosity. But a gushing river? What a delightful discovery. Maybe she would try her hand at fishing later. She had caught a Carp once upon a time – so why not? It wasn't as though she was busy doing anything else. Fishing sounded like a calming new hobby.

Her parents had chosen their new home wisely. She was pleased that it was big and remote. Happy that it was close to the sea and that the gardens had lots of interesting hidden spaces. It was pure escapism, and she knew that was exactly why her family had purchased this very place. It was an escape route and an exit from their old way of life. A life she missed, but one she had now outgrown.

Following its course away from the sea, and against the flow, she saw an image in the distance. Moving closer, she soon made out the silhouette of a person squatting on the side of the river. It was a young girl dressed from head to foot in a purple and golden sari. She was washing her clothes, smacking them against the rivers boulders with immense determination. The scene she had stumbled upon, looked more like a documentary; one filmed by the shores of the River Ganges. She approached the back of the girl, and recognised the long mahogany plat falling down her back. She knew it was her sister Nina, and yet she didn't know if she should address her by her own name or her assumed Hindu name of Anju. Bloody hell; she couldn't remember what the doctors had said. Would she encourage the multiple disorders if she acknowledged them or not? She should have asked Baba May about it. Her grandmother had told her that her sister's condition had a new name and they should use the correct terminology. Dissociative identity disorder – yes, that was the posh psycho-babble term. Clarah was surprised she had even remembered it. She should have looked it up online before meeting Nina again. She reproached herself for being too forgetful or too lazy to care, or at least… care enough.

Molly Malone suddenly let out a loud neigh, followed by a wet nasally snort, complete with several inches of dripping gunge. It frightened Nina, who let out a tiny gasp as she jumped to her feet. The girl stood paralysed for a moment, perhaps recognising the white mare, but not its rider. Clarah could see the face of her sister, but something was missing from her eyes. The eyes didn't belong with the rest of the body. Rather than twins being reunited, it felt more like two strangers meeting in a chance encounter.

Clarah jumped down from her horse and held her hand out to Nina, but the girl was frightened and stepped away from the outstretched arm. 'Nina, it's me, it's your sister Clarah. I have just flown back from my long travels. I only got back yesterday. Sorry but I couldn't find you when I got back, but then again, I spent most of yesterday sleeping. Hey, thank you for the welcome home poster and the balloons. That was so sweet of you, and at least I knew where my room was.'

Nina looked too frightened to respond.

Clarah was concerned and asked, 'are you okay Nina? You do remember me…don't you? 'Nina said nothing. She looked as though she was in shock.

Clarah tried again. 'Do I address you as Anju? Do you prefer to be called Anju?'

Once again, the question was met with silence. Clarah cried inside her heart. Had her sisters brain been damaged when the accident happened? She had seen the blood drip from her head, but hadn't considered it to be anything serious. It was just a flesh wound – wasn't it? Nina didn't appear to recognise her. Maybe it was her hair braids and weight loss? After all, Clarah looked so different now. Yes, that was it – that was why Nina was confused…surely.

She tried again, 'Anju, do you understand me? Do you know how to speak English?' The girl spoke in a language that Clarah could only presume to be Hindi, as she replied, 'main keval kuchh shabdon ko samajhane.'

This time it was Clarah who backed off. She stood in silence and looked at the girl facing her. She looked long and hard; studying the contours of her face and the stance of her body. Finally, she broke her silence. 'I don't know who you are Anju, I don't know what you are doing in Nina's body, and I don't even know if you can understand what I am saying – but I do know that you are not my sister. I can see a stranger in her eyes. I want my sister back and I am going to find a way to make you get out of her skin. You don't belong there. My sisters body wasn't yours to take. I don't care what the psychiatrists say about this condition. As far as I am concerned, you are a lost spirit who is possessing my little sister. Know this much- you cannot mess with a Roma woman. I will do what it takes to be rid of you.'

With that, she turned away, took hold of Molly's reins and walked back towards the stables. She had a deeply worried look etched upon her face. She would need to talk to Baba May about this. Surely her grandmother, with all her Romany mystic skills would have some solutions tucked up her witch's sleeve.

'What have I come home to?' She nodded her head in disbelief.

Clarah walked back into an empty house.

She called out the names of her relatives, 'Baba May, Kane, Aunt Mary….Ma.' There was no response aside from an echo.

She was alone in an empty hallway.

'Where is everybody?'

It felt much colder in here than it did outside. It was more than cold – it lacked human warmth. No; it was something more. Something chillingly sinister, but she couldn't put her finger on exactly what it was. She decided to investigate her new home.

She walked into each of the reception rooms; rooms which had names she didn't understand. Clarah had been raised in a small fiberglass frame on rubber wheels. Hers was a space that didn't boast a reception room, family room, snug, lounge, drawing room, music room and so on and so forth. In her mind, they were all useless empty places. Unused useable space, which in her old life would have accommodated several beds to sleep several people. How could a house have two kitchens? One used for cooking and the other for show? Why two staircases? One for the servants and the other for the served. Was this how the rich gaje conducted their upper-class lives? She was astounded. So much room, for so few people. It seemed so…wasteful. So, considered how so few have so much, whilst so many have so little.

The next thing that she noticed, was that there was no dust. Not one single trace of it – anywhere. Gypsy women always kept a clean caravan, but this was a sprawling big mansion. Aunt Mary could hardly lift a dustpan with her crooked fingers, Kane was a useless drunk, Da was away playing at being a high roller in Vegas, her Ma was away having something nipped and tucked…and so that only left Baba May. How could Baba May possibly keep this large house so spotless? Baba May was fit for her age, but still an elderly lady.

Clarah ran her finger across the top of the dining table and uttered, 'not a blimin dust mite anywhere.' It seemed unnatural. It was unnatural. It wasn't possible- even by OCD Gypsy standards.

The second thing that she noticed, was that the house lacked a Romany personality. It was plain and sterile; and that just didn't fit with tradition. It should have been packed with ostentatious bling. She would have expected family photographs packing cabinet tops. Lots of porcelain ornaments *(especially of horses)*, would have been crammed onto every shelf, and with their new money – pure brazen grandiose flash should have been on show. If it wasn't gilded, it wasn't Gypsy. Again, she muttered to herself, 'the place is as bloody boring as shite.'

She went to open the fridge. It was packed full of food – but how? There was no car in the driveway. Come to think of it…did they even have a car? She hadn't seen Da's old white van parked outside, but concluded that he had probably got rid of it anyway. After all, it was scrap on wheels and a rusting-metal excuse for a van. She thought out loud, 'so how does anyone buy any food then? Maybe Baba May had learned to conquer her phobia of on-line shopping. Yes, that would be it – the internet.'

She decided that the only explanation was that her family had found 21st century, cyber supermarkets.

But where was everybody?

She decided that maybe the unfriendly limo driver had taken them all into town. What town? All she had seen on the drive in, was some tin pot village. Perhaps she would take a stroll into the village. After all, it was a warm September day *(warmer outside than inside)*, and perhaps the fresh air may help wake her up. Her head was still muffled by severe tiredness, and whatever stuff she had allegedly swallowed during the flight.

As much as she tried to remember, she still had complete amnesia about the journey home. She considered that it may be beneficial to blow out the cobwebs from her ears and have some thinking time. Yet, only an hour earlier she had been trying not to think, but that was before she met Anju.

Her sisters unwanted tenant, had presented a whole new challenge. This was an odd problem; a mind-blowing paranormal freaky situation and something she would have to consider carefully. Yes, she needed some thinking time. Yet more thinking! Her brain was starting to hurt. She wished she was back in Bali, curled up next to Konnor's tanned body. But then she thought about his brother Ash, and as the vomit rose in her throat, she dismissed all memories of Bali.

***

Clarah closed the front door, supposing that there was no need to lock it. If she was to be frankly honest with herself, she didn't really care if the house was burgled anyway. She decided that a bit of carnage may inject some excitement into its wishy-washy sterility. She decided to take the short cut through the church yard; the one that Baba May had mentioned to her. Retrace her brother's drunken steps so to speak.

She was shocked to walk past a freshly dug grave awaiting its beneficiary. Baba May told her that this was a small place and they didn't have funerals very often – yet here was another one looming on the interment horizon. She reasoned to herself that maybe lots of elderly retired folk lived in the area. She didn't know what else to think.

Walking through a small gate and over a wobbly bridge, she found herself on the main High street. She looked directly at the occasional passers-by, but either they were locked inside their own private thoughts or were deliberately ignoring her. She had experienced this before. She had endured this from the gaje all her life. Yet, she was sure that her family would have hidden their Roma heritage from the locals.... not because it was anything to be embarrassed about. Quite the contrary-they were massively proud of their culture, but more because they didn't want to bring attention to themselves. Her kind didn't want trouble and attention often meant trouble. Yet it was as though folks didn't see her, but what the hell; she was long beyond caring.

She thought back to her childhood again, and the amount of times she and her siblings had taken a short sharp slap upon the heads, with the words. 'don't you be going bringing problems to our door.' The memory made her shiver.

***

The village was pleasant enough. It boasted some old cobbled alleyways and crooked medieval buildings. She especially liked the steep roads and multitude of thigh torturing steps. She felt at ease with the respite of a congenial tea time stroll. Clarah meandered from street to street, with no particular route or ambition - thought free at long last.

But just then, when she least expected it, she walked past the Red Lion pub and recognised a familiar face. Sitting alone, with a pint of cider in hand, was her brother Kane. He looked distant…almost empty. He obviously hadn't recognised her.

She sat down beside him. He hardly even noticed, and it was evident he still hadn't recognised her several minutes later. Clarah had seldom felt so isolated in all her life. To the Roma culture, family was everything. Now she was the stranger – the unseen stranger that everyone ignored. Family, villagers, pet dogs. Was she invisible?

She introduced herself, and even then, there was hardly a shred of emotion on his face. He finally looked up at her and spoke.

'Your eyes are red, you look tired Clarah.'

She responded, 'your eyes are yellow, you look sick Kane.'

Her comment was meant to be a meaningless jibe, but her mockery failed to raise a smile. She waited for some sort of conversation to begin, but it was obvious that her brother wasn't going to instigate anything. She cast her eyes upon him with slow deliberation; scanning his body from top to toe. She couldn't help but utter, 'my God Kane, you look wretched.' It was an old word; one not often used in modern times – but it fitted his appearance.

He looked up at her with a cold stony stare.

'You have no right to condemn me sister. Take a good long look at your own actions first. You have a lot of apologies to make to a lot of people.'

What could Clarah say to defend herself? She knew he was right.

She changed the subject.

'Nina – what has happened to her. Her mental state is so much worse. What do you know about this Anju creation of hers?'

Kane was either not willing or able, to strike up much of a conversation.

'The girl is a mad dog. Someone ought to put her down. She is crazy.'

That was it. That was all he could say. Clarah felt deeply sad and disappointed. She had lost Nina and now it was more than obvious she had lost Kane. She would leave him to his solitary drinking and head back home…to the house…to the place that pretended to be a home. It was a place she was already starting to fear, although she couldn't rationalise exactly why. Just a feeling…

***

Night was starting to fall, and Clarah felt unusually anxious as she took the same short cut back through the church yard. The September air was damp, and yet because it was unseasonably warm, fog had started to descend upon the cemetery. As mist snaked around her ankles and severe tiredness impaired her judgement. she was beginning to understand how easily her drunken brother could have fallen into a hole. All be it, that the hole was an empty grave.

With each tentatively placed step, visibility grew worse. Clarah let out a huge sigh of relief as she reached the driveway to the house she believed to be home. A welcoming avenue of Victorian lanterns guided her towards the entrance. As she walked through the front door, she called out and awaited answers. Yet again, no friendly reassuring voices hollowed back at her. No heartening aromas of apple pie and freshly baked bread greeted her nostrils as she walked down the hallway. No trite violin music blasted its chimes from the general direction of the music room.

The house was cold and empty. She was alone – completely alone. She whispered under her breath – even seeing her breath as it left her mouth.

'Fine okay- so they have all deserted me. Not a problem - I will get some shite microwave food, grab a bottle of wine, lock myself in my room, watch braindead TV and get hammered.' Clarah did just that. Maybe that was exactly how her brother had coped? She considered that perhaps this was how he had become an alcoholic? Who was she to judge? She whispered to herself, 'hey don't judge a drunkard until you have walked in his shoes.'

She already knew that she wouldn't be staying in Whitby for too long. Something about the place spooked her. She may have loved the beach, but she hated her new home, and she just about tolerated the unfriendly gaje village. This wasn't for her. She had no idea what was for her, but that was a question for later. For now, she was tired and hungry.

Maybe she had time for one last Facebook, Instagram, WhatsApp message or email before bed. She would drown herself in social media and attempt to contact him yet again. Why wasn't Konnor replying? Why wasn't anybody in the world replying?

The tangled web of deceit wasn't a game she was well-versed in playing, yet she was adjusting to this game. Clarah was hiding something from Konnor – something she had to hide. She was good at keeping secrets. Denny had given her some useful first lessons in the betrayal department.

She then tried texting the two French girls she had first met in Cambodia. Alone and frightened in a strange country, Anais and Valentine had come to her rescue, befriended her and recognising her vulnerability- basically salvaged her from a ship wreck. Yet, even they weren't responding to her messages.

Clarah swore out loud, 'shite, what has happened to everyone?' For a moment, she suspected the entire earth had died and she was the only person still breathing.

She threw her phone down on the bed as though it was its fault. She had no idea what was wrong with either of the Baratolli brothers. She had no idea what was wrong with everyone. Her parents both knew she was back home, yet it seemed could not be bothered to make the effort to welcome her back. Baba May and Aunt Mary had vanished off the planet

... she knew not why, where or come to think of it – how. Kane could not string two sentences together- even when sober. Her elder sister Katalyn no longer wanted to know her, nor she her. Her younger sister Nina drifted in and out of some strange Hindu never never land and as for Denny...she had no idea where he was, and neither did she care... or care that much. Well - maybe she cared a little, but more out of nosiness.

Yes, indeed – aside from Molly Malone she was quite alone. The feeling of isolation was as alarming as it was restful. Time for more wine! She wondered if this is how it all starts – the downwards slope into the pits of depression. Probably!

The tiredness was beginning to take its toll, and with jet lag still playing havoc with her system, Clarah's eyes slowly closed.

CHAPTER 6

Saturday 26th September 2015
ASPEN COLORADO

Meanwhile on the other side of the Atlantic, Konnor was driving through the most stunning of geographies. This had to be one of the longest driveway in the whole of the USA, but boy…what a drive. In the midst of the autumn fall, the trees were every colour of red and orange that one could imagine. In the distance, snow-capped mountains cast their doppelganger images onto the lake. The portrait emerging from outside the car window was further blessed by a spectacular sunset. As the sun bid the day farewell, it contributed a hue of flushed pink to the glistening mountain peaks.

Konnor's grandparents lived in Colorado, and he had stayed with them on many occasions. He was quite accustomed to the magnificent splendour of the area. However, he had never grown complacent about its incredible beauty. Summer, spring, winter or fall…especially fall – this little slice of planet Earth never ceased to amaze him- and now he was back for the weekend. Back in a yesteryear place he once loved, but on this occasion, it was for another reason. It was a reason that left him feeling nervous and uncertain. However, for the moment he was driving with the window open and the sweetest of air was blowing through his golden locks. On the radio, the song "Good Life" by "One Republic" played, easing his journey with its soft melody and pertinent lyrics.

The driveway continued to go on and on. Konnor began to wonder what type of house belonged to a driveway like this. Winding its way through the autumnal forest, it was the pumping artery that fed visitors into the stomach of the Lezemel family home. Such a place for such a family was bound to have the highway to hell as its conduit.

Konnor shuddered as he mentally spoke their name. He couldn't believe that his sister Armarni was getting engaged to playboy lothario Ze'ev Lezemel. Tonight, was their engagement party and Konnor was on a behaviour warning from his older sibling. Armarni didn't trust Konnor and she was right to do so.

As a 20-year-old guy, he felt uncomfortable pimped up in a formal suit and bow tie; much preferring to be back on the campus of USC in torn jeans and baggy tee-shirt. In fact, he had much preferred to be back on the island of Bali with Clarah, however he guessed that maybe she was now just a fling from the past. She had hardly contacted him since he had been back in California. Konnor had a sneaking suspicion that Asher had stayed behind with her in Bali, despite all his brother's protestations that he couldn't stand the girl. He simply didn't trust Ash...not as far as women were concerned. Asher was just a bit too similar to his father Reed, having inherited his sultry good looks and seductive charm. Konnor tried to cast the thought from his mind. He was a sensitive soul, and the thought of double betrayal would wound him deeply.

With a turn of the corner, the Lezemel mansion finally came into view. It was as he expected it to be; a hungry monster extending its lizard-like tongue towards the end of the endless driveway. Two large rectangular windows ran the full length of the house, and even had the appearance of eyes. Konnor had a fertile imagination, so the large porch covered doorway soon became a nose and a mouth. It had a face. It was watching him with its wooden face. Konnor considered it to be a timber framed ogre. The Lezemel winter retreat has been built in a typical forest-lodge design, but bigger, bolder, brasher and…he couldn't explain. He had run out of words. He just didn't like the place.

He drove over to the welcome committee of valet parkers at the terminus of the forever driveway. As he had expected, security men stood rooted to the spot as though they were mannequins. They had the usual wire plugged into their ears, obligatory sunglasses *(even though it was getting dark),* and he concluded, probably armed enough to deal with a military coup.

Aspen was one of the many homes of the multi-billionaire Lezemel family. The underground gossip mills rumoured them to be a dynasty of Satanist and illuminati leaders – all unconfirmed of course. History and conspiracy theorist professed that they had made their wealth through slavery, although politicians and accountants had spun a very different story. Konnor didn't want to think about it too deeply and shuddered at the thought of having Ze'ev as a brother-in-law.

The hired men in black opened the car door for him, and Konnor did his posh-best to disembark with a degree of dignity. His legs were stiff from the long drive and he already felt nervous. However, a quick scan of the area revealed no headless chickens dashing about the place and a distinct lack of severed heads dangling from any tree branches. He gave a heavy sigh of relief as he was guided towards the large oak door, but oh no…there it was. The "Seal of Solomon" in all its magical Kabbalistic glory, was engraved into the wood. Perhaps Konnor had been too premature in castigating his overly-wrought imagination. Perhaps the Lezemel empire was as it was rumoured to be – strange magic of the blackest kind and here he was…about to walk into the viper's nest.

Downstairs, the basement had been converted into a nightclub. Dug into the bedrock, it was perfectly insulated. No noise could escape the thick basement walls – not that there was anywhere for it to escape to. Not that there was anyone around to hear anything anyway. Its isolation was both convenient and disturbing. The floors and walls were awash with psychedelic images. Vibrant swirls and spirals, rotated along the dancefloor, then meandering up the walls like vibrant pythons.

His sister's young friends were perched on bar stools and partaking in the world of molecular mixology. Multi-coloured drinks misted with liquid Nitrogen, made their way across the rainbow illuminated bar. Giddy young females laughed hysterically at the crude titles given to many of the concoctions; their tipsy giggles almost drowned out by the hypnotic dance music. Around the corner of the L-shaped room, roulette tables were manned by an army of professional croupiers, and alongside blackjack tables and slot machines, the ambience was one of a Las Vegas casino in all its decadent glory. To add to the flavour and further lower the tone, partially clad showgirls swung on precarious swings braced into the mirrored ceilings. Armarni considered the whole thing to be vulgar, but her in-laws had contrasting opinions and after all, it was their house. No amount of pleading with Ze'ev had made the slightest difference, and so basically, she had to shut up and put up. Armarni had been instructed that many of their high-profile guests required privacy, and hidden amongst the mountain forest of Colorado, this was a place that assured total discretion.

Meanwhile the upstairs party could not have been more of a contrast, as the more mature guests sipped on demure Martini's and chitter chattered about share prices, with the occasional political snipe.

A pianist played bossa-nova lounge music in the background. It was blandly inoffensive. The notes virtually disintegrated underneath the sophisticated babble of the rich, famous and well-connected.

Reed cringed. As a musician, bland music did not fall into his ears with ripples of orgasmic delight. He had requested that he should attend his daughter's engagement party under his new, *(original name)* of Tony Mort. However, the Lezemel party organisers had objected. With their constant thirst for sensationalism, the name of Reed Baratolli with his much-reported fall from grace, added a wicked sparkle to the guest list. Tony Mort was merely associated with a homeless shelter in New York, and somehow that didn't quite have the same garish appeal.

Feeling less than at ease, his smile broadened when a young man with a tuft of unruly yellow hair made his way into the human zoo. Konnor rushed over to his father and gave him a sociably unacceptable bear-hug. Reed moved his son back so he could gaze upon his tanned boyish face.

'You have no idea how pleased I am to see you,' proclaimed Reed. It had been at least six months since they last met and Reed struggled to keep his emotions suppressed. Konnor was not one to mince his words and cut to the chase.

'I have missed you too Dad, but what the hell are we doing here with these crazies? Remind me again, but why is my sister marrying into this family – aside from their astronomical wealth that is?'

'Don't judge her too harshly,' responded Reed. 'Armarni was born with a silver spoon in her mouth. But then one day she woke up and the spoon was replaced by a plastic straw and it was all my fault. You know, it's always easy to go up in life Konnor, but bloody hard to come down.

Simple rule of thumb - you don't miss what you have never had, but you do miss what has been taken away.'

Reed took a large gulp of Scotch and continued, 'a downward trajectory hurts. Trust me son... I know. But hey, let's chill. We are stuck here, so we may as well blend. Let's head for the basement bar, get some of those strange vaporising cocktails and find the bride-to-be. Is Asher planning on being here?'

Konnor went quiet. Reed repeated the question. His son shrugged. Reed repeated the question yet again.

'I don't bloody know Dad – I last saw him in Bali about 7 or 8 weeks ago. There was a girl...'

Konnor didn't say anything more. He didn't need to. Reed understood. During his marriage to Konnor's step-mum Eenayah, he had been a rogue, a philander, a flirt and every other adjective used to describe a shameless cheat. He remembered many a conversation with his best friend Fabien, which began with the line, 'there was a girl.'

If anyone understood the call of the siren, it was Reed. Asher was a good-looking boy and a son he adored, but alas he was also a seasoned charmer. He took after his father. The moment was awkward. Reed knew to change the subject.

'So, if we see him, we see him, and if we don't – whatever. Ash will turn up if he wants to I guess.'

Father and son made their way down towards the basement noise and shrieks of merriment far more appealing than the upper-deck morgue.

They passed by Tia Lembugo and her fiancé Nico as they descended down the diamond encrusted staircase. The couple were so wrapped up in each other's company that they failed to notice anyone aside from one another. Konnor nudged his Dad.

'Err, did we just walk past a world-renowned chef and his famous actress girlfriend by any chance?'

Reed had met many famed people in his life, so wasn't as easily impressed as his credulous youngest son.

'Tia and Nico, yes indeed. Unlikely pair, but they seem all loved up. I believe they are getting married next year. Now stop acting so starstruck Kon and let's try to find your sister.'

Armarni Baratolli had just come out of the aptly named ladies powder room, with a few tell-tale particles of white powder still visible on her upper lip. Her pupils were overly dilated, and Reed recognised that his daughter was unusually talkative and elated. His heart sank. She wasn't doing anything that he hadn't done before, but the sense of disappointment weighed heavy in his heart. It may have been hypocritical of him to mentally condemn her, but he had hoped she would have turned out to be a better person. At least a better person than he had been in his tempestuous youth.

She hugged her father and threw herself at her brother in an overstated show of sibling love. Konnor and Reed gave each other a knowing look. They then looked up at the semi naked girls swinging from the ceiling, each adorned with bestial masks which covered their pretty faces with snouts.

Konnor looked around, remembering the sweet charm of Bali; now comparing it to this place of diabolical wantonness. It had an atmosphere of depraved impiety; thinly disguised as an engagement party. Drugs, drink, gambling and debauch nudity. This was hardly the norm for a family celebration.

'Do we think we can meet Ze'ev?' asked Reed, keen for an introduction to his future son-in-law. Almost like a rabbit appearing from a top hat, and spot on time, Ze'ev appeared hanging onto the arms of TV presenter Maddox Burnham; both laughing like tipsy schoolboys.

If Reed could have uttered one word at this first meeting it would have been the word "false". He disliked Ze'ev instinctively, but then again Reed would have despised any man who came close to his only daughter.

Ze'ev shook Reeds hand and thanked him for attending the party. To Reeds surprise, he found Ze'ev polite, courteous and intelligent. Reed wanted to dislike the man. He would have preferred that Ze'ev fitted some immoral stereotype, but surprisingly there wasn't much to dislike. Ze'ev displayed genuine affection for Armarni, and scolded her for the powder-room powdering event.

Armarni had always been a wild child; especially after her mother Julia died. When Reed considered it logically, Ze'ev was the better outcome of the many fates that may have awaited Armarni. Memories came flooding back; her running away from home, her bulimia, her drinking, her bouts of self-harming. He considered that perhaps this future marriage was the preferred destiny.

Ze'ev put a protective arm around Armarni and made her swallow some water. The son-in-law to be, was acting the gentleman and doing all the right things. Reed felt an immense sense of relief.

Konnor sulked in the corner, deeply regretting his decision to attend what he considered to be a superficial celebration. Sure, the girls were pretty. Most of them were probably models in search of a rich husband, but Konnor was neither husband material or rich. He wondered where his brother was, and then wondered where Clarah was. He wondered if they were together. He had left them alone together in Bali. Surely that had been a mistake?

Reed spotted the depressed aura which seemed to shroud his son in a dark desolate energy.

'A penny for them?' he asked. His son let out a resigned sigh.

'Just thinking about an English girl, I met on my tour of Asia. She was unusual. Nice, different, funny. I tried not to like her but... you know how it goes sometimes? I think she may be with Ash now. They have both gone silent on me and they stayed behind in Bali together. I just sense that something isn't right. Nothing I can do about it I suppose.'

Reed tried to change the subject, so pulled a book out of his man-bag. He handed it to Konnor saying, 'your step-mother had this book written for me before she went missing. It's all about my family history. She even took some of the photos of the town my grandfather came from. A place called Leigh in Lancashire, England...a million miles and a million lifetimes away from here. I suspect these may have been some of the last photos Eenayah ever took. It was a present for my 50th birthday. You know son, I didn't take care of her as much as I should have done. I didn't even take care of this book as much as I should have done. Sometimes we just forget to care. Anyway, out of all her stepchildren, Eenayah loved you the most y'know. It belongs to you now.'

Konnor had never seen the book before. He hadn't even known of its existence. He fingered the cover and sniffed its pages. He wasn't sure why he sniffed the pages. Perhaps some books can tell a story with a smell.

He asked, 'what's with the heart shaped hole carved into the cover?' Reed smiled. It was the forlorn smile of regret tinged with guilt.

'That hole once contained a heart shaped ruby. It was a genuine gemstone. She loved your Aunt Ruby so much.'

Konnor ran his fingers along the shape.

'What happened to it.'

'Someone stole it, 'replied Reed. 'As I said before, I didn't take care of it and when you don't look after something, someone else can come along and take it away from you. You understand what I am saying, don't you son.'

Konnor understood perfectly.

'You know what Dad, I have booked myself into a motel in the nearby town and if it isn't too impolite, I am going to check in early. I have had enough of this circus. Can you send my apologies to Armarni? I may even make a start on this book. I would prefer to sit quietly and read about your ancestors, than stay here at this wacky party.'

Of course, Reed understood. He would have done the same himself, had it not been for the fact that Ze'ev's family insisted that he stay at the family home.

He watched as his son left the room, silently wishing that he could have followed him. He tried not to yawn, but he yawned anyway.

It was at that exact moment, that a blonde woman approached him holding two glasses of champagne. She wore a figure hugging crimson gown, with a flesh revealing side split; one that extended up to her hips. 'Hello Reed,' she whispered seductively, 'are we keeping you up?' Reed could not believe his misfortune. He looked at her, looked away to slap his forehead and then turned to face her again.

'Bloody hell Emmanuelle. What are you doing here?'

Emmanuelle laughed. 'What? You are surprised to see me at a party hosted by an alleged dynasty of devil worshipers? Did you expect me to be selling fairy cakes on a charity stall in aid of a new church roof?' Reed couldn't help but laugh. Emmanuelle always did have an impish sense of humour. However, he also reminded himself not to be complacent about her playful charms. It would be all too easy to get sucked into her world. Reed had made that mistake once before. Emmanuelle was a clever demoness and one that could delicately manipulate her victims to do her bidding.

Reed repeated his question, determined not to be side-tracked.

'Come on Emmanuelle. I know you like a good party, but I also know that you don't waste your precious time on anything that doesn't promise a pot of gold at the end of the rainbow. Why are you here?'

Emmanuelle handed Reed one of the champagne flutes, then alluringly sucked on the cherry at the end of her cocktail stick. She considered her answer carefully.

'Actually, 'she replied, 'I came to talk to that lovely young son of yours. It's a shame he had to leave so early.'

Reed instantly became concerned. Memories of how Emmanuelle had killed his first wife Julia in a car accident, came flooding back to mind.

'Please don't do anything to Konnor, 'he begged. A tremor was now obvious in his voice.

'He is only a kid. What could you possibly want with him?'

'It isn't him I want Reed. It's the girl he met in Asia. The one who keeps tugging at his pathetic heart strings. The one his brother seduced the minute Konnor's back was turned. Two brothers and one woman –

seems like a bit of an on-going theme in your family. Didn't your second wife do the whole brother's thing?'

Reed ignored the bitchy snipe, feeling relieved that Emmanuelle's attention was focused on someone aside from his son. He knew very little about this girl, only that his son had met someone, someone he was struggling to forget.

'Who is she Emmanuelle? What do you want with her?'

The demoness flicked her crystal grass with her index finger in mock boredom. Avoiding the question, she looked around and waved at a trio in the corner.

'You must surely remember Océane. She was your "once upon a time" musical prodigy. We had such fun in the recording studio. Happy days Reed. Oh, and look – there is Arabella, your "once upon a time" PA. Not sure if you have ever met Tobiah however. He is sort of related to the Lezemel family. Bet you didn't know they were connected to Jack the Ripper ah? It can be quite interesting – all this ancestry stuff.'

Emmanuelle had brought along her entourage of lesser demons. Reed found it ironically amusing, that despite all the probable conjuring's of the Lezemel clan… the real deal was actually standing in their basement club and they didn't even know it.

Pathetic as it was, he waved back at the trio.

He repeated his question. 'Who is this girl you refer to? What is she to you?'

Emmanuelle brushed her long platinum tresses behind her shoulder and replied, 'her name is Clarah. She is very special. Actually, I don't want to kill her – I need her to stay safe, but I am afraid I had to do something very bad to her to keep her safe. Despite what you think of me

Reed, there are some things I don't like doing and hurting the unborn is one of them. It was a necessity.'

Reed looked alarmed and confused.

She continued, 'make sure that Konnor stays away from her. He shouldn't get involved with someone such as her. She is the wrong kind of woman. If you see Asher any time soon, tell him to do the same. She is trouble. Remember what happened to you Reed. You don't want anything bad to happen to your little boys now do you. That's all I will say. They must stay away from Clarah. I have a plan for her and it does not involve your sons.'

With that Emmanuelle turned and walked away. Reed was rooted to the spot – quite unable to move. The word 'petrified' seemed appropriate for his condition. He looked to the floor. He was in shock and was visibly shaking. By the time he looked up, Emmanuelle and her devilish team had vanished. He still couldn't move. The thought kept invading his mind, 'who the hell is this…Clarah?'

CHAPTER 7

Saturday 26th September 2015
MEETING THE DEVINE AURA

It was 3am, and Clarah was slumbering in an agitated hot/cold, half-asleep/half-awake, dry/sweaty state; drifting in and out of lucid dreams and strange nightmares.

Occasionally she drifted back to the lost moments on the aircraft and the journey back from Indonesia. Something strange had happened on that flight – she knew it, but she couldn't be sure what it was. Something bigger and something ultimately powerful, wasn't giving her the privilege of that final memory.

As she tossed, turned and wrestled with the gremlins of amnesia, the heavily quilted bedspread, made its way down below her chest. In her sleep like state, she pulled the cover back up to her neck. A sweaty leg made its way out from beneath the tapestry quilt, as again the cover descended down the bed. As the sweat cooled her body down, she unconsciously pulled the cover back over her by way of a reflex action. This charade repeated itself several times, until the exhaustion of the night lulled her into unconsciousness. No longer correcting the dissident cover, it made its way below her waist. As a sudden chill submerged her into coldness, a swift action heaved the sheet down below her knees.

Her eyes opened wide.

It was a sudden awakening; a dramatic realisation that something… something profusely unnatural was removing her bed cover. Bit by bit, the material was making its way off her body. A sudden wrench on the quilt confirmed her worst fears as it fell upon the carpeted floor. The absent duvet left her body feeling strangely exposed and vulnerable. There had been a womb like assurance about being enclosed by thick warm blankets, and for now this protective fluffy shield was missing.

Clarah shot upright like an angry spark spitting out from a fire. A dark pixelated shadow seemed to glide across the room.

'Bugger it, 'she thought, 'there's a bloody ghost in my room.'

She let out a pathetic scream, and then was immediately aware that maybe nobody would hear her. She was alone, or was she alone? She could see her own breath. Why was her room so cold?

In a sudden assault, which came from nothing and nowhere, she was thrown back onto her bed. Her throat felt constricted as a heavy presence seemed to press upon her chest. She couldn't breathe. She had been sat upright, but now something weighed her down. She tried to scream, but she couldn't. For one split second, it was as though something blocked her airways. She tried to cough, but nothing happened. Her body was paralysed, yet she screamed inside her head. If she couldn't make the sound, at least she could make the thought of the sound.

The weight pressed down upon her hips. Rancid breath settled upon the nape of her neck. A sudden jab, and it seemed as though blood spurted from the vein in her throat. She mentally cried for help. She was being attacked. Her throat was being attacked. 'What the hell,' she screamed inside her head. It was as though something was actually invading her veins.

Unbeknown to Clarah, her grandmother was now back home and Baba May heard Clarah's silent cries for help. She was a psychically tuned Romany lady. She could hear every groan and creak of the woodwork. So of course, she could hear the psychic howl of her own granddaughter.

She rushed into Clarah's room, and picked up the distressed girl – rocking her in her arms like a baby.

'Hush, hush my sweet darling. I am here now – nothing can hurt you.'

Clarah relaxed. She could smell the familiar rose-water scent on her Grandmothers clothes. It lulled her back into a childlike state. Lavender or roses, both were equally calming and reassuring. Exhausted, she closed her eyes, comforted by the warm rocking movement of Baba May. Her grandmother stroked her forehead, as tears fell down from her cheeks. The grandfather clock struck 4am, as Clarah finally drifted off.

9.41am and once again her eyes were open wide. Her immediate awakening thought was, 'what the hell just happened? Was it a dream? A nightmare? Some sort of illusion, or was any of that shit real?'

She ran out of her room, down the stairs and into the kitchen. Baba May was always up with the crowing of a rooster. She would surely be sat at the kitchen table, drinking tea, eating toast and watching the breakfast news. That was what she always did, but the kitchen was empty. The kettle was cold, as was the toaster. The TV was switched off.

Clarah then ran from room to room, looking for signs of life. Aunt Mary's ground floor adapted room was starkly void of clutter. She hadn't been in there before. Clarah scanned it with detective-like precision. Indeed, it had been kitted out for a disabled person, with all the wall bars and so on, yet everything was simply too perfect. The bed was neatly made up, but with not a single crease in the sheets. The thought suddenly occurred to Clarah, that the room looked unslept in – yet she had spoken with Aunt Mary the day after she had got back from Asia. Where was Aunt Mary now? She had not seen her mother's sister since yesterday. Somewhere in the back of her mind she had considered it odd, but then dismissed her concern as nothingness.

Come to think on it - where was Baba May? She was sure it had been her gran who cradled her after the nightmare. She ran upstairs to her grandmother's room, and with some relief it did display signs of being lived in, but looked as though it had been abandoned in a hurry. Used towels were lying by the sink, and a full laundry basket commanded attention. However, the room was still empty- lived in or not.

She started to panic. The empty house was now teasing her. Yet Baba May had come into her room and comforted her. Opening door after door, she finally found her brother Kane's room. She knew it was his abode before the door was fully opened. The smell that met her nose was putrefying. Her brother was snoring heavily in a deep whisky induced sleep. She noted old vomit on his pillowcase, and a mouldy plate of chips by his bed. His face was smeared with mud. She resolved that she really needed to speak with someone about Kane. His pallor was pale and blotchy and his nose swollen and reddened. He didn't look well. What the heck, she wasn't a nurse. Now was not the time for tea and sympathy. Right at this moment she was running scared and needed to find someone – anyone. Where was everyone?

She then ran to Nina's room, with hope against hope of finding something slightly normal behind the door. A startled Nina was sat on the bed reading some teenage music magazine. As her long absent sister rushed in, she gasped and ran over to hug her.

'Clarah, Clarah – when did you get back? Did you like my welcome home poster and the balloons?'

Clarah was confused. She pulled away from her.

'Anju, are you Anju,' she asked?

Nina giggled in a childish way.

' Oh no – don't be silly. Anju was a friend, but she has gone now. I am back again. This is me – your twin sister…Nina.'

Clarah started to cry as she hugged her beloved sister. At first, just small minuscule tears, which soon grew into big heartfelt sodden floods of emotion. She squeezed Nina tightly.

'My God, it's good to have you back Nina. I cannot begin to tell you how much I have missed you. I am so sorry I left you. I panicked. I know that's no real excuse. Please forgive me.'

Nina looked confused. She wore the face of a child, too full of wonder and happiness to bother with such minor issues as recrimination. 'There is nothing to forgive Clarah – you are here now. We will be together forever. I won't let you leave me again.' Nina hugged Clarah.

At that moment, the doorbell rang, followed by an insistent wrapping. Clarah concluded that it must be her Grandmother. Baba May had always been an early riser, so had probably popped out to the village for something or the other. Maybe she had gone to the butcher for some fresh bacon. Breakfast sounded like a good idea as her tummy was beginning to rumble, and besides – she needed to ask her Grandmother about the strange invisible visitor to her room.

'Stay here Nina, don't move. I am just going to open the door for Baba May.'

Nina was confused and shouted after her, 'but she already has a key to get in. She can come and go as she pleases.'

Clarah didn't hear her, and ran downstairs anyway.

A fresh faced young lady was standing on the doorstep. The unexpected caller quite took Clarah by surprise. The girl was of a similar age to Clarah, and had the biggest whitest smile she had ever seen. Clarah couldn't quite work out her ethnicity. She looked quite oriental, yet her skin was radiant alabaster. Her eyes were as blue as the sky, yet complimented by her jet-black air, they looked even brighter and bluer. She was carrying a basket of eggs which she unpredictably thrust into Clarah's arms. Clarah stepped back in surprise, clinging onto the old-fashioned egg basket as best she could.

'Hi, my name is Aura. I hope I'm not intruding. I know it's quite early in the day, but our hens have laid too many eggs and I wondered if you would like some. Always best eaten fresh.'

It was a direct, and even slightly forced introduction. Within the Gypsy community, Clarah had rarely mixed with strangers and so the niceties of first meetings was something she had yet to adjust to.

She wasn't sure quite what to say.

'Oh…that's very kind of you Aura. My name is Clarah.'

For an awkward few seconds, they stood in silence, neither of them quite knowing what to say next. Clarah then suddenly found her tongue. 'Where are my manners; please come in Aura. I have just woken up after a bad night's sleep, but I would die for an omelette. Thank you for bringing along your surplus eggs. Please…come in. I will put the kettle on.'

Clarah tried not to show it, as her kind did not show weakness, but she was sorely relieved to finally have some company. The stillness and silence of the house, had been starting to play tricks with her mind.

Aura followed Clarah down the corridor, observing every picture on the wall, and noting each knot in every beam. Her eyes were large with wonderment and sheer delight.

'I have always been curious about this house Clarah. I live up on the farm, and from my bedroom window I can just about make out the roof amongst the tree's. It's a strange thing isn't it. The less we can see of something, the more we want to see it. Thank you for inviting me in by the way. I hope I didn't come over as too pushy. It is just a joy to be here.'

Clarah was puzzled by her young visitor's obvious enthusiasm. Being a non-house dweller, she had probably taken the 17th century house for granted. It was just a place to sleep, indeed a very nice place to sleep – but aside from being a glorious historical shelter, she had no emotions towards its ancient wattle and daub.

She replied, 'you are welcome Aura and yes the house is sort of remote, isn't it? I am guessing that's why my parents purchased this place. It's far from the road, hidden away in acres of fields and just very peaceful …and most of all it is private. I have only just come back from my travels, so I haven't really had time to explore anywhere yet. The jet lag has really screwed my bloody clock up. I can't quite puzzle where the time has gone and I remember nothing at all about being on the plane. What day is it?'

Clarah may not have been overly endowed with the minutiae of social etiquette, but even she recognised that she had told her new friend too much too soon. The girl seemed to have a deep interest in the house, so Clarah concluded that maybe it was best to change the subject and focus on that. Too soon to hang out the dirty laundry.

With that very thought, Clarah asked, 'so...If you are local, and you sound as though you may be – perhaps you can tell me all about this place while I cook us breakfast. I take it that you are joining me for breakfast?' Aura beamed with a smile that stretched right across her face.

'I would love to, and just for the record – today is Saturday,' she replied. 'I grew up on the local farm. Those are all our fields over to the left. My dad is a farmer. Doesn't sound too glamorous does it. I am the youngest daughter; in fact, I am the only daughter. Growing up amongst brothers, I sort of missed female companionship. The village folk are mostly elderly. The younger population tend to move out to the cities for work. If you are not a farmer, butcher, publican, fisherman or a clergyman– then there isn't a whole lot of employment around these parts.'

'So why are you still here?' Clarah suddenly felt unusually inquisitive. 'Oh, I am sorry – I didn't mean to be nosey.'

'That's okay. I don't mind talking about it, 'responded Aura. 'My father has a big farm to run, and my mother has advanced multiple sclerosis. I am her main carer. My Dad couldn't cope without my help. So here I am.'

She sighed and then smiled again. Never one to stay down for long, Aura always seemed to smile and then smile yet more.

By now they were in the kitchen and Clarah had started to beat the freshly laid eggs.

'I am sorry about your mother Aura. My Aunt Mary is disabled, although I'm not sure quite why or how. Maybe it's arthritis – something like that. My Gran looks after her. It must be hard for her, looking after her own daughter and all that, but my Gran is a very strong old lady. Being a carer is such an important job, but a big responsibility I guess.'

As she poured the mixture into the frying pan, Clarah started to become curious about her unexpected guest.

She asked, 'tell me Aura, how did you know I was here – seeing that the house is hidden away in the tree's and all that?'

Aura smiled yet again as she replied, 'I saw you walk into the village yesterday. You sat down next to Kane. Nobody ever sits down next to Kane, so I sort of figured you must be related. We all know that Kane lives up at the big house, so it wasn't rocket science to work out where you lived.'

'Hmm, I guess that figures,' responded Clarah. It seemed like a reasonable explanation.

'Would you like ham and cheese in your omelette Aura?'

'Yes, pile them both in. Why have you put out three dishes by the way?'

Clarah winked at her as she went to the bottom of the stairs and shouted Nina's name. As she went back to the kitchen she replied, 'one of the plates is for my twin sister. She is totally sweet, but a bit on the simple side. I am not totally sure if she is autistic, suffering from some psychiatric thing or even possessed by evil spirits – but something isn't quite right. Just pre-warning you. Try not to judge her. She is smart, but in a different way…oh and her heart is pure. Oddly enough, she is the happiest person I know. Perhaps that's what happens when you don't think too deeply about life. Perhaps with no thoughts, one finds peace.'

'You have a deeply philosophical attitude to life Clarah – it is unusual. I have never seen Nina before. I suspect many of the villagers don't even know she exists. So …where are the rest of your family? I have noted some comings and goings from your house, but you mostly seem to keep yourself to yourselves. The villagers talk, and gossip and wonder, and then before you know it the imagination takes over…and then they create a painting from a few splashes of ink. You know what small places are like? We are all just nosey neighbours.'

Clarah knew exactly what she meant. She had spent her life in a small community, so she didn't need any lectures about the wrath of small talk.

The two young women sat down at the kitchen table, whilst the empty plate awaited Nina's decent from her bedroom. Clarah looked uneasy. She liked her visitor. Aside from the two French girls she met in Cambodia, she had never had a gaje friend before and welcomed the opportunity to download her worries. However, she still needed to remain cautious. Clarah wasn't sure if a gaje could be trusted.

'So, here's the deal Aura. I have just come back from a year back-packing around Asia and Australia. If that sounds fun, then yes it was – but in truth it was more of an escape than a vacation. It's a long story and I don't want to go into the nitty gritty right now…just explaining why I have only just arrived here and why I have this silly hair.'

She then turned around to catch her reflection in the glass door of the oven.

'My God, this style now looks totally inappropriate for a British autumn in a place within ear shot of the cold North Sea.'

Aura leaned over to touch her new friend's braids.

'Hey Clarah– I style my Mum's hair all the time. Would you like me to sort this out for you? I can give you a whole new look.'

Clarah exhaled with a hefty sigh of relief.

'Please do something with this tangled mop Aura. The whole "fresh off a Thai beach" look, doesn't fit in with my life anymore.'

'No problem, responded Aura, 'I can put in some soft brown/copper tones in if you like. A warmer look would suit you. Anyway – back to my question. Where are you hiding the rest of your family?'

As Nina bounded into the kitchen like a giggling schoolgirl, Clarah pointed in her direction.

'Well – this is my sister Nina. Kane is upstairs snoring and the less said about him the better. You know about Kane anyway. My mother is allegedly at some health farm or spa thing, and I am told that my father is in Las Vegas. I don't think they expected me to be back this week, so it's not their fault. It was a last-minute flight… yet another long story about a bounty hunter and a price tag. I probably caught them on the hop. I am sure they will be back soon…hope so anyway.'

Clarah's face sunk into a sulk as she focused on the kitchen tiles. Aura felt sorry for her.

'I have been away a long time,' she continued, 'and I really miss them. I dread seeing them though. I am in bad books – very bad books. Humongous big trouble.'

Aura looked at her with yet more sympathy.

'Don't say it- another long story ah? You seem to have a lot of long stories Clarah.'

Clarah wondered about her new friend with the strange name. She had stood on her doorstep with a basket of eggs, an infectious big smile, and a massively positive demeanour. She has marched down the hallway, and into her kitchen with an unwavering note of marvel and mirth. Her beaming face had rescued Clarah from a chilling lonesome nightmare and a moment of panic. She liked the girl from the farm and enjoyed consuming her surplus eggs. But now, the sudden switch to what she could only decipher as compassion was confusing. Aura was beginning to figure her out, and starting to question her about her many untold long stories. It was too much, too soon. Clarah suddenly became uncomfortable.

Aura started to push more buttons. Her inquisitiveness was becoming a runaway train.

'You mentioned your Aunt Mary and your Grandmother. Are they around? I would love to meet them. I have caught sight of them a few times in the village, but they seemed like they didn't want to be approached. People can do that sometimes. It's as though they wear a "keep off the grass" sign.'

Clarah almost chocked on her cheesy omelette, and without thinking went on a mini rant.

'You would like to meet them? Hey join my club, as so the bloody hell would I. Here's the puzzling part of all this, we don't even have a car or anything. Maybe the odd broomstick in the cupboard, but nothing mechanical. Yet they never seem to be in the house. I haven't seen my aunt since the day I arrived, and as for my grandmother…I call her Baba May by the way…she seems to float in and out like a blinking apparition. Talking of which in the early hours of this morning something….'

Clarah cut her sentence short. She was blabbering on too much and giving far too much away. She hardly knew Aura. She shouldn't tell her about the strange incident in her room. The moving of the covers, the choking, the stabbing sensation on her throat, the weight on her chest. She shuddered.

Aura probed for more information, 'something…what something? What happened? What did this something do to you Clarah?' Aura had made it an impossible question not to answer.

With some reluctance Clarah replied, 'something came into my room last night and whatever it was pulled the duvet off my bed. It was a man; I am sure it was. You are a local Aura. You must know the history of this area like the back of your hand. What do you know about this house? Is it haunted? It feels haunted to me.'

Aura took the empty plates away and walked over to the sink to wash them. She played the role of obedient daughter who did everything for her mother, so tidying up after herself was an apparent reflex action. It seemed to fit the situation. She went to sit back down, bringing Clarah a fresh mug of tea. The smiling stranger had most certainly made herself at home.

Aura eventually replied, 'well your house is both the oldest and the biggest in the village – and probably in the entire area. Locals know it as Morladron Diank. Someone once told me that this means "pirates escape". No idea if that is linguistically correct or not, but it is possible. There are supposed to be tunnels in your cellar that lead directly down to the caves; caves reputed to be used for smuggling. Maybe you saw the ghost of an old pirate looking for his hidden treasure.'

Aura stifled a laugh as she continued, 'but then again, an old man once lived here. My family only knew him as Jacko. He was a bit of a recluse and the house was ignored for decades. It got into a terrible state. He died here and nobody found his body for quite a while. Few villagers would ever come to this house. I find that both sad and shameful, that someone could just die and nobody would even notice. That is tragic – don't you think Clarah? Anyway, it was purchased by some investment company. Folks who are expert in renovating listed buildings. It took many years for the developers to get it looking like this – lots of red tape and hurdles to jump through. However, from what I can see they did a good job and then your family moved in just over a year ago. That's all I know. Thank you for letting me see it on the inside.'

Clarah was sure her visitor was embellishing the truth. Aura frequently turned her back to her, then walking back over to the kitchen window. She had noted that her visitor did that several times, mostly when she wanted to hide the expressions on her face. As Aura washed her tea cup, she gazed out at the panoramic view from the window. Even to a local who had seen the dramatic rocky landscape of sea and beach a million times, it still captivated her with its beauty. It was as though she was seeing it for the first time, and yet allegedly she lived here. It didn't add up.

She addressed Clarah, 'do you know that your house actually sits on a small island? I mean, it's not technically an island as such, but it's only connected to the main land by a small bridge and a rocky path, but only when the tide is out. When the tide is in, you only have the bridge. It's a wobbly old thing. The restoration company should have repaired it, but they seemed to lose interest in this place very suddenly. Who knows why? The bridge only spans a narrow stretch of water, but the sea below is full of nasty under currents. Rumour has it that many a man may have drowned in that water. It's quite deep and totally treacherous. Then when the tide is out, you may think you are safe – but the beach below the bridge is made up of quick sand. You should never go there. It will suck you in and kill you. Without that wee bridge, you are quite trapped here. Quite, quite trapped. Maybe that's why the smugglers liked it here. One man's idea of hell is another man's paradise and all that.'

Oh, the harbinger of doom. Clarah was not amused by her sombre friend. Despite overdosing on nicotine patches, she now had a deep need for a cigarette. Was it too early for a shot of Whisky? She so hoped Aura would just smile again, but her new friend was now in a sombre mood. She kept replaying the words in her head, "quite, quite trapped". Her words sounded more like a warning than a health and safety announcement. Just when she was beginning to think company was desirable, it seemed that the silence of her own company was preferable.

Aura wasn't for giving up yet and continued, 'the villagers call this John Stephenson's Rock. Same name as the famous Whitby pirate –so I guess it's possible that he once lived her. This is a very old house Clarah, and if it could speak, it would probably have many stories – maybe even as long and as complex as your secret tales. So Clarah, perhaps you did see a ghost in your bedroom, or maybe you just picked up on some residual energy. Then again, you are probably still exhausted from a long journey and the mind can play tricks when its tired. You should go back to bed and get more rest. I will come back later and sort your hair out.'

More rest – she had to be joking. The local farmers daughter had just told her that she was "quite, quite trapped". Not just one "quite" but a double "quite". This was not exactly a restful thought.

Clarah couldn't help herself – she blurted out, 'can I come over and stay with you Aura – please?' She felt ashamed and embarrassed as soon as the words had fallen from her mouth.

'No, I am sorry, 'replied Aura. 'My mother isn't well and besides; you have Nina to look after. Why don't you sleep in her room tonight? Safety in numbers and all that. Maybe your Grandmother will be home soon. Sorry; I need to get back to the farm now, but it was lovely to meet you both. I will come back tomorrow with some scissors and hair dye. Would 1pm be okay?'

1pm– yes that sounded like a plan.

As Aura took one last look out of the window, she noticed the stables. 'Do you have horses,' she asked?

'Yes, a stallion, a mare and four Shires for the four horsemen of the apocalypse. I am sorry Aura, but your bridge story quite freaked me out. Anyway, the horses are Kane's, he is horse mad. Always has been. They are all he really cares about. I am told that the mare is mine, but in all honesty, he does all the donkey work, or I presume he does. I have yet to witness him move very much.'

Aura looked concerned.

'Maybe you should go and check on them Clarah. The last time I saw Kane, he didn't look in a fit enough state to cope with hard physical labour. Mucking out stables isn't work for the job shy. You should make sure that someone has been feeding them. Anyway – I love horses so maybe you can introduce me to them when I come back later.'

With that, Aura collected her empty egg basket and made her way towards the front door.

'See you soon. I will bring Shepherd's Pie and wine next time I call over. Oh, and homemade damson jam – its divine. 4 o-clock tomorrow - don't forget.'

She left as quickly as she arrived. The door was slammed shut.

Clarah hardly listened to her last few sentences. The comment she made about Kane made sense. She suddenly felt extreme concern for the horse's welfare. She rushed out through the back-patio door, down the garden path and towards the stables…almost tripping over her own feet as she rushed.

What stables? What horses? She didn't know what to think. What had once been stables now looked as though they had long since been converted into a tool shed – one that had not been used in many years. Cobwebs covered the doorway. Garden implements were buried in inches of dust. Spiders scurried into the corner as she opened the door. This was a place that time had forgotten. She scratched her head in confusion. What horse had she ridden upon? Where was Molly Malone? It was quite clear that no horses had been stabled in this place for a very long time. Sure, they had been here once. A horseshoe had been nailed onto the door to collect good luck. This was also a Gypsy tradition. The shoe was rusty. It had been there for a long time. Everything had.

She looked back up at the big white house. A fog had suddenly crept in from the sea and was now shrouding the white rendered walls in a white blanket of mist. It was all too much for tired eyes. Why was the house playing with her? Something was very wrong in her mixed-up inside out, upside down world, but she didn't know what or why.

Clarah was starting to hate her new home. Her sanity was being tied into a knotted sheet of madness. She must have imagined everything. Could her imagination have been so real – so persuasive?

Perhaps sleep was a good idea. Her body ached with profound exhaustion. She should rest. Why she was so tired? Perhaps she was ill? She considered this possibility. Yes, she was tired, sick and delirious. She should go back inside.

CHAPTER 8

Saturday 26th September 2015 - late evening
WAS IT A DREAM OR A MEMORY

Clarah's eyes closed as soon as her head sunk into her humongous pink pillows. As her weary body began to shut down, her head spun into action; overly excited neurons digging up the bones of long buried events.

She drifted back to the 12th July 2014. It had been a fine night after a morning of heavy showers. A big orange moon hung in the clear sky, dallying perilously close to the horizon. Threatening to collide with earth, it illuminated the camp site with venomous precision.

She remembered that night with excruciating crystal clarity. She had been alone in her caravan; curled up into a ball as stomach cramps stabbed deep within her pelvis. It was that time of the month, and her engorged uterus was in constant spasm. She could hear the rest of the girls giggling outside, excited for her hen night…. the hen night she was now too sick to attend.

Her brother in law (Peter), had been persuaded to drive the hens into Newcastle and had hired a stretch limo for the evening. At the insistence of the menfolk, he had also been bullied into being a chaperone for the night. Roma fathers would never have let their daughters loose in a big city without some sort of bodyguard. Her sister's husband was a big guy, around 6ft 5, and a body builder. The hen's fathers felt secure in the knowledge that Peter would be watching over their cherished girls.

Clarah had wished that she could join her giddy bridesmaids, but in her present state, dancing the night away in a Geordie night club was not a welcome option. With that thought, another cramp like spasm made her cry out in pain.

'Why now, why tonight,' she uttered? 'What shite timing!'

After Peter and the girls had left, Clarah decided to go into town to buy extra strong Paracetamol and tampons. This was a risky manoeuvre, but heavily bleeding and in agony, she had little choice in the matter.

The travellers had pitched up on unused common land, but none the less it was still considered to be a local beauty spot. In the morning, it was frequented by dog walkers, in the afternoon by mountain bikers and picnickers and at night by courting couples and dogging pervs.

The locals were attached to this overgrown wasteland and quite naturally were angry by the presence of the gypsies. Masked protestors sometimes collected around the front entrance and taunted them as they came and went, sometimes throwing rotten eggs at their vans.

They were out again tonight. Clarah didn't want to risk the wrath of the locals, so took the long route over to the town centre. She had found a seldom used bike track at the back of the woods. It was a bit overgrown with nettles, but came out behind some skips at the rear of the bakery. A narrow-cobbled alleyway then led out onto the main street. It was a little-known route and one she had discovered by accident.

She pulled her long dark hair back from her face, tethering it into a tight ponytail. Borrowing her brother's duffle coat, she concealed as much of her face as she could. Dressing in the untypical feminine attire of jeans and Wellington boots, she made her way towards the back of the woods by the side of the lake. The lake had been fenced off in parts, and finding the secret track entailed negotiating barbed wire. To set yet further challenges, a morning of heavy rain had partially submerged the path.

However, Clarah was a determined young lady and before long she was on the main street and making her way out of the chemist shop. Every time she passed a group of people, her heart pounded anxiously. She hoped against hope, that her shopping expedition had been a successfully executed undercover mission. As a Gypsy girl, she didn't trust the gaje settlers and the last thing she wanted, was to be recognised.

It was Saturday night and a group of drunken revellers were making their way out of the pub. She tried to avoid eye contact and hoped that wearing her boyish gear and makeup free face, she would not attract their attention.

With a mere curious glance, she noted their faces. She was sure she had once seen Kane with these boys, but then dismissed the idea as impossible. Her brother would never have mixed with these local lads, even though in truth he seemed to have more in common with them than his fellow travellers.

One of the lads then seemed to have clocked her softly featured face. She put her head down and quickened her step. She was sure they were following her. On turning the corner near the bakery, she ran down the side alleyway and hid behind the skip. She hoped that these local lads didn't know about this secret route into the woods.

She held her breath. Silence. Nothing. No footsteps, no clatter of boots along the alleyway. She concluded it must have all been in her imagination, so when she felt the coast was clear, she made a dash through the wet thickets.

She cursed the big full moon as it cast a shadow against her frame. With a sense of urgency, she thrust herself into the undergrowth, and once again hid for a few moments to ensure she wasn't being followed. The car park behind the bakery remained empty – she was safe. Time to make a move. She whispered to herself, 'run Clarah, run.'

As relief descended upon her shaking frame, she continued with her journey, plastic bag of painkillers, tampons and acne cream, dangling from her arm and cutting into her wrist.

The slimy rain-soaked path was full of precarious puddles, so forcing Clarah to walk through the birch wood. The long thin trees were huddled so close together, that they were almost impossible to navigate. As she kept changing direction to find a safe way back, she soon realised that she was quite lost.

Earlier in the day, she had scoured the common with army like fastidiousness, and had come to understand the geography of her new temporary abode better than most. The terrain had been scouted out with military precision, but now, in the darkness and even with the assistance of the big moon, she had lost her bearings.

In the distance, she heard voices – the voices sounded familiar. She had no choice but to head in their direction and hope it was the camp site.

As she moved closer, the sounds became louder and the familiar twang of Gypsy accents sounded in her ears. She felt reassured that she was heading in the right direction.

Suddenly she found herself very close to the epicentre of the boisterous noise. Too close. Far too close. She dived quickly behind a holly bush as a shocking scene met her eyes.

She curled herself up tightly like a startled hedgehog. She hoped she had not been seen. Slowly she raised her head and dared to peek out from behind the bristly leaves.

She saw her sister Nina. She could hardly believe what she was seeing. It was too horrific. Her poor sister's arms had been tied up above her head and she was hanging from a tree. Her long white skirt was covered in mud and ...was that blood? Yes, it was drips of blood...falling from a deep cut on Nina's forehead. She was naked from the waist up. One of the boys was trying to climb up onto the branch to reach her. There was too much noise; lots of angered commotion. Nina just hung there in silence. No screams, no cries – just this bewildered look of total shock on her pale childlike face.

Clarah had to get help. How could she get help? She didn't know where she was. She only knew that she was unnervingly close to this sickening scene. One false move, one crunch of a twig underfoot, a mere rustle of the holly leaves – and she would be discovered. She had to get away undetected. She had to get help. Slowly and gently, she crawled along the woodlands leafy carpet.

She felt like a forest animal, as though she had returned back to some primeval natural state. She decided that she was a fox. Yes, that was it, moving slowly and stealth like in the long grass like a stalking fox. She didn't even notice the nettle stings on her cheeks, or the holly shrapnel sunk into her wrist. Shots of adrenalin flowed through her veins, even taking away her throbbing period pains. It anaesthetised her better than any Paracetamol ever could.

Eventually she came across a clearing, and made a dash towards what she believed to be the right direction. The mud was thick and heavy on her boots. Every step was challenging, as the slimy pathway pulled her down, seeming to suck the soles of her feet into the earth.

She then heard a deep moan, coming from somewhere. It was a soul rendering noise, like the cry of death. She turned. Slightly to her left, she saw the shadow of someone on the ground. It wasn't ground though. It had a reflection like a mirror. It was water. Then almost by a deliberation of fate, the cloud covering the moon moved to one side, allowing the person to be illuminated in lunar light.

She gasped in horror. It was her brother Kane. She recognised his red corduroy jacket. He was half in and half out of a small pond. As she watched him, his grip on nearby reeds slipped and he started to sink into the green slimy water. She gasped yet again, and let out the faintest of screams as she rushed over to his side. She grabbed his sinking hand and pulled as best as she could. His hand was cold and wet. Her hands were cold and wet. He was heavy; his clothes soaked in pond water. As his head slumped forwards, his nose and mouth became totally submerged. A few bubbles escaped, bobbing up and down and mixing with the nearby frogspawn like a gurgling cocktail. The reality hit her like a hammer from hell – he was sinking into the pond. Her brother Kane was actually in the process of drowning – of dying.

Again, a shot of adrenaline zapped into her bloodstream. With a strength, she never knew she possessed, she tugged and tugged at his arm until he was half out of the pond. After this monumental effort, she lay exhausted by his side for around ten or so minutes. Panting and breathless, her heart raced and her lungs struggled to catch any breath. When she eventually recovered, she remembered Nina. 'My God – Nina,' she gasped. She checked that Kane was breathing, pushed him onto his side as best she could and then covering him with the duffle coat she had been wearing, ran off to get help.

Panic stricken and crying as she ran, she must have scurried around in aimless circles. Time stood still. She had no idea how long she had been lost, but it must have been at least half an hour or so, because by the time she made it back to the camp, Nina had made it back before her. She assumed that the boy on the branch must have cut her down and let her go or even carried her back. She hoped that was the case.

The sound of sirens could be heard close by. Blue and white flashing lights could be seen driving up the dirt track. The camp had been thrown into mayhem. Screaming, shouting, yelling, crying, hollering – it was a communal commotion. It was a sound she had never heard before, a collective racket containing every type of human emotion. Ambulance men could be seen leaving her parents caravan, and she could tell from the arm dangling off the stretcher, that they were carrying Nina.

She wanted to tell people about Kane. She tried to get some attention from everybody, anybody, somebody…but they were all so consumed in the moment that nobody listed.

She then saw her father. His face was red with a rage she had never seen before and wet from the rain that had just started to fall. She tugged at his sleeves.

'Please Da, please can somebody come with me. Kane is lying half drowned by a pond. Your son needs your help as well.'

Her father took note. His eyes became wild…almost animalistic; raging with a mixture of sorrow, disbelief, confusion and raw anger. He shouted to three of his friends. 'Dave, Pat, Robbie – get over here. I need help. Kane's in trouble.'

The men followed Clarah to the spot where she had left her brother. The three friends helped Mick pull his sons legs from out of the cold dank water and then Dave and Pat carried him back to the camp.

Robbie ran ahead to call for help, shouting as he ran 'call for another ambulance. Kane is half drowned and hypothermic.'

Mick looked at his daughter. He noticed that her face was pale with shock and her body was covered in mud.

He asked, 'what where you doing out in the woods Clarah- so far from the camp? I thought you were too ill to go out with the girls tonight. You look a right state lass. What has happened to you?'

Clarah spewed out a gush of gibberish, as though she couldn't talk fast enough to tell her story. All her father could hear was a jumble of words about Paracetamol and chemists and skips and then.... he heard her mention Nina.

'You saw what? You saw Nina tied up? You saw who? What lads did you see Clarah?'

It wasn't intentional. She just told it as it was.

'I think it was Peters brothers. The lad climbing up on the branch was Paddy. I am sure it was.'

She didn't think to say that maybe the boys were rescuing Nina. Perhaps they were untying her? She didn't know for sure. She hadn't the time to explain, or even time to finish her sentence. With a look of pure recrimination in his twisted face, her Da marched off before she could stop him. Clarah shouted after him, but he was gone.

She panicked. What to do? She decided she should go and find her elder sister Katalyn. She needed Katalyn to call her husband Peter, and then get him to drive back from Newcastle immediately. Sod her stupid hen party – this was an emergency. She knew she may have given her Da the wrong information and with the look of fury etched upon his face – he was capable of anything. She had never seen him look so angry before.

Katalyn's caravan was on the edge of the camp. She had two young children and so she and Peter had always parked on the outskirts …somewhere usually quieter.

As she darted towards her sister's brand-new Clubman SE, she heard strange noises coming from the inside. She opened the door – it was unlocked. She saw that her little ones had fallen asleep in front of the TV and their mother had thrown a fleece over them. They each sucked on a dummy. They were fast asleep. Clarah pulled the fleece up to their necks and gently kissed her niece's foreheads. They smelt of baby talcum powder. She loved these little girls so much.

Then from the direction of Katalyn's bedroom she heard low pitched male moans, alongside higher pitched female sighs. The mattress made a familiar creaking noise. She was listening to the sound of sex – she knew it. She couldn't understand why Peter was at home rather than chaperoning the hen night as he had promised but…maybe it was for the best.

She hated to interrupt a married couple in their heights of intimacy, but Peter's brothers could be in trouble and she needed his help. As she went to knock on the door, she hesitated. It felt wrong. She was intruding. When the bedroom became silent, she slowly and nervously entered. Curled up onto her side, was her sister Katalyn with a self-satisfied smile on her face. Tiny droplets of sweat caught by the moonlight, glistened like tiny diamonds. Spooning her, was a bronzed muscular figure, nuzzling affectionately at the nape of her neck. However, the man lying naked besides her wasn't Peter. This was not her husband.

Clarah recognised an eagle tattoo on the man's bull-like shoulders. It was her own boyfriend - Denny. The man that she, Clarah …was due to marry in just 2 weeks' time.

Clarah was frozen to the spot, yet the loving couple hadn't even noticed her. They were still wrapped in that hazy "after sex" glow and entwined in one another's sweaty skin…lost in a sensual world of their own making. She was nothing more than an intruder into their clandestine world. She was invisible, a nothingness, an outsider, an impostor in their private moment of betrayal. She was but a pimple, a carbuncle on an otherwise scene of perfect loved-uppiness, (to quote a Baba May word).

Clarah was numb, paralysed in disbelief. She cursed the full moon. First it had delivered her with an agonising heavy period, and then the sight of her sister Nina hanging from a tree, followed by her brother Kane partially submerged in green algae and now…bloody hell, and now the evening had been nicely topped off, by allowing her the vision of her boyfriend screwing her sister.

Baba May had been right about the curse of begrudgery – she was sure of it. Someone had jinxed her happiness. Someone jealous of her family's good fortune was now set to destroy them, and by all accounts they were succeeding. This was all so unnatural, so unlikely, that Clarah deduced that a curse was the only probable explanation.

She said nothing. Such was her trauma, that she wasn't capable of speaking. She tiptoed quietly out of Katalyn's shiny new caravan and walked back to her Ma's van. The cheating two-timing couple, had not even known she had been there. Their dirty little secret had been discovered, and yet they wouldn't even know it.

When she arrived back at her own van, it was pure bedlam. A second ambulance had arrived – she presumed for Kane, and now the police were also on the site. At that moment, she thought, 'is this what it feels like to have a complete mental breakdown?' She just stood there. It was as though she was watching a movie. She was in it and yet – outside of it. All around her there was turmoil and madness, yet she was silent and still as the world wafted by in complete pandemonium.

A strange calmness descended upon her. It was a coldness and a lack of emotion she had never experienced before. She decided she must be in shock, so unnatural was this feeling. She walked into the van and into her room; the one she shared with Nina. Opening up her bedside drawers, she removed her passport and purse and placed them into her backpack. She scrunched the plastic chemist bag inside, along with her pyjama's, toothbrush and a change of clothes. She went into the tiny bathroom, and splashed her face in ice cold water She wanted to rinse all the tears away and wipe any traces of hurt from her face, or at least that was the intention.

Shedding her mud stained clothes like a snake sheds its skin, she dressed herself in the turquoise jump suit hung up by the shower. It was the one she would have worn to her hen party. She now so wished she could have gone out with the other girls and missed all of this bedlam, however fate had other plans for her. Clarah was surprised by how serene she felt. Her heart had gone into total shut down and now her brain was taking over – encouraging her to make what she assumed to be rational decisions.

She phoned for a taxi, requesting that it meet her by the gates to the common. The world of the travellers had been ripped apart and tipped upside down, yet nobody noticed her leave and neither did she notice them stay. Even the police with their detective like super vision, failed to notice her. It was as though she was walking through some parallel universe. Clarah was at the epicentre of the very core of the chaos, yet strangely removed from it.

The taxi came as requested, in itself almost appearing and then disappearing unnoticed. It had arrived quickly, almost too quickly – but she paid no attention to the time.

'Drive me to a cash point,' came her request.

Once she had withdrawn as much cash as the hole in the wall would allow, she then asked of the driver, 'do you know this area?' He shook his head to confirm he did.

'I was born around here my love,' came his reply.

'That's great, 'she responded, 'then drive me to the most expensive poshest hotel you know. Money is no object. I haven't booked anything, so can you hang around outside of wherever you are going to take me – just in case they don't like the look of me? I am used to rejection.'

The taxi driver appeared to be puzzled.

'Is this bit of an spontaneous break miss?'

'You could call it that,' replied Clarah with cool demure clarity.

'I didn't exactly plan for any of this.'

That was the end of the dream…perhaps less of a dream and more of a memory. Part of her hidden past had slotted into the frame like a missing piece of a jigsaw puzzle.

***

Clarah woke up shivering, little beads of sweat growing like mushrooms on her forehead. For a moment, she was confused. Was she in Whitby, in Scarborough or in Newcastle? The dream had been so clear, so real.

For several minutes, she just lay there before she remembered that it hadn't been a dream. Her unconscious mind had just replayed her a tape of something that had actually happened, something dark and terrible. It was a memory that she had tried hard to supress. Yet Clarah had finally connected to her past. A single solitary tear escaped from her eye; it was the first time she had allowed herself to cry about the events of that night. Despite all of this, she was a little rich girl now and so had been blessed with a well-funded escape route. Yet in truth, no amount of zeros on the best side of a decimal point could fix the pain. It was still raw; like an open wound that had healed on the surface, but bore the brunt of scar tissue beneath the skin.

As she lay in her bed, she considered her family.

Kane was fine, well…sort of fine. After all, he had recovered from his near drowning experience. He may be a filthy drunk, but he was alive. She resolved to get him some treatment. They were lottery winners. Surely, they could now afford to send him to some celebrity rehab clinic; expertly able to treat his addictions. She decided that helping Kane was the next project on her agenda.

Nina was fine – in fact having shed the invasive personality of Anju, she now seemed almost normal. Okay, so she had some sort of autism and would always be simple-minded and child-like, but she seemed happy enough.

Plus, their mother and father would soon be back from wherever and life would become happy and normal; just like it was for other people. Other people always seemed to be happy. She wanted a slice of that cake.

Clarah had spent most of her life being on the outside, looking through a window into other people's lives and reluctantly observing their mundane happiness. Ordinary people playing, loving, laughing, eating, drinking and living in their centrally-heated domestic slice of lemon-drizzle paradise. She had watched them as she stood outside on many a cold dark night, often dripping wet in the torrential rain. Now, she was the one on the inside. Surely life could only get better?

She heard banging downstairs. It was the familiar sound of Aunt Marys walking stick as she limped along the wooden corridors. She heard what she thought was her bedroom door as it was slammed shut. 'Aunt Mary is back home,' she gasped to herself, then assuming that Baba May must be with her. She jumped out of bed feeling light and joyous. She had faced the past, staring it in its green jealous eyes, and now she had moved on. Her memories had been dismal, but now that she had been forced to confront them, she was ready for a new beginning. Indeed, the hope for a fresh new future was a lovely feeling. She opened the window and let in the rays of a stunning autumn morning.

Sunday mornings – how she loved this day of the week. In the near distance, the church bells called its worshippers to prayer. The smell of a fried breakfast was already wafting it's tempting aroma's in her direction. She heard the newspaper fall through the letterbox. She loved reading the Sunday papers, delighting in their playful gossipmongering. She decided that this would be a perfect day.

CHAPTER 9

Sunday 27th September 2015
REED FACING UP TO A LEDONITE

Konnor sat outside on the motel patio, casually smoking a roll-up and sipping a black coffee laced with heaps of sugar. The autumn sun kissed his face with its golden embrace. He extended his neck backwards; holding his face upwards to enjoy the last tease of the years warming rays. All too soon winter would descend upon the Colorado mountains. The orange and reds would be replaced by white and silver. At that exact moment, he understood why ancient man ritualised the passing of the sun. In some strange way, he was also saying goodbye. He wasn't sure why he had that feeling…he just did.

Childhood memories came flooding back as he reminisced about his grandparents and holidays spent fishing or skiing. The memories were cruel and a stark reminder of what once was, and what could no longer be. He saw his past life in black and white; just like an old photograph. He preferred to view his past through the imaginary lens of a camera. It kept pain at a distance. The reality of what actually happened to his Grandparents was simply too traumatic to bring to mind. Yet at the time, he felt more sorrow for his father's loss than for his own grief. Amidst all his father's trauma…in as much as losing his wife, his business, his money and his estate – he had also lost his parents.

Konnor had no idea how his dad had found the mental strength to survive. Reed Baratolli's fortitude surprised many. His Dad had often told him that he had a guardian angel holding his hand, and he said it as though he meant it. Konnor did not doubt it for a second.

A bleep on his mobile interrupted Konnor's thoughts. He had been glad of the intrusion as he had been sinking into some deeper darker place. Konnor was a joker; the eternal clown who was the life and soul of the party. Deep and dark was not part of his shallow and light demeanour. If only they knew.

He picked up his phone. It was a text message from his brother.

'HEY bro, just bout to jump on a plane to NY. Soz I missed the engagement party. Will come and visit ya soon in LA. Clarah flew home Weds night & not heard from her since. D'ya know if she got back okay? She was a bit freaked out before she left. Some guy had been following her & then she took off all of a sudden. Let me know if you hear anything. Tell Armarni I am sorry.as couldn't get a flight back in time. Will make it up to her. See ya soon bud. Keep the beer & the babes on ice. Cheers Ash. x

Konnor threw his phone on the table and gestured for more coffee. He mumbled to himself, 'so that girl is trouble, is she? Those are the exact words Ash said, yet now he is concerned for her welfare all of a sudden. I wonder oh I wonder.'

He lit another cigarette. Suspicion, mistrust, doubt – this wasn't a state of mind that sat easily on his young gullible shoulders. It wasn't so much that he didn't trust Clarah, it was more a case of not trusting Asher. His brother viewed any attractive female as his for the taking and had limited morals in that department. Konnor couldn't help but think out loud, 'so - Clarah came back 4 days ago and in all that time she hasn't made any effort to call.'

He stirred his coffee much longer than required, as though looking into the brown whirling liquid would act as some sort of oracle. What was it about the colour brown? In a moment of unexplained telepathy, he could see that Clarah hated the colour, yet that made no sense.

All in all, her silence spoke volumes. With social media and multiple methods of communication, it wasn't as though she was relying on a carrier pigeon. Konnor was over thinking the situation. He resolved to remain cool, calm and impassive. He put his feet up on the chair opposite and reclined backwards to grab the last little snippet of summer sun. Clarah was old news and not worth the mental torment that was screwing with his brain and turning it into sentimental mush.

At that moment, a 2nd text came in. This time it was from his father Reed.

'Hi Kon. Hope you are awake. Wanted to catch up with you before you headed out to Pitkin County. What time is your flight? Let me know where you are staying and I will drive over after b'fast. BFN DAD x.'

***

Reed had begun to realise that the Lezemel mansion was less of a home and more of a party retreat for the family's secluded, exclusive and very private entertainment. He couldn't quite put his finger on it, but it lacked the warmth of a loving home. What family abode incorporated a fully functioning nightclub in its basement? Likewise, the breakfast room was like something one would find in a hotel. Breakfast food was set out in a self-service capacity, so that guests were free to sleep late and then help themselves at their leisure. A few waiters walked amongst the tables to take orders for hot food, but aside from the hired help, the breakfast area was mostly empty. Hangovers a plenty, he presumed.

Reed grabbed a glass of fresh orange juice and a croissant, and then wandered out onto the balcony. It was a perfect Sunday morning. The sky was the purest blue and the air was crisp and fresh. Reed took a deep breath of the pine infused oxygen, filling his lungs with the honeyed fragrance of nature. Occasional log fires had been lit amongst the tables, however it was a warm morning and so they were almost superfluous to requirements.

Reeds table was close to the edge of the balcony, and so he was able to view the artificially created waterfall cascading over artistically placed boulders. It was art imitating nature at its splendid best. He had already calculated that such an overly-stated construction must surely have come at a price? Putting his mental calculator aside, he resolved to enjoy the sound of the splashing water and the serenity of the mountain vista – that was until his moment of escapism was interrupted.

A man approached his table. His face was familiar.

'Do you mind if I join you,' he asked? Reed was surprised.

'Sure, but do I know you,' he replied?

Nico placed his tea and toast on Reed's table and introduced himself. His name jolted Reed's memory, although he recalled taking far more notice of the exquisite young actress draped on his arm, than on the facial features of her escort.

'Ah yes I remember you now. Pleased to meet you. I am Tony Mort. I run the VOTS homeless charity in New York, although you may remember me as Reed Baratolli. So…you are thee Nico, the world-renowned chef. My housemaid Roserie purchased all of your books and by default I have eaten several of your amazing recipe's. Thank you for many years of delicious food.'

He stood to shake his hand and then continued.

'I understand that you are now engaged to the lovely Tia. I must say, congratulations Nico. You are a very lucky man. When is the wedding?'

The Italian chef enjoyed the compliments and the trivial social niceties of small talk, yet was in a serious mood.

'The wedding is next June and thank you for your compliments. Yes, Tia is lovely and indeed I am very lucky. Did you see the magician last night? Some guy by the name of Soul. He was truly amazing. We are thinking about hiring him for our wedding.'

Reed simply shrugged.

'Sorry, I had an early night. I missed the show.'

It was an abrupt reply, but Reed was mindful of the time and didn't want to engage in a deep conversation over breakfast. However, Nico had a different agenda and was not going to be so easily ignored.

He asked,' on another subject, did you know that we are connected?' This wasn't a question that Reed expected.

He shook his head, and looking puzzled stated, 'erm no. I mean I guess everyone is connected to everybody else in some way, but I can't imagine how our paths have ever crossed.'

Nico continued, 'my brother Amedeo is the hotel manager of a place in Wales called Darwydden. Does that sound familiar?'

The colour rushed from Reed's face. The mere mention of that word covered his body in goose-bumps.

'Yes of course I know of Darwydden. My sister-in-law Ruby and her husband are the owners. Small world indeed - quite a coincidence.'

'Yes, it is,' agreed Nico. 'Ruby's best friend is Becky and she married my brother. It is a very small world Reed.'

Nico went very quiet after this revelation and focussed on consuming his breakfast. The sudden silence brought about an awkward moment. Reed tried to lighten the atmosphere.

'So, Nico, what do you think about my new in-laws. I was a bit worried about Ze'ev to begin with, but the guy seems well mannered and treats my daughter well. The tabloids don't paint such a good picture of the guy, but then again you are looking at someone whose life was destroyed by inventive journalists, so I may as well give him the benefit of the doubt.'

Nico remained in a solemn mood.

He responded, 'do you refer to Ze'ev's playboy reputation, or the Lezemel family's association with the darker side?'

Reed shrugged and looked at his watch without trying to appear too obvious. He was keen to see his youngest son before he went back to UCLA and time was passing. Nico was steering the conversation down a blind alley and this was a place he didn't want to go to. Reed slurped down his last remnants of orange juice to send out clear visual signals that the conversation was over. He mopped his mouth with his napkin, threw it down on the table and stood to leave. Nico grabbed hold of his wrist to detain him. The action was forceful and shocked Reed.

'I noticed that you were talking with Emmanuelle last night,' pronounced Nico.

'Erm…well yes. I was talking with her for just a few moments. Do you know her or know of her?'

Nico continued, 'it's so sweet that you describe Emmanuelle as a her, when we both know she is an … it.'

Nico emphasised the word 'IT' so to give it more of a dramatic effect. Reed was somewhat flabbergasted that anyone else could possibly be aware of her true demonic identity. He was curious.

He sat back down and asked of Nico, 'what do you know of Emmanuelle?'

Nico sipped his peppermint tea and smiled. It was the self-assured smile of one who believed he had some superior knowledge of the universe. Nico exuded the smug assurance of one who supposed himself to be special – the keeper of an extraordinary secret.

After a few moments of thought Nico replied, 'I am a Ledanite and one of the many descendants from the line of Sheol. I know that you know exactly what that means. I take it that when Emmanuelle hired you to do her dirty work, that she explained the prophesy of Tamar to you.'

Once again Reed was in shock.

After a few shaky moments he replied, 'I knew I should have stayed in New York. I knew I should have kept the blighted name of "Reed Baratolli" locked away in a cupboard forever. It was a mistake coming here. Yes, yes, yes – I know of the Tamar prophesy. That blasted stupid story has been a scar on my life. I lost everything – and I mean absolutely everything because of it. I don't know why you have stopped to talk with me over breakfast Nico, or if this little chat was by accident or design, but I am no longer in league with Emmanuelle. I want nothing more to do with the whole "line of Tamar" piece of crap. You and your Ledanite friends need to leave me alone. Just count me out. I need to go now or I will miss seeing my son before he flies back to LA.'

With that Reed stood up once again and turned to leave.

Nico sniggered to himself, knowing full well that he could make Reed spin on his heels and turn back around with just a few words. He decided to give it a try.

He shouted after him, 'hey, do you know who was keeping your son Konnor company in Asia? None other than Anais and Valentine. Nice young girls. Do you remember who they are Reed or should I say – Tony?'

Nico had played his cards right and felt a degree of egotistical self-satisfaction. Reed stopped dead in his tracks. He turned around to face Nico – almost as though videoed in slow motion.

'Anais and Valentine,' he repeated. 'Do you mean Fabien's daughters? How would you know this? How would you know my son's name, or where he was, or who he was with?'

On this occasion, it was Nico who stood up to leave, completely understanding the power of the walk-away.

As he gathered his phone and sunglasses from the breakfast table he replied, 'I am sorry to be the one to break this news to you Mr Baratolli, but Fabien- your dearest closest pal, is also a Ledanite as indeed are his daughters. His task was to protect your wife Eenayah and in order to do that, he had to get close to you. Do a bit of simple mathematics dear Reed. 2+2 sometimes does add up to 4. Surely even you can presume that if his Ledanite daughters have been with your son, that they have been there on a mission of some sort. Ledanites don't do coincidental. Who else was in the backpackers group alongside Konnor? Some Gypsy girl maybe. You know Reed, perhaps it's time to have one of those father/son conversations. If both Emmanuelle and the Ledanite are on the scene, it seems to me like the prophesy of Tamar is still knocking on your door. Ciao bella Reed.'

With those words Nico turned to leave, whilst an ashen faced Reed remained rooted to the spot. The last thing he wanted or expected was for some ancient plague to revisit and infest his life – yet again.

'Who the hell is this Clarah girl?'

It was a thought that plagued his mind as he made his way back to the car. Whatever and whoever she is, he knew Nico was right – somehow, she mattered, and mattered as much to the living as to the dead.

CHAPTER 10

Sunday 27th September 2015 – midday
MEANWHILE – BACK IN WHITBY

Baba May looked as shocked to see her Granddaughter rushing down the staircase, as Clarah was to see her gran standing in the hallway. Neither of them could read the expression on the other one's face. It was confusing. Her grandmother was pleased to see her, yet unhappy. She was surprised, and yet not. The elderly lady hesitated before opening her arms to hug her.

Clarah found that most strange, and asked of her, 'Baba May – where have you been? You had me worried. I haven't seen you since yesterday. You just sort of…disappeared into thin air. What have you been doing? Where did you stay last night?'

The old lady was quite taken aback by the machine-gun questioning and seemed to hesitate just a few seconds too long; long enough for Clarah to think her gran could be lying.

'I have been at the hospital and I stayed overnight,' responded Baba May – her voice hoarse and sullen.

Clarah noticed the dark circles around her reddened sunken eyes, so presumed that there must have been a problem with her aunt.

'Is Aunty Mary okay now,' she asked? 'I heard her in the hallway and then she just slammed her bedroom door shut – quite aggressively I may say. Has she been poorly?'

Her Grandmother looked away; not wanting to respond in case either truth or fib accidentally escaped from her mouth.

'Best to leave your aunt alone,' she replied – not wanting to either confirm or deny. The old lady shut the conversation down as fast as she could.

Her Grandmother was a about to walk away, when an overly enthusiastic rapping at the door caused them both to spin around on their heels. Clarah opened the door to find her new friend Aura standing on the doorstep. She was clutching a large bag and a bunch of purple Michaelmas daisies. She had arrived as promised… dead on 1 o'clock.

She jokingly made a scissor action with her fingers, 'hi it's me, I'm back. Aura Scissorhands. Are you ready for me to cut those braids out Clarah?'

Baba May stepped out from behind her granddaughter and declared, 'over my dead body. Gypsy girls wear their hair long.'

Clarah's guts clamped into a spasm as her Gran uttered the "G" word. Years of persecution, discrimination and racial abuse came to the surface like unwelcome vomit. Clarah coughed back the acidic secretion that burned the back of her throat. It was impossible to miss her extreme reaction.

Aura tried to reassure her, and put a comforting arm around her young friend.

'It's okay Clarah. I had already figured out that you guys were the Gypsy family who had won the lottery. The whole village had it worked out from the moment you folks moved here. Nobody minds. Nobody has an opinion. You need to swipe that victimisation chip off your shoulder, because the more you think about it, the bigger and heavier it gets. Now enough of this serious talk. I have hair dye and matching extensions in my bag. With 21st century beauty enhancing technology, I can get these knotted locks of yours, back down to your waist.'

She looked over at Baba May and added, 'would that be Gypsy enough for you Granny BM?'

Baba May stood to one side and gestured that they should both go to the kitchen. She looked concerned, worried, maybe even slightly angry. The visitor confused her. She had an unusual look about her face. She knew Aura from somewhere, but couldn't quite put her finger on it. The introduction had been unsettling and she couldn't help but wonder what Aura wanted with her granddaughter.

Clarah yelped as the tightly knit peroxide braids were delicately undone one by one.

'I don't think you granny likes me very much,' stated Aura.

Clarah shrugged. She didn't have an opinion. There were far more pressing things playing on her mind.

'Tell me, do you find this place a bit strange Aura? I mean you are a local yokel. What do you know about the house?'

Aura replied, 'not as much as I would like to. The infamous John Stephenson was supposed to have once lived here. He served under the Jolly Roger for Bartholomew Roberts – one of the meanest brutal pirate captains of all time. He and his crew of 51 men, were executed in 1722 and Stephenson was one of them. The villagers often report seeing a man in pirate's attire on dark murky nights, but then again that could just be Kane.'

They both laughed at that comment and the bizarre vision it incited. Baba May also overheard the gibe made about Kane and was less than amused. None the less, she was impressed with the miracle Aura was creating with Clarah's hair. It was almost back to how nature intended, as long luscious chestnut locks now cascaded down to her granddaughter's waist. It reminded the old lady of how she once looked in her former years.

Aura noted that the house had no mirrors on the walls downstairs, and so she commanded, 'go to the bathroom and check out your new look.'

As soon as Clarah left the room, her grandmother approached Aura – touching her skin as though testing the heat of a Sunday roast.

'What are you?'

Aura looked over at the old lady, smiling with the original beaming white grin that first got her over the step.

'What do you want me to be?'

Baba May was a resilient old lady and not one to suffer fools.

'What do you want with my granddaughter?'

The young woman got up from her seat and tidied her hairdressing paraphernalia away. She responded without looking the old lady in the eye.

'There are others aside from me Baba May. Clarah is in a perilous place, and others will come for your granddaughter. You are lucky - I am one of the better ones. Believe me when I say that I am trying to help her, so be grateful that I got here first. Baba May, you are a wise old woman, so try to understand that Clarah needs to find herself before anyone else can find her. She is suffering from amnesia and the sudden shock of the truth would be too much for her to take in. But sometime soon, she does need to remember. You cannot keep her trapped in this world of illusion forever. She needs to know what happened to her, just not quite yet. We should both be patient. Slowly slowly catchy monkey.'

Baba May grimaced, not sure how to react to the strange visitor. Aura continued, 'I also know that you are a lonely old lady Baba May.

Being both needy and powerful is a potent combination, but nonetheless you shouldn't hang on to the souls of your loved ones. The dead need to move on and it is selfish to entrap them. You need to let go. As for Clarah, she is special – you do know that, don't you?'

Baba May's face turned an unnatural shade of white as she replied, 'yes I do know all of this and yes I can handle this myself. Please leave now. Whatever creature you are, I need you to be gone from my home.'

Aura smiled yet again and with her haberdashery of beatifying items exited the kitchen.

With one last backward glance, she replied, 'have it your way May Loveridge. I have done what I came to do for the time being, and anyway – it's time for me to get back. My father is on shepherd duties today and whilst he is out tending his flock, there is nobody around to look after the rest of the household. See you later – I am sure.'

She was gone before the door was even shut.

Baba May couldn't figure out what Aura was. She only knew that she wasn't human. She feared so much for Clarah. How was she ever going to handle this situation?

Clarah bounced back into the kitchen like a new born lamb. Her newly created tresses rebounded from side to side as though they had a life of their own. Looking around and unable to spot her friend, her expression immediately became sullen.

'Where is Aura?'

Her Grandmother was busy pulling a partially knitted shawl from out of her huge "Mary Poppins" style handbag. Untangling a ball of wool, she replied,' she has gone back home. She says she will be back, and I do not doubt that for a second. You look nice Clarah. Your new hair suits you. It's good to see you happy again.'

At that moment the kitchen door opened with slow deliberation…the hinges squeaking eerily on its frame. In shuffled Aunt Mary, hobbling with a distinctive limp…audible by the forward thrust of her Zimmer frame meeting with the stone floor and the echo bouncing off the bare walls. Clarah rushed over to greet her – hugging her as though she didn't want to let go.

'Baba May tells me you have been in hospital Aunt Mary. Are you okay now?'

Mary shot her mother a look of scorn, disapproving of Baba May's fibs, even though suggested rather than spoken.

'Yes, I am fine child, but I can't stand up for long. Please help me to a chair.'

Clarah did as she was instructed and linking her beloved aunty, guided her to the table.

'Fetch me some of Baba May's tea concoction,' she commanded. I could smell it brewing from out in the hallway. Nothing oils my springs better than my Ma's cuckoo tea.'

Clarah understood the instruction. Her grandmother was an expert in blending all types of herbs into tea's, but the one most favoured by her aunt was indeed the strangely named cuckoo tea. Baba May would take freshly boiled moon water and then add a few crushed teaspoons of rose hips, with a sprinkling of Butcher's Broom, Yellow Dock and Mugwort. Once the brew had cooled and just before serving, she would add a small knob of solid honey, a teaspoon of Mead and scatter some elder berries so that they floated on the surface. She prepared her creation in an old white and blue enamel jug; a tatty looking vessel which looked as though it had been around since forever.

As Clarah brought the steaming crock over to the table, childhood memories came floating back with a rush of tear-stained nostalgia. She hadn't noticed it before, but their new home was sadly lacking in any adornments from their former life. It was as though some upmarket designer had been given a handsome cheque and the authority to purchase paintings and ornaments which would best coordinate with each other. Maybe this was why she found her new environment sadly lacking in warmth – like a home without a heart. However, this vintage blue and white jug; the one Baba May had always used for her healing drinks, was the one connection to her past. It made Clarah feel sad. She started to crave for the life she had before, yet knew there was no way back. She was back on the brown mountain; walking around in circles, yet unable to go anywhere or come from anywhere.

Noting the woeful look on her niece's face, Mary reached over and stroked her hand in a soft and soothing way. Clarah looked down upon her aunt's misshapen fingers with their knotty swollen knuckles, feeling pitifully sorry that arthritis had twisted her body so cruelly. Just like her mother, Mary was one with inborn psychic abilities, although it wouldn't take one so gifted to read the mien in Clarah's eye's.

'Drink some of your grandmother's cuckoo tea, 'urged Mary.' You look pale beneath that sun-tanned skin of yours. This drink will do you some good.'

Again, Clarah did as she was instructed and poured herself some of Baba May's unusual brew.

As she sipped the strange sweet tea she asked, 'why is it called cuckoo tea?'

Mary gave a response that provoked more questions than answers. 'Ah well dear Clarah, I was always told that in Roma tradition it was given to a widow. Of all the songbirds in the sky, the cuckoo was thought to have the saddest melody. It calls and it calls, but none answer. As such, it became the symbol of a woman who had either lost someone she loved or one who suffers from some illness or misery. That would be me on both counts I guess.'

Mary exhaled a long-drawn-out sigh, as though breathing out a lifetime of regret. Of course, she was both a childless widow and a woman tortured by chronic pain. She ticked the cuckoo box twice. She sometimes considered the contrasting luck of her twin sister Violet, and as much as she hated it, often felt a nuance of jealousy and resentment. It was a feeling she hated, and so shook it off as soon as it paid an unwelcome visit. Begrudgery of a sibling would bring bad karma – indeed, it already had. Poor Violet. Tears shone in Mary's eyes as she thought about her twin sister.

Her aunt continued, 'maybe something in this tea warms a cold heart. Others believe there is more magic to it than that, and that the cuckoo is a gatekeeper- one who dwells between the worlds of the living and the dead. Tis more of a mysterious explanation, don't you think? Whichever way- it is a blood tonic, so drink up dear Clarah. By the way, how is that heart of yours these days?'

'Oh no,' came forth the response as she buried her head in her hands. Clarah knew that at some point, someone in the family would raise the subject of Denny. After all – he was her fiancé and she had run out on him just weeks before their wedding. Abandoning her entire family was bad enough, but deserting a future husband was not something a Gypsy girl was supposed to do…ever. She needed to cut this inquisition short.

'Denny cheated on me aunty. I don't want to say how I know, or with whom. Just trust that I am telling you the truth. I did love him, but he broke my heart and after that there was no turning back. It was on that night – the night Nina was attacked. I saw him…I saw them…together. That was a bloody awful night. Out of nothing more than interest, do you know where he is now? Just curious? I am over it – honestly I am.'

Clarah's grandmother put her knitting down; suddenly taking deep interest in the conversation.

Mary replied, 'dear child; I heard that Denny met someone else and has settled down now…with a gaje girl of all people. Can you believe that? He lives back in Scarborough and works as a farm hand. He tends the wild stock and drives a tractor. He has moved on and so should you.'

At that point, Nina sauntered into the room with a masculine stride. She was wearing one of Kane's suits – the posh Pierre Cardin one that he only wore to weddings and funerals. She had painted a black moustache on her lips and tied her hair back into a bun. She took a beer from the fridge, slugging it down as a bloke would do. She then sat in the corner with her legs open wide, just as a bloke would. She pulled one of her brothers roll ups from his pocket, lighting it and taking long slow drags.

The three-woman looked upon her in silence; accustomed to Nina's many alter-egos. Sadly, nothing that Nina did would surprise or shock anymore. Clarah was pained. For a few moments, she had thought her twin sister was getting better – but clearly that wasn't the case.

Clarah asked Baba May, 'where is my brother? Where is Kane? He worries me.'

Her aunt replied, 'The last time I saw him, he was going out to ride his horse. When he isn't drunk or asleep, he is out on the beach.'

Clarah didn't believe a word. She didn't believe anything anymore. What horse in what stable? She had seen the old tool shed and felt the cobwebs as they had become tangled in her hair. Besides that, riding took strength, desire, passion and sobriety. Kane seemed incapable of any of those attributes. Why was everybody lying to her? What was going on? What was it that they were not telling her?

For a moment Clarah sat quietly. The energy seemed to be draining from her body. She felt disorientated…confused. The kitchen suddenly became cold and her bare arms were covered in goose bumps. Her grandmother had just finished knitting a pink and white shawl, which she lovingly placed around her granddaughter's chilled shoulders.

She said, 'Clarah, your aunt and I need to go away soon. We have to go back to the hospital and we may be away for a few days. Will you be okay here? I need you to keep an eye on your brother and sister?'

Clarah was horrified by the idea. Her grandmother was her rock, her backbone; the only essence of stability in a very wobbly world.

Baba May knew she had to go, knew she had to leave Clarah to figure things out on her own.

Clarah protested with her eyes, yet was completely aware that she was wasting her time. Baba May seldom changed her mind, not once it had been made.

Her grandmother helped her daughter Mary to her feet. Mary's face was coiled up in agony as she tried to stand. Baba May turned to face Clarah as she uttered a grim warning.

'It is a full blood moon tonight Clarah. We all remember what happened on the last blood moon. I will cast a protection spell for you before I leave, but please…try not to go outside. Take heed of my words and stay where you are. I can shield you in this house, but I can do nothing for you should you wander outside. Out there you are alone, completely alone. You do not look well my dear. It would serve you best to catch up on some rest.

Why did everyone insist on trying to scare the wits out of her? Her grandmother described her as being "completely alone" and Aura told her that she was "quite, quite trapped". No words of cheery comfort from either party.

Indeed, Clarah did feel under the weather, as well as feeling suddenly cold and inexplicitly fearful. She so hoped her new friend Aura would visit and spend some time with her.

The kitchen door was slammed shut- and that was it – her gran and aunt were both gone. The nature of the nomadic Gypsy life was such that folks knew the art of a quick goodbye. Moving out and moving on – it came easy to a traveller.

Clarah knelt down to look at Nina. Maybe she could make some connection with her or whoever she believed herself to be. What happened next caused her to fall backwards in shock and astonishment.

She held her sisters hand.

'Nina, Nina – are you okay my love?'

Her twin hissed back at her as though she had transformed into a wild animal. She growled rather than spoke.

'I am not fuckin Nina. I am Paddy and your shite father killed me for no shitin reason. Go check it out for yourself, arsehole. Your murdering father is banged up in prison and your pathetic mother is dead.'

Nina's eyes then rolled to the back of her head, as a dribble of saliva escaped her mouth. She then raised her head and spat at Clarah like a hissing serpent. It was animalistic, maybe even demonic. A chill ran down Clarah's spine. She let out a small scream…maybe more of a gasp. She ran out of the kitchen, calling for her grandmother and her aunt – but they had already left. How could they have vanished so quickly?

She ran to the door and watched as she saw the black limo leave the driveway. She couldn't make out the driver. Was it the same guy who had collected her from the airport?

As she looked down upon the doormat, she saw part of the line of the circle of salt. Her grandmother hadn't been joking – she really had used witchcraft to protect her. She squatted down and touched the salt with her finger, even licking it to make sure it was salt. She was sure she would feel safer outside, rather than be supernaturally locked indoors with her deranged siblings and the menacing quietness of some former pirate's den.

Why had Baba May gone to so much trouble? It was just common sea salt, so surely it had no power. Her gran was an old Romany lady and she believed in such things. As for Nina and her possessed snarling; maybe she just had some chemical imbalance in her brain. Perhaps her medication was due? Yes, that was it – it was just part of her condition. Logic explained everything. Or did it? She could not be sure.

Her Da in prison and her mother dead? No way, not possible. Nina was deranged. Baba May had no reason to lie.

CHAPTER 11

Sunday 27th September 2015 – late afternoon
NEVER GO OUTSIDE ON A BLOOD MOON

5.30pm and darkness was falling upon a north Yorkshire hamlet; a mere cluster of tiny cottages hidden somewhere on the outskirts of Whitby. At this time of year, the light didn't hold much beyond tea time.

A full blood moon hung on the horizon in all its ominous glory, and later on in the early morning, a total lunar eclipse would grace star gazers with an astronomical spectacle.

However, for those with their sites centred on more mystical matters, this was not a night to venture out. Yet against all counsel of the spiritual kind, venture out she would.

As a self-assured travelling girl, Clarah wasn't one who usually needed companionship, yet now she pined for the comfort of a friendly smile. She grabbed her hat and Burberry trench coat, and did the one thing her grandmother warned her not to do – she stepped over the protective line of salt and walked outside.

At the end of the long driveway, she crossed the bridge over to the main road. Looking down below, she could see that the tide was moving out – exposing the killer rocks and grasping quicksand. This was the treacherous place of death Aura had warned her about. The bridge was old and not in the best of conditions. She made a mental note to mention this to her Grandmother, lest it collapse and she be left alone, stranded and quite, quite trapped.

Once over the bridge, she could either take the familiar short cut through the cemetery, or take the longer route down the lane. Noting the sinister shadows cast by the full blood moon, she elected to follow the hard tarmac. She had no idea why she should find the lane a safer option. After all, it did wind its way through dense woodland. In itself, it was fairly isolated. Aside from lunar illumination, it was as dark on the lane as the very pits of hell.

A hooting owl in the distance made her skin crawl and the hurried scurry of some creature under rotting bark made her jump. Her senses were on heightened alert. The forest was alive and noisy, not willing to assist her with the comfort of a peaceful walk. In hindsight, she considered that perhaps the path betwixt sleeping bones may have been the better decision. Too late now. She was marching up the tarmac, pupils dilated, heart racing, primeval instincts on fire.

After 30 or so minutes, she spotted Aura's farm house on the top of the hill. This was the very place that Aura had pointed to. The place she had said she lived. Clarah felt immense relief, and focussed on the path to the hilltop. It represented safety, sanctuary and the ears of a kind listening friend. She hoped her impromptu visit wouldn't been seen as intrusive. She was sure Aura's family would understand, certainly if they were nearly as kind and chatty as Aura was. She then remembered – she hadn't brought them a gift and as yet, Aura had never visited her home empty handed. She was sure they would understand. She vowed to bring them something extra special next time she called over. She felt excited to meet the family of her new best friend.

The farm house was in darkness. Surely, they couldn't all be asleep at this time of day? She was aware that farmers were often early risers, so maybe this also required an early night in bed – but surely, not this early?

Aura had mentioned that she had a big family – many brothers. With such a large family, why would the house be so dark? She opened the gate slowly and with deliberation. Something didn't feel right.

She approached the front door. Japanese knotweed grew over parts of the pathway. It looked as though it hadn't been trodden upon in ages. The door knocker was rusty and she struggled to make it move enough to afford her an audible rattle on the door.

She looked around. She was alone on top of a dark hillside. The farmhouse looked unlived in. Clarah became afraid. She started to doubt the wisdom of her decision. Why had she not obeyed her grandmother and just stayed at home?

She then summoned enough courage to wander around to the back of the house. Most of the windows had cobwebs dangling from around the frames. These were not new cobwebs, but years and years of spider's weaving thread upon thread. Corpses of long dead insects littered the glass. The glass – too soiled to afford her a peek into its domain. The rusty latches had not been used in years, many years.

She found the back door…it was ajar. Holding her breath, and with some trepidation, she slowly pushed it open. The hinges creaked.

Everything seemed to be so – unused. The kitchen was little more than a ruin. Taps didn't run. Cookers didn't cook. Even in the darkness, it was obvious that nobody lived in the farmhouse, not just now- but in a very long time.

Clarah was confused. Why would Aura lie to her?

Memories of the stables came flooding back to mind. Was she going crazy? Was this how madness started, with weird imaginings of things that didn't exist?

Fear shot through her veins. After all, it was the night of a blood moon. Baba May was superstitious about such things. Why was she out on such a night? Why? Stupid, stupid, stupid. She scolded herself without clemency.

Clarah slowly turned around and then she ran. She was not in the best of health. She was weary and completely exhausted. None the less, she picked up her heavy feet and made them move as best she could. Her muscles ached, but she ignored their plea for rest.

At the bottom of the path, she had a choice. It was either the short cut through the cemetery, or the long lane through the woods. Desperate to get back, she headed in the direction of the church. Somehow, in her desperation to get home, the dead seemed less of a threat. They were just skeletons. How could bones hurt her?

The unkempt gravel path of the cemetery made a loud crunch underfoot. It had been raining, and in the darkness her feet kept plunging into unseen puddles. She spotted a clear way through a line of headstones, leading up to the little gate onto the bridge. It was a well-worn unofficial footpath. The moon lit up her way with an eerie orange glow, so she headed off towards the bridge-gate. Panting and puffing, she could hardly breathe. Weary feet met with uneven ground, and before long she went tumbling.

Clarah found herself strewn upon the ground, chin embedded in the grass and face eye level with some cheap solar lamp. She often wondered why grieving relatives placed such things, seeing that the dead could not voice their appreciation. She had decided it was more to comfort the living than the dead.

Her eyes then glanced upwards towards chiselled words in the masonry. Words that would change her life forever.

"Our beloved daughter Nina Lee, 1995 – 2014. Rest in peace".

Clarah rubbed her eyes. She pulled herself to her feet, crouched down and rubbed the headstone with the damp grass. No amount of rubbing would make the words go away. It just left green skid marks on the cold stone. She then removed the solar lamp from the ground and shone it upon the words that followed.

It read, *"also her loving mother, Violet Lee, 1974 -2015. Forever missed".*

Her sister and her mother – DEAD! Buried here. It was not possible. 2014, that couldn't be right. Nina was in the kitchen, playing at being a boy… as Nina sometimes did.

Her mother was at some reclusive spa. Baba May had told her this much, and why would her grandmother fib about something so important? None of this was possible. It was a nightmare surely. She would wake up soon, she was sure of it. However, she was beginning to realise that nothing was certain in her life anymore.

She had been sure that the stables existed, sure of where Aura lived. Yet, they were cobwebs and dust – just shadows of what had once been. Even the horses were imaginary, and yet she had ridden her mare down the beach. How?

The poor girl was shaking. Her fingers trembled as the clumps of grass fell upon the cold ground. She sat down upon the grave, as though her legs could no longer support her body. She was in shock.

In the near vicinity, she thought she heard a bluebottle. It was a faint, yet distinctive buzzing noise. How could that be? Bluebottles didn't live through to late September and even if they did, they slept at night.

Then came the stench – putrid and vile. It was like the worst possible stink of rotting flesh. She turned, and saw a mud-caked figure hovering over her. It was Kane. He looked terrible. She was shocked to see him in such a state. She held out her hand so he could pull her up. She pointed to the headstone.

'How has this happened?'

Before he could reply, a wind descended from out of nowhere. It screeched and howled with a bestial turbulence. The trees blew from side to side, battered and beaten by the sudden gust. A figure appeared. It didn't walk in or crawl in. Whatever it was, was not there and then it was there. It just materialised. All Clarah could make out was a gowned shape; a shadowy figure cloaked in deep crimson.

A hand grasped the top of Kane's head, supernatural sharp talons sinking into his skull. Blood trickled down his face.

All Clarah heard was the words, 'I have been waiting for you Kane. Now, you are coming with me.'

Then they were both swept out of the cemetery by a gust of wind. It all happened so fast, like a video being fast-forwarded. Such was the speed of their exit, that all Clarah saw was a flash of red mist, as they vaporised into the far wall. As soon as they were gone, the storm subsided. A few leaves and a loose branch fell from a nearby Sycamore, and then a strange ethereal silence fell upon the churchyard. It was all so quiet, much too quiet. Still sat in the grass, Clarah was visibly shaking.

A woman appeared by Clarah's side.

She also "just appeared" ... as though from nowhere. She had a kindly face, and she smelled of summer flowers. She took hold of Clarah's hand and with a reassuring motherly voice said, 'you shouldn't be out here alone. There is evil in this place. Come, Clarah, we need to go – we should hurry.'

With that, Clarah was back in her kitchen. She didn't walk up the driveway, nor struggle to locate the key, or unlock the door or follow any of the usual "getting home process". She was simply back at home, with just the blinking of an eye. The nice woman was gone. She felt abandoned and vulnerable.

Clarah ran around the house in a panic -turning on every light.

Nina's room was empty, as was Kane's. She phoned Baba May, but she didn't pick up. She tried her Aunt Mary's number, and she didn't answer either. There was no trace of Aura, whatever or whoever Aura should be. She was indeed quite quite alone and she felt quite quite trapped.

She lit a cigarette, inhaling nicotine quicker than the cigarette could oblige. She then lit another, and another – chain smoking her way into chemical calmness. She downed a neat whisky and then another and another. No matter what she did, she couldn't wipe out the words on the headstone. They had been carved into her memory, as deeply as they had been carved into the granite.

She asked herself, 'what just happened?'

Nobody answered. Even she couldn't answer herself. She fell asleep in front of the kitchen TV, with the sound turned up as loud as was tolerable.

***

It was sometime around midnight, and the witching hour was almost upon her. Clarah was still asleep. It was a restless uneasy sleep. She was still sat at the kitchen table, with her head resting on a plate. Her body was still quavering as she dozed.

A presence entered the room. It was a female, probably aged around 50 and wearing some sort of uniform – maybe a maid's outfit. The woman turned off the noisy TV, and sat down besides Clarah – stroking her perspiring forehead so to comfort her.

Clarah began to rouse – slowly at first and then becoming more alert. Her eyes popped open wide with a sudden startled awakening. She found herself gazing upon the face of the nice woman from the churchyard. She recognised the smell of summer flowers. It was like a bouquet of gardenia. Clarah sat bolt upright. Her head hurt, and the room was spinning ever so slightly.

'Who are you,' she asked? The woman had the sweetest of smiles, and Clarah instinctively sensed that she meant her no harm.

'My name is Roserie,' came the reply.

Clarah stumbled to her feet to pour herself a large glass of tap water. She turned to face her unexpected guest.

'I am sorry. I don't normally get a hangover until morning.'

She looked at her watch.

'Just past midnight – wow this is early for me. I must have put away a shit load of booze. Nice lady…Roserie…whoever you are…I have just had the weirdest of dreams. More like a nightmare - it was no bloody nice dream. Anyway, erm Rose… whatever you call yourself, why are you in my house? Are you a friend of my grandmothers?'

'I have known your grandmother for many years Clarah,' responded Roserie, 'but not in the way you think.'

What did she mean by that? Clarah wasn't thinking anything. With her head still revolving around on her neck, she felt too sick to think about cryptic messages too deeply. Roserie put a motherly arm around her shoulder.

'Clarah, I am sorry to tell you that what happened in the cemetery was neither a dream nor a nightmare. What you saw was real. You can go back in the daylight and see for yourself. I am sorry child, but you stumbled upon the grave of your mother and your sister.'

Clarah stared at Roserie with a mixture of disbelief, confusion and horror.

'How can they be dead? Nina lives here. I have seen her every day since I have been back from my travels. She put a welcome home poster on my door. She is not dead. I can't comment about my mother, but as for Nina -100% she is alive – I swear that she is.'

Roserie shook her head, not wanting to verbally challenge the young woman. She had delivered this message many times, to many people, over many years, and it never got any easier.

'Clarah, your sister died the day after her accident. Her head was hit by a stone and she developed a blood clot in her brain. The doctors tried to save her, but the damage was too bad.'

'No, no, no, no – that cannot be, 'yelled Clarah. 'She was here. I have spoken with her. She thought she was called Anju and she spoke Hindi. She turned the village cash machine into a shrine and washed clothes in the river. She has some mental disability and sometimes she changes personality. That my sister is dead – no, that cannot be true.'

Roserie's heart sank, and yet she was obliged to explain.

'Your grandmother, Baba May – she is gifted with psychic powers. In truth, so are most of your family, but only your gran chooses to use her abilities. She couldn't let Nina go, so she held onto her spirit. It was a selfish thing to do, but she is an old lady and she needed the company. Bereaved people often do that – I mean, they often cannot or will not let go of loved ones.'

'Can this be true?'

'It is all true Clarah. Nina was waiting for you to find out about her in your own time. In the afterlife, her mind is no longer diseased. Her thoughts are no longer locked in a strange world. She is free now. The spell Baba May bound her by, has been broken. She has passed over. Nina will always be around you in spirit, and forever in your heart, but she is no longer within this earthly realm. For your own sanity, you must accept her passing.'

Clarah did not want to believe her, but there was something about the way Roserie spoke which demanded respect and acceptance.

She asked of her, 'are you some sort of angel Roserie?'

The woman nodded, 'aye, I guess you could land me with such a title. Trust me, my work is not as glamourous as you may think. I don't have wings and I can't play a harp. I am an earth-bound angel. But, I do have your best interests at heart. You can trust me.'

Clarah paced up and down the kitchen, from the sink to the cooker to the refrigerator and back again. Mostly her head was bowed as though deep in thought. Occasionally she looked up at the woman who called herself Roserie. Under any other circumstances, she would have found the angel story totally unbelievable, but...there was something about Roserie that seemed credible. Her presence was soothing and her touch was like a kiss from a perfumed heavenly breeze. Yes indeed, by some illogical reasoning, her claim was convincing.

She moved back to the table and addressed Roserie directly.

'You saved me from something in the cemetery. I don't know what it was. It was covered in a red cape- I couldn't make out its shape. It felt evil. Where did it take my brother? Where is Kane?'

Roserie sighed. This was going to be a long evening. She hadn't wanted to tell Clarah so much, so fast – but it seemed unavoidable. 'Kane is also dead. He drowned, but not immediately. He lived for a week or so after Nina had passed, but the muddy water he inhaled destroyed his lungs. I know this must be hard for you. This is a lot of information for you to take in. It wasn't planned to be this way. Kane wasn't supposed to appear in the cemetery, and you weren't supposed to take the short cut home. Your presence in the churchyard triggered something, especially with the moon being as it is. Sometimes destiny gets screwed up. It happens when humans are allowed to make their own decisions. I wish that the living would just leave things to me sometimes.'

Clarah retorted, 'but hang on here – his name wasn't on the gravestone. I am sure of it. He can't be dead because he would have been buried with my mother and sister. Unless…unless…did Kane do something bad? Is that what it is? Have they buried him somewhere else because he did something bad?' Roserie simply nodded to confirm.

'Was it to do with Nina?'

Roserie didn't need to answer. Clarah had worked it all out before she could speak.

'I knew I recognised the gaje boys in the town. I had seen them hang out with Kane. It was them, wasn't it? They killed Nina. Oh shit - it wasn't Peters brothers. I told my Da it was them. Somehow, my brother is connected to her death. It has to be something very bad for my family to disown his corpse. Gypsies don't disown their dead unless they did something very bad. This is the only thing I can think of. Tell me what you know…please?'

Roserie had a heavy heart. Clarah's situation was far worse than most, and it wasn't over yet. She still had plenty of bad news to deliver. Softly and respectfully she answered.

'Kane had an issue with drink and drugs. You do know that don't you Clarah?'

Roserie didn't need to add anything further.

'Fuckin drug dealers, 'Clarah uttered, 'I bet he owed them money. But…he was wealthy. My Da put as much money in his account as he did in mine. We were each given the same. Oh no, I think I know what happened. Kane would have haggled with them. He always did try to get things for a knock down price, or even for free if he could. I just bet they knew all about his hidden money and that annoyed them. Gypsy family wins the lottery. It was in the news. My lord, they were threatening him with Nina. She was the bait. I suppose that they didn't actually mean to kill her, but it all went wrong for them didn't it. A stone to her head. I don't think they meant to do it, but it just happened.'

'You are very astute,' replied Roserie. 'They were found and convicted of manslaughter. Yes, Kane was implicated, but he was in the ground before it came to trial. Your family knew.'

'Where did they bury him?'

'Same churchyard, just as far away from your mother and sister as possible.'

'What creature took him? I saw it sink its fingers into his head. I mean – they penetrated his skull. It was a female hand. What was that thing…some woman?'

Roserie stood in order to face Clarah and address her directly.

'She is a powerful demoness. She calls herself Emmanuelle. She is made all the more potent by her ability to appear human, and whisper thoughts into empty heads. She is exceptionally intelligent, and can twist, manipulate and manoeuvre lesser beings into being her slave. She has an interest in you Clarah. That is why I needed to get you away from her fast, even though I broke many universal laws to do so.'

Clarah was confused. It took her a while to drink in all the information.

'But you said, or I think you said, that I triggered something by being in the churchyard. Roserie I am puzzled. What exactly do you mean by that?'

Roserie had not meant to take the conversation to such a deep level, but she recognised that Clarah's mind must be quite muddled, and that the young girl was probably in shock. She tried to deflect the question.

'You haven't asked about your mother yet. Do you not care to know why her name was also on the headstone?'

Clarah replied, 'my ma was a mother first, above and beyond everything else. She was selfless whilst I was selfish. I have been a terrible daughter. I had no idea that my brother and sister had been so badly injured…that they died just after I ran away. If only I had known that things were really that bad, that critical, that terminal...I would never have left.'

Clarah started to weep. As she did, Roserie moved back to her side and once again wrapped her arm around her shoulder.

'I am sorry,' uttered Roserie, 'I should have guessed that you were avoiding the subject of your mother. I should have known it was too painful. We don't need to talk about this right now.'

'Yes, we do,' snapped Clarah. 'I was the worst ever daughter. She needed me and I wasn't there.'

Clarah stopped to blow her nose, still blubbering as she spoke. Through her sniffles she continued, 'I knew something had happened to her. Baba May was aware that I was coming home. For heaven's sake, I was on the other side of the equator and it was a long-haul flight. My ma had time to come back from wherever she was. She wouldn't have stayed in some fancy spa knowing I was back home. I knew Baba May was lying, and besides....' Her voice tailed off as she wept into a soaked tissue.

'Besides what, 'asked Roserie?

Clarah continued, 'I think my mother's spirit came to me when I was in Oz. I was working at this station up in Queensland. I used to help out with the horses, mucking out the stables and that sort of thing. My family had hired a detective agency, and they got this investigator bloke to try and find me...persuade me to come home, I guess. I didn't want to be found. I had run away for a reason. I tried to dodge the bullet, but the detectives were good. No matter what I did, where I went - they always picked up on my trail. Anyway, I was with the other jillaroo's one night. We were all mucking about, sitting around the camp fire. We had drunk far too many tinnies. Then...I saw a light in the corner of my eye. To be fair, I thought I was pissed. I blinked a few times, but it was still there. It was up near the ranch entrance. It was weird. I was like a moth driven to a flame. I just had to keep going towards the light. I couldn't stop myself. Then I saw her.'

Once again, Clarah broke off in tears, blowing into a tissue that was barely surviving the onslaught of her secretions.

'Go on,' requested Roserie.

'The light just morphed into my ma. I could see her as clear as clear. She told me that I needed to go home. She said it was time. She told me that a man called Simon would come for me and put me on and plane and that I had to do as I was told. I didn't do as I was told though. I ran away...again. I jumped on a flight to Bali after that. I disobeyed her. But I knew... I just knew she had...died.'

Roserie went to find new tissue supplies from the bathroom. When she returned, she said, 'Clarah, tonight has been too much for you. Yes, you needed to know the truth, but not this much and not this fast. All your questions will be answered tomorrow, but not now. You cannot take anymore. I am calling for time out. Come -follow me.'

Roserie took her by the hand and led Clarah towards her bedroom. She pulled back the duvet for her, as a mother would for her child. She then tucked her into bed, in the same motherly way.

'Dear child, you are protected in this house. Your grandmother is a gifted witch, and that ring of salt around the perimeters will keep out anything evil. Once I kiss your forehead, you will fall into a deep sleep. You will dream. You need to dream. You have to understand what happened the night you left the campsite. In the morning, you will wake up and everything will be much clearer. Then your new friend Aura will come and visit you. She will tell you about all the things we haven't yet discussed. She will tell you who you have become. But for now- just close your eyes.'

Clarah's eyelids grew heavy. Sleep was already wrapping itself around her weary body. She just about managed to ask, 'who and what is Aura by the way? Is she an angel as well?'

It was a question which caused a giggle to fall from Roserie's lips. 'My oh my - Aura an angel? Most certainly not. What a funny thought that is? However, she is your friend. She will tell everything when you see her next. For the moment Clarah, you need to rest...and dream. Shush.'

With just the promise of a kiss upon her crumpled brow, eyes were shut. Roserie vanished. Outside, the lunar eclipse had begun.

CHAPTER 12

Saturday July 12th 2014
HADES HALL - A JOURNEY BACK IN TIME

The dream had begun and amnesia was being challenged.

Clarah had returned to the night Nina had been attacked. Her mind went back in time to 2014 and to the caravan site in Scarborough. She had returned to the cries, the confusion and the total mayhem of July 12th.

She then found herself in the back seat of a taxi. It was a deep blue Mondeo and it was driving her somewhere, anywhere…as far from the flashing blue lights as it could go. She didn't know where the taxi driver was taking her; she hadn't been paying much attention. The brutal events of the night were still leaping around in her head like a mad box of frogs. The cruel memories were a distraction. All she knew for sure, was that she wasn't in a city centre of any kind; not even on the suburban outskirts. It was too dark outside. No street lights, no illuminated windows, not even a single floodlit car park outside a solitary pub. Aside from an impish moon peeping from behind clouds, and the beam of the driver's headlights; not a shred of electricity brightened up the pitch black of the outside world. Clarah knew that she was in the middle of absolutely nowhere…and she didn't care. Not a jot.

In the distance was the obscure suggestion of mountains. They were peppered with little white dots she presumed to be sheep. She soon recognised that there was no way she could be on the A19 heading north up to Newcastle. At best, this was a "B road" and at worst a farm track.

She was now certain that she must be heading west into the heart of the remote moorland.

The North Yorkshire Moors – beautiful, wild and yet desolate at the same time. She knew them well, both loving and hating the geography of the terrain in equal measures.

Logically, she should have been scared, or at the very least concerned – but she wasn't. She didn't care if the taxi driver was an escaped mass murderer planning to dispose of her mutilated body in some secluded heathery grave. She felt numb. After what she had just witnessed back at the campsite, she now felt blasé about her own fate.

In a strange way, she actually felt grateful not to be in Newcastle now. Thinking about it logically, she didn't want to risk bumping into her own rowdy hen party; especially with Peter hanging around like a redundant escort. How could she possibly look him in the eyes…knowing what she knew?'

Peter - her thoughts drifted back to his wife…her own sister Katalyn. She balked at the memory of her sister lying naked with Denny. My God - she hadn't seen that one coming. If cheating people inadvertently give away subliminal signs of treachery, then she had been too blind or complacent to see it.

She shuddered, sad yet angry at her own trusting ignorance.

Too many bad things had happened all at once. She considered that life could be cruel like that. One day the garden could be an avenue of Cherry Blossoms and then the next – a tornado tears up the roots, rips off the branches, crushes the pink buds and it all changes.

Her mind tried to make sense of it all but her thoughts were shipwrecked and useless, like the tangled strands of a broken fishing net. She resolved to stop even trying to reason with the unreasonable.

Clarah then looked out of the taxi window; trying to spot any signs of life on planet Earth. She placed her hot forehead on the cold glass, hoping the window wouldn't become a mirror and show her how desolate she really looked…far more desolate and lost than the windy moors outside the cab.

Finally, at the end of a very long dark twisting country lane, lights began to appear…lights that illuminated a forever driveway amidst a remote handsome country estate.

The word "driveway" gave her a sudden vision of some young blond lad driving down a similar long driveway, feeling equally as anxious. It was a strange experience – like some leap into a future time. Clarah understood that she had inherited some of the dranengri abilities of her Roma grandmother, and so it was not unusual that a random experience would take her on a flight of fancy into another time zone. She wondered who the young blond boy could be. Perhaps he was someone she was destined to meet at some future date, she concluded…or rather, hoped.

As they approached the hotel, the driver looked through his rear mirror. He caught Clarah's eyes as she peered outside with both wonderment and bewilderment.

'My friend is the head waiter here,' he told her. 'I hope you don't mind, but I have asked him to book you a room. In your sorry state, you look like you are in need of somewhere quiet and you don't get much quieter than this. I hope that's okay with you Miss. I can drive you into Newcastle if you don't like it here.'

Clarah responded with a dry husky voice, 'no no – it's okay. This looks fine. In fact, it looks perfect.'

In truth, she didn't care. She just needed to be away…somewhere, anywhere, nothing really mattered. Whatever location she was in, was just some numerical longitude and latitude on a map. A place, any place…was just a position to pass through at a given moment of time. After all – she was a Gypsy, a nomad, a traveller, a drifter…a wanderer through life. Passing through- that's what she did best. That's what she always did.

The driver carried her bags into the large marble floored reception area. Clarah couldn't help but look up at the vast 7ft wide chandelier, with its multiple candle lights demanding praise and attention. It rested inside an extensive dome, with the most opulent ceiling moulding she had ever seen; deep indigo with gilded neo-classical cornices. She gasped and the words just slipped out, 'wow, holy shit,' Clarah then shuddered with embarrassment, as she realised she had cussed out-loud in the poshest of lobby's.

A young woman approached her. Clarah guessed from her soft baby-face, that she may be of a similar age to herself, yet she carried herself as though she was much older. The lady-girl wore a designer bell-sleeve crepe dress; one that oozed class and sophistication. Her long strawberry hair was pulled off her face by a high ponytail, and she wore dark cherry lipstick that matched the colour of her dress to the exact shade. In fact, everything matched; nail varnish, shoes, hair piece – she was perfectly co-ordinated. Clarah looked her up and down with a tinge of envy, then deciding that she was a bit too flawlessly matched for the average teenager. The word "false" came into her head, and yet again her psyche connected with someone else who had thought the same thing, somewhere else, somewhere far away. Why was that?

Something just didn't seem right about lady-woman, and her face… she looked familiar. Clarah was too mentally exhausted to process these thoughts any further, so shut the lid on her Pandora's box of ponderings.

The young woman held out her immaculately manicured hand to greet her.

'Hello, I am pleased to meet you. I understand you are a friend of a friend. My name is Océane and I am the owner of Hades Hall. We have a room reserved for you. Let me take you over to the reception desk where Arabella will book you in.'

Clarah look down upon Océane's cold thin hand, a hand adorned with jewellery; Carnelian art-deco rings and Garnet bracelets co-ordinated effortlessly with the rest of her attire. Clarah then looked down at her own turquoise off the shoulder jumpsuit…apparel more in keeping with a Gypsy hen night in Newcastle. She dreaded to think how her face must look, absent of all makeup accept perhaps the occasional mascara smudge. She knew she must look awful.

She wondered if the hotel staff would guess she was a traveller. Many of her friends had tried to book venue's like this for their weddings, but as soon as the hotel manager realised who and what they were, the event would suddenly become overbooked and dates mysteriously cancelled. It had happened too many times to be mere coincidence.

She suddenly felt quite self-conscious and had to constantly remind herself that she was a rich girl now. However, the wealth had been too recent to leave its mark. She still bore the look of a commoner, although her bank account would beg to differ.

Clarah turned to pay the driver, pulling a grubby fake Ted Baker purse from out of her plastic supermarket bag. Océane pushed it away, 'we will take care of the taxi fare Miss …err …what is your name exactly?' 'Lee, Clarah Lee.'

Océane continued, 'Clarah Lee – that's a nice name. No need to worry about such things Clarah. It's all part of our service. We take care of all your requirements at Hades.'

Clarah was starting to dislike her flawless hostess. She begrudged the fact that Océane oozed supreme self-confidence. She despised the soft sensual tones of her French accent, and her kitten-cute pronunciations of English words. Océane spoke as though her tongue could cut through butter with a knife made from silk. Clarah felt it unfair that Océane didn't have one single pimple on her perfect skin, irrespective of popping stage. She knew that her hostess had seen the anti-acne cream in her plastic bag and had probably inwardly smirked at not needing such pharmaceutical assistance. Toned arms, with pert breasts and concaved stomach – it didn't seem fair. Clarah was jealous and begrudged the girls beauty. Envy was one of the 7 deadly sins she loathed the most, yet she could not deny how she felt.

She wondered if Denny would have still have cheated on her if she had looked even a tiny bit like Océane. She hated that thought- it was like self-punishment directed to the victim by the victim.

Océane seemed to know the driver. She turned to address him, 'Tobiah, go and see the concierge. He will sort you out with some money.'

She then grabbed Clarah's hand and guided her towards the reception desk.

'Arabella will assist you. All she needs is some sort of plastic and then she will show you to your room.'

Before walking away, Océane looked back at Clarah, as though she had just read her mind. She smiled reassuringly, 'thank you for your unspoken compliments Clarah, but let's not forget that I have to work to get all of this. I am working right now. You are not – I am. Everything comes at a cost. The bigger the reward, the higher the price tag. Never forget that. Anyway, I have other guests to attend to. I will leave you in Arabella's capable hands.'

With that, she strutted out of the lavish reception area with the composure of a super model, leaving her windswept guest somewhat overwhelmed.

Clarah was nervous. She had to fill the registration card in and it was asking for a home address. As a Gypsy girl, she had no home address. Aside from this fact, she hardly knew how to write. She could tap away on an iPad without any issues, but holding a pen felt strange.

Arabella seemed to sense her discomfort.

'It's okay Miss Lee, a debit or credit card will suffice. I will fill the rest in for you.'

It was a relief. This exceptionally upmarket establishment seemed to be staffed by exceptionally nice people, and ones who could read minds. After the gruesome night she had just experienced, the last thing she needed was yet more tension. The quiet solitude of a warm bed and the sanctity of sleep, was all she really required.

If Clarah had nursed any expectations, then the room she had been allocated lived up to all hopes and dreams. Arabella unlocked the door, winked mischievously and then stood to one side to watch Clarah's reaction. She couldn't help but gasp as her eyes met with a queen sized 4-poster bed; with matching duvet, throws and scatter cushions…all swathed in rich burgundy, dark chocolate and burning gold. Arabella had placed her in the turret room, which was an executive suite over three floors. Handing her the keys, Arabella left her guest to explore her new temporary abode.

Clarah climbed the wrought iron spiral staircase to an upper room which boasted a lounge, complete with its own self-service kitchen area. Opening the fridge, she noted it had been stocked with snacks and drinks. On the granite work top, a bottle of Louis Roederer Cristal Rosé champagne, was sat on ice. Clarah had never tasted champagne before.

Climbing to a 3rd floor, she found a bathroom suite, which she initially thought looked like *"The Star Ship Enterprise"*- from the TV series she was once addicted to. She first noticed a rectangular mirrored steam-shower cabin, complete with state of the art chromotherapy lighting, Tri-Jet Steam System, and even a Bluetooth compatible touch control panel. A notice on the wall informed her that she could download an app and control the shower from her mobile phone. Clarah giggled like a child overcome with wonder at Christmas. She then noted a Jacuzzi hot tub in the corner and taking centre stage; an old-fashioned free-standing copper bathtub. Directly above the bathtub was the glass dome at the apex of the turret. She could imagine that lying in the bathtub before bed, would offer up the most awesome view of the stars.

For the 3rd time that evening, a jumble of words seemed to take on a greater meaning. She repeated the words "view of the stars" – VOTS. It had some significance and yet….what?

She refocused her thoughts on the anticipation of sipping champagne whilst lying in the copper bath tub. The terror of the night's earlier events, although not vanquished from her mind, had now been replaced with the sheer excitement of being in such an extra-ordinary setting. For a traveller girl, this place was akin to paradise.

Then at that precise moment of euphoria, a timely bursting of her bubble occurred when a message came over the intercom. The voice made her jump.

'Miss Clarah Lee, could you please come to your door so we can take your room service order?'

Clarah ran down the spiral staircases to her bedroom door, and upon opening it noted Océane waiting with a pen and a menu with lots of tick boxes.

'Oh, erm come in. Sorry it took me so long. I was investigating the bathroom. I didn't expect to be served food in my room,' stated Clarah apologetically.

Océane smiled as she strode into the room as though she owned it; which of course she did. Clarah secretly wondered how someone possibly younger than herself, could have such an acquisition. She then remembered that she was also a wealthy young woman and mentally began to calculate how she could also use her new-found wealth.

Océane interrupted her train of thought. She began, 'I heard your stomach rumbling when you walked into reception, so I figured you must be hungry.'

Clarah had quite forgotten about her stomach, but then suddenly realised that Océane was correct. She hadn't eaten in about 10 or maybe even 12 hours.

Scanning the menu which Océane had thrust into her hand, she then realised that she couldn't understand a single word. Her reading skills were basic at best, and not at all suited to deciphering French cuisine. Océane could see that her young guest was struggling.

Sympathetically she asked, 'let me help you with this Clarah; is there anything that you don't like?'

'Yes,' came the rapid response, 'I don't like the fact that my brother and sister are in hospital and obviously I am not there with them. Oh, and I don't like the fact I have just found my boyfriend…make that my fiancé, in bed with my sister. These are the things I don't like Océane. Anything else on that posh menu of yours will suit me just fine.'

Océane was taken aback by the stark candour of the girls reply. She literally did take a few steps backwards. After a couple of awkward seconds, she replied, 'oh I see. So, that is what brought you to Hades Hall in the middle of the night? I was wondering why you were dressed so inappropriately…I would say in last season's Versace clubbing attire, yet with just a few belongings in a grubby backpack and a plastic shopping bag. It made no sense to me. Tobiah informed us that he picked you up from outside a Gypsy camp. When he phoned to book you a room, he said we should take pity on you as you looked quite distressed. Now I get it. Your heart has been torn to shreds – you poor thing.'

Clarah couldn't tell if her perfect hostess was being cruelly sarcastic or genuinely concerned.

'Why take pity on a Gypsy girl? Nobody else does. My kind are thrown out of posh places like this all the time. Mostly we can't even make it past the front door. What makes me any different?'

Océane cocked her head to one side and smiled.

'What makes you so different Miss Lee, is an American Express Centurion Card. Of course, we had to make the appropriate security checks, but it proved to be legal. Gypsy or not – you have money dear girl. It takes a fair amount of cash in the bank to warrant such a card, so I think I can guess who and what you are. Whatever your ethnicity, this plastic buys you respectability, ma pauvre petite fille riche.'

Clarah was finding the superior attitude of her teenage hostess both unnerving and irritating. She wanted to tell her she was 'up her own pert arse', but then again, didn't want to be rude to someone who had rescued her from an awful situation.

'Okay, la Mademoiselle of Hades Hall, let's play the honesty game. Yes, I am from the Gypsy family that won the lottery. I am guessing that this was your assumption. My parents gave me £500K to spend, so that's why I have this Centurion thingy card. It only happened recently, so I haven't had time to upgrade my appearance in keeping with my new wealth. Just adjusting to changing times…if you know what I mean. But then again, you probably have no idea what I mean. You and I come from different worlds.'

Océane admired the girl's feisty response. She looked her guest up and down and for a while said nothing. Finally breaking the silence, she replied, 'well, I guess that being nouveau riche must be a challenge. Thank you for being partially honest with me Clarah, and you are quite correct, we are from different worlds, but that doesn't mean that I don't want to help you. Perhaps a tad more honesty may come in useful as a communication aid. I mean - I know for a fact that it takes a bit more than £500K in a bank account to get you the bit of plastic you have in your tatty purse. I believe that 2 tickets bore the same winning numbers. I reckon you had the other winning ticket Clarah. Yes indeed; you had it and you didn't tell anyone, did you? What was its value - erm 8,9,10 million? Tell me when to stop counting. Now, that sort of amount will get you some mean killer ass plastic. Just be straight with me Clarah and I can help you sort your life out. So, let me ask you the question again – food wise, is there anything that you don't like?'

Clarah was stunned. This Océane girl was impossible to outwit.

'Erm no, I can eat anything. I don't really care.'

'Good,' responded Océane, 'so let me choose for you. Soupe de poisson for your first course, followed by pigeon with warm foie gras sorbet and followed by café gourmand. I think you will enjoy that – it's a small black expresso presented alongside lots of miniature puddings. I believe that for tonight's menu, our chef has prepared a petit brownie triangle with an eggcup-sized crème brûlée and clafoutis. They are just a collection of nibble sized puddings, so should be easy for your uncultured tummy to digest. Do you prefer white or red wine?'

Clarah hadn't understood a single word Océane had uttered.

'I would have been happy with a pork pie and a mug of tea,' she replied, 'but no big deal. I guess you can't have everything on that menu of yours. I will eat what you suggested and as for red or white wine – a glass of each will be fine for me. I like to mix my drinks – that would be mixing them together by the way, so also bring me a plastic tumbler with a straw – if you don't mind Mademoiselle.'

'Très bon,' responded Océane, 'trying not to look offended at the mere suggestion of mixing wine's.

'I am glad that you are letting me help you Clarah. Your food will take about 50 minutes to prepare, so please avail yourself of the shower and complimentary dressing gown. I suggest you get some rest after that. Not meaning to be rude Miss Lee, but you look awful. Tomorrow morning Arabella will go out and buy you some appropriate clothes and footwear. Don't worry about it, she has good taste and a fabulous eye for fashion. We can guess you size and just charge it to your bill. You don't have to move a tiny little muscle my dear. You are rich now and this is all part of our service. Once you are scrubbed clean, well fed and rested, we will find which hospital your siblings are in and you can make some decisions on what you want to do next. Right at this moment, you need to take some time out for yourself. Time to think about your options, time to be strong.'

Clarah's eyes became moist. Even though she knew that Océane was only doing all of this because she was a member of some upper-class plastic card club, she still appreciated Océane's help. She couldn't ever remember anyone wanting to help her before...not really help her. She held out her hand as a sincere gesture of gratitude and simply said, 'thank you.'

Océane took her hand, noticing her guest's grubby bitten fingernails and the thin silver band that she wore on her engagement finger.

'Remind me tomorrow Clarah, but we also need to get a manicurist to call in and fix those nails of yours. As for that cheap engagement ring, I am presuming that you are no longer in need of this thing?'

Océane held out her hand in expectation.

Clarah looked down at the ring, pulled it off her finger and placed it gently into Océane's outreached open palm. Océane then lifted up the sashed window and tossed the ring out onto the lawn.

'One day, many centuries into the future dear Clarah...when this lawn is at the bottom of a sea, some archaeologist will find that babble and wonder how it got there. They can wonder, but they will never know. They will never comprehend the tears of its owner. The passing of time hides so many secrets.'

Clarah gasped as her engagement ring went flying through the air.

'Why did you do that,' she screeched in horror?

Océane turned to face her and replied, 'because underneath the skin of the plump frightened little Gypsy girl who now stands before me, is a rich, slim, confident young woman, who deserves a man who will be faithful to her, and that is why.'

With that, Océane winked at her and walked out of the door.

This was not what Clarah had expected.

Only this morning, she had woken up in a cold bunk bed in the room she shared with her twin, Nina. She had not anticipated that the next time she lay down her head, it would be in a place like this. She had looked at her exclusive American Express Centurion Card, and then hidden it back in her purse. Her win had overwhelmed her and she didn't know what else to do with it. Neither had she anticipated, that she would end the day no longer engaged to Denny. Life certainly was a strange unpredictable beast.

***

She began to stir from her sleep. Somehow, she had fast forwarded back from whence she came – September 2015.

Roserie was sitting beside her. As she saw her emerald eyes open, she pressed a finger on Clarah's forehead.

'No, no, no Clarah. Go back to sleep, there is yet more for you to see.'

With just those few words, Clarah was back inside her dream. She drifted slowly back in time, back to her memories, back to a place she didn't want to be, and difficult moments she would rather forget– the night of the blood moon July 2014.

Clarah

There was more she had to see. Amnesia had been a kind and patient friend, but now that acquaintance would end. It should end. It had to end. Clarah needed to remember.

CHAPTER 13

Sunday July 13th 2014
INSIDE THE DEMONS LAIR

Maybe it was all just one big illusion; a nasty consequence of mixing white and red wine to create a new Rosé, or maybe she really had hit the reverse gear. Time travel – was it truly possible? Whatever and however, she was lying in a strange hotel bed and September 2015 had been moved back to July 2014.

Her legs were plump and blindingly white, as they had been once before. This was before her calves had trampled the tea plantations of Sri Lanka and walked the great wall of China. These were her hips before daily swims in tropical lagoons had evaporated stubborn cellulite. This was a body as it had been, pre the aerobic hike around Khao Luang, when blubber had been transformed into muscle in just a week. This was the flabby tum before a bespoke diet cooked by her own personal chef erased the love-handles. This was the old Clarah. The one she hated. The one she wanted to run away from. The dumpy pudgy Clarah that men cheated on.

She was nuzzling her head deep into huge cotton sateen pillows, when a pheasant cackling under her window rudely awoke her from her slumber. It took a while for her eyes to adjust to the light. It then took a few minutes longer for her to realise where she was. Then the memories came back to her – slowly at first and then with the haste of a runaway train.

She tried not to see it, but closed eyes could not shut out the awful pictures inside her eyes.

Nina hanging by her arms from a tree; her head cut and face covered in blood. Kane, half drowning in a stinking algae coloured pond. Her father Mick and the sheer anger and venom in his eyes, a look of rage she had never witnessed before. The cries of her mother, heart wrenching pitiful cries that no daughter should ever have to witness. Then of course there was Denny; the man she was engaged to. Denny, with that blushed afterglow of carnal gratification, lying naked next to her older sister Katalyn.

'Oh my God,' was the only words she could utter as she sprang bolt upright in bed.

As she sat up a sharp pain rebounded inside her skull, bouncing off bone like it was a trampoline. She looked at the empty bottle of champagne on the bedside table. None of this could be real. It wasn't possible. Yesterday morning, the only problem on the horizon was an inconvenient period pain, and the realisation that she may not be fit enough to participate in her own hen night. Just a mere 24 hours ago, that dilemma was the total epitome of her worries.

'Now- but what the crap has happened now?'

She repeated the words several times inside her head and started to cry. Small tears to begin with, then escalating to full on sobs.

The mattress sank. Someone or something was sat next to her. She held her breath- not daring to move. She could feel the weight pulling down on her duvet. Her hands were covering her tear stained face. She parted her fingers slowly, and then pulled her hands away fully. She gasped in shock.

'Who the hell are you,' she demanded?

The woman's face was familiar, yet kindly. She could see her own eyes in the woman's eyes…as though they were related in some way. The woman didn't reply. For some reason Clarah wasn't as afraid as she should have been. Here was a complete stranger sitting on her bed…and yet she was oddly accepting of this intrusion. She couldn't understand why that should be.

Clarah asked again, 'do I know you? Are you a cousin?'

Her voice was raspy, as though she was either coming down with a cold or had smoked too may cigarettes. Then she remembered the cigars, none other than Fuente Don Arturo AnniverXario. Why had she smoked cigars? Just because they were there and just because she could, came her own answer to her own question.

The woman got up and walked to the window. Opening the curtains, she sighed, 'they never did find your engagement ring Clarah. Perhaps some things are best gone forever. Still, it is sad to have lost something once so precious, especially by a careless fling. That ring meant a lot to you once upon a time. Those emotions all seem such a long time ago, long ago to me that is. Still raw to you I guess. Shame - many a heart has been broken by a fling.'

Clarah shot out of bed. 'How do you know all of this? I only erm, lost the ring last night …I think. It wasn't long ago at all. Who the hell are you? Why are you in my bedroom? How did you get in here? How do I know you?'

Clarah was growing agitated by the vague comments of the familiar stranger.

The woman moved back to the bed, all the time looking around the room with a faraway nostalgic glimmer in her eyes. She continued talking.

'I woke up in this room once, just like you did this morning. I was beside myself with grief, just as you will be soon.'

She held out her wrists so Clarah could see them.

She continued, 'I don't think I actually wanted to kill myself. I don't know why I cut my arms. I am ashamed of this disfigurement now. I came here to take these scars away. Hey, you think these welts are easy to live with? Try being in a humid rain forest near the equator and having to wear long sleeves out of shame. This mutilation is an embarrassment Self-harm is a useless bucket of shite. If only I could stop just one person in the future from doing this…but I can't. The scars don't vanish Clarah. The only way to fix this is to go back in time and prevent it from ever happening. Do I regret taking a knife and slashing open my wrist? Yes of course I do. What the hell did it solve? It was just a moment of temporary insanity, a moment which led to a life time of disfigurement. Such a sad bloody shame. Please don't do this to us Clarah.'

Clarah jumped out of bed and visibly scanned every hair on the woman's head. She noted every minute line on her skin and each mole on her arm. It took a while, but eventually it clicked.

She announced, 'I cannot believe I am actually going to say what I am going to say, but for some weird reason, I think you may be me. Are you the me of the future?'

The woman clapped in sarcastic applause.

'At long last dear Clarah of yesteryear. I was wondering when you would recognise yourself. Have I really changed that much?'

Clarah almost choked on her words as she replied, 'if I have just heard what I think I have just heard, and then you ask me if you or me or we have changed, seriously – my God… a big fat bloody yes. My lord, just compare us. Age is supposed to drag our tits down with its gravitational pull…all the way down to our tombs I believe, and yet you are beautiful. You are slim. Your hair is…amazing. You can even talk better than I can. Your voice is nice. You sound like you are in control, like you are smart…really smart. How did I ever get to be this amazing? This is crazy.'

'Well, praise indeed. Thank you Clarah v1. Having lots of money does help enhance one's appearance. Wealth changes people – always does, always will.'

Clarah shook her head in disbelief. She glanced over at the champagne bottle, wondering if Océane had doctored it will some hallucinogenic drug.

She continued, 'I am fairly certain that I will soon wake up back in the caravan, and find out that the last 24 hours have all been some spaced out delusion. However, whilst I am still in this dreamlike state, can I ask you Miss Clarah Lee v2 of the future, what are you doing here? Why are you back in a past that must be painful to revisit? The last 24 hours have been a living nightmare. I wouldn't choose to come back to this date…but hey, you are the future me and I did. So, why did we decide to come back here?'

The Clarah of the future smiled a knowing smile. She replied, 'well dear younger me, I wanted to prevent these bloody scars.'

She walked over to a finely serrated knife, still lying on last night's room service tray.

'If you don't mind Clarah v1, I will just take this with me. It is best not to leave anything to chance.'

With that, the woman held out her arms. The scars vanished before their eyes.

'Result – it worked. Thank God for that. I prevented something terrible from happening, something we would always regret. Isn't that just awesome. I was warned not to meddle with the past. Something to do with a time/space inconsistency loop, but hells bells - what's so bad about scar prevention?'

Clarah slumped back on her bed, muddled thoughts marching through her head like an army of ants.

'I don't get it, 'she exclaimed. 'So, you are the "me" of the future and by the looks of you, I have obviously done okay in life. It would seem that I have recovered from Denny and other recent shite events, spent time in a rain forest and lost lots of weight, but…how can you, can I… shit how can the collective "we" just time travel? Surely that isn't possible?'

The future Clarah sat down next to her predecessor and tried to pick her words carefully.

'*Enchantment under the Sea,*' came her reply.

The present Clarah shrugged, 'I don't understand.'

The future Clarah continued, 'you must surely remember the film – *"Back to the future"*. Marty went back to Hill Valley High in 1955 and visited the dancehall where his parents had their first kiss. Come on Clarah – you…I mean we, we loved that film.'

The present Clarah nodded in agreement.

'So,' continued her future self, 'you must remember the words of the Doc when he said, *"I foresee two possibilities. One- seeing herself thirty years in the future would put Jennifer into shock and she'd simply pass out. Or two, the encounter could create a time paradox. The results of which could cause a chain reaction that would unravel the very fabric of the space-time continuum and destroy the entire universe!... Granted, that's the worst-case scenario."*

Clarah v2 giggled to herself as she enjoyed replaying the scene in her mind. Meanwhile, the Clarah of 2014 remained befuddled.

'A time paradox. I don't understand. What's that?'

The future Clarah put a reassuring arm around her younger self and replied, 'I don't understand either. I only know that me being here could be dangerous. I have already changed our future by distorting the past, but one day you will thank me for not having to live with the scars, aside from the fact that maybe you won't, because you will never have the aforementioned scars in question. The only way I was allowed to come back and do any of this, was to agree that you will forget all about our meeting. That was the deal. Lucky girl - you will never know the pain and the shame I have endured.'

'So, I will forget about all of this? Forget ever meeting you?'

'Selective amnesia? Well yes, for now V1 you will forget. One day, we will show you all of this in a dream, but before that happens there are things you have to find out for yourself, about yourself. If I tell you too much, too soon – in some way it could alter who I am right now, which of course impacts on your future. Bad shit happens for a reason. It teaches us, it makes us strong. You just have to work your way through it, that is aside from cutting your wrists in self-retribution.'

'So, let me get this right, 'asked the present Clarah. 'You can travel where you want to and go back and forth in time at will? That must be amazing. Hey you can travel to next week and tell us the lottery numbers…if only I needed the money, which I don't. Oh bugger…. I mean…. did you? Is that what happened? Was it you/me/us? Did we do that? I always blamed Baba May and her sorcery, but was it really you?'

Her future self, hung her head down low. She touched Clarah's cheek softly and replied, 'these things are not for you to know right now. You have already suffered enough v1. Amnesia is Mother Nature's anaesthetic. It takes away the pain of something that is too hurtful to remember…something so agonising that the very memory becomes life shattering. All you really need to know for now, is that you will recover, life will get better and you will turn into someone very special and exceptionally gifted. The pain you are feeling is just for this tiny moment in time. Believe me when I tell you this. I know Denny broke your heart…hey, I was there as well, but be patient and soon the hurt will stop. You will forget about this conversation until the time is right for you to remember. Oblivion will be your best friend for the moment. Trust me on this.'

'So, do tell me, 'asked the present Clarah, 'you must have visited Denny, because that is what I would have done. We loved him and he let us down. Maybe I need some sort of closure…but please, where is he in the future? Who is he with? Is he with Katalyn? I am sure you know something, because if I could just walk through walls into someone's secret past, he would be the first one on my list of visitations.'

The future Clarah understood her plea, and replied with a heavy heart.

'Dearest Clarah form the past, you can read me so well, but then again I am you. Yes of course I was curious. The human heart isn't just a box that can be opened and emptied by turning it upside down. So yes, naturally I went to see him. I wouldn't exactly use the word "stalking" but for a while there was an element of that and with my present skill set, observation can be boringly easy. Hey, who needs browser search history when one can travel in time? As you said…we needed closure, so I wanted to know the truth.'

'What did you find?'

'What I found was a cheating liar. You must surely recall all his multitude of excuses; the alibies, the pretexts, the ruses for being here there and everywhere. Maybe it was an important meeting, a football match, a sick uncle, a stag night in Prague? There was always a perfectly valid reason for him to be away. I am sorry Clarah v1, but even as he was due to walk up the aisle with us, he was in a relationship with another woman. When out of town, he was living with a gaje near Birkenhead. Our relationship with him was just a scam. Perhaps he just liked the idea of spending our millions.'

'I am shocked. I honestly didn't know.'

'Well that's because he was clever – a seasoned adulterer. I am afraid that Denny was screwing around with any skirt he could get his hands on. It wasn't just Katalyn…she was one of many. He didn't have an ounce of loyalty in his pencilled-dicked body.'

'And now?'

'He finally settled down. Time and maturity can change a person y'know. He now lives on a farm near Scarborough. He seems happy enough. He tends to his sheep and rides his shire horses up and down the hillocks. He has a pleasant little life. Some other unfortunate lady has to keep the reins on him now, so let's hope he keeps his zipper closed.'

'That's funny. He became a shepherd and I became a time traveller.'

'Life can be funny ol thing Clarah. I just find it sad that for now, you will forget all of this. I want to tell you to be happy that the ring is off your finger, and that those wrists of yours are uncut. I want to tell you that Denny was never really ours to have and to hold. For now, these words will be forgotten, but one day you will see and hear all of this in a dream. In the meantime, you will just have to toughen up and brave the heartbreak.'

The younger Clarah had taken a liking to her older self.

Clarah v2 had been right to visit her. Maybe it had jeopardised some space-time continuum paradox, but the decision was a good one. She now knew that she would get over Denny. She also knew that one day she would be the proud owner of Barbie-doll slim legs.

She addressed her older self.

'You are going to leave me now, aren't you? Must you go? I mean – I know you must, but I like you. It has been a privilege. I think I will enjoy being you one day.'

The future Clarah smiled with the self-assurance of knowing that she had left her former self in a good place.

'What a result. The Clarah of 2014 has almost decided that she likes herself. Let's raise the flag kiddo. Hey, I am still here and still going strong, so that means you must survive to become me. I cannot give too much away, because I don't want to alter our destiny, however just one thing for you to know before I go. Right now, you are in a place of demons. You should have guessed as much by the name of the hotel, but then again you aren't as well travelled or as well read as I am. You will get smarter. Knowledge and wisdom will come with time.'

'DEMONS – what? Really?'

'Hey, don't go all manic and tense on me just because I mentioned the D word. I notice some rigidity around you lips and is that froth coming from your mouth? Look, the owners of this place may be bad, and I mean really bad. After all, they are demons and they don't do charity coffee mornings, but on this occasion, they mean you no harm. The me you are about to become, will be far too useful to them in the future. They need you to stay safe, so just enjoy their hospitality. But don't go smoking any more cigars …lung cancer and all that.'

The visitor from the future noticed the strained look on her younger self's face. The trauma of the last day had become too much.

'I need you to rest now Clarah. Your hostess will wake you soon enough and will guide you through what you should do next. She will put you on an aeroplane and you will travel far away. Money is no object, so go wherever you like. You will have a wonderful time, visit many countries, meet many new friends, experience new things, grow as a person. Do not fret, it will all be okay in the end. You will grow up to become me. However, just for the moment, you will forget this meeting. It would be confusing otherwise. I will catch up with you in the future. I only came here on a scar removal mission, and look…all gone.'

Clarah had every reason to be confused, and so she was. She held her hand out towards the woman who referred to herself as v2. She didn't want her new self to leave. She liked this confident beautiful version of her plump uncultured self.

Clarah v2 held onto her predecessor's hand, feeling a deep sense of nostalgia and a longing for the past, as imperfect and difficult as it may have been.

'You know what little v1, we always see yesterday as a better place. The sky was always bluer, the snow was always whiter and deeper, the grass was always greener. Our mind can be selective as to what it chooses to remember. The reality and the memories do not always match. You will sleep now. Part of you will wake tomorrow and plan a trip around the world. But another part of you will wake up next year, having been around the world and then come back again. Don't try to work it out – it gets way too crazy if you try to rationalise it. For now, just sleep "little me of yesteryear". Sleep in the knowledge that we will be okay. Things will work themselves out.'

***

The alarm jolted her awake with a loud rude tone. 28th September 2015- that was the date on her iPhone. How long had she been asleep? Had she been asleep? A house of demons – what the hell, had she really been in a house of demons? Hades, God of the Underworld. Had she been there? Had she been to some weird underworld?

Clarah jumped out of bed. Where was Roserie? What was Roserie? She had gone. She was alone in the house, yet again. Quite quite trapped. The words made her think of Aura. Who the hell was Aura? Why did Aura lie to her?

House of demons – what did that mean? Yet it was true – the taxi driver had taken her to Hades Hall the night Nina had been attacked. Nina was dead. Kane was dead. Her mother was dead. She could time travel. She saw her future self, visit her former self. Denny was a shit – she wished she had known all of that 2 years ago.

Did she see a demon in the graveyard? It stuck its nails in her brother's skull for Christs sake. How did Roserie get her back in the house so fast? They didn't even walk. How did that happen? Where was Aunt Mary? Where was Baba May? What was happening to her? Could she really time travel?

The room started to spin. It whirled and whirled like a spiral, until Clarah collapsed on the floor. The reality of the madness was too overwhelming. She lay unconscious. She lay quite quite still…hardly breathing.

CHAPTER 14

28th September 2015
VIEW OF THE STARS – NEW YORK

Tony Mort aka Reed Baratolli, was back in his comfort zone. Back in the world of needy vagrants and the successful corporate entity that housed and fed them. Back in the midst of a most unusual business, an enterprise which converted tramps and beggars into a desirable workforce. Tony was happy to be back home in the city of his birth, a city which appreciated the work he had done with the homeless of New York.

Sat in the humble cabin that represented VOT's HQ, he tried to concentrate on the numbers presented on a financial spreadsheet. Yet no matter how hard he tried, his mind could not focus on the necessary mathematics. Reed was sorely disappointed to have missed seeing Konnor before he flew back to LA. He had wanted to ask him about the mysterious young woman he had met on his travels. Whoever or whatever she was, she had attracted the attention of a devious demonic entity, and anyone that fell within Emmanuelle's radar was either dangerous or in danger.

Reed was also deeply concerned and still unnerved by his brush with a Ledanite follower. He held his head in his hands, as though the gravity of the situation was pressing down on his skull. He mumbled to himself, 'why did I walk back into that world?'

He stood up and looked outside the cabin window. The camp was a hive of activity – the helpless having become the helpers. Tramps and vagabonds manned the soup kitchens, changed the bedding, re-erected tents blown apart by last night's storm and swept up the general litter of lives and leaves entangled with rubbish and heartbreak.

He was proud of his VOT's homeless charity, and if ever life became unbearable, then just watching the salvation of so many hopeless souls seemed to inject him with a dose of hope.

He turned on the radio. Aside from being a savour of the homeless masses, the only other thing that cheered him up was music.

'Once a musician, always a musician,' he thought. The lyrics of Tom Petty's song *"wont, back down"*, resonated in his ears. The part about being stood up at the gates of hell, sent a shiver down his spine as Emmanuelle came back to mind. Indeed, he had been stood at those very gates.

His morbid reflections were interrupted by a knock on his rickety office door, and without waiting for an answer, Dr Frank O'Byrne strode in with all the confidence of a man who feared nothing life could throw at him. Dearest Frank, was a portly man with vivid carrot-red hair and matching beard. He was a Dubliner in every sense of the word, as well as an ex-priest and ex teacher of theology. Moving away from his various ex-professions, Frank was now an associate in the VOT's franchise and ran several of the homeless camps located in Glasgow, Manchester and his native Ireland.

With a broad smile and massive bear hug he almost suffocated Reed – a man he only knew as Tony Mort.

'Tony, bloody good to see you my friend.'

Reed's heart rose and sunk at the same time. He was always happy to see Frank, but at the same time he knew he had promised him the accounts for his localities, and as yet they sat on his computer minus any totals. No matter the numbers, maths only make sense once added up.

Reed looked distracted and distant. He patted Franks back and in jest, and mimicked his Irish accent.

'Top of the morning to you Frank. You are looking in rude health my good man. Welcome back to New York. Please take a seat.'

Reed looked over at his PC screen and sighed. Frank was a perceptive type of bloke. Years of listening to various confessions, followed by years of listening to various excuses from various students about why various items of homework were missing or late, had given him the skill of detecting circumvention. He noticed that his boss was looking pale and tired. Something was weighing heavy on his mind – he was sure of it.

Reed handed Frank a mug of hot coffee and bounced back into commercial mode. Years of negotiating contracts with wannabe musicians, had honed his negotiating skills to perfection. Although more comfortable with a guitar in his hand, he was equally as accomplished with a calculator.

'Look mate,' he began,' I know you came here to talk about the London project, but land is expensive there Frank and although the need is great, the numbers don't stack up. Yes, we are a charity, but we still need to pay for stuff.'

Frank said nothing as he tried to control the self- satisfied smirk that badly wanted to invade his face. He pulled an envelope from his inside pocket and handed it to Reed.

'God works in mysterious ways my friend. We have just received a handsome donation Tony, and when I say handsome …in your native language I mean mega-bucks. This was posted to our Manchester offices.'

As Mr Anthony Reed Baratolli Mort opened the envelope and scanned the contents of the letter, he wasn't sure which part of it shocked him the most – the amount or the benefactor's name. He gasped as he read the contents.

'Dear Mr Mort; this letter is to inform you that upon his death, Mr Paul Bucklow bequeathed a share of his residuary estate to the 'View Of The Stars' homeless rescue charity. The amount donated to the charity is £7,000,000. Please contacts the solicitor's office detailed below to make the required arrangements.'

Reed turned a whiter shade of pale and collapsed into his office chair. For one who was the recipient of a large sum of money, his face was intensely serious as opposed to joyous. Frank erased the wide smile that had just swathed his face and switched on his priestly empathetic persona.

'I am sorry Tony. Did you know the chap?'

'Paul Bucklow…my God, Paul Bucklow - yes I certainly did. It was a long time ago. He used to be my wife's father-in-law. Eenayah was married before she met me. Her first husband died young. Paul was his father. I guess he must have saved up a bob or two over the years. From what I recall he was a professional footballer. He was quite good…very good. One of the best. I think he played for Manchester United…or maybe it was City. I am not sure which. Hey I am an American, so no big expert on the world of British soccer. I really don't understand why Paul has done this. I mean, sure I am grateful Frank – of course I am, but I only met the guy once or twice. Paul only had 2 sons and both died, quite young, so I guess there was nobody else in his life.'

Clarah

Reed looked genuinely baffled.

Frank suddenly realised how little he knew about his elusive business partner. He had no idea that his boss had been married before, but then again, he had never asked. Tony Mort's past seemed to be a deeply protected secret. Of course, there was the occasional gossipy tittle-tattle. Some said that he had once been a multi- millionaire musician. Others said he was a reformed sinner and one who had sold his soul to the devil. Frank hadn't really paid much attention. The more private a person is, the more people tend to wonder about them, and after all, Frank had skeletons a plenty in his own cupboard. He understood how the past should sometimes remain in the past, so he had always respected Tony's need for discretion.

He stood up and got the Bourbon from Reed's cabinet. He poured two glasses and handed one to Reed.

'I think we should drink a toast to Paul Bucklow, irrespective of whatever Manchester team he played for. God bless his soul. This money can help us buy the brownfield site we have been looking at in London. Here's to a new VOT's in England. Tis a cause for celebration Tony ol pal.'

Reed chinked glasses, confused yet relieved and grateful. Because of Eenayah's former father-in-law, a problem had been solved.

At that same moment Darcy entered the room. She was shocked to see Frank and Tony hitting the bottle so early on in the day. Noting her look of surprise, Frank handed her the letter.

'It's a donation from the Will of Tony's ex-wife ex father-in-law,' exclaimed Frank. 'I know that sounds complicated, by just look at the numbers after the pound sign.'

Darcy looked at the name on the letter. She knew the name – Paul Bucklow. He was Ledanite, as indeed she had once been. The connection came as a shock. She had only ever known Reed as Tony Mort, but now knowing the name of his wife's father-in-law, she had also uncovered Tony's true identity. Tony was Reed Baratolli. She said nothing. Her mind was bombarded by a million questions. She could not believe that some random wind of coincidence had wafted her away from the Ledonite hot spot of Darwydden and into the evil clutches of the foe.

Darcy handed the letter back to Frank, and in her sing-song Welsh voice stated, 'that's good; I mean sad for the guy who died and all that, but good news for VOT's I guess. Congratulations to both of you. Shame a man had to die for this, but well done nonetheless.'

She seemed dismissive. Her reaction was as cold as her frozen response. From somewhere deep inside her memory bank, she recalled the night she spent with Eenayah at Darwydden. They were both drunk and in her tipsy state, Eenayah had made a shocking confession. She had told Darcy that Paul Bucklow had seduced her. Of course, Darcy knew that there was nothing vaguely accidental about this incident. The whole seedy encounter had all been pre-planned. Paul was a Ledonite and Eenayah was one of a few remaining Tamar clones. As such, she had to become pregnant whilst still fertile. It was a task that her husband Reed could not assist with. Reeds vas deferens had been cut and he had been rendered infertile. That night at the manor house was special. It was the last time that Darcy ever conversed with Eenayah. After that, her friend lay in an unconscious heap hidden deep within a Welsh mountainside – held prisoner until her twin boys had been born.

The whole episode had been distasteful…shocking. Darcy left Darwydden soon after Eenayah's twins were born. She retired her membership of the Ledonite cult and flew to New York to start a new life.

Unbeknown to her at the time, Darcy had travelled the Atlantic to work alongside the man who had been married to Eenayah. The man who had betrayed his wife many times and in many ways. A man whose name was associated with so much shame and dishonour, that he had to change it. Tony Mort was that man. Tony Mort was Reed Baratolli. Darcy knew that now. It was a revelation she found hard to accept.

Darcy said no more. She threw the letter on the table, left the office and gave the door a good old slam on her way out.

'What just happened' asked Reed?

'How the shite should I know' responded Frank.

'Can you go after her,' asked Reed?

'As long as you don't expect these wobbly legs of mine to run,' replied Frank.

Frank did as was instructed and went in pursuit of Darcy. Reed paced up and down the room, frequently looking outside the window. He could see what he presumed to be an intense conversation. Arms were flaying all over the place, with the occasional finger being pointed in his direction. Darcy's reaction to the letter had been unexpected. Why was that? Reed was mystified.

As the conversation outside continued in earnest, Reeds mind turned cartwheels. Could it be that Darcy knew Paul Bucklow? He was Welsh, she is Welsh. Maybe all Welsh people know each other. Was Wales a small place? Reed was American and he didn't have the vaguest idea about such geography. He peered outside the window. Whatever Frank and Darcy were conversing about seemed to be serious.

Almost 10 minutes had gone by. Reed scoured his memory banks. Past events were never welcome or happy visitors. They galloped all over his conscience like a herd of wild horses, carelessly leaving divots in a heavy heart. He felt ashamed of his former self. Mortified by the way he had negotiated fame and fortune in exchange for preventing his 2nd wife becoming pregnant. Guilt ridden for the way he had capitalised on Eenayah's depression, by keeping her medicated into a zombie like state. Ashamed by his engagement to Amanda Primetta whilst still married to Eenayah.

My God, the realisation that Amanda had been 23 years his junior had just registered in his brain.

'No fool like an old fool,' he muttered to himself.

Then there was poor Eenayah, cursed by some ancient legacy of which she knew nothing about. The "prophesy of Tamar" had been a blight which had secretively haunted her life. A sacred spell cast by some woman who live thousands of years ago. A woman who had cloned herself through generations of twin girls. The line of clones had to be contained. The likes of Eenayah had to be stopped from breeding. The mutant dna sown far into the future, had to be restricted, even expired. So, his wife remained childless because Emmanuelle and her pack of demons, commanded it to be.

Reed shuddered at the mere sound of the demon's name inside his head. He had sold his services to Emmanuelle. In return for wealth and success, he had kept his wife as a childless depressed medicated prisoner in a gilded cage. It backfired. It all backfired badly, tragically and cataclysmically. So now here he was, hiding beneath the name of Tony Mort and hiding inside a pathetic little wooden cabin.

15 minutes had now passed and they were still outside. Franks head was tilted to one side, as though he was listening intensely to whatever Darcy was saying. Reed continued to pace up and down the room, as his past life continued to flood his thoughts. His first wife Julia came to mind, and the way she died with her lover Bert by her side. He had needed to get Julia out of the way so he could marry Eenayah. He had caused his children to be without a mother, but he had needed to do what he needed to do. He thumped his own head as the words 'why, why, why,' spewed forth from his mouth.

At that moment, the cabin door was flung open. Frank walked in. He looked upon Reed with a glare of condemnation.

'Darcy knows who you are,' pronounced Frank. 'Why did you not tell me? Why did you lie, Mr Reed Baratolli?'

'Would you want to be called Reed Baratolli,' replied Reed?

'Where do you keep that American whisky Tony? I think we need a drink and a serious chat. Do you mind if I continue to call you Tony as I don't think I can say the name Reed? I am bloody gob smacked pal. I didn't see this one coming.'

'Bourbon – it's called Bourbon Frank. Take a seat. Tell me about Darcy. She came to work at VOT's about 8 or so months ago. She seemed to be a hard worker - bright, friendly, approachable, smart...but now I am wondering who the hell I have hired. Who is she? How does she know me?'

Frank took a gulp from the glass placed before him. He shook his head as though still disturbed by the news that his associate was not who he thought him to be.

'Her full name is Darcy Kyfin…it's an unusual name,' replied Frank. 'Did you not realise that she had the same surname as your wife's twin sister… you know, the one called Ruby Kyfin, married to Owyn Kyfin?'

The realisation hit Reed like a hammer between his eyes. Of course, why had he never made the connection before? Prior to her employment with VOTS, he had never met Darcy in person, but he knew of her. Eenayah had told him about the crazy night she spent with Darcy at Ruby's gothic manor house, the infamous Darwydden Castle Manor. She had shrieked with laughter down the phone, as she had told Reed about getting drunk with Darcy and exploring the dungeons and caverns beneath the house. It was one of the last conversations he had with his wife, that was…before she went missing. She had been so happy on that day. Yet again, the heavy toll of guilt had placed itself upon his shoulders.

Frank noticed the look upon his friend's face.

He continued, 'Darcy knew Paul Bucklow. They were practically neighbours, give or take 20 miles. As soon as she saw the name and you explained your connection to him, she figured it all out in an instant. Why did you change your name Tony?'

'I didn't. I was born Anthony Reed Baratolli Mort. I have always been known as Tony Mort. I grew up as Tony Mort. But then, when I became a musician I just thought my middle names had a sexier ring to them. But then Reed Baratolli became a bad boy, in more ways than one. My wife went missing and it became public knowledge that I had been unfaithful to her.

Then if you recall, I was suspected of the contract killing of Katia Beselovaya. I was the last person she spoke to on the phone, a phone call that had been bloody recorded. Can you believe that? Whoever records a phone call? It all got very nasty and yippee... the police could listen to every single nasty word exchanged between us.

Then would you believe it, the bloody killer made his way over to Miami after he had done the deed. Guess what? Yes, that's where I lived. Fuckin Miami. Of course, the police thought I had arranged the whole thing. Why wouldn't they? It was all too much of a coincidence.'

Reed topped up his glass and knocked the contents down in one.

'Why do I feel that you are a priest and I am in a confessional?'

'Because I used to be a priest ...once upon a time. Obviously, I still have the knack. Tell me, why was the conversation with Katya so nasty, I mean...so much so that the police thought you may have killed her?'

'Because she more or less accused me of attempted rape, that's why.'

'And...was she correct?'

'Oh yes...she was spot on. The old Reed Baratolli was quite a nasty guy and the public got to read all about it. They learned how I tried to hide my money away from my wife in an offshore account. They learned how my accountant "Alexia Towers" went to prison for stealing it. Thank God, I wasn't the only one on her list of stupid rich fools, but none the less I was on a list people could read about in the tabloids.

Oh, and I haven't even mentioned getting engaged to some political gangster's daughter whilst still married to Eenayah.

Now my dearest Frank...now do you understand why I wanted to shed the name Reed like a snake sheds its skin. The gossip around here is correct. I did sell my soul to the devil and now I am here, doing all of this good stuff by way of repentance. Maybe I am trying to buy myself back. I don't know if that is possible, but I am trying – under the name of Tony Mort...and that my friend, is actually my real name.'

Frank wasn't sure how to react. He didn't know if now was the appropriate time for him to disclose his association to Eenayah. Perhaps honesty was the only way to recover a damaged relationship. Or maybe honesty would be the straw to break the camel's back. He had to give it a shot…either which way.

'Tony – I also knew your wife. I didn't know her in person. I had never met her. However, my dear friend Professor Roland De Vede wrote a book for her. I believe the book was a gift for you.'

Reed was shocked at hearing this for the first time. As with Frank, he had no inclination that they were somehow connected.

'My God, yes. I know that name. It was written in the credits. It was a book about my family. Professor De Vede did all of the research. How strange to be talking about the book again. Only the other day I handed it over to my son Konnor as a keep-sake. How strange.'

'Life can be very strange sometimes. I know it was Roland's daughter Mercy, that Eenayah turned to for protection. I know that Mercy was heartbroken when Eenayah fell from a cliff and hurt herself…seriously hurt herself. Mercy felt that she was to blame. Her detective agency MeDeVe had been hired to protect her whilst she was in the UK, so Mercy took it personally…like she hadn't done her job thoroughly.'

Reed topped his glass up and slurped it down in one.

'Oh, please don't tell me you also knew Mercy De Vede. Do you know that I was even accused of her murder? She was Katya's best friend. She was the one who got her to tape the phone call with me. It all adds up, doesn't it? I mean – once the police pin that guilty thing on you, suddenly you have committed every crime known to mankind.'

'Maybe attempted murder rather than murder, Tony. There are those of us who suspect her death was a set-up so she could get her backside out of the UK and harm's way. Don't forget that Mercy was ex CID, and high up the police rankings at that. She was one of them. She could pull strings. I hope that is the case anyway. I liked her and I don't like to think of her as dead.'

'Well whatever Frank, it was a shit period of my life. How can I describe it? My life toppled like a stack of domino's. You know the game - you line them all up, you give one of them a push and then the rest all start to fall over. I almost killed myself at the time. I came close. I had the gun and my finger was on the trigger.'

'What stopped you? Why didn't you pull the trigger Tony?'

'If I was to tell you that an angel stopped me, would you believe me? I mean, would you believe someone like Reed Baratolli?'

'Try me. I am an ex priest. Believing in angel's sort of comes with the job description.' On this occasion, it was Frank reaching for the near empty bottle. He urged Reed to continue.

'She was my housekeeper, or at least that's what I thought she was. She just turned up at my door when I married Eenayah. I actually assumed that Eenayah had hired her and she thought it was me. It was years before we realised that she had just invited herself in and neither one of us had done the whole hiring thing. Anyway, her husband had died back home in Iceland. I think she herself was Spanish or Mexican – heck I have no idea what she was. I only knew she wasn't Icelandic. She had these 2 cute kids in tow, and I think we both felt sorry for her. Eve was about the same age as Armarni and her son Saul was roughly the same age as Asher. They all grew up together like one big family. She took very good care of Eenayah and she loved all of my children like they were her children. I knew she was a good woman, but I had no idea she was something else – I mean…something like an angel.'

'I assume you are talking about Roserie?'

'My Lord…dear Frank. Please don't tell me that you know her as well. Do you know everybody I know?'

'It would appear so Tony. It's most peculiar. All this time we have worked together superficially…as mere colleagues, and yet there were much deeper ties binding us together. We were connected but never realised it.'

For a moment both men sat in silence, dumbfounded by the their newly disclosed commonality of associates and experiences.

Frank finally broke the silence.

'Perhaps I should confess a few of my own secrets now, Tony. You see, when I was a priest I fell in love. I wanted to get married to this woman…who just to complicate matters happened to be a nun. Of course, a priest cannot be married, and neither can a nun. I argued with my conscience. Night after night I prayed and asked for guidance. This soft female voice with a hint of a Spanish accent would answer me. It was Roserie. At the time, it was just a voice, but then I met her for real. It was here at the VOT's site – New Year's Eve 2014. She told me what happened to Eenayah. It gave me some closure. I appreciated her visit. She encouraged me to join VOT's and to help you set up the franchise. That's why I am here. That's why I am helping you with all of this. It is because of Roserie.'

For the first time that morning, Reed smiled.

'Bless her. I had no idea. Well I for one am glad you are here Frank. Tell me, did you get married? You describe yourself as an ex-priest, so I take it that you left the priesthood?'

'Yes, I did and I did. I had many a happy a year with my wife. She passed away a few years ago. We were not blessed with children and so now your charity has become my child. In many respects, it has saved me and so has Roserie, many many times over. I understand salvation, and I understand absolution. You cannot ask for forgiveness unless you forgive yourself. I will never refer to you as Reed, but you should give Reed a break. He was a bad boy, but he has done more than enough to say sorry. Show the guy some compassion. The past is the past. You cannot undo it, but you can learn from it and make the future a better place.'

Reeds face then became intensely sorrowful and serious.

'I am sorry that you had no children Frank, but VOT's is lucky to have you. Plus, I agree with the whole "forgive and move on" motto. I am trying my best.'

Reed then paused a little as though struggling with the next question.

'We need to track down Darcy and have a good chat with her. I want her to understand that I am not the person she thinks I am. Reed was in the past. Tony is the here and now. I also have just one last question Frank. What do you know about the Ledanite followers?'

Frank spat out the Bourbon that had been making its way down his welcoming throat. It was not a question he expected and one he was unsure how to answer.

'Shite, that took me by surprise. The Ledanites ah. Well, yes, I know of them. I believe they are well intentioned…hearts in the right places and so on. They just want to protect all the lines of Tamar and all her clones. I take it that you were aware that Eenayah was such a clone?'

'Yes of course I was aware Frank. Don't forget, I batted for the opposite team. It was my job to stop her getting pregnant, so she didn't go on to produce more lines of mini-clones. I failed in that job. Not sure how, but I cocked it up. I believe she had twin boys. Not sure of the significance of that. I am guessing it was fairly important, as I believe it was the Ledanites that kidnapped her from the ambulance and hid her away until she gave birth. No idea who the bloody father was. I am sterile so it sure in hell wasn't me.'

Frank couldn't help but cast his eyes towards the discarded letter on the table as Reed said the words. Reed followed his line of sight.

'Crap! No way! Bloody Paul Bucklow. Is that why you are looking at the letter. Is that why he left my charity millions in his will. Guilt money for impregnating my wife…is this what this fuckin cheque is about?

Frank put a comforting arm around his friend, but it made little difference.

'When was the penny ever going to drop Frank? What a fool I have been.'

'You are many things Tony, but you are not a fool.'

'I should have worked it out…perhaps paid a bit more attention to my Sunday school bible studies. Tamar…Genesis 38. She got it together with her father-in-law Judah, after marrying both his sons who then died. Shite, I knew that Greg and James were brothers and Eenayah was engaged to one and married the other. Paul was her bloody father-in-law. Why didn't I see it? I had already figured out that she was living the same life path as Tamar. I mean, that's why the Ledanite were so interested in her. She wasn't just one from another line of clones. She was another Tamar. She was the one who was meant to give birth to the sons. That's why Emmanuelle wanted her out of the way. My God, when Eenayah became pregnant, it must have been Emmanuelle and her team of demons that tried to kill her. One of them pushed her off the cliff. I get it now. I am so stupid. Why has it taken me so long to work all of this out?'

Reed started to weep, something he rarely did.

Frank filled the kettle with water and switched it on.

'I need to brew some tea. I think it's about time we both sobered up Tony, because we need to have a serious conversation with Darcy. You are right. All that you said is correct. When I was outside earlier, Darcy told me the whole story.'

'My God; I employed a bloody Ledanite.'

'So yes, okay she was a Ledanite, but she didn't agree with what happened to Eenayah. She saw the twins being born. She was there...in the cave. She knows where Eenayah's body is buried. She came here, to New York to get away from the Ledanites. She was born to be one of them, but she isn't one of them anymore. Right now, she hates you, because she hates the Reed that the world grew to hate. However, I believe she still holds Tony Mort in the highest regard. She can fill in many of the missing gaps. I am sure she will help.'

Reed snuffled back his tears, obviously still in a state of shock.

'Dear Frank, my wife Eenayah has gone. I have always known that she wasn't just missing...that she was dead. I cannot repair the past, but I can protect the future. I am worried for my children and they are my only concern now...nothing else, just them.'

'You are a dark horse. I didn't know you had children Tony.'

'They are from my first marriage to Julia. A Las Vegas showgirl would you believe. She died.'

'I am sorry.'

'It's okay. It was a long time ago. Just Google it. You can read all about it. Reed Baratolli has few secrets.'

'So, what worries you about your children?'

'Where do I start? Well, my oldest son Asher has inherited the traits of his father Reed, and we all know what a shit-head Reed could be. I am sorry to say that he is turning out to be just like me, and no matter what I say to him, he refuses to change. God help the women of the world.'

'Do you have a daughter?'

'Oh yes, materialistic Miss Armarni. Her pretty brainless head is quite empty, aside from a few granules of Cocaine that is. She has just gotton herself engaged to Ze'ev Lezemel. The boy seems alright, but his family are as creepy as hell.'

'Yes, I have heard about the Lezemels. Personally, I think it's all wind and no sails. I wouldn't get too wound up about it Tony. Kids have to make their own way through life, and I am sure Armarni will walk a path strewn with diamonds.'

'It's not so much the older ones Frank. It's the youngest lad who gives me sleepless nights?'

'What's his name?'

'Konnor. He is a lovely looking boy…the image of his mother Julia. Blonde, beautiful and brave. He has such a lovely caring spirit. You should meet him. He is coming over to New York soon.'

'I would love to meet him. He sounds great…so what's the big worry?'

'Konnor met a girl whilst he was backpacking around Asia. Her name is Clarah. It was just a summer romance thing, but maybe it was something more. He keeps talking about her.'

'So, what's the problem with that?'

'Frank, have you ever heard about a creature called Emmanuelle?'

'Dressed in red, long platinum hair, mother of some wannabe French singer that Reed Baratolli took under his wings. I was at the dentist waiting for a check-up once and perusing the magazines on a table, I saw some photos of you and her and her daughter with a name I can't remember. Mother and daughter both quite stunning.'

'Océane – that was the daughter's name.'

'Yes, it's coming back to me now. She was all hyped up for fame and fortune and then she just disappeared – vanished into thin air. I think Reed Baratolli came under suspicion for her disappearance as well.'

'Reed Baratolli was blamed for everything my friend. However, you should know that Emmanuelle is no mortal and neither is her daughter Océane. Emmanuelle is a powerful high-ranking demoness and her daughter a demon slave.'

Frank almost choked on his cup of tea.

'Oh...oh dear. You have kept some interesting company over the years Tony.'

'Emmanuelle has an interest in my son's girlfriend. It is an interest that worries me. She wants Konnor to steer clear of her. This Clarah person has caught the demon's attention.'

'How do you know all of this?'

'Armarni's engagement party. Emmanuelle was there. I also rubbed shoulders with a Ledanite the following day. A chap called Nico –

famous chef. You have probably heard of him. He has his own TV show. He told me that the daughters of an old French doctor friend of mine, are also Ledanite and that they have been following Clarah on her travels. They have followed her in order to protect her. That can only mean one thing Frank.'

Frank asked, 'are you saying that the girl your sons have met, is a clone of Tamar.'

'It cannot mean anything but. Who else do the Ledanite stalk? However, the prophesy also says that for a clone to walk in Tamar's step, the brothers she sleeps with have to die. I don't want my boy's dead just to tick a box on some ancient scroll.'

'Hang on Tony. This girl has only been with your son Konnor. What has your other son Asher got to do with any of this?'

'He was with them both in Bali. Konnor flew home to go back to university. Asher stayed behind with Clarah. As I told you before – Ash is a chip off the old block. I know what I would have done, if say…left alone with a beautiful girl on a paradise island. I know what Reed would have done…let's put it that way.'

'Hell's bloody bell's. If she has also followed the path of Tamar and been (in the biblical sense) with both brothers, that could be worrying for you Tony. It makes you the father-in-law dear friend. Dear oh dear.'

'But I am infertile Frank. I had a vasectomy after Julia died. If they are targeting me as someone who could father a second set of male twins by way of heir and a spare, then they need to know that they have picked the wrong bloke. Shit- what if they don't know that I am firing blanks. What if I am part of some plan? How do I tell them? Why aren't they happy with Eenayahs twins anyway? Surely, they have what they want now? The prophesy has been fulfilled. Surely all this is over now?'

'I cannot answer you Tony. Maybe the boys aren't showing any supernatural abilities? Maybe at some point in the future they get taken away from the Ledanites and they lose control over them? I do agree with one thing though…this girl, Clarah…she sounds like trouble. We should talk to Darcy. Let me approach her first and tell her how things have changed with you. I can say how repentant you are, that you are not the Reed she remembers. She will help, I am sure she will. She understands the Ledonites. You make the tea and I will find her.'

Frank left the cabin and walked around the camp. He looked everywhere. He called out her name. No answer. Finally, he saw a note propped up against his briefcase. It had been written in a hurry.

'Sorry Frank. I love it here but I cannot work in the same place as Reed Baratolli. His wife Eenayah was my friend and her twin Ruby is my sister-in-law. Too close, too personal, too painful. I will never forgive him. It is best that he finds himself another assistant. Good luck with everything. Darcy xx'

Frank had a feeling that this may happen. He had seen the look of fear in her eyes. He wished he could have spoken with her first. Too late, she had gone. It was always too late.

CHAPTER 15

Monday 28th September 2015 – morning
A HOSPITAL IN MANCHESTER

Baba May hated hospitals. She always felt awkward is such places. In particular, the intensive care unit brought about its own set of challenges. The daunting technology behind the machines overwhelmed her. Tubes, bleeps, alarms, syringe drivers, bags for draining stuff out and bags for putting stuff in – it was all too much for a humble caravan woman.

She felt that her family must surely be cursed, certain that it was the Gypsy amria of begrudgery. Yet again, Baba May was sitting in a stark white room, watching another of her grandchildren fight for life. First poor Nina, then Kane and now…now her darling Clarah. Clarah who stood out from the crowd. The one who knew her own mind. The free spirit. The one who was bullied and browbeaten, yet still picked herself up and hit back. The kindly sister who protected her vulnerable twin. The caring niece who helped her aunt Mary wash her hair when Mary's arthritic fingers could no longer squeeze the bottle of shampoo. Now…this. How had it come to this?

She stroked Clarah's braided hair. Her grandmother wasn't keen on her new style, but with her tanned skin it suited her.

'Bless you,' she whispered. 'You look just like that Bo Derek woman.'

In truth, she had never seen Clarah look so healthy. Yet, Baba May knew that the bronzed glow was but a superficial illusion. Under her skin, Clarah was a desperately sick young lady.

The old lady was lost in her thoughts, when a young nurse tapped her on the shoulder.

'Ma'am – Dr Forshaw is able to see you now. Please follow me - I will take you to his office.'

Baba May turned to her daughter saying, 'Mary, stay here with Clarah please. I doubt we will be long.'

Tomas Forshaw was a handsome young Consultant. Part Polish and part Welsh, he had an unusual sing-song voice, and kind toffee coloured eyes. He was most respectful of the elderly lady – pulling out a chair so she could sit down and attentively asking if she needed a glass of water. However, as a busy doctor he didn't have time to beat about the bush with social niceties.

'Mrs Loveridge - can I address you as May?' Baba May nodded in agreement.

'I understand that you are Clarah's next of kin?'

Again, Baba May nodded.

'Yes, I suppose I must be doctor. She does have an older sister Katalyn, but the lass has young babes and is too busy to come. Her father Mick… well, let's just say he is away somewhere, so I guess that leaves me. I am her gran. Her mother Violet is…I mean she was my daughter. Violet passed away Dr Forshaw.'

Dr Forshaw had only been working at the hospital for a few days, but some of the nurses had already filled him in with the background. It sounded as though the family had been beset with a catalogue of tragedies piled upon tragedy. His heart sympathised with the old woman.

'I have only just started working at this hospital May, but your granddaughter seems strangely familiar. I am sure I know her face. Has she ever lived in North Wales by any chance?'

Baba May answered the doctor with a very strained, 'no,'

'She has never left the vitsa Dr Forshaw. Our girls stay with their families until they are married off. We keep them under wraps – it is the Roma way.'

The doctor scratched his head. He seemed confused.

'Hmm, strange. She looks very similar to an ex patient of mine. Just a coincidence I suppose. Anyway, I digress. Do you know what happened to your granddaughter?'

'All I know for sure doctor is that last Thursday, which I think was about 4 days ago, she was on her way back from her travels and she collapsed on the plane. It was just as it was coming into land at Manchester airport. Clarah has always been a fit healthy girl. She had been away for about 14 months, doing that back-packing thing that some young uns do. This has come as a big shock.'

Tomas Forshaw flicked through her notes, chewing on the end of his pen whilst deep in thought. After a minute or so he continued, 'your granddaughter had a DVT on her flight home. That is a blood clot in the leg. It can sometimes happen on long haul flights, because people are sitting still for many hours. Anyway, it seems that the clot broke free and ended up in her lungs. We call this a pulmonary embolism. I believe that Clarah had a cardiac arrest just after the plane had landed. She was fortunate in that there were doctors on the flight who were able to resuscitate her. However, as you are no doubt aware, the end result of all this is that your granddaughter is now in a coma.'

Baba May played with her fingers, twirling her loose wedding ring around. It was a habit; something she often did when in deep thought. Of course, she had already known that her granddaughters heart had stopped as the plane wheels had hit the tarmac. She already knew Clarah was in a coma. She hadn't known the medical details of what had caused it and she guessed it was interesting to learn, but none the less it didn't change anything. Clarah was in a desperate situation. Her eyes were as dry as cold stone, but her heart cried.

'Have you any questions May?'

'How long can she be in a coma for, doctor?'

'Usually 2 or 3 weeks, however as yet we cannot determine the level of damage that has occurred. It is impossible to say how long she went without oxygen. I wish I could be more specific, but it is still early days. If she remains like this after 4 weeks, we would say she is in a persistent vegetative state. Time will tell. The next few weeks are crucial.'

'How much time Dr Forshaw? If she went into that vegetation thingy, how long could she remain like that?'

'It could be as long as 15 years, May. Some people have survived an amazing number of years in this limbo of half-life. However, there are other complications that could occur in the meantime. The main thing right now May, is to stay hopeful. I was told that she seemed to flinch when one of the doctors put a central line in her neck, so that in itself is a positive sign. Keep talking to her – it helps. Aside from that, I am sorry but it is a waiting game. Maybe other family members could help out. I am concerned that you are taking all of the strain on your own shoulders. You don't want to make yourself ill, do you now?'

'There aren't many family members left, but thank you for your concern doctor. I will be fine.'

'I believe that you live in Whitby. That is a long way for you to travel. If things don't improve soon, we will discuss transferring her to Scarborough. I am sure that will make these visits easier for you.'

'Yes, it would. I would appreciate that.'

With that, Baba May walked out of his office and back to her daughter Mary, who was lovingly holding Clarah's hand.

'Is everything okay, 'asked Mary?

'Yes,' replied Baba May. 'He was just telling me how the accident happened, and that we should keep talking to her.'

Mary looked rather sheepish, not knowing quite what to say next, or how.

'Ma, there is something I must tell you.'

'What?' Baba May looked alarmed.

'I am quite happy to stay here with Clarah, but I think you need to go back home. I can sense that something happened at the house last night. It is more than just a feeling Ma. The house was visited, I know that for sure.'

Her mother seemed annoyed.

'You should have told me sooner. The circle of salt should have done its job…unless she disobeyed me and went outside. Silly girl. I bet that's what she did. Clarah has never been one to obey instructions. I should go. I will see you later Mary.'

With that, she kissed Clarah's hand and her daughter's forehead.

Baba May grabbed her coat to leave. She knew her daughter Mary well enough to know she would instinctively feel such things. Poor Baba May felt torn in half. She was but an elderly lady, divided between home and hospital and not knowing where she was needed the most. The last 14 months had taken their toll.

***

Dr Forshaw had been just leaving his office, when he witnessed Baba May's departure. His secretary Susan Jones was stood at his side, trying to balance a pile of notes in her arms.

He turned to face her asking 'Susan, did you just see that old lady leave?'

Susan peered over the heavy mound of paperwork.

'I didn't get the clearest of views Tomas, but yes, I saw her go. That is Clarah's grandmother. She has been here every day, bless her. Everybody feels so sorry for her. She lives in Yorkshire. It is such a long journey for the poor dear.'

'But, she kissed someone,' he stated.

'Yes, I saw her take Clarah's hand and kiss it. So very touching.'

'No... I mean yes, she did that.... but she kissed something else. Thin air. She kissed thin air. It was a though she saw someone or something, something we can't see. Am I going completely crazy, or is there an invisible person sat next to Clarah?'

'I can't see anyone,' replied Susan. 'But then again, if they were invisible I wouldn't...would I? Don't beat yourself up about it Tomas. You were on call last night and you must be shattered. Maybe you should catch some rest whilst the unit is quiet.'

Tomas nodded in agreement. He walked away, yet checking over his shoulder as he left. He could have sworn he saw May Loveridge kiss the air. Odd - most odd!

***

A gaggle of demons were sat in the corner. They were hidden from sight. The nurses worked around them, totally unaware of their presence. Of course, Mary could see them, and as soon as she did they quickly vanished into another corner.

Emmanuelle looked over at Baba May's comatose granddaughter and giggled to herself. She was pleased with her work.

'Well, at least Clarah's fertility shouldn't be a concern for the foreseeable future,' she declared.

Océane responded, 'I don't understand Mother. The twin boys have already been born. They must be nearly 18 months old by now. The prophesy has been completed. So surely, doesn't that mean that any remaining clones are less of a threat? Eenayah had the twins as prophesied. They won, we lost. Isn't that game over?'

Emmanuelle threw Océane a look which would have frozen a volcano.

She snapped back, 'firstly, and just to correct you with some biological technicalities Océane, you are not my daughter and I am not your mother. I borrowed a corpse before it began to rot. I needed to acquire a musically gifted daughter and so this whole parental façade was a mere convenience. I did not do that ghastly giving birth crap, so please do not address me as your mother. Secondly, Saskia is my only biological child and even now I cannot believe that I put myself through that agonising scenario. Thirdly, never assume that our job has been done. Until all the Tamar clones have been driven into extinction, they remain to be a threat. There are only a handful left, so we are close to at least winning that battle. Extermination of the mutant DNA is our only option.'

Clarah

Océane had a skin as resilient as rhinoceros hide. She was accustomed to Emmanuelle's caustic comments and cruel taunts. However, sometimes she simply couldn't resist the opportune gibe.

'I understand what you are saying mother…erm I mean Emmanuelle, but if that is the case, how did Violet and Baba May escape the curse of sterility? It would appear that these Gypsy Tamar clones slipped through your net. They both reproduced, and you didn't manage to stop them.'

Emmanuelle was less than amused, but recognised that she was being goaded by the younger demon. She respected Océane's derisive attitude, after all, she wasn't exactly mentoring a nun.

Emmanuelle replied, 'the Gypsies are a tightly knit community. Their suspicion of outsiders and intense cultural closeness, made them difficult to infiltrate. Even the Ledonites couldn't penetrate their pack. However, Clarah committed the cardinal sin of shunning her kith and kin. As soon as she left the safety of the campsite, she was ours for the taking. From the moment she stepped into Hades Hall, her fate was sealed. Our mission was to divide her from her family, and well done Océane – you succeeded. The baby fawn is vulnerable away from its mother and the safety of the herd. Cum patientia Océane.'

Océane was deep in thought for a few mome

Eventually she asked, 'but hang on a moment, if Clarah's family had not won the lottery money, and if Denny had not had been unfaithful and if Kane had not been a drug addict, then surely Clarah would never have deserted her kith and kin. So, my question for you Emmanuelle is, did you create those situations, so that Clarah would break free from the vitsa?'

Emmanuelle smiled. It was with a proud look of self-gratification.

'Dear Océane, the prime ammunition for any demon consist of money, sex and drugs. However, we don't force humans to crave money, desire sex and abuse drugs. They do that all on their own. We just feed on the evil already in their hearts. Sometimes, human fragility makes our jobs so very easy. Clarah's leaving was a very happy accident. Don't blame it on the sunshine, don't blame it on the moonlight, don't blame it on the good times, blame it on the human desire for excess.'

Now, they both giggled…laughing uncontrollably and sadistically for a good 5 minutes.

The attention span of a demon is short, and so they soon became restless…bored with the mundane oppressive atmosphere of the intensive care unit. As it no longer amused them – the two demons simply vanished.

Mary watched as the sniggering demons left; vaporising into some other deeper darker realm.

CHAPTER 16

Monday 28th September 2015
A MAGICAL TRIP TO ROBIN HOODS BAY

The kitchen door wasn't just pushed open, it was blasted open with the mighty roar of, 'what the bloody hell are you doing in my kitchen, how did you get into my house and who or what in hell are you anyway?'

'I have just made hash browns and black puddings for breakfast Clarah. Your timing is great. Do be seated. Coffee or tea?'

With that command, Aura dropped a steaming hot breakfast plate on the table and smiled demurely. She had quickly worked out that food served as a great calming technique in the Lee household.

Clarah was in no mood for social niceties.

'I am fed up of this game Aura. You lied to me. I went to your house last night, and what I found was little more than a derelict ruin which hadn't been lived in for years…maybe even centuries. Why are you doing this to me? There was no sickly mother in a wheelchair, no older brothers watching football on TV, no shepherd father out tending to his flock. No nothing, just lots of dust and lie after lie. You need to start being honest with me. The truth, or get out of my house on your blimin broomstick or whatever it is you use for transportation.'

'Ooo fighting talk. I like that about you Clarah. You have attitude. Okay, so I will come clean, but this could be a long conversation and some of it could get quite complicated. You haven't been back home long. What is it now? Monday…not long at all. Still fresh off a plane. I wanted to give you time to recover. It seems to me that you are almost ready for the truth…but not quite yet. I am going to ask you to do a lot of deep thinking, and the concern I have right now, is that your blood sugar levels are low. Trust me – my eyes can see into your veins and detect your biochemistry. The human brain needs to be fed in order to think. Glucose metabolism sustains basic physiology and all that. So therefore, I am going to leave you to calm down for 10 minutes and when I come back I expect to see an empty plate. Then we will talk. Oh, and you were going to ask me for coffee, so here it is, with a heaped spoon of sugar just the way you like it. Let's escalate those glucose levels.'

As Aura turned to walk out, and with Clarah always being the type who liked to have the last word, she shouted after her.

'Fine, okay – so you are right. I am hungry. But just so you know, I haven't come back home. This was never my home. I have no home. I am a traveller. The clue is in the name. It is as it says on the tin. Just so you understand.'

***

10 minutes later and spot on time, Aura walked back into the kitchen. She began, 'I take it that your stomach is full, your mouth now closed and your mind is open. Can we start again?'

Clarah responded, 'sure, but you need to understand that I am suffering from partial amnesia, and not having recent memory recall is a bit of a bummer. That's aside from being zapped back in time last night. I landed head first in dreams that were so vivid, that I am sure they were real. Hey get this; at one point, me from the present was watching me from the past, having a conversation with me from the future. Talk about 3 being a bloody crowd!'

'Sounds fascinating,' added Aura.

'You think that sounds fascinating. Wait until I tell you what happened in the cemetery. I mean, most folk are gently eased into the fact that their mother, brother and sister have passed away, but nope...not me. I have to go nose diving into their tombstones, and I really do mean nosediving. All that, after finding that your farmhouse was actually an ancient ruin, complete with spiders and years of neglect. My life gets weirder by the second.'

Aura tilted her head sympathetically. She wasn't overly familiar with the human species, but she still recognised that Clarah had been severely traumatised by recent revelations.

She stroked Clarah's perplexed brow.

'You can tell me all about your nocturnal adventures later. Right now, hold onto my hand. You and I need to go somewhere with a few more negative ions. Just to add, negative means positive in the ionic molecular world. Hold on tight Clarah; we are heading for somewhere with a bit of a breeze.'

There was no slow pixilating, dematerialising and rematerializing. No flashes, no bangs, no dramatic exit or spectacular entrance. Quite simply, one minute they were in the kitchen and the next they were sat on top of a cliff. It was that quick, that easy and that unimpressive.

'How did you just do that,' asked Clarah?

'Truly, 'replied Aura, 'it is not as difficult as you think. When you travel in your dreams, you don't need to jump on public transport, do you? Your brain takes you on a journey that doesn't require fossil fuel...and by the way, you humans need to stop using that shit. Yes, the brain is more powerful than you give it credit for. Simply think of yourself as being somewhere, believe in it, and POW! It just happens.'

Clarah laughed at the batman style expression. Her new friend was…unusual.

'I am sure you have vastly underestimated your mental transportation ability Aura. I doubt it is always this easy.' Looking around she then added, 'but by eck lass, you pick your locations well. This place is awesome.'

Clarah gazed around at the panoramic vista and took a sharp deep breath of the crisp sea air. The copper toned autumnal leaves contrasted perfectly against the forever horizon, and the rolling hills with their tiny yellow flowers, framed a wild blue sea. She beamed in appreciation as she watched the seals on the rocks below. Inhaling the salty air, she asked 'where are we?'

'Robin Hoods Bay. We could probably have walked here if we had an hour or so to spare, but my method delivers us faster.'

'Stunning. Robin Hoods Bay. Yes, I like it here, but despite the visual seduction, I really need to hear the truth. The past few days have been the strangest in my life and I need to figure out what is happening to me. So, let's start with, what and who are you Aura? You have lied to me – consistently fibbed I may add. Plus, you can move me to places just by holding my hand. It isn't natural. By the way, this is not my first experience of this stuff. An angel did the same thing to me last night. Quite impressive. Quickest exit from a graveyard ever. So, is that what you are? Are you an angel?'

Aura sniggered, 'me…an angel? I am way too bad to be good, and for the record…far too good to be bad. No, I am not an angel Clarah. I am not sure why humans are so obsessed with titles. You seem to have an obsession with putting a label on everything. Your planet would be far more peaceful, if you didn't brand one another with a category, and then compete between yourselves. What a tribal bunch you are.'

'I don't understand. What point are you trying to make?'

'Okay, so for example…did you know, that both the ancient Mayans and Egyptians believed there were 9 Gods? It is also said that there are 9 ranks of angels, whilst others talk of 9 types of demons. So, it shouldn't surprise you to learn that 9 differing aliens have visited earth – 8 in competition for your DNA, with the remaining group acting in a judicial way. 9 is the number of judgement… so to speak. So how do you not know for sure, that these 9 whatever's, are not one and the same? One culture may give an alien the title of a demon or an angel the title of a fairy from the bottom of the garden. These are all just titles Clarah?'

The young Gypsy girl fell silent for a moment. She hadn't anticipated such a complex reply.

'Stop skating around on the mucky edge of the ice, 'she eventually responded.

'I am a label sort of an earthling, and a Yorkshire one at that - so hit me with a title. What are you?'

'A deva,' came the reply.

Clarah tried hard to stifle a giggle, but unable to resist she eventually spat out in a loud broad northern dialect, 'what?'

She continued, 'do you mean a deva such as in Tia Lembugo…all fur coat and no knickers? Are we talking diamonds and attitude?'

On this occasion, it was Aura's turn to laugh.

'No, no, not at all,' she responded.

'I am a deva as in the original meaning of the word. I am a deva of the hidden Delvic world. I am guessing that you probably haven't heard about the Delvic kingdom?'

'Got that in one Aura. I sure haven't. However, I suspect that your explanation is going to be "off the scale" weird, so is there any chance I could magic myself some chilled Chardonnay whilst taking in the views of Robin Hoods Bay. I doubt I am going to forget this conversation in a hurry.'

'Just think about it. Trust in the power of your thoughts Clarah.'

The young Gypsy girl almost flew off the grassy cliffs as the wine appeared in her hand. Aura could hardly contain her amusement.

'Dear sweet Clarah. You have ordered your wine in a plastic throwaway cup. What are we going to do with you?'

'But that's exactly how I drink it Aura. Anyway…it's just a drinking implement. Surely you are not going to be obsessed with the labels of tumblers, flutes and the nuances between crystal and glass stemware? All just titles my dearest deva.'

Game, set and match; the humble traveller had made her point. Clarah was secretly delighted that she had used an expression such as "nuances". She didn't know if it was entirely appropriate, and wasn't quite certain what it meant, but she had heard it said on some TV show. It felt like a good word to use. Nuances…she repeated the word a few times to herself.

Aura enjoyed the companionship of her new assignment. She had warmed to Clarah's earthy normality and straight-talking Yorkshire mannerisms. She loved the fact that her young friend was a complex cocktail of child-like innocence, with street-cred toughness.

'You underestimate yourself you know. You are a smart girl Clarah, and you amuse me, but…do you want to know what I am or not?'

'Yes, fine. Go for it. What does being a deva from devaland mean? Hey - I have a tumbler of white wine which has been miraculously transported into my hand, so you could say that you have my full attention.'

She raised her hand, saying 'slange var' as she took a sip of her Chardonnay.

Aura recognised that she was being challenged by her encounter with the earth person, yet she still delighted in her young friend's company.

She replied, 'What you refer to as "devaland" is in fact the Delvic realm – a state of being which exists partway between the astral and ethereal plane. I don't really expect you to understand right now. Just know that I am not an angel or a demon. I am not living or dead, and neither am I human or alien.'

'Hey slow down Aura. I mean…that doesn't leave you with a whole lot of other options. You have out-titled yourself.'

Aura sighed and scratched her head, unsure how best to explain such complexity to a young woman such as Clarah. A young human who had lived a fairly simple life, that was up until a lottery win turned it upside down and inside out.

She began, 'devas are spirits of nature, and by that, I mean we represent all elements of the natural universe. For instance, my peers may govern fire, water, trees, gravity, smoke, volcanos, solar flares and the air and so on. All elements of the natural world are allocated a deva. I oversee the spirit and as such frequently encounter lost souls. These are spirits who are disembodied and find themselves in places they shouldn't be.'

Clarah drank more wine and looked out to sea, seemingly confused and yet strangely unconcerned. For a minute or so, she felt as though she was in yet another dream. Surely none of this was real – the wine, the sea and even the salty breeze blowing her hair away from her face. All of these sensations felt strangely spurious. It was a bizarre yet surreal situation. She remained silent and unresponsive. Aura became frustrated with her lack of communication, clicking her fingers in front of her eyes, so to bring Clarah back to the moment.

'I lost you for a minute Clarah. Don't worry, that happens sometimes. Your consciousness is drifting between different situations, so it is only normal that you will lose yourself occasionally. This is symptomatic of a misplaced soul. However, time is against us, so I need to work fast. Are you okay listening to some condensed lessons about the world of the outlier spirits?'

Clarah was still partially disconnected, as though in shock.

She replied, 'yes hit me with some facts. Last night I believe that I saw a demon drag my brother down into hell, so I doubt that there is anything you could say which would shock me more than that appalling vision. I keep replaying it in my head. It was awful Aura. I think that maybe Kane was a lost soul. I guess that he was one of those you failed to waft along on your spirit wind.'

Aura ignored the comment. The truth would hurt too much and besides, now was not the time for an ethical debate about Kane's moral compass. She stood up and putting a hand up to shield her eyes, looked far out to the sea.

'I don't know how much attention you are paying to me Clarah, but if you can focus for a moment, this is important. Can you see that ship out in the distance?'

Clarah nodded to confirm.

Aura continued, 'it is following a shipping lane. The lane is invisible. It isn't as though Picasso drew a couple of lines in the sea between the occasional masterpiece, yet the captain knows they are there. If he obeys the rules and keeps his ship within the lines, he shouldn't sail into shallow water and run aground. He will avoid hitting any hidden rocks, and he shouldn't go bumping into other ships coming in the opposite directions. These lanes of travel will keep him and his crew and his cargo safe.'

Clarah finished her wine with one last thirsty gulp, and then rose to her feet. She followed the direction of Aura's stare. The autumn skies were a wintery pale blue and the cold North Sea looked wild and untamed. She identified with its unruly might. The wrathful waves were rolling the ship from side to side without mercy. On the horizon, thunder clouds were gathering and the occasional glint of sheet lightening, created a dramatic exploding seascape. She stretched her arms towards the sky and yawned.

'Please go on Aura, but I have no idea why a shipping lane should concern me. What is your point?

'Rules Clarah...rules. The entire universe is made up of both physical and spiritual laws and they exist for a reason. Everything on this world of yours and the many worlds hidden from your sight, depend upon a delicate balancing act. Far out at sea a storm is brewing. If that ship gets flung off course, it may run into trouble. The spiritual winds I govern, are similar to the shipping lanes. They steer all types of souls from all kinds of planets, into a divine pre-determined direction. Dear sweet Clarah – you are man overboard. You are an outlier. You have run adrift. You are in a strange ocean, sometimes drowning, sometimes floating. You swim towards the shore but the undercurrents pull you back. This is why your life has become so peculiar. This is why your reality is out of synch. This is why I am here.'

Clarah was beginning to understand. The explanation was extraordinary, yet by using the example of a ship sailing across choppy waters, Aura had found the perfect metaphor.

'Am I dead? On the odd occasion, I have thought that maybe I have died.'

'No, not quite. You are in a coma Clarah?'

'A coma. How?'

'You had a heart attack on the flight back from Bali. You nearly died.'

'But…I am healthy. I am young. How?'

'You had a blood clot. It broke free and became stuck in your lungs. It can happen on long flights. You were immobile throughout the whole journey. However, someone or something gave you a sedative. It tranquilised you to such a degree, that it probably contributed to your condition. You were also given something else that caused this to happen. Some medication. I am not sure what or by whom.'

'Shit. Oh, my god that's awful. Where am I. Where is my body?'

'You were taken to a hospital near the airport at Manchester. Complicated name – begins with W. I will try to find out for you. Your grandmother has been sat by your side nearly every day. That is why she keeps leaving the house. She catches the train in the morning and it takes her 5 hours to get to the hospital. She has stayed over in a local hotel once or maybe twice. She worries about you.'

'I just presumed that she was taking my Aunt Mary to the hospital for treatment.'

'Clarah; I am so sorry. I hate to tell you this, but your Aunt Mary died many months ago. She had an accident. She fell downstairs and broke her neck.'

'No, no, no. That cannot be possible. I have seen her around the house. We have spoken. She has even told me off...given me a right ol ribbing for running away.'

'You have also spoken with Kane and Nina, and they died over a year ago. You have been living in a house of ghosts. In your spirit state, you can see other spirits. They will appear as real to you as the wine you just believe you have consumed.'

'I am shocked. Poor Aunt Mary. Where is she buried?'

'She was cremated. It was her wish. Mary's ashes were thrown out to sea from this very spot where we now stand. It was one of the reasons I brought you here. I know you loved her. I thought you would like to see...'

'But...these...ghosts, how and why are they still here? Should they not have moved on?'

'Your Baba May is a powerful Romany witch. She was lonely. She didn't want to live in that big house all by herself, so she conjured up the spirits of those she loved – aside from your mother that is. She left her daughter Violet in peace. Your Baba May broke many rules and she is aware that I am angry with her. She is steering a course from outside of the shipping lane. She drifts in dangerous waters.'

'This is plain crazy. How the bejesus can I see ghosts? Aren't they just clouds of spooky images, normally invisible? I am struggling to get my head around the fact that for the last week I have been talking to ghosts. Am I in a dream?'

'No, not in a dream, but neither are you in your physical form Clarah. I am talking to your spirit. You see, the soul normally escapes its outer shell at the point of physical death. Those are the rules. You should have died, but you didn't. You were resuscitated, yet somehow your spirit escaped its body just before your heart started to beat again. Modern medicine and a ventilator is keeping your body alive, but right now your body is nothing more than an empty carcass. Everything functions as it should and your organs are alive, but the real Clarah – the person who is you, is standing on a cliff at Robin Hoods Bay. It is unusual, but you are not the first and probably won't be the last.'

'Am I brain dead?'

'That's the strangest thing of all, but no you are not. You have been drifting in and out of different realities. On one occasion, a doctor was threading a central line into a vein in your neck. You were in a coma, but you felt it. You were in your bedroom, and you thought that Dracula was attacking you. I guess that's what happens when you live in a place such as Whitby. Every now and then, you will feel what your body feels. It will be confusing. Your spirit could be in the middle of a desert, but if your body feels cold you may start to shiver. You see, you have not completely disconnected from your physical being. The soul still longs to return, so it won't let go of the girl in a coma. You are straddling two disconnected worlds, neither really in one or the other. You are an outlier.'

Clarah paced up and down along the top of the cliff edge, occasionally looking out at the metaphor ship now disappearing beyond the horizon. She pinched her skin. It hurt. The pinch left a red mark.

She asked, 'how can you say I am not flesh and blood. I still feel like a living person.'

'All sprits feel the same way. They still possess all senses as though they were still alive. You are no different. A person whose leg has been amputated, can still feel the missing leg. They call it phantom pain. So sometimes, you can feel what your body feels. It can be confusing.'

'So, if I throw myself off this cliff, are you telling me that I cannot die?'

'Just give it a go. I am not stopping you.'

Clarah wandered to the edge, as close to the edge as she dared. She looked down and watched the angry waves as they berated the rocks. A dizzy feeling of vertigo enveloped her. She was so close to the sides of the cliff, that she could even feel droplets of the spray being spat from the sea.

'I can't do it. I do believe you Aura, as wild and as ridiculous as your explanations sound. But... I feel so real. I feel so alive. I can't do it.'

'Yes, you can,' and with that Aura pushed her over the edge.

She went tumbling through the air, falling and falling. She hit the water with a loud splash.

CHAPTER 17

Tuesday 29th September 2015
A BUMPY LANDING INTO THE TRUTH

Clarah woke up sprawled across her bed, upside down and half dangling off the mattress. Her damp head was suspended just inches from the floor, causing her hair to mingle with the rug, which was of the exact same colour. A glint of sunshine from the partially opened curtain, propelled a sharp beam of daylight onto her sleepy eyelids. Sudden consciousness made her jump, causing the rest of her body to join the rug. As she lay in a disjointed heap upon the floor, the sound of laughter finally brought her to her feet.

Aura could hardly contain herself, 'not the most elegant of landings dearest, but after all that sea air, at least you had a good night's sleep.'

'You pushed me. You… nasty lowdown sneaky evil deva bitch. You pushed me off a bloody cliff.'

Aura shrugged nonchalantly.

'I can push a spirit anywhere I like. You are not in a physical form. I cannot brake you. How else could I make you believe me? For the journey we are about to take, belief is mandatory. In fact, belief is the essence of your imagined existence.'

Clarah looked down at her hands. They were neither cut nor dirty. She pulled up her skirt to look at her knees, and likewise they were not even mildly scuffed. Nothing was broken… not a single joint had been knocked out of place. Just a mere trace of mud and grass stains from falling in the graveyard, marred her near perfect presentation.

The realisation then hit her, that she had fallen…or rather had been pushed from a great height, and yet it had not left a mark upon her skin.

'My God, I am not real, am I?'

She started to shake, yet with all the grit and resilience she could muster, she did not breakdown. It took all the inner strength she had, not to collapse into a crying heap.

Aura was sympathetic. Outliers often felt distraught at this stage of their discovery. She put a reassuring arm around her shoulder.

'You are real Clarah. You are alive, but your physical body is in a hospital bed somewhere in Manchester. In my realm, the spirit actually has the greater power. We view the physical body as an incumbent passenger. To us, it is weak, vulnerable, degenerating and easy to break. The spirit is eternally youthful and truly magical. Try not to fret too much about this.'

Clarah merely nodded, pushing the slight trace of dampness away from her cheek.

Aura continued, 'you are actually quite rare and also incredibly blessed. You have an amazing opportunity to enjoy this period of your existence. As an outlier, you can travel wherever you want, and do so with just a thought. You can cross continents and even an entire galaxy, with just the blinking of an eye. You can be visible or invisible according to the situation. You can move around time with relative ease, backwards or forwards. You have been given this gift for a reason – so use it wisely little traveller. In the meantime, there are rules – things you should know.'

Clarah was in shock and somewhat dumbstruck. She could just about manage the word, 'what?'

'First you should eat. You are pure energy, and every time you use your energy to do something, you drain yourself of power. You should treat your spiritual self, the same as you treat your physical self. You still need to eat and rest.'

Clarah was still in shock. She simply nodded in compliance.

'I will need to leave you soon Clarah. I have others to attend to. Trust me, there are many disembodied outliers drifting around in the aether. However, before I do, I will train you how to ride on the spiritual wind.'

'Sounds fun.'

'Do you remember the ship we saw yesterday?'

Clarah nodded a compliant affirmation.

'Well,' continued Aura, 'there are also otherworldly shipping lanes you need to navigate. I will now go downstairs and shall cook you an omelette. Whilst I crack open some eggs - you should try to think of yourself in the kitchen. The first time you attempt this, it may take a little while…but persevere. After I leave, you should practice moving around without the use of your legs. You have become a new sort of traveller now dear Clarah. One without the need of caravan wheels.'

Aura then vanished.

***

Clarah sat on her bed. Her mind was spinning, if indeed she had a mind. No matter how articulate the explanation of her condition was conveyed, she still could not believe the words. Her body and her soul, once connected, were now separated. She tried to jolly herself up. Perhaps this travelling thing could be fun. She should give it a go.

She closed her eyes and she tried. She then closed them tighter, as though that would make some sort of difference. Nothing worked. Exasperated, she fell back onto her bed. Was it that she didn't believe enough? This whole situation was ridiculous, so of course she didn't believe enough. Yet with that thought, she remembered the cliff. She was definitely pushed. She looked down at her grass smeared clothing, and with that she remembered the graveyard and falling at the foot of the family headstone. Then she remembered Kane.

The most pungent stink pervaded her bedroom. It was akin to the vile smell of rotting flesh mixed with caustic manure and rancid butter. It was so pungent, that some stomach contents ascended into her throat and for a moment, she thought she was going to throw up. The offensive odour made her heave. Then she saw him. She had been thinking about Kane, and Kane had appeared. He was crawling towards her on all fours like a tortured animal. He had manacles around his ankles. They appeared to be fettered to chains that seemed to melt into the ground. He held up his face and looked her directly in the eyes.

'I am sorry sister. Forgive me.'

With that, his body started to levitate a few feet from the ground. It did not stay there for long, before an arm appeared from out of the carpet. With long red manicured fingers, the hand grabbed at his ankle, and with one mighty pull, wrenched him into the floorboards. He literally fell into her bedroom floor and then vanished. Clarah heard her brother cry for help just before he was dragged down into whatever and wherever.

Clarah was traumatised. Panic stricken she screamed, 'get me out of here'.

It was a prayer from the heart; one beseeched with sincerity and urgency. Just a simple yet powerful command and that was all it took. A wish made with an extraordinary force of determination.

***

Aura was just serving up the omelettes, when Clarah appeared in the kitchen…sitting on the washing machine. Aura applauded her unusual entrance.

'Well done, I was wondering when you were going to join me. I have been waiting for at least 15 minutes, but hey, you made it eventually and that's all that matters. I erm…take it you were thinking about dirty clothes when you teletransported?'

Clarah looked down at the washing machine she was sat upon.

'Oh heck. Well yes. I guess those green skid marks were bothering me. Gypsy girls always like to look clean and well presented.'

'You need to be careful Clarah. Your thoughts are powerful. When you are thinking about being in any one place, at any one time, with any one person – just be sure that no other random notions enter your head.'

Clarah understood. She had thought about Kane and he had just appeared. He was not a welcome sight, or smell. She shivered. Aura caught her reaction and understood.

'Do us both a favour Clarah. Until you have learned to master your new skill and have practised moving from room to room, it is best that you stay within the confines of this house and garden.'

'Surely my Baba May will become suspicious, I mean…with me floating in and out of places and all that?'

'Your gran already knows that you are here in spirit form. Don't forget, that she is the one watching over your body. I suspect that you won't see much of her during the week. The long journey back and forth from the hospital is tiring, and so she will probably book herself into a local hotel. I guess that for most of the time, you will be home alone. Quite quite alone.'

Clarah's face became sombre. She hated her new home, and now she hated it even more. She had considered it to be haunted, and now that fact had been confirmed, she also knew that she had the ability to see her spectral visitors. Not just see them, but have a conversation with them. Heck, maybe even swap ideas about the latest ghosting methods. She looked over her shoulder…nobody was there. Nothing was there. Yet, she was in a house of ghosts and maybe was one herself. She had no idea what she was anymore.

Aura noticed her silence.

'Clarah, you will be fine. This time of solitude will be good for you. It will give you space to practice being the new you. You can always read a good book, go fishing in the river, hey maybe you could even learn to cook. I noted that you are lacking in the culinary department. So few humans can find the time in their hectic lives to be stress free, pain free and simply stand still for long enough to absorb life. You are such a busy species. I like that about your race, but sometimes you need to follow in the steps of your great prophets and learn the art of silence and stillness.'

Clarah giggled to herself. 'You don't know me very well do you? Trust me, I am fairly good at doing nothing. I won't be bored. Troubled yes – bored no.'

'I am relieved to hear it. Your body is in a strange state of suspension and you are still connected to it. It is weak and sometimes it will drain your spirit of its energy. It is best that you rest up.'

Aura started to walk away but Clarah tugged at her arm, pulling her back.

'Aura, before you leave, I have a request.'

'What?'

'My Da...I don't know what happened to him. I don't really know where he is. I can no longer believe the inventive yarns of my gran. Baba May can spill a few fibs from her mouth when it suits her purpose. Is he alive? My Ma, how did she die? With these questions on my mind – how can I be still? Sure, I can sit and do nothing, but my head won't stop spinning. I need to know these things.'

Aura smiled sympathetically. She felt genuine compassion for her latest outlier.

'Today you should rest. Imagine your horse "Molly Malone" and she will come to you. Go for a gentle gallop along the beach. Tomorrow morning, I will return and I will take you to a place and time which will answer all your questions. We can practice invisibility and learn all about the things we should not do when cloaked from sight.'

'Like opening doors?'

Clarah laughed at the notion.

'Yes, like opening doors and picking up pots and pans and throwing them. We don't want to frighten the mortals. You are a quick learner. Enjoy the rest of the day little human.'

With that, Aura left.

*****

Clarah had never felt so alone in her entire life, even when backpacking around Asia as a solitary wanderer. Of course, that was before she had met up with Anais, Valentine and of course Konnor and his brother Ash. Her mind wandered away from her latest surreal experiences, and found its way back to the ruins of Angkor Wat.

She had been visiting Cambodia and had found herself outside a crumbling Buddhist temple. To a humble Yorkshire lass, it had seemed like another world. She had likened it to some manufactured filmset from a Hollywood Indiana Jones production. Clarah had been enthralled by the crumbling presence of the Bayan temple and lost in a world of her own. Paying little attention, she had picked her way over some stones that were partially blocking a crumbling gateway. Ancient faces came from out of the stone walls, almost teasing her as she tried to navigate the slippery boulders. Huge tree roots had climbed up the building. Like woody tentacle's, they were possibly the only structures holding the exotic jungle shrine together. The air was steamy, spicy and almost smouldering with the spectres of the former Khmer inhabitants. She wasn't paying attention to the mossy platform on which her foot now rested, and then she fell. It was only a small slip, but enough to ensure her ankle had become stuck in the giant tree roots. She had chosen to visit Angor Wat just before sunset, to avoid the vast crowds of selfie-taking tourist. However, lying trapped in a heap of rubble akin to a *"Tomb Raider"* backdrop, she was regretting that decision. Usually happy in her own solitude, Clarah was now quite terrified.

The jungle noises were changing, as the chirpy trills of the tropical birds became silent, and the creatures of the night began to awake. As the sun began its descent, shadows of the ancestors seemed to come to life. Angkor Wat was transforming into something quite unworldly. Never had she been so relieved to hear the sniggering guffaws of silly young people, as a group of fellow backpackers spotted her wedged white limbs beneath the monster tree roots.

That was how she met the group...Valentine and Anais, (the French sisters), along with Asher and of course his brother Konnor. From that moment onwards, she was never to be alone.

She travelled with them on whatever route they elected to take – which was soon to be Australia's gold coast, then ending their journey in Bali. She let them do the thinking on her behalf and they seemed happy to steer the course. It was the most fun she had ever had in her entire life. For a girl who had travelled around from layby to scrubland in a caravan, life became wonderful and exciting. Paradise truly existed, and now that she knew it did, she could not undo that knowledge.

***

Clarah was climbing down from the most amazing roller-coaster ride, so depression began to sink in as reality hit home. She wondered why none of her new friends had responded to her many texts and emails– but then she remembered. She was in a coma. She had almost died. Her heart had stopped. She believed herself to be real, but she wasn't…not really. Maybe she only thought about sending those messages, but hadn't actually pressed send. Could her imagined fingers make contact with laptop keys? She didn't know for sure. Maybe just maybe, her messages were in her imagination…just like Molly Malone. She missed Konnor, but didn't know if she would ever be able to see him again, or he see her.

Clarah sat down on the floor and curled herself up into a fetal position. She sobbed, and then she cried and then she howled. She felt sorry for a body that was struggling to live. It had a fight on its hands. Then she realised that she had just thought of her body as an "it" and now she knew she had truly divorced herself from… it. She was she and it was an it.

She picked herself up and turned on the radio. The song "I'm learning to fly" by Tom Petty came on the radio. It was an old song. She loved it, but the lyrics made her cry again. Indeed, she had started out down a dirty road. Started out all alone and was still alone. More alone than ever. She wondered where Konnor was right now. He was somewhere out there in the big world, and totally ignorant of her situation. At least she wasn't thinking about Denny and that was a plus. She then remembered Aura's warning to be careful of her thoughts.

So...Clarah had to learn to fly, but not yet. Not until she could control her thoughts. Aura had much to teach her.

CHAPTER 18

Monday 19ᵗʰ January 2015
BACK IN TIME - A FLY ON THE WALL

Katalyn chewed on her fingers, biting each nail off one by one. She was visibly edgy and ripped her index nail off until it bled. For one so vain it was an unintentional defilement, yet a sign of extreme nervousness.

She was sat in a busy café in York. It was a charming oldie worldly establishment, tucked neatly behind York Minster Cathedral. It was old age, yet ever so slightly new age, with a large Buddha taking pride of place amongst a few sandalwood scented candles and joss sticks.

Under more normal circumstance, she would have mused over a cappuccino and crunched on slender almond biscuits; watching the passers-by as they wrestled with their umbrellas. However, on this occasion, she sat and stared at the floor, not wanting to make eye contact with anyone. Not wanting anyone to notice her furrowed brow and tense manic nail chewing.

***

Clarah felt uncomfortably voyeuristic, as though watching someone take a shower.

'Are you absolutely sure she can't see me Aura?'

Her Deva friend was eternally patient.

'You are spirit. You are invisible. You assumed that the villagers were ignoring you because you were a Gypsy and yet you were mistaken. They simply couldn't see you. When you are ready I will teach you how to materialise a physical body illusion, but for now just observe and learn about a meeting that you never knew about. We have gone back in time by about 8 months. You had just spent the day wallowing on a white sandy beach at Koh Samui, and around about now, you were ordering your first Kamehameha of the day.'

Clarah licked her lips at the mere thought of her favourite Eastern tipple. She considered that perhaps later, she could materialise the Thai chili-infused vodka, subtly drizzled with lemon and coconut milk.

Aura could sense that Clarah was drifting, and so nudged her in the ribs.

'We came here because you wanted answers about your mother and father. Pay attention Clarah, or all of this will have been a waste of time.'

She silenced her thoughts and continued to observe her sister.

Katalyn heard the jingle jangle of the door as it opened and she instantly knew who was walking through it. Her mother Violet sat down silently beside her and pulled her daughters hand away from her nibbling mouth. It was an unwelcome scolding and not the most appropriate of greetings for a much-needed reunion.

'How are you Kattie,' Violet asked?

Katalyn struggled to keep her eyes dry. She looked at her mother's headscarf, noting the tell-tale sign of someone enduring cancer treatment. Katalyn tried to make light of it.

'Have you not got a wig you can wear Ma?'

Her mother smiled back.

'I have about 10 in many different colours, but on a wet and windy day like today, I decided to play safe. I still don't feel right about wearing a wig, although it can be an interesting experiment. Folks react differently to different hair colour's, you know. I find it all quite amusing.'

Her mother tried to lessen the tension in the air, but any attempt at humour failed. Katalyn's face wore a dark sombre expression.

'So Katalyn…enough about my hair, or lack of it. I am going to get myself a big mug of Yorkshire tea. Would you like a drink?'

Katalyn jumped to her feet, 'let me get these Ma…2 sugars?'

Her mother gestured for her to sit back down.

'I am not an invalid child. I walked here from the train station without any assistance, so I think I can walk to the counter and order the drinks for bugger's sake.'

Katalyn scanned her mother's frame as she went to order their tea. She had lost a lot of weight. It suited her. She considered that some folks would look ill and drained from so much sudden weight loss, but as her mother had been a bit on the plump side beforehand, ironically, she looked the better for it. No traces of sagging skin either. She hoped that her Ma's enduring collagen was an inherited trait. With her heavily made up face, her mother was disguising her illness well, or at least she was making every effort to do so. Yet the charade hadn't fooled her first-born child.

Violet walked back to the table.

'The waitress said she would bring our drinks over, 'she uttered. 'I have also ordered some slices of buttered Parkin and Brack cake.'

Katalyn stared deep into her mother's eyes. They bore the sadness of someone who had seen too much, lost too much and had slept too little. No matter what fancy high price cosmetics she now smothered on her face, the emotional scars were still obvious. Some things could not be masked by paint and powder.

Mother and daughter sat in silence for a short while. It was a moment suspended in time, like that spooky twilight zone when seconds feel like minutes or even hours.

Katalyn broke the strained muteness by pulling out some recent photos of her toddlers.

'We had these done at a proper photo studio in Leeds Ma. These copies are for you.'

An instant smile enveloped Violets face, as she stared at her granddaughter's cheeky smiles and radiant eyes; eyes alive with life and hope. Her heart was immediately swathed with total love, as every cell in her body ached for a cuddle.

'I wish I could see them again. Will you bring them to see me next time? Please Katalyn. They are only babies; they don't remember anything. They have no scars from the past.'

Katalyn rebuked her mother with a harsh response.

'Why don't you come and see them for yourself. Come back to the camp with me. There's a lot of people who would like to see you Ma. A lot of people who miss you. They know about your illness and they feel sorry for you. They forgave us…they forgive you. Please come back Ma.'

Violet stroked her daughters hand, protectively placing her palm over Katalyn's tightened knuckles. Her fingers were clenched so tight, that they had turned quite white.

She looked at her daughter directly as she stated, 'you do know that I cannot come back Katalyn. July 12th last year. How can I forget that date? It was a Capricorn full moon; a time when the planets reveal the wisdom of the ages. It was an ominous omen of karmic evil. We should have kept Nina inside. We should have all stayed inside and locked our doors. A moon like that can drive folk's crazy. That's where the term lunatic comes from y'know. It's science and everything. A big moon pulls at the water inside the brain. I think that's what happened. It made everybody's brain go mad. Aside from that, I do believe that my family was cursed by someone in the vitsa. Someone who was so jealous, that they had been smitten with green eyed begrudgery. They cursed us all for what? A bit of money and the blessings of good fortune.'

Violet sighed deeply and continued, 'no, I am sorry Katalyn. I know you are happy with your life and with Peter and your baby girls. I know you love the whole wanderlust existence, but I am through with all of that. I wouldn't know who to trust anymore and besides, Baba May isn't getting any younger and your Aunt Mary can hardly walk. I miss little Tillie and Keziah so much that it hurts. I miss Peter; that handsome young husband of yours. He is a good man. I miss you more than anyone Katalyn- but I cannot come back. Too much water has flowed under that bridge. I am sorry. That part of my life is over.'

***

Clarah's eyes became moist.

'Hmm, just noticed that she didn't mention me on her "missing you the most" list. Ma always did favour Katalyn.'

Aura shot Clarah a disapproving look.

'Just watch and listen Clarah. You are too impatient, and anyway, she was referring to going back to the camp and at the time, you had run off to the other side of the world…remember.'

***

Violet took a large gulp of tea as she watched the hailstones pelting the passers-by with their icy fury. They made a loud pitter patter noise on the roof of the café, and for a few moments drowned out any attempt at conversation. It was a welcome respite and gave both women thinking time. The hail then stopped as suddenly as it had started.

Violet looked over at her daughter stating, 'Kattie- I wish I could come back. If I could wave a magic wand and turn back time, then I would. But even Baba May with all her weird herbs and hexes cannot conjure that kind of magic. Just look at the weather outside. These lungs of mine wouldn't hold up to breathing in the chill of a cold caravan – not anymore. I am sorry my dearest daughter.'

Katalyn's watery eyes looked away. Deep down inside she knew her mother was right. She stared at the steamed-up windows of the café, as though she wanted to be lost inside their misty glaze. She had tried her best and had failed. With hope against hope, she had truly endeavoured to fix things with all their friends and cousins in the vitsa, but all too late. Everything was all too late. It was unfixable. Sometimes some relationships just break beyond repair.

As with her other siblings, a bank account had been opened for Katalyn and £500,000 deposited inside. Somewhat rashly, she had already spent most of it trying to appease the rest of the vitsa. Yet new cars, caravans and gifts of clothes and jewellery, had been accepted with an edge of steely resentment. In truth, she wasn't really happy there herself, but she wanted her girls to grow up within the Roma culture. It was their birthright, and besides, Peter would never leave. Her husband was Roma to the bone.

Katalyn got up to walk to the restroom. She was now resigned to having a family divided, so resolved to try and enjoy the rest of the morning with her poorly Ma. That was the least she could do. She began to realise that making peace with her estranged mother was really all that was left. The clock was ticking and time was running away with itself. Katalyn knew she was possibly having the last ever conversation with her mother.

***

As the scene unfolded, Clarah felt miserable to the core.

'What date is this Aura? Where in the world was I when all this was happening?'

'It is the 19th January 2015. At this very moment, you were sat in a restaurant, laughing and joking without a care in the world. You were with some new friends. People you had just met whilst travelling. You had just placed an order for sablefish with caramalised sweet ginger. You were getting drunk and having fun. You were flirting with the cute blond haired lad.'

Clarah was ashamed and filled with guilt.

'So, when my mother and sister met in this place…probably for the last time, I was on the other side of the world getting pissed and making out.'

'That's the problem with facing the truth full-on my little human friend. Most of the time you don't hurt as much as maybe you should do, because you don't often have the bitter-sweet privilege of being a fly on the wall. Now that you have that capability, you may find yourself being disappointed in yourself many times over. What is it you say on earth? Yes, now I remember the phrase…ignorance is bliss. Welcome to the harsh stark light of reality Clarah. There is no bliss in truth.'

***

When Katalyn finally made her way back to the table, her mother was part way through a selection of cakes. Much like the tougher women of her generation, she had a habit of bouncing back, and was now consuming calories with extreme gusto. Katalyn sat down beside her coyly… edging her way along the church pew window seat.

As she sat, Violet mumbled, 'it's great to eat and not get fat. I'm making the most of it.'

With a swig of tea; simply by way of oral preparation to wet her mouth, she moved on to the next cake.

Attempting to start their meeting afresh Katalyn asked, 'so Ma, how are you keeping?'

Violet made light of her situation.

'It's my own fault for going under those blasted sun beds when I was a youngster. We didn't know about skin cancer back in my day. Forget putting Factor 10 on the skin, we would coat ourselves in olive oil and vinegar and lie basting on tin foil. Us silly young girls would roast ourselves like fried chicken. We were so bloody ignorant back then. You would think with having Roma blood that my skin would be okay, but no…I got one of them mole things. It was on my back so I didn't see it for ages. I mean…who ever looks at their own back places?'

Yet again, Katalyn was choking back tears.

'But Ma, they cut it out. Surely you should be okay now?'

Violet was made from sturdy stuff. A life on the road had sandpapered down all her soft edges and now was not the time for dressing up the truth in a fluffy cardigan.

'Yes, they cut it out,' she replied, 'but by the time they got to it, the bugger had seeded itself elsewhere. I now have other things in my lungs. I think they are called nodules. The doctors gave me some radiotherapy and chemo and all my hair fell out, but the medicines won't cure me

Katalyn. You need to know that. What I have got inside of me, it is terminal. It will kill me. However, I am told that the treatment will keep me going longer and make the condition easier to live with. This is one of the reasons I cannot live the traveller life anymore, and also why I so long to see my little granddaughters. Will you not bring them to my new house in Whitby? Please bring them soon, they will love it. I am not on the other side of the word Kattie. One day I will be unreachable, but for now we are only talking miles.'

Katalyn had been verbally and emotionally pinned against a wall. Her mother had dealt the knockout punch. She hesitated.

'It's still a long way from York Ma. They are only babes. It's a big journey for them. Let me think on it. Tell me, what's you new house like anyway?'

Katalyn tried to recover, using the tactic of changing subject.

Violet replied. 'it's big and old and it's been rendered white. It overlooks the sea and sits on top of a cliff; not a big cliff. More like a bit of a hill really. You can walk down a path and there's a golden beach at the bottom. It's not private- we don't own it or anything. However, other folk (we call them the public), can only reach it when the tide is out. So, when the water is up to the rocks, only we and we alone can reach it from our garden path. So, I guess that makes it sort of private. The girls would love it there. They could make sand castles and everything. Oh…and there is a pirate's cave. The rumour is, that there is a tunnel that goes from the cave into the cellars below the house…some kind of smugglers run. I haven't been down there so I wouldn't know. It's supposed to be haunted by the ghost of a smuggler; a man who was hanged for piracy hundreds of years back. There is bound to be buried treasure somewhere – surely? Some even say that on a clear day you can spot mermaids in the water. It's like dreamland for little children. I mean shit, Hollywood has to make up all of that stuff, and we have got it for real on our own doorstep. Did I mention the local ice-cream? They make it with clotted cream from the local farms. The girls like ice-cream...don't they? Why don't you bring them over in summer...or sooner? Maybe sooner would be better?'

Katalyn knew exactly what game her mother was playing.

'That was quite some sales pitch you just delivered Ma. Even I am amazed as to how you got to fit pirates, mermaids, treasure, ghosts, sand castles and caves into just a few sentences.'

'You forgot about the ice-cream,' chortled Violet.

For a few moments, the mood was lightened and they laughed a little. The mood could not stay light for long. Violet had a train to catch and a long journey back to her Whitby version of a Hollywood film set. Yet they still had serious things to discuss.

Katalyn asked of her mother, 'have you heard from Clarah? Do you know where she is?'

Violet held her daughters hand as she replied, 'you know dear, there are private investigators out there who can trace anyone. Now that I have the money, I can afford to hire such people. So yes, I do know where she is, although I don't know if I can pronounce it.'

Violet pulled a grubby sheet of paper from her 60' style Dior handbag.

'Somewhere in Malaysia it says here, but that was 2 weeks ago and she moves around a lot. I am told she is safe and making friends. The detective people know what they are doing. They have her in their sights. She is having fun.'

Katalyn nearly choked on her drink.

'The bitch! She is having fun. She is having bloody fun. How can you stay so calm Ma? We have been dragged through the pits of hell and back, whilst my younger sister is in Asia somewhere having bloody fun.'

'Calm down Katalyn. You shouldn't judge.'

Her daughter bit her lip, but the words still tumbled out.

'She ran away when Nina was still in intensive care Ma. Her twin sisters brain was bleeding. Kane had been drinking mud in a ditch and was on his death bed with pneumonia. How can you tell me not to judge?'

Her mother looked at her with a knowing look. She knew those things only a mother could know.

'Pull your halo up Katalyn, its fallen down to your ankles girl. What exactly was you doing when Kane was drinking mud and Nina was dangling from a tree?'

Katalyn was shocked. Did her mother know? How could she know?

Violet continued, 'have you not been to visit your Da? Manchester isn't far from York.'

Katalyn again looked shocked.

She responded, 'why call it Manchester. Why don't you call it by its proper title rather than its location? The place is Pathways, Pathways prison…and no, I have not been to visit him in prison and neither do I intend to.'

Violet looked embarrassed and scanned the room to see if they had been overheard.

In a hushed tone she whispered, 'I didn't want to use that word in here Katalyn. Have you no self-respect?'

Katalyn shrugged nonchalantly.

'He attacked Peter's brothers. For Christ's sake Ma, all the lads were trying to do was cut Nina down from the tree. Why the hell did he go after them? What possessed him?'

'Are they okay, 'enquired Violet, her face etched with sadness and shame?

Her daughter helped herself to a spoon of her mother's pie for a deliberate sugar rush, as she replied, 'well I guess so. Paddy is blind in his left eye. Jim's nose has been fixed so it doesn't bend to the right anymore, and Dan is still going to the Orthodontist to have the last of his implants done and sure his leg is out of plaster now. The limp should get better with physio. Paddy still has some damage inside his head though. The doctors cannot be sure he will be fine in the long run.'

'Oh, well I guess that's partially good then,' responded Violet.

Katalyn had to use every inch of her inner strength to remain calm.

'Good! You just said good. They are my husband's younger brothers Ma. They are my family. Why oh why did Da ever think the boys would do something like…. that…. like what happened to Nina? It was just………'

Her speech trailed off. She didn't or couldn't say anything more, but deep down, she still ached for her younger sister. Nina. The word couldn't make its way from her lips.

Violet held her daughters hand again.

'See what I mean about the water under the bridge? How can I possibly go back to the camp and face the boy's mother, knowing that my husband attacked them? I know exactly what he did Katalyn. He almost killed Paddy, and that's why he is now locked up in…Manchester.'

Violet sighed, it was a deep regretful moan from the heart. 'He is so sorry about everything. He was in shock at the time, but that doesn't right a wrong. Your Da is very angry. He was given the incorrect information. I don't know who told him it was Peter's brothers, but someone told him. I would love to know myself. He says it was Clarah, but I can't believe she would say such a thing. Anyway, the police caught the real criminals in the end. Some settler boys from the local town I believe. I am so relieved it was none of our lads.'

Katalyn shook her head, as though still in a state of disbelief.

'But Ma, I heard that the gaje lads did it because Kane owed them money. The rumour is that they were drug dealers. Surely Kane could have just paid them what he owed? You won the fuckin lottery. You had given him a fat load of notes. Tell me ma, why would they want Nina dead? My little sister was just a baby inside her head.'

Katalyn hid her head in her hands, not wanting the happy middle-class teenagers serving at the counter, to see her grief.

Violet looked at her watch and walked to the counter to settle the bill. She then made her way back to their table, but remained standing.

'This has been an emotional meeting Kattie. As nice as we tried to make it, we couldn't make it nice.'

Her mother looked down at the stone floor and with a heavy heart continued.

'July 12th 2014 tore a hole in my heart, and not just my heart. Many suffered as a result of that cursed moon. My family has been destroyed. There are those you may hate right now child, but please don't hate me. I have done nothing wrong.'

With that, she removed a card from her bag. Inside the card was her address in Whitby. She added, 'please come to see me. Bring the girls. If

Peter can ever look me in the eyes again, please bring him as well. It would do you both good to take a trip together- as a couple. You know what I mean by that Kattie. You have a marriage that needs some attention. Anyway - I have a train to catch now.'

Her mother turned around one last time. She added, 'get Clarah back if you can. I know you hate her for running away, but she had her reasons Katalyn. Here is the business card of the agency we used to find her. The name of the main detective is Simon De Vede, and his contact details are on the card. His company has been paid in advance. They are very good. These are the people who found our Rory when he disappeared in Greece. I don't how long my health will hold up. You are now in charge. Please keep in touch with him.'

***

Clarah suddenly piped up, 'that was him. I remember now -Simon De Vede. It's all coming back to me. He was the chap who kept following me. He was the detective that put me on the plane in Bali. I am starting to get my memory back. Simon De Vede – well I never.'

'Clarah – please shut up. It's really great that all the jigsaw pieces are finally falling into place for you, but your Ma and Katalyn are about to see each other for the very last time, so we should respect this moment for what it is and pay it some attention.'

Looking like a scolded school girl, Clarah did was she was told.

***

Violet bent down and gently kissed her daughter's forehead. It was a last kiss, and they both knew it. As the jingle jangle of the bell marked Violets exit from the café door, Katalyn suspected that she would never see her mother again. It was a strange thought. With that Katalyn's chair seemed to be pulled from underneath her for no logical reason. She ended up on the floor with half her cup of tea soaking her hair and ruining her white designer blouse.

***

'I cannot believe you Clarah. The first time I take you on a trip to the past and you become violent.'

'Just experimenting Aura…that's all. Just needed to know how much I could make the non-physical me, create a physical act in a past situation, and one that I was never even involved in at the time. A mere scientific experiment and I must add, an illuminating experience. Hey, but as a positive, it was easier than I thought. I am getting the hang of the tele- kinetics stuff.'

'Well, don't do it again. It was a gross misuse of your abilities. Have you learned all you needed to know?

'Well yes, you could say that. I certainly understand why I am so hated and I don't blame them for hating me. I was a deserter. I get that. Shame that Katalyn didn't confess her part in all of this…the cheating bloody bitch. Still, it was lovely yet sad to see my Ma again. It is very sad about Ma's cancer. I'm sorry I wasn't here for her. I wish that the Simon detective person, had explained that to me. I would have come back sooner. I am also shocked that my Da is in prison. That was all my fault. I told him the wrong story. I want to go and see him if that's okay. That part hurt me the most. This has been a painful experience Aura. I feel drained. Can I go home now?'

'Hold my hand. Close your eyes and imagine your kitchen as we last saw it a few minutes ago. Try not to think of your sister's tea-sodden clothes or you will end up crashing into the washing machine again.

Clarah please promise me – do not attempt any time travel. Just keep a low profile and practice moving from room to room.'

With her fingers crossed behind her back, Clarah shut her eyes tightly and promised Aura that she would behave herself. However, she was a rebel by nature. The term "low-profile" didn't exist in her vocabulary. Besides that, now she could move around without caravan wheels, and roam through time and space as an outlier. She was free and more than that, she was exceptionally special.

CHAPTER 19

Saturday December 5th 2015:
MERCY DE VEDE - SOMEWHERE ON THE RHINE

Simon De Vede looked out of the boat window on a cold and frosty eve. He was cupping a hot mug of vin chaud and watching the world go by. Part timbered «pan de bois» houses, with their steeply pitched red clay roofs, screamed out pure Alsace charm. The young detective was sat on a water taxi as it steered its way south along the part French and part German, River Rhine. A stone's throw behind the riverside buildings, he could just about see the narrow-cobbled streets as they descended down to the waterside. In the fading light of early evening, illuminated shop windows with their slatted shutters, created a cascade of flickering colour. Yuletide lights, wrapped around tree branches and lamp posts, added to the effect. Indeed, this was "Hansel and Gretel" fairy tale scenery, paying full magical homage to the Brothers Grimm.

As the boat sailed further away from the beckoning charisma of Strasbourg; a gothic city that filled the Rhine air with cinnamon…Simon began to recognise a journey from his childhood. The smells, the sounds, the leafy riverbanks… they were all familiar. Cherished memories of Christmases long past started to tug at his heart strings.

Several kilometres later, past the main bridge from France to Germany, the boat neared the Réserve Naturelle de la Forêt d'Erstein. The water taxi then slowed down as it prepared to moor up in front of his grandfather's childhood home. Simon had not visited this place since being a young boy, yet even now as an adult, it was just as grand and impressive. His eyes drank in the large renaissance style house, with its white rendered walls and terracotta "queue-de-castor" roof tiles. Feeling unusually sentimental, he lifted his small suitcase from the taxi, and then finding his sea-legs, walked up the gravelled pathway. He remembered the heavy oak door, with its castle like shape and ornate strap hinges. As a small child, it was too heavy for him to pull open. He recalled being scared by it, although he couldn't recall why that should be. He had only been a little sprite, and the door seemed so big and foreboding. However, on this occasion he needn't have worried. It was partially ajar – his arrival had been long overdue, and much expected.

Walking into the archetypal Alsace hallway; a charming fusion of French and Germanic architecture...he could smell freshly cooked gingerbread. Its beckoning aroma was wafting over from the general direction of the kitchen. He remembered that tomorrow was Saint Nicholas day in the region, and wondered if his Grandfathers family had mannele already baked and awaiting consumption. With yet another wave of nostalgia, he recalled sitting on his grandfather's knee and dipping the fluffy pasties into a dish of hot chocolate.

These were all agreeable yesteryear thoughts, but pushing them to one side, he reminded himself that he was here on serious business. Visiting his poorly grandfather in his sickbed was one of his priorities, but being summoned by his formidable Aunt Mercy was yet another.

The name of "Mercy De Vede" was enough to make a lesser mortal quake in their boots. From hardnosed London detective to CEO of her own global investigations company, she was not a lady to mess with.

Simon pondered the thought, 'what could she possibly want that was so important to make her break cover?' As a detective himself, Simon knew how difficult the decision had been to shut shop and quit the

UK. Only an extreme threat of a serious nature would have caused her to abandon her company and feign her own death. Simon never did get to the bottom of the story. Almost forgetting where he was, he soon roused himself back into professional mode, with the promise of mannele and hot spiced cider, to come later in the day.

The housemaid "Aline" was a long-standing family employee of many years' service. Simon didn't see her standing behind him, so as she softly touched him on the shoulder, he almost fell backwards in shock. He spun around to find a middle aged friendly face smiling back at him. Her waist had expanded, her eyes bore the signs of crow's feet and her thinning lips had been smiling too many times for too many years - but he could still recognise the housemaid he had last seen some 12 years erstwhile. Her deep brown eyes showed both delight and concern.

'Monsieur Simon, it has been so long. You were only this big when I last saw you.'

Aline pointed to an area just below her shoulders. Simon smiled and kissed both her cheeks affectionately.

'You have come to see your grandfather, have you not? Follow me, I will take you to him.'

Simon wasn't sure if this was a question or a command, but assuming it to be the latter, he followed Aline up the broad spiral staircase.

On entering the room, Simon was shocked to see the physical state of his grandfather – the once eminent and renowned Professor Roland De Vede. His pale gaunt face, was drooping ever so slightly on one side. His arm was resting on a pillow, as though it was too weak to support its own weight. An oxygen mask was attached to a cylinder, delivering noisy air into his sleeping lungs. Simon touched his grandfather's hand.

It was blue and cold to the touch. By way of a reflex action, he pulled his own warm pink hand away. The iciness of the old man's fingers, sent a chill up his spine. It was upsetting to see him this way. An intellectual man who had travelled the globe, now lying so helplessly in bed. Gasping for oxygen, yet deeply asleep. The needed had become the needy.

'Don't be so afraid Simon. He has been like this before, and then when we least expect it, the old bugger just jumps back to life like a spring chicken. He will be sat at the kitchen table before you know it.'

Simon turned to face the woman who could only be his remarkable Aunt Mercy. He noticed her white gloves first, and then the Avoca faux fur hat perched precariously on her vintage finger-wave hairstyle. Along with her Maximilian fur coat and matching snood, she looked every inch of a 1950's film star.

Removing her overly warm coat, she continued, 'it's lovely to see you again Simon. You are a little early, but you know that I cannot abide late comers. Thank you for your punctuality. So, my little detective nephew, are you here just to see your Grandfather, or did my email trouble you enough to pay us a visit?'

Simon was speechless, slightly over awed and not too sure if he was being played.

On removing her coat, Mercy appeared as though dressed for an occasion. Wearing a red tartan pencil suit nipped in at the waist and of course matching high heeled footwear, she was immaculately presented as per expectation. Simon knew that this was daily attire for his aunt, who at all times appeared as nothing less than perfect.

'I am sorry Simon. I have just come back from shopping. Aline told me you were here. Please come.'

Retrieving her coordinating clutch bag, Mercy gestured that he should follow her. Still in shock at his Grandfathers appearance, he obediently followed his aunt into a room he presumed to be her office.

'It is lovely to see you again Aunt Mercy, but I didn't realise that my Grandpa was quite so ill. It has shocked me. Has my father been to see him?'

Mercy sucked on a vapour cigarette, then casually responding, 'he has pneumonia. A week of antibiotics will see him right. Since he had his stroke, he doesn't move around much and you know the old saying darling – "use it or lose it". Oh and no, your father hasn't been to visit. You should call him. Change of subject - how's my old company these days?'

Simon glanced around the room. His aunt had informed him that she had retired, yet her office looked well used. Stuffed files were crammed full on uneven shelves. A global map with an array of coloured stickers had been pinned to the wall. He counted at least 4 computers with as many differing mobile phones and various other gadgetry. She was up to something…that was for sure. Retired? He doubted that the formidable "investigator supreme" could ever hang up her Dior hat.

'The company's new name is SiDeVe, 'responded Simon, 'and MY new company is doing very well dear aunt.'

Mercy looked up as though trying to visualise the name in imaginary neon lights.

'Hmm, not bad, but I do think the name MeDeVe had a certain je ne sais quoi.'

Simon ignored his aunts slight note of resentment. He sympathised with the extreme circumstances by which she had been forced to abandon her company…even feigning death to disappear from the public gaze, however she had retired and he was very much still working.

Mercy grew impatient.

'Simon dear, a lovely young lady once taught me the importance of 5pm. Tonight is St Nicks Eve and we have a party planned. If we are to talk in a professional capacity, you have just 20 minutes left before I switch my brain into recreational mode. We should grab the moment whilst the clock is in countdown. So…rumours have is that you are doing some work for Reed Baratolli? Why?'

Simon sunk into his Grandfathers antique green leather chair. He stoked the arms, as though connecting with long lost memories. Mercy coughed loudly, so to bring him back to the moment.

He began, 'Tony Mort as he has now known, tracked me down. Grandpa wrote a book for his wife Eenayah, and his name was on the credits. Reed was aware that Eenayah had hired you to protect her. He must have figured out the connection. De Vede is an unusual surname, so it didn't take Tony…I mean Reed, very long to find out the who, what and where.'

Mercy's pupils dilated. She sat down as though expecting some terrible news.

'Go on Simon. Tell me the story from the beginning.'

'Long before Reed aka Tony contacted us, we had been hired to track down a missing girl and the circumstances were…unusual. I believe this case will interest you.'

Mercy leant forward, seeming to be attentive and yet in denial of her own curiosity.

'How old was the child, 'she asked?

Simon felt slightly embarrassed as he replied, 'erm about 20. My missing child was (he coughed) …20.'

Mercy controlled her surprise (and laughter) as she responded, 'so not a child then. More of a young woman. Did you believe this woman had been killed Simon? Just curious as to why you accepted the job?'

Her nephew was struggling with the conversation, as even he was finding his own words unconvincing.

He answered, 'no aunty. The family believed her to be alive. We found that she was back-packing around Asia. Her family had recently been subjected to a huge amount of personal grief and they wanted her to come home. For some reason, she resisted their multiple requests. Her family were rich - nouveau riche. They could afford our charges and chasing her around Asia didn't come cheap.'

Mercy could hardly contain her stifled look of disdain and disbelief. 'Simon, you worry me. Money is money and reputation is reputation. Sure, we all need to earn a wage, but are you seriously telling me that someone paid you to track down a 20-year-old woman…a woman who had taken a legitimate gap year to go travelling? Backpacking is not exactly an uncommon thing for a 20-year-old to do. This story doesn't make sense to me. What is her name?'

'Clarah Lee. Part tinker, part Romany, she is part of an insular community. She isn't just another woman on a globetrotting adventure. Her family took her absence seriously.'

'A Gypsy indeed. How unusual that someone of nomadic birth right should go a roaming. So, what happened next? You persuaded her to come home I take it?'

'Well yes – eventually. I caught up with her in Bali a few months back and did just that.'

'Bali...nice, but bet that looks dodgy on the company accounts. So dear nephew, did you travel back with her or award yourself a few extra days' vacation in Bali?'

'It's my company Aunt Mercy. SiDeVe Ltd - the clue is in the Si bit. So, what if I took a few extra days break?'

'So what? So, you didn't complete the assignment Simon, that's what. You found the girl yes...but you should have gone with her on the plane. I take it that you don't know where this Clarah is right now or what happened to her on the flight home? No- of course you don't. I know all about it and I will fill you in with the details later, but in the meantime...how does she connect with Reed aka Tony?'

'What the hell happened on the plane? Is she okay? How would you know anything about Clarah?'

'Be patient - I will tell you what I know when you tell me about Reed Baratolli. Why does he want to hire you?'

'His son, or should I say his sons as in the plural, both became involved with Clarah. They were also backpacking in Asia and they met up with her. For some reason Tony...I mean Reed, became edgy about the whole situation. He wouldn't say why, but he looked seriously concerned. He wanted me to dig around and find out what I could. Of course, I nearly died when I heard the name. I wasn't sure if taking on the case would mean some sort of conflict of interest. So, when you emailed me, I came over right away. Ta-Da…and here I am. It's your turn now. Is Clarah okay, and how would you know about her anyway?'

Mercy now looked equally serious as she replied, 'do you remember Tomas Forshaw?'

'I know the name but I can't place who he is.'

'July 2013 – he was a doctor who worked in intensive care in North Wales. He was the Consultant who was looking after Eenayah before she was kidnapped. He was the same chap who was looking after me after the car crash and called the police when he found I had faked my identity.'

'Nice guy. So, someone you don't really like a great deal…I suppose.'

'No, no – quite the contrary Simon. When the police needed a fake death certificate so I could roll over and pretend dead, Tomas was most obliging. It probably broke a zillion rules, but we kept in touch. He is kind of cute.'

Mercy winked at her nephew as she tried to subdue a wayward smile.

'So,' sighed Simon, 'what has your Dr Forshaw got to do with Clarah?'

'He has moved hospitals now,' responded Mercy. 'He works in South Manchester. A few months back a young woman had a heart attack as a Qatar airlines flight was coming into land. She was admitted to the intensive care unit where Tomas now works. Her name is Clarah Lee. He called me a few days later. Something about her was puzzling him.'

'What was it?' Mercy had caught her nephew's attention.

'The woman had bleached her hair peroxide blonde and she was about 19 years younger than Eenayah Baratolli, but Simon thought her features were strikingly similar. The circumstances also seemed to conjure up a bit of déjà vu.'

'How?'

'She was in a coma and pregnant. Tomas told me it felt like the Baratolli case all over again. However, unlike Eenayah, Clarah had a miscarriage.'

'I am sorry. I had no idea. I feel so irresponsible now. You are right aunty. I should have got on the plane with Clarah.'

Feeling ashamed and embarrassed, he hung his head low.

Mercy patted him on the back.

'Don't feel too bad about it Simon. Clarah had a DVT; that's a blood clot to us mere mortals and non-medics. It would still have happened even if you had sat next to her on the flight home. However, there is something else that you should know.'

'What?'

'When your grandfather was investigating Eenayah's family tree and the line of Tamar prophesy, he took some cheek cell samples from Eenayah to compare them with her grandmother Harriet. They were found to be identical, which is how your grandfather confirmed that the myth about a line of clones being reborn throughout time, was in fact actually true. We kept some of the samples in a lab, and with Tomas's assistance, we ran a comparison with Clarah's dna. I think you can guess what I am about to say next Simon.'

'My God – she is a clone. No way. Clarah Lee is a bloody clone.'

'Yes, indeed and scientifically verified. I recall my father telling me that there were still about 5 of them left on the planet, although we can't be sure how many of them are of child-bearing age. After our recent experience with Eenayah, we all know what that means.'

'The demons will try to exterminate any Tamar clone or at least prevent a pregnancy from reaching full term. If I recall rightfully, they are trying to close down the line. So…do you think it was them, I mean her blood clot and all that.'

'Tomas ran some toxicology tests after she was admitted…just to be on the safe side. She had been sedated during the flight…not enough to make the cabin crew suspicious, but enough to keep her fairly immobile. She had also been given diuretics, so she was dehydrated as well. Tomas also believes she could have been given a hypercoagulation agent to thicken the blood. The clotting agent is still in the research phase and not licenced for use. Tomas believes it comes from the Siberian Beselovaya plant, which is partially owned by the Lezemel dynasty. You must recall my friend Katya?'

'The one who was murdered in Atlanta?'

'Indeed, one and the same. Her father owns the manufacturing company that produces the agent. Bit of an odd coincidence one would say. Anyway, all of that aside, Clarah was pregnant and so up to 10 times more likely to develop a blood clot anyway. Add to this the risk posed by a long-haul flight, and one has a toxic cocktail for disaster. It was an accident waiting to happen. The worrying thing is though, it all seemed to point towards natural causes. It was only because Tomas recognised the facial features of Clarah that he ran the extra tests.'

Simon had been stunned into silence. He walked over to the water cooler and poured himself several glasses of water which he drank with haste.

'It gets even more complicated aunty. When the team were trying to locate Clarah, we dug up a few other connections that may interest you.'

'Go on Simon. Its 5 minutes to 5, but you have my attention.'

He continued, 'you must recall the Rory MacDonald case. It gave much needed publicity to MeDeVe Ltd as I recall.'

Mercy simply nodded in agreement. She had been very proud that her company had cracked a case which had befuddled the police. None the less, she still had no idea where Simon was going with this.

He continued, 'Rory's parents are Bernice and Ennis MacDonald. Do you remember the family?'

'How could I forget them Simon. They were the tenants of our researcher -Don Morris. They were homeless and desperate as I recall. It was because of Don, that we agreed to drop our fee's and find their son without billing them for any charges. They were in a terrible state. The police had all but given up on ever finding Rory alive. Solving the MacDonald case was career changing publicity for us. We succeeded where the police failed. My lord. Bernice and Ennis...those are names from the past. But how are these lovely folks connected to Clarah?'

Simon was reeling in her curiosity. Feeling victorious in being able to contribute to some of the one-sided conversation he replied, 'Bernice MacDonald is the sister of Mick Lee and Mick is Clarah Lee's father. She is their niece. However, there are other associations that will interest you.'

Mercy rose from her chair and paced the room. She only ever did this when the thrill of a chase was captivating her into movement. She signalled to her nephew, 'go on.'

Simon turned on his iPad and located his notes. After taking some times to locate his summary page, he finally replied, 'Clarah disappeared on July 12th 2014. The travellers had pitched up at some local beauty spot near Scarborough, and some of the locals were protesting about the situation. They wanted them removed. The police were already at the park entrance, along with a small crowd of overly wrought towns folk. It was already turning into something of a drama, and then Clarah's sister Nina was found half unconscious. She had been seriously assaulted. Nina had some sort of learning difficulties, so the fact that she was a vulnerable young woman just made the situation many times worse. The police had to pull Mick Lee off a couple of boys he was throttling. It was a serious attack, so much so that he was later sent down for aggravated assault. At the same time, her brother Kane had been found half drowned in a small pond. Witness statements describe the scene as chaotic. In amidst all of this disorder, Clarah took off in a taxi and hadn't been seen since. It was out of character for her to just run away leaving both her siblings seriously ill in intensive care. They were a close-knit family. Plus, she was due to be married soon. She had no reason to leave like she did.'

He had caught Mercy's attention.

'Did you locate the taxi firm and the driver,' she asked.

'Yes and no,' he replied. 'There were enough people in the area at the time, taking videos on their phones, as well as CCTV footage, so the taxi and registration plates could be identified. So yes, we have spoken with the taxi firm, but the taxi driver himself has left the company. It transpired that he had given a false ID anyway, making him near impossible to track down. However, one bit of luck is that the firm tracks the location of all their cars and they know where the driver took her.'

'And that would be….,' asked Mercy?

'Hades Hall,' replied Simon.

Mercy was intrigued.

'I have heard of this place. Isn't it the only 6-star hotel in the north of England, or maybe even in the whole of the UK?'

'That's the one,' responded Simon.

Mercy's curiosity had become aroused.

'Why would a taxi driver, pick a young woman up from outside a Gypsy camp, more than likely registering the fact that she was a traveller herself, and then take her to the most expensive B&B in the whole of the country? That just doesn't make sense.'

'It does when you understand that her family had just won millions on the national lottery Aunt Mercy. Clarah Lee had been given a considerable sum of money, so she could afford to stay in Hades Hall.

'I do keep up with the English newspapers Simon. Since being retired and looking after my father, I don't have much else to keep my mind busy, so yes...I heard all about this big win. Now you have told me that Clarah was a beneficiary, it does explain how she was able to finance her global adventures. Her sudden departure to warmer climes may be out of character for a poor Gypsy girl, but to me it seems totally in character for a rich one.'

Her nephew then located a photograph on his iPad.

'Get this - Hades Hall has one owner. A young girl of only 17 or maybe 18 years old. Don't you find that odd? Here is a photo of her. I am sure you will recognise the proprietor.'

Mercy looked visibly shocked as she announced, 'Océane Poulain, my God. I never thought my lips would ever utter her name again. How could such a young woman possibly own Hades Hall?'

Simon smiled, visibly pleased to have caught his aunt's attention again.

'You may recollect once sending me to Toulouse on covert surveillance. Océane Poulain was a musical prodigy of Reed Baratolli' s when she was about 15 years old. She had a couple of hits, and then she suddenly vanished from the music scene around about the same time as Reed nose-dived into oblivion. Hey, maybe she sold enough records to afford Hades Hall legitimately, although even I have my doubts about that. My concern relates more to her mother, or certainly the female who claims to be her mother.'

Simon then swiped the screen of his iPad to reveal another image. Mercy took the iPad from him and sat down. She looked long and hard at the photo. Simon could not read her reaction. She looked more sad than angry. Eventually she spoke.

'Emmanuelle – the demoness. She was the bitch that almost killed me. She was the fiend that gave my father…your grandfather a bloody stroke. She is clever, beautiful, and dangerous. I hate her. Does Clarah Lee connect with her in any other way?'

Simon answered, 'we found that someone took Clarah's American Express Centurion card, and went on a shopping binge with it. We have identified transactions in York and Leeds. None of the sales assistants can recall seeing someone of Clarah's description. Some of them do recall a young woman splurging out on an array of very expensive outfits, but describe her as a dark-haired goth type person. We also traced the online flight booking from Manchester to Bangkok. Zac managed to hack into the travel agencies server and locate the email IP address. The booking was done from Hades hall. The manager denies that Clarah ever stayed there. She wasn't even registered onto their computer system for some reason, and yet we can tell from other online transactions that she was there. I mean, why would they find the need lie about such a thing?'

'Hades Hall sounds like a nest of demons,' responded Mercy. 'I guess the clue is in the name. It sounds to me that they had their claws stuck into Clarah from the minute she left the safety of the Gypsy camp.'

Simon shrugged his shoulders.

'I am sorry that SiDeVe let her down aunty. We tried our best we really did. For a small company like ours, it was just a massive geographical challenge. She was either hiking up a mountain, waddling through a paddy field, swinging through a jungle, sunbathing on a beach, swimming in some tropical sea or galloping through the Australian outback. We could only track her when she crossed a border, submitted her passport, or spent money on her cards. Honestly, in hindsight…if we had known she was connected to the whole line of Tamar thing, I would have called you sooner. There was just no reason to make the connection. I feel so bad about this now.'

Mercy looked at her watch – it was 5pm. She poured herself and her nephew a glass of champagne from the chiller. Handing him a crystal flute of bubbles, she commented, 'don't beat yourself up Simon. You are not the first detective to have let down a client. I let Eenayah Baratolli down big time, so trust me…I have trodden this weary path of regret before you. If these demons have some interest in Clarah, then they must have some motivation driving their interest. These creatures never do anything for nothing. Emmanuelle is a beast in sheep's clothing.

Although I am retired, I also have an interest in Emmanuelle…possibly because she nearly destroyed me and no human has ever come remotely close to doing that. I am proud to say, it took the likes of a mighty demon to bring me to my knees, and even then…I survived.'

Simon was flicking through the photos on his iPad…listening to Mercy and yet distracted by some random thoughts.

'So Océane of Hades Hall, is the French girl that was contracted to Reeds music label? She is Emmanuelle's daughter? Am I correct?'

Mercy topped up her champagne flute and commented, 'as far as I am aware, Emmanuelle only had one natural born bone-fide daughter, and Océane was not that child. If my memory serves me right, we could not find any history about Emmanuelle's legitimate offspring. No hospital or school attendances. No friends, no gym membership. None of the normal activities and associations one would expect of a teenager. As for Océane, she was probably the name given to some corpse that Emmanuelle resurrected back to life. That is how the bitch acquires her human servants. Océane isn't human, but neither is she some brainless zombie creature. She is most likely a very clever demon living inside human skin and being controlled by an even smarter demon. Simon dearest; I believe we have concluded that Emmanuelle and Océane are interested in Clarah because she is a clone…but I am innately curious to know why the hell Reed B is tied up in all of this…yet again. This is like history repeating itself.'

She peered at her nephew over the rising effervescence from her glass.

'Tread with care Simon. I would share certain information with Reed, but also try to find out how much he knows. I am just interested…nothing more than that. Just curious.'

Simon simply nodded. He could read his cunning aunt like a book.

'Sure – if he asks I will tell him. I was just naturally concerned about becoming involved. As you said, Emmanuelle nearly killed you and my grandfather. I know what the Baratolli case did to you aunty. Remember that I was working for MeDeVe when all of that weird crap happened. It has sort of…put me off. I am not sure I want to take on Reed's work. I am tempted to tell him what I know and then just walk away.'

Mercy stroked her nephew's hair softly.

'We have a party to get ready for Simon. We can discuss the intricacies of next steps some other time. For now, I just have this to say. Bernice and Ennis MacDonald were lovely people – salt of the earth honest souls. I feel very sorry for Clarah, especially now I know that she is their niece. It may be too late to protect her, but if you need to do anything to protect them – please just do it. Yes, it may be risky, but you are the CEO of a company Simon. You need to bring work into SiDeVe Investigations Ltd because you have overheads and wages to pay. You cannot just run away from a case because a big bad demon says BOO…but promise me you will be careful. Come on – lets drink up. After all, somewhere in the world its 5 o-clock and right now Simon- that place is now and its here.'

Simon was disheartened with his aunt's response. He was privately hoping that she would support him in his decision to drop the case. He hadn't expected the opposite reaction. He had always suspected that somehow, someway…she still kept tabs on him. It would be difficult to disobey his aunt. He knew she would find out…she always seemed to find out everything. Even though SiDeVe was his company. (following

MeDeVe' s demise), he couldn't help but treat his aunt as though she was still his boss.

As he followed Mercy down the garland laden staircase, he couldn't help but mutter under his breath. Despite the promise of mannele, he was far from happy. He knew only too well that he was treading through deep, dark, shark infested waters. He was filled with dread.

CHAPTER 20

Monday 7th December 2015
PATHWAYS PRISON - IN SEARCH OF A FATHER

The outside of the building was grim and Victorian. It reminded Clarah of a Dickensian workhouse. The image that met her eyes was framed by the gloomiest of rainy days. She could easily imagine the misery, poverty and starvation of pauper children in the industrial north... yet this was not a poorhouse. Neither was this the 19th century—this was a 21st century prison in the middle of Manchester.

Clarah had obeyed Aura's instructions and focused on a picture she had found on the web. Whoosh - suddenly she was there. From Whitby to Manchester within a millisecond. It was the first time that Clarah had ventured into the outside world, yet she found it surprisingly easy. If anything, the ease of mind-travel was disturbingly simple. If this was so effortless, what else was she capable of doing? The question seemed too immense to consider. In her own mind, she was just a humble caravan girl and until now...nobody very special, or so she had believed. She only knew that none of this was normal. She wasn't dead, and yet her body and soul had become separated. How far from normal could this spiritual explorer wander?

Clarah stood invisible in the centre of the spiral exercise yard. As a traveller, she had experienced many shades of grim, yet this was possibly the worst. It wasn't just the bleak location, but the hopelessness of the lost souls trapped within the spiral. Inmates walked around and around in a meaningless circle. She could hear them curse and swear as they uttered total garbage. They sucked on hand rolled cigarettes and coughed incessantly as the cold damp air inflated tar filled lungs. It reminded Clarah of the brown mountain of limbo.

She had begun to believe that maybe just maybe, such a place did exist within another realm. A place torn from the world of Dante's Inferno…floating between heaven and hell. Yet this wasn't in another realm – it was here. Her memory had been shaken and stirred and the truth glared her in the face like a bogeyman in the night. The circular path from nowhere going to nowhere was in the here and now. The brown mountain was at Pathways prison. Had she been here before? She must have been here before. Why would she have remembered it otherwise. Perhaps she had not just vaulted over miles of fixed terrain, but possibly through time itself.

Clarah was confused. She looked up to the sky to feel the rain droplets on her face. Perhaps the tiny polluted smidgeons of water could convince her that she was real, although she knew the wet sensation was a mere illusion. She was nothing more than energy. She only felt what she thought she should feel.

As she looked up to the Manchester skies, she watched as drones openly delivered drugs to the inmates. Clarah could not believe that the guards had failed to notice the drug drops. It was all so obvious. One man punched another in a battle to retrieve the drop. Within minutes a fight had broken out. Clarah had seen many a campsite fist fight so none of this phased her, yet to witness it within the confines of a custodial building came as a shock. The guards looked the other way. Battle weary, they had witnessed this scene many times before.

She wandered inside, unchallenged by the thick stone walls. She saw prisoners making weapons that they called shivs. She observed an inmate as he pushed two razor blades into a toothbrush. She could only imagine his twisted reasons for creating such a weapon. It was an object that could shear skin – pushing it apart to reveal the underlying muscle, veins and tendons. It was an innocent looking toothbrush, yet one that only existed to create pain, suffering and a river of blood. She felt sick.

The smell of stale sweat and the ketonic odour of alcohol withdrawal saturated the atmosphere. Pumped up male testosterone snaked down the inner walkways like a serpent. It licked at each of the closed cell doors, mocking those confined within. Clarah walked unseen within the confines of the angry walls. She hated the place, yet she had to find her father. She crouched down in a shadowy corner, trying to avoid the stained remnants of ancient vomit. She pictured her father's face. She clearly saw his tanned skin; weather beaten and leathery. His hair was a mass of thick dark curls, kissed by subtle shades of grey. His eyes – green on the inside and hazel on the perimeter. His hands were huge. Her mother always called them farmers hands. They were like shovels…that's what her mother used to say.

Aura had instructed her that all she ever needed to do was just think. Her thoughts were powerful, they were her vehicle…her magic carpet into any place, any time. She just needed to focus. She mumbled to herself, 'where are you Da'?

A dark figure squatted down beside her. It came from out of nowhere and it could see her. It knew she was there. What was it? She could not make out its features. A black smoky mist seemed to envelop it.

'What are you? Who are you?'

The thing laughed at her. She couldn't hear it, but she knew it was taunting her.

'Who am I indeed? Have you forgotten me so soon?'

She recognised the voice. It was young, male and disdainfully patronising. The accent was from deepest darkest Yorkshire with a hint of Irish. The veil of mist started to clear, and she was horrified by the image that pixilated into view. She gasped, 'Paddy.'

'Aye Paddy. That's who I am lass. I am Peter's younger brother. You remember Peter don't you. He married Katalyn…that two-timing slut of a sister of yours. Your shite father killed me and it's all your fault. I was trying to get your fuckin sister down from the tree. I was trying to rescue her, but you told him I was the one who strung her up. I had to beg him not to kill me. I went down on my knees in the crappy mud and bloody pleaded for my life. I told him that I didn't touch Nina, but he didn't believe me. Sweet little Clarah would never tell him a fib. He almost knocked my fuckin brains out. He nearly killed my other brothers as well. Why did you lie to him Clarah? Why did you do that?'

Clarah was frozen to the spot. With tears rolling down her cheeks she mumbled, 'I made a mistake. I am sorry Paddy. I had no idea that my Da hurt you so badly, bad enough to kill you. I am sorry…. I saw you…I saw you…I just thought…'

'You thought wrong, bitch. You took my life away.'

'I am sorry. It was a mistake. I am just here to see my Da.'

'Oh yes and so you are. Your timing is spot on as usual. Let me take you to his cell. Let's have a nice family reunion.'

With that Paddy became shrouded in the black mist yet again. Some part of him…perhaps his hand, grabbed hold of her arm and before she knew it she was flying through the air. They soared over the criss-cross metal barriers, over the central dome, and straight into a cell on the opposite side.

The body was still swinging. The head was cocked to one side as though the neck may have been broken. The hands…those big farmers hands, swung loosely by his side. Hands still warm, and not yet blue. A makeshift noose had been created from his leather belt and prison trousers. His eyes were closed. His face bore no expression. It was blank, like a crumpled sheet of paper, but one with all the writing erased. Letters rubbed out one after the other, until nothing remained. Until nothing was left to live for. All gone.

Clarah screamed, 'Da, Da – no. This cannot be. Paddy pull him down. Help me Paddy, pull him down.'

Paddy shrugged.

'The last time I pulled a bloody person down it got me into heaps of trouble. No way, I'm not helping him.'

Clarah thought she saw his hands twitch.

'He is still alive. I need to get help. I don't know how to do this.'

She zapped herself through the cell walls and went in search of a guard. She saw a man in uniform. He was leaning on the metal barriers and looking down at the floors below. How could she become visible? Aura told her that if she thought about it, she could appear to be as real as any other person. Desperate to help her hanging father, she squeezed her eyes shut.

'See me, see me, see me…please just see me.'

The guard almost collapsed, 'how did you get in here? How the hell…'

'Never mind that. You need to come with me.'

She grabbed hold of the guard's arm, and with just a thought and nothing more. they were both inside the cell. No doors needed to be unlocked.

'Cut him down, cut him down now. I think there may be a chance to save him.'

Aura appeared inside the cell. She looked up and watched as the guard climbed up on the chair; the same chair Mick Lee had used in his suicide attempt.

Kane also stood in the corner, watching the dreadful scene unfold with a degree of sick curiosity.

'Clarah, your maiden flight into the outside world was not what I would have anticipated. However, I guess that you needed to be here at this very moment. There is an air of fate about your timely intervention, but I need to take you away from here right now. It is dangerous to stay in such a place. Come with me.'

***

'Oh my God – what just happened?

Aura shot her a look of disapproval.

'Well my little human, you are safely back home in your kitchen now but what just happened was not so impressive. You lost your focus and I did warn you that when travelling on the spirit wind, you need to concentrate on the task in hand. Your thoughts can take you to places, but they can also bring other lost spirits into your domain. Some of these spirits are not exactly cardigan wearing Sunday school teachers.'

'I am sorry Aura. I have never been into a prison before and I got distracted by the people and the place and the terrible way they live. The drugs, the violence, the smell, the noise– you could cut the tension in the air with a knife. My thoughts just got lost.'

'Yes, they did. You focussed on the negative aspects of prison life and suddenly you had troubled spirits for company. Think hopeless and you get hopeless. Paddy is a vexed soul. He hates you and your family. Kane is a troubled soul. He knows he is mostly responsible for Nina's death and that knowledge will torment him for eternity. Clarah, you need to keep your mind clean, pure and positive or otherwise the vexed and the troubled will come knocking on your door.'

'Did my Da live? Did the prison guard pull him down in time?

'Officer Sam Drummond did a fine job. Your father is alive, but I am sorry to say that he did brake his neck. He will be paralysed from now on. His life has just taken another turn for the worst. I am sorry.'

Tears fell down Clarah's cheeks.

'Oh, the wretched curse of begrudgery. It plagues our family. When will it ever go away? Have we not suffered enough already?'

Aura felt sincere sympathy for her young student and hugged the shaking girl as she sobbed. She brushed Clarah's hair away from the stream of tears meandering down her face.

'Time is a strange thing,' she told her. 'In my sphere of existence there is no such thing as time, but I can see how important timing is in a world that does live by the clock. A few minutes less spent in the exercise yard and perhaps you could have stopped your father from making that noose. A few minutes later inside his cell, and maybe he would have died. As it stands, he is alive and paralysed from the neck down.'

Clarah was shocked by the harshness of Aura's words. The truth was delivered in such a matter-of-fact way.

'You make it sound like his fate was my fault.'

'Well dear, so sorry to be the harbinger of doom, but in all honesty, it probably was. How would you like me to dress it up? Should I pipe some icing on the cake?'

'Nicer – just a bit nicer. You could have made it fluffy and less offensive.'

'Sorry but truth is truth. I will try to knit it a woolly hat next time. Hey and you haven't even asked about the prison guard. I mean, some random ghost appeared from out of nowhere, whooshed him through walls and commanded him to take down a hanging man. How do you think he must be feeling right now?'

'I don't care?'

'Well you should care. You have abilities Clarah, powerful abilities that are unique to you. No other human can do what you can do. Escaping a living body was a freak accident and one that should have never happened. Every time you invade time or space, you can create change. You need to think more carefully about what you are doing.'

'Okay, so how is the guard? Will he be okay?'

It was a reluctant question.

'No, he will not be okay. He will become the laughing stock of the prison service. The more he repeats his unlikely story, the more his colleagues will poke fun at him. He will be put on sick leave and sent for psychological assessment. He will never return to his old job, but his brother Jack Drummond will find him employment somewhere else and he will find contentment with a new career. He wasn't happy as a prison guard anyway, so for Sam the change will be for the best.'

Clarah was hardly listening. Instead her mind was focused on Aura's earlier statement…she could invade time and space.'

'I've got it,' she proclaimed. 'I will go back to the prison as it was this morning. I will visit my father in his cell and get him out of there before he does what he did. That way he doesn't feel so hopeless and won't attempt suicide. I can go back in time and make everything alright.'

Aura smiled sweetly. She really did have the most wonderful of smiles. It lit up her entire face like a celestial beam from a star.

'I was wondering when you would figure that one out Clarah. Yes indeed, you can travel back in time. You are an outlier – a free spirit. You do not operate within the constraints of a shipping lane. There are no rules in Clarah's kingdom. However, understand this, when you change one thing, you also change many other things. Like…Sam Drummond; the young guard who helped your father. His life would have changed after seeing you. But if today never happened, Sam Drummond will stay as he was. He hates his job, but he will keep doing it because nothing has spurred him into doing otherwise. He will become stressed, become an alcoholic and his wife will divorce him. The children that they were meant to have, will never be born. Think carefully Clarah, with great power comes great responsibility.'

With those final words, Aura vanished.

Clarah had much to consider. Today had been a strange day. Every day from now on, was a strange day.

Round and round the brown mountain – she was caught in a spiral every bit as hopeless as the ones the prisoners walked.

CHAPTER 21

Monday 1st February 2016
SI-DE-VE PRIVATE INVESTIGATIONS - LONDON

Central London - just off Fleet Street and hidden at the end of a shaded cobbled alleyway, was an unpresumptuous office building. Its slate roof was bowing and the timber frame had been punctured by woodworm, yet this remnant from the past blended in with an altogether more modern London skyscape. Rebuilt after the great fire, the proud name of SiDeVe Ltd swung from a sign over the door. On a windy day, the sign creaked and whipped up images of Samuel Pepys or Dr. Samuel Johnson as they made their way to the inn opposite for a mug of sweetened warm ale with a dollop of nutmeg. It is said that one of Jack The Ripper's victims; Mary Jane Kelly, was a visitor to the same inn.

Simon De Vede was a young guy in his 20's, and so he embraced the vibe of the London lifestyle. On a Friday after work, on many a summer's eve, he loved nothing more than to stand outside the many pubs and wine bars with all the Fleet Street journalists and join in with their banter. It was an expensive location for offices and his aunt Mercy had warned him against the move from Oxford, but perhaps Simon wanted to make his own stamp on his own company – so he dismissed her advice with the know-it-all arrogance of youth.

Simon had a new recruit starting today. He wasn't sure if another pair of hands fell within his tight budget, but JD had persuaded him to hire his brother. Simon didn't want to lose a talented guy such as JD, and so he caved in to the request.

Although marketing themselves as an investigation company, many of their recent contracts had been more aligned to personal protection. As an ex-SAS soldier, JD was in heavy demand and Simon could do with another JD type of employee. He had been assured that ex-prison guard Sam Drummond, was that very person. With that very thought still lingering on his mind, his office door opened and in walked JD with his brother.

'Don't you ever knock?'

'Coffee?'

'Yep in the corner. Get one for me while you are at it.'

Simon stood and shook his new recruits hand.

'I presume you must be Sam. I am Simon De Vede, please take a seat.'

For such a tall muscular man, Sam looked uncomfortably nervous.

'I take it that you are an ex-soldier like your bro?'

'Yep.'

'This isn't an interview Sam. At the end of the day I need another JD. Jack Drummond is my top man and whatever he wants, he usually gets. Don't ever tell him I have paid him a compliment, but if you are even half the man your brother is, you will do well at SiDeVe.'

'Too late. Heard you. Feeling the love Simon. Milk no sugar?'

JD was like a peacock pruning his feathers. He beamed from ear to ear as he placed a couple of coffee cups on the table before his boss and his brother. He sat down to join the conversation.

Simon continued, 'did JD explain that you will be earning less money here and we don't have any work pensions in place. Financially this will be a backward step for you Sam. I take it you are married and have a mortgage and bills to pay?'

Sam was apprehensive, but believed the truth to be the better path to walk.

'Yes, married just over 6 months, and yes, I tick all the other boxes as well, but I also value happiness and sanity above money. I hated being a prison guard. I know what JD does for you and I want a slice of that cake. The job sounds interesting.'

Simon took a sip of his coffee and smiled sympathetically at his newest employee.

'I take it that you had a strange experience at Pathways?'

'I don't really want to talk about it… if that's okay.'

'Yeh, that's fine. I wasn't about to judge you anyway. If anything, your bizarre little experience could be an advantage. Over the years this company, both when it was run by my Aunt Mercy and then by me, has investigated some really weird stuff. We have specialised in many cases that the police couldn't crack; mainly because such cases involved secret cults and other such mysterious happenings. We prefer our employees to have an open mind to such things. A closed mind is dangerous in our line of work. You can't do this job with your eyes shut. So…would you say you have an open mind Sam?'

'JD told me about the Baratolli case. I am aware that you work on some strange oddities. Trust me, I am sure I will fit like a hand in a glove. Mr De Vede…after what happened to me a couple of months back…let's just say that my mind is as open to anything and everything.'

'Good, very pleased to hear it Sam and please call me Simon. So, without further ado, let's launch you in at the deep end. I have a meeting at 10.30am and it's one I would like you to be involved with. You have just told me that JD has already brought you up to speed with the Baratolli case. That's a good thing as it will save me a lot of time. It was a complex situation and it destroyed my aunt's company, but now some of it has come back to haunt us.'

'Sound's fascinating.'

Sam edged nearer to Simon, eager to hear the story. He already felt at ease with his new career.

'Reed Baratolli - now known as Tony Mort from the renowned VOT's charity franchise, is sending a representative to come and visit us. Our visitor is Dr Frank O'Byrne. He is an ex-priest, ex-theology teacher and an old friend of my grandfather, Professor De Vede. He is a nice guy, with a personality larger than life itself. You will like him.'

'Why isn't Reed coming over in person?

'I am told that Reed hardly leaves New York these days. He has shunned his former life and if you know some of the man's history, you will understand why.'

'What JD didn't tell me, I have read about in the newspapers anyway…so yes, I get it.'

'Well in that case, I will hand you over to Kerry to cover off all the HR stuff. Kerry is my PA, receptionist and fixer of all things. She will show you around the place and introduce you to the rest of the team. If you can get back here for about quarter past, we can prep for our meeting. Welcome aboard Sam. Hope you will be happy with SiDeVe. I like to think that we are a good team.'

With that, Kerry took Sam by the hand and walked him out into the high-tech backrooms; a star-trek setup which defied the character of the rickety old building.

***

Frank O'Byrne was punctual as usual. He gave Simon a warm hug. Frank adored seeing his best friend's grandson and didn't hold back from openly showing his pride and affection for the young lad. Trying to impress his new recruit, Simon tried to remain professional and kept his distance.

'So, what brings you to London Frank? I believe you are quite the international jet-setter these days?'

Frank giggled at the mere thought of meeting that description in his winter years of life.

'Well, since you ask…we are opening a new VOT's camp a few miles up the road. Bagging London has long been my dream and now a charitable donation has made it all possible.'

Frank could hardly contain the look of victory that shone from his rotund face.

'Congratulations. I am not the biggest fan of Reed Baratolli, but I am in awe of what he has achieved with his charity work. On another subject, what else brings you to my offices?'

Frank was slightly taken aback by the directness of the question, but he had noticed the newbie sat in the corner, and soon figured out that Simon was keen to assert his authority.

'Tony…erm I mean Reed, asked me to come and see you. I am sorry but I only know Tony to be Tony and it came as quite a shock to discover his real identity. One can go through years hating the thought of a person, but then to find out that the person you thought you hated, is someone you work with, and also someone you like and admire…well, it sort of throws the whole hate situation up into the air. I guess it's the same with soldiers who fight a war, and then have to face the human they just tried to kill…somebody's son, brother, nephew, husband…all just flesh and blood. Bloody hell, I am a former priest and I shouldn't really say this, but sometimes it's easier to just carry on hating. It stops us from having to question our own morals.'

Frank had drifted off into a world of his own, looking down to the floor and obviously doubting his own ethics and integrity. Simon tried to pull him back.

'Here's the situation Frank, Reed aka Tony, contacted me by email and asked if I would investigate a young woman by the name of Clarah Lee. I was concerned about a conflict of interest. Clarah went missing back in July 2014 and her family hired us to find her. We did, and she came back home about 5 months ago. Now, you are sat here in my office as Reeds deputy…but I am not exactly sure how I can help.

Frank pulled out some photographs from his briefcase, and started to explain.

'These are photographs of Clarah with a young lad called Konnor – that's Reeds youngest son. She was with him and a group of other kids in Bali. Reed has asked if you could find where out she is now.'

Simon glanced at the photos and placed them on the table in front of Sam. The new recruit said nothing, but his face went ashen.

'Please deliver this news back to Reed. Regrettably Clarah Lee suffered a blood clot on the flight back to Manchester. She is in hospital and she is in a coma. I understand that her condition is chronic. She is in PVS, that is a persistent vegetative state. I think I can understand Reed's concerns about the girl. He is a smart guy and I am sure by now that he will have figured out that she is a Tamar clone. However, in her present condition she can pose no threat to his son. I am sure that this news will give him some reassurance.'

Frank was shocked into a moment of silence.

'Oh – this is not what I expected you to say Simon. Not at all what I expected. I guess there isn't much else we can discuss about the subject. I mean - what of Clarah's twin sister? I am presuming that she must have a twin. Couldn't she be the clone?'

'Poor Nina…hell no. She died not long after Clarah ran away on her backpacking adventure. So, you see Frank, this branch of the line of Tamar has been closed down. The demons won the day and the Lee line has been expired. Clarah is no more, or should I say, of no more threat.'

Frank stood up, still shaking his head in disbelief.

'Well, I will let Reed know. I guess it's up to him as to how he shares this information with his son. What of your grandfather? Can I visit my old friend Roland?'

'Sorry but that isn't my decision Frank. I will ask but I expect the answer to be a resounding no. He picks up any infection going and so the family try to keep him as germ free as possible, and that means minimal visitors. Plus, he has dementia. I am sorry Frank, but I doubt he would even know who you are.'

Frank took a handkerchief from his coat breast pocket. He dabbed the corner of his eyelid.

'Sorry, just got a speck of dust bothering me. Erm…you will still ask, won't you Simon…please.'

Simon stood up to shake the old gents hand.

'Yes of course I will ask. I have your number.'

As Frank left the office, Simon turned around to see Sam Drummond looking pale and deeply worried.

'You look like you have seen a ghost lad. Are you okay mate?'

Sam pointed to the photographs which Frank had accidentally left on the table.

'I know this woman. I know her father. I know her granny. I don't think she is quite as comatose as you believe her to be.'

He had caught Simons attention. A severely sombre look was forged into the young man's frown lines. He suddenly looked older than his 25 years.

'Sam, this is important. You need to tell me what you know. It doesn't matter how ridiculous it may sound.'

Sam paused. This incident made him the laughing stock of Pathways prison. He had presumed that by leaving the place he had left the history of his employment behind – but no, it had followed him. He hesitated.

'Sam, please. In this job, I have had to battle demons. As weird as it may sound to the rest of the population going about their daily lives, I know that this stuff exists. You say you know Clarah and her family. How?'

Sam relented, but with reluctance.

'Her father Mick Lee was in prison for manslaughter. The only visitor he had was a little old lady called Baba May. I saw her once. Sweet old dear. Poor thing looked exhausted and besides herself with worry. Anyway, back in December, Mick tried to hang himself. I was on the upper corridor. Shit...have you got a glass of water Simon?'

Simon poured him a glass from the water cooler.

'It's okay Sam – go on. What happened next?'

'This face. It was the same face as on the photographs, although the hair was a little different. The face came right up to mine. Maybe there was an inch between us. It was as real and as physical as your face is now. The look – my God the expression on the face…it was horrified. I would say in a state of panic. This thing – it grabbed my arm. Those cell walls are solid Simon. Honestly, they are several feet thick, but we just went through it as though it wasn't even there. I saw Mick Lee hanging from the ceiling. I just got this instruction yelled at me. I was told to cut him down. I just went into auto pilot and did as I was told. I tried to resuscitate him. I didn't look around for ages, but when I did the woman had gone. The cell door was still bolted; locked from the outside. Hell, I was trapped in there myself and had to radio for help.'

'Shit.' It was about the only word Simon could utter.

Sam continued, 'I didn't know who the woman was, but I do now. It was the person in that photograph, it was Clarah Lee. I am an atheist Simon. Your mate Frank O'Byrne was right about the soldiers in a war. Sometimes you have to switch a part of you off, so you become less human. I switched God off. I couldn't operate with a conscience sat on my shoulder. I believed in nothing, but I believe in what I saw that day. Clarah may be in some hospital in a coma, but her spirit isn't. It's out there, and she looks as real as any other person. I don't know how she has done it, but she has.'

Simon thought for a moment and then said, 'well, I guess in the army they teach you to face your fears. So, I am asking you to face yours Sam. Your first assignment is to find Clarah Lee. Find any family she has left. Try to get to the bottom of all this. As much as I despise the man, I should let Reed know.'

'What? Do you actually believe me?

'You have your first assignment Sam. I wouldn't give you the job if I doubted your story. Whatever happened to you caused you to quit your job. That all sounds fairly real to me, but if you have changed your mind, hey most things in life have a reverse gear. The door is just behind you.'

'Thanks Simon and thanks for the offer, but I won't be hitting the reverse gear any time soon.'

On that note, Simon winked, gave him a thumbs up sign and left the room. Sam Drummond had been assigned first posting - to find Clarah Lee. He couldn't believe the ironic twist of fate – that the person who caused him to quit his job was the person he now had to confront.

CHAPTER 22

Sunday 14th February 2016
VALENTINE ROSES

For one so young, Clarah felt as though she had lived for an awfully long time. She often wasted her surplus minutes watching daytime TV and consuming a copious number of calories. She felt perfectly at ease feeding the energy of her spirit, in the smug knowledge that none of the food was being sucked into her fat cells. She had no cellulite to worry about, after all she had no body. Yet no matter how hard she tried, she could not get it into her head that she was a soul adrift from its fleshly parts. It was all too strange, yet it was a condition that had its advantages.

She lay draped across the settee like a wearied Greek goddess. All she required to complete her fantasy, was a bunch of ripe grapes and a hunky Adonis. She idly watched as Nina played a game of Gin Rummy with her Aunt Mary. Nina was winning. Despite her twin's obvious lack of mental capacity, Nina could be wiser, shrewder and more astute than any card shark anywhere. It was so sweet…watching Nina smile again, especially after all she had been through.

For once Kane was clean, and sober. She presumed that her Baba May must have given the boy a good talking to. He sat reading the paper, studying the racing form for the 3.20 at Southwell. He was muttering something about a horse called "Hoofalong". Nobody took much notice. Kane was addicted to the horses, and as the family considered this the safer of his addictions, they let him get on with it.

She could hear her mother Violet singing in the kitchen as she made mamaliga, a form of unleavened corn bread. The aroma of mushroom and hazelnut pie came from the kitchen. It may not have been top cuisine to a gaje, but to travellers living from the hedgerow, it was comfort food. For Clarah, this was the safety blanket of her childhood. But was it one she was creating in her own mind? After all, what she thought, usually became. As that deliberation swirled around inside her head, she began to realise that she didn't know if she was living in a house of ghosts, or manufacturing a cosy scenario just because she could. She pulled herself up from the settee and went in search of the only actual living person (as far as she knew) - Baba May.

Baba May was busy brewing a fresh pot of cuckoo tea and seemed to have a permanent grin on her face. Clarah understood. Why shouldn't her grandmother be happy? It seemed that in her Romany wizardry she had surrounded herself by her family; her grandson, both her granddaughters and now both her own daughters. Ironically all the millions in the bank now meant nothing to this family of ghosts. Hers must surely be the strangest of families, and one which had recently expanded.

The materialization of her father Mick had shocked Clarah the most. Shocked, and yet pleased her. She knew that his broken body had resided in the next bay to hers, coincidentally both in the same intensive care unit. The coincidence had amazed her, yet Baba May had always told her there was no such thing. Baba May believed in fate, but then again, she read the Tarot cards for money, so the concept of destiny was a sales pitch to her customers.

Clarah watched her beloved Da as he sipped his mother-in-law's strange concoction. It amused her to think that these ghosts did not see themselves as dead. She could not explain it to the living people. They wouldn't understand.

Clarah was pleased that her father had been spared his time in prison and of course the greater prison of all - paralysis. His broken neck had virtually disconnected his head from every nerve below his throat. She now so wished she had not asked the guard to pull him down. The guard- oh yes, the man Aura had given her a complete guilt trip about. The guard whose future happiness she had to spare by not going back in time just a few moments earlier. She did as was told, and because of it her father had died. Or had he? Looking over at the tanned muscular man who raised her... the tinker with the kindest of eyes and big spades for hands, she had never seen him look so alive. A song came to mind. *'With his sparse witty talk, he was cock of the walk, as he rolled the dames under and over. They all knew at a glance when he took up his stance that he sailed in the Irish Rover.'*

She smiled to herself. That was her Da – the ultimate Irish rover.

Her moment of quiet contemplation was interrupted when Baba May appeared in the kitchen with a huge bouquet of red roses. She thrust them into her granddaughter's arms, 'they are for you.' Clarah was naturally stunned. She read the card. 'Remember me. Happy Valentine's day – love Konnor xx.'

Clarah fell into the chair conveniently waiting behind her. She sniffed the blood red flowers and caressed their petals.

'Oh, Baba May. Konnor has found me. He knows where I live, but he doesn't know what I have become.'

Baba May took the bouquet from her. A thorn had pricked Clarah's finger, yet no blood came from the open sore. Clarah rubbed the scratch, all too aware that she hadn't bled. It crystallised the thought – she had no blood to bleed.

'They are beautiful. I will put these in water for you child. However, that boy you refer to…Konnor, well he is here.'

'Where?'

'He came to the door. I sent him out to the back. I thought you may need some time to compose yourself – you know, make yourself visible to mortal eyes. You need to be honest with him love. He won't believe you, but still…you should try to explain.'

Konnor walked around the side of the big white house and wandered into the coppice. Although February and technically still winter, it was a fine dry day. The sun was low in the sky and cast strange shadows against the trees. The sky itself was the deepest blue, marred with just the occasional smudge of white fluff. The young American sat upon a little mound of earth and looked out to sea. He liked the peace of the place. It was calm and welcoming. Only the sound of woodpigeons and the distant splashing of water on rocks, disturbed its gentle tranquillity.

Then, out of nowhere a wind picked up and shook the trees above his head. The sudden gust blew up the last remnants of autumns discarded leaves and carved them into a tiny tornado. From out of the oranges and browns of this funnel, walked a young woman. Her hair was the same colour as the leaves, and each melted one into the other. She was wearing a white lace nightgown which was almost translucent. She had placed one of Konnor's roses behind her ear. Konnor gasped. She was like a surreal vision. She held out her hands as she walked towards him. They kissed.

'Konnor, how did you find me? What are you doing here?'

He stroked her long auburn hair. It looked different. He had remembered her with blond braids.

'Your hair – it suits you.'

'Well, this is actually my natural colour.'

'Yes, I figured that much.'

As the sun caught her face and highlighted her features, he could now see the resemblance to his step-mother Eenayah. He now knew that all he had been told about Clarah, about her being a Tamar clone - was true. He hadn't believed it at first, but now…

'Clarah you don't need to explain anything to me. My father hired some detective company and what they told us was mad – I mean completely bonkers…just unbelievable. I couldn't get my head around it. Then Dad sat me down and told me more, so much more. He explained what happened to my step mom, and why he was concerned for me…and for Asher. Look…I don't care what happened between you and Ash. If anything did happen I am guessing that he just took advantage of you anyway. My brother can be a shite.'

Clarah didn't know what to do or say. Honesty wasn't always the best policy. Once upon her time she told her Da a tale and it ended up with 4 boys in hospital. Paddy later died from his injuries, and her Da was found guilty of manslaughter. At the time, she hadn't fully understood the velocity of a man's anger. Yet Konnor was different. He was a gentle soul. Should she tell him the truth?

'Konnor, I am sorry to tell you this, but I was pregnant. It was your brothers baby. I hated Ash. He always ridiculed me and looked down upon me as though I was trailer trash. Work it out Konnor. How do you suppose a woman could get pregnant by a man she can't even abide?'

Konnor face went pale. His eyes looked directly into hers as though piercing her very spirit with a knife.

'He raped you?'

'He was drunk. He is a big guy. He was strong. If you ask him he will deny it, but Romany girls don't sleep around. It isn't in our nature.'

Konnor looked down on the ground and shook his head in disbelief.

'The bastard. I suspected as much.'

'Don't be angry Kon. The past is past. It's gone so let it go.'

'I visited you in hospital Clarah. This detective chap took me to see you. Sam Drummond…nice guy. He told me all about you, and how your father tried to hang himself. I know the truth about you Clarah. The doctors have involved the police. They believe that your blood clot – well, maybe it wasn't an accident after all.'

For a moment Clarah went deathly quiet. She could hardly believe that Konnor knew the truth and yet he was here. He had not forgotten her. Eventually she replied.

'I know. I visited myself. I can travel anywhere these days Konnor. No walls can contain me. Even time cannot contain me. I am not dead. I am not a ghost. I can be real, just as I am now. However, I can also just exist as energy and do pretty much as I please. I overhead the doctor looking after me. He was speaking with someone on the phone. He was talking about some test results. He thought someone had given me some medications that had caused the blood clot.'

'Who would do that?'

'I don't know…who would want me dead.'

'The demons,' replied Konnor.

'When my father explained about Eenayah, he told me she was from the line of Tamar. He said that there were demons who would do anything to end the line, and that means preventing future clones from being born. You do know that you are also from the line of Tamar, don't you?'

'Oh yes, I had that all figured out. When invisible one gets to be a fly on the wall. Sam Drummond - the guy who took you to visit me, well he was the prison guard who I saved from the fate of career unhappiness. He seems to talk about me a lot and I have been listening over his shoulder.'

'Is it always interesting, or just small talk?'

'I don't think the words small talk and Clarah Lee would ever appear in the same sentence. But it can get boring in Whitby sometimes and I like to visit folks…see what they are up to and all that. I have learned a lot about myself in the last few weeks and all from the lips of total strangers. What really blows my mind though, is that if I wanted to, I could go back in time and unravel everything in a micro second. I can change everything. I still can't get my head around that.'

'Bloody hell, you are more powerful than I realised Clarah. I am not even sure that you comprehend how awesomely powerful you are. If you can just go back in time and re-set the future, then why don't you go back and stop Asher from raping you?'

Clarah smiled and flicked a blond sun-kissed curl from out of Konnor's left eye, then kissing his concerned young brow.

'You don't understand Kon. With great power comes great responsibility. Anyway, that's what Aura has tried to teach me and don't ask me who or what Aura is. That's way too big of a conversation. You see, everything I alter in the past has repercussions for the future. Think about it…if I hadn't have become pregnant, perhaps the demons wouldn't have tried to kill me…if your theory is correct that is. So now my body wouldn't be in a coma in some hospital and I wouldn't be here in spirit right now.'

Konnor nodded, trying to keep pace with her train of thought. He was confused. Clarah continued…

'We had broken up back in Bali if you recall. We both accepted our time together as just a holiday romance. In that instance, your father probably wouldn't have become involved and wouldn't have hired the detectives and by the way Sam would still be a prison guard. Without Sam and the detectives, you wouldn't know where I lived or maybe even had a reason to find out. I wouldn't have the beautiful roses you have just given me, and instead they would be sat in another lucky woman's vase on Valentine's day. Instead – they are my roses in my vase, minus the one that's in my hair. That's how life works. Do you now understand how difficult this is for me? How I have to think everything through so very carefully.'

Konnor gulped. He understood, or at least he thought he did.

'Well oh well Miss Clarah Lee, you seem to have this all worked out. I don't know what to say. I have never thought about things like that before. This isn't exactly a normal conversation.'

'It's the good ol time paradox, 'responded Clarah.

'What?'

'Hill Valley High 1955 in the film "Back To The Future". It's all about the fabric of space-time continuum. I so loved that film. One of the greats…don't you think?'

'Yes. I agree. So okay, I think I get it now.'

'Changing the subject, what are you going to do Konnor? Now you are in England I mean. What are your plans?'

Yet again a gust of wind seemed to come from nowhere and rustle the branches of the tree's. It was as though they were not alone, as though other ears were listening.

'I am off to Wales to visit my family?'

'Oh- you never mentioned you had family in the UK.'

'I didn't? Oh…sorry about that. What did we talk about in Bali?'

'I don't think we did much talking Konnor.'

Konnor laughed, also blushing with embarrassment. He kissed her cheek. It was warm, and that confused him.

'Yes, I have an Aunt Ruby and Uncle Owyn and a young cousin called Harry. I also have grandparents from my step-moms side. They used to live in the Isle of Man, but then relocated to Wales to be with my aunt. I also want to visit the wonderful woman who brought me up. She cared for me when my Dad was away on tour, or my stepmom was doped up with sleeping tablets. What an angel? Her name is Roserie. She worked as a housemaid when we were in Miami, but she was more like a mother to me than a paid employee. She has now moved to the UK and looks after Harry. I haven't seen her in such a long time. We were all raised together alongside her own kids – Saul and Eve. We are all more or less the same age give or take a few years. God, we had so much fun back in the day. Not sure if Saul can be there, more's the pity. Of all things, he works as a magician now, even renamed himself as Soul. He was the entertainment at Armani's engagement and nobody even told me. I am gutted that I missed him. Anais may even pop over – she said she would try.'

'Wow, when you said you had family over here, I didn't think you had so many. Where do they all live? Not under one roof surely?'

'Yep, under one very big roof. I can hardly say the name. Darwydden – I probably pronounced that wrong. It's like some gothic manor house connected to a castle.'

'I know the name Roserie. It's an unusual name. Is your Roserie mortal?'

Konnor giggled like a 7-year-old and pinched her side in an infantile gesture.

'Don't be silly, she was our housemaid. Anyway, why don't you come over and join us? I would love to show you the place.'

Clarah pulled herself from the grassy mound replying, 'let me think about it. Come on, let's go inside. I want to introduce you to my Baba May. I need to know what she thinks about you. Oh, and yes, I would love to visit this Darwydden place. Just text me when the coast is clear – yes spirits can use technology… and I will be with you within a second.

With that they smiled, held hands and walked indoors. As reunions go, it was nice. Clarah was happy. The situation may have been unusual – unique even, yet all seemed very normal and quite pleasant. That apparent normality was about to change – and soon.

CHAPTER 23

Tuesday 16th February 2016
DARWYDDEN FAMILY REUNION

The journey from North Yorkshire to North Wales was gruelling, but for someone who lived in a place the size of the USA, a mere 5-hour drive was a walk in the park. Konnor had loved spending time with Clarah, but was equally as happy to vacate her possessed abode.

He couldn't see the unseen dwellers, yet he knew they were there. They would creep up on him and blow down his ear, tug on his shirt sleeves or tickle his ribs. Doors would slam and plates would fly through the air. Sometimes Clarah would laugh at some invisible gesture and then go suddenly quiet when she saw him watching. To Konnor, it seemed like a multitude of private jokes that came in waves, and yet the secret laughter excluded him. After all he was a gaje and he had a pulse. It was a double negative- he was the outsider. It unnerved the young American.

A house of ghosts would alarm the strongest of hearts, and his was not the strongest. His was the sad heart of a boy whose mother Julia had died when he was very young. A mother who had been unfaithful to his father. He knew Reed wasn't really his biological father, yet in all fairness to the millionaire music mogul, he had raised Konnor as one of his own. If anything, his father loved him more than his own biological offspring.

Konnor was aware that his half-brother Asher knew the truth and hated him for it. Konnor the bastard child, yet the child that everybody adored. Bouncy blonde hair, blue eyes, a cheeky smile and a wicked sense of humour – Konnor had it all, aside from his biological parents.

He thought about Clarah and what his brother had done to her. He knew that in all probability, it was his brother doing it to him. This was spite – pure spite and begrudgery. That was it. Ash begrudged him of all the affection showered upon him, and especially that coming from their shared father. Taking Clarah had been his way of saying – 'I can have anything that belongs to you.' That thought crushed him.

Clarah on the other hand, was a tough nut to crack and had simply shrugged it off. Rape was just another notch in the bedpost of her toilsome life. Yet, her casual dismissal of the incident was almost the greater tragedy. Acceptance of such a callous violation confused the young lad, and yet he knew that in all probability, woman around the world faced similar defilements, yet had no other choice but to accept their lot. It seemed unfair. Indeed, it was a man's world. He shivered as he considered the bestiality of his own gender.

Yet it was Clarah who had tried to assure him.

'Don't fret Konnor. The curse of begrudgery always comes back to kick the beholder.'

He debated the thought in his head. Maybe she was right. Perhaps that was why Asher had stayed away from home and avoided his sister's engagement. It had confused him at first. Why was Asher avoiding him? But now he knew the truth…now he understood. How could his brother look him in the face, when a green-eyed monster gazed back without an ounce of guilt or shame? It then occurred to Konnor, that Asher wouldn't know that he knew. Clarah would have flown back to England and that would be the last that anyone would have seen or heard from her. He wondered. Suspicion flooded his mind. His thoughts hadn't taken form. They hadn't evolved into a theory…but something didn't smell right.

As he descended into the valley leading to his aunt's vast home, he tried hard to focus on the delights of a reunion and push his brother's ravenous debauchery to the back of his mind. Long journeys presented the driver with too much thinking time and he hated the road for that. He turned the radio up and played the Cults "She Sells Sanctuary" at ultimate volume. This was his favourite running music when ascending the San Gabriel Mountains range on a Sunday afternoon. The loud guitar rhythm drowned out his melancholy thoughts. Maybe the louder the music, the greater the silence inside his head.

Then he saw them. He had not seen this sight since being a young boy and he was immediately taken back to a youth that seemed so much better than it probably was.

The twin turrets - that was the vision that presented themselves in all their Celtic glory. They poked their pointy heads above the treetops long before visitors dropped down the lane to Darwydden. They both welcomed and warned in equal measure.

The gravel driveway was icy and the tiny stones cracked beneath the car wheels. For some reason Konnor felt nervous. He had tried to distance himself from his step-mom's disappearance. It was a mysterious abduction, and an event too painful to contemplate. Konnor wasn't sure if seeing his Aunt Ruby again…her twin sister, would bring raw emotions flooding back. He braced himself for the worst.

It was winter in the Welsh valleys of Snowdonia, and with the sun low in the sky, it wasn't long before daylight crept behind the mountain range.

A sheet of navy blue dusk fell upon the area. The trees on either side of the drive hung dramatically over the road and when caught by the car headlights they looked foreboding and ominous; their branches like tentacles reaching down as if to scoop up any passing vehicle in their wake.

He remembered his step-mom telling him how much she hated her twin sisters strange home. Eenayah was convinced it was haunted and as a young boy he was impressionable enough to believe her. Konnor tried to ignore the hungry finger-like twigs reaching out to him, and focused on the large iron gate at the end of the twisting lane. Once through the gate, the scenery became far more welcoming. A multitude of flickering fairy lights illuminated the line of conifers and iron-framed oil lamps lit up the drawbridge as though it was the backdrop to some medieval film set.

Konnor parked his hire car and walked across the cobbled courtyard into the reception area. The wonderment of this oddity of a building still enthralled him as much now, as it had done when he was a boy. The entrance door and the turrets were part of the original 11th century castle. Rumour had it, that the dungeons, casemate and undercroft all still existed. His uncle Owyn once took him into a small vaulted chamber underneath the rampart. He recalls screaming and running away, tripping up and ripping his knee open on some steep granite steps.

Looking up at the newly converted hotel, his eyes followed a line which almost seemed to follow a line of construction through history. Connected to what remained of the castle ruins, was the black and white timbers of the Tudor period. This was the era that had given the house its clandestine meeting places, hidden hideaways and priest holes. His uncle once told him about the secret passageways…walls within walls. It caught the attention of a young imaginative boy from Miami.

Following on from this were the large Victorian rooms, with their tall ceilings and then came the Edwardian period with its elegant sash windows and gentleman's library.

Darwydden castle hotel was like an architectural time machine. Although he had yet to visit the caverns beneath Darwydden, he had been reliably informed that the 21st century had left its mark, with the most amazing holographic computer-generated imagery.

His step-mother's family had turned their gigantean home into a hotel, and his uncle had transformed the underground caves into an amazing illusionary wedding grotto. Owyn had even won some sort of awards for his technical wizardry. Konnor couldn't wait to see it. He knew how much Ruby and Owyn had struggled financially to convert their ruin into a 5-star hotel and he was full of admiration for their achievements.

He was also more than aware that his step-mom had financially contributed towards the conversion – it had been the very last thing she had done before she went missing. In fact, this was the very last place Eenayah had visited before she went disappeared into thin air.

Konnor hadn't been here since 2013. He had turned down all invitations, afraid that old memories would be stirred. He was a young guy, and as yet death was a concept he couldn't come to terms with.

Everybody…both privately and publicly, assumed Eenayah must be dead. It was an acceptance of her absence that still confused him.

Nonetheless, over 18 months had passed and it was time to put some ghosts to rest. Ghosts; he laughed at that word as he then remembered Clarah's Whitby home. He now feared humans more than ghosts.

Konnor took a deep long breath, then braced himself for an emotional rollercoaster ride. He now had other ghosts to confront…those locked up inside his own head.

He pensively entered the reception hall, which was now lined with knights in armour and stag's heads. As a child, the entrance hall had been a large bare square of nothingness. His aunt and uncle hadn't been able to afford such grandiose decoration. Not that it mattered back then. They seemed to have enough warmth in their hearts to light up the place, even though part of their home had no electricity.

He recalled a huge Christmas tree in the hallway. He had pretended it was a city and each of its branches had been roads to sparkly villages. He moved around the wooden nutcracker soldiers within the tree and made up imaginary games in his head. He also recalled being taken up to his bedroom on Christmas Eve. His step-mom and Aunt Ruby were slightly drunk from brandy and port. Neither of them could stop giggling or hiccupping. The grand oak staircase had been draped in holly and ivy and outside the snow had just started to fall. He felt a warm glow inside his soul – a feeling that had eluded him since childhood.

These images were nothing more than shadows from the past, yet they were amongst the happiest memories of his life. Times long past and now gone forever. That made his sad. Yet here he was – back again. Back in a Christmas scene from his youth. He felt joyful yet sorrowful at the same time.

His nostalgic mental wanderings were then disturbed by the voice of the young receptionist.

'Can I help you sir. Have you a reservation?'

Konnor had almost forgotten that the once family home, was now a business. A business with guests, with staff, with bookings and profit to be made. The grand hallway now housed computers, and an ATM cash machines. His aunt and uncles home was a commercial entity…yes of course it was.

He turned to respond to the receptionist, but the vision of beauty that met his eyes, quite took his breath away. She was very attractive and he immediately became overwhelmed with guilt. Had he not just professed his love for Clarah? Yet the young woman had a look of her. The girl's slinky auburn hair was short and perfectly framed a pixie like face, yet she most certainly had similar features. He tried to convince himself. Yes of course, that's all it was. He saw the receptionist and she remined him of Clarah. He was missing her – that's all. No need to feel guilty.

'I am Konnor Baratolli,' he announced. 'I am Mrs Kyfinn' s nephew. Is she around? If not, then maybe my Uncle Owyn is available?'

The young receptionist blushed, silently reprimanding herself for not recognising him. Yet how would she know what he looked like? She knew to expect a young American male, but nobody had told her he was this gorgeous. She felt her pale skin redden as that thought played havoc with her hormones.

Indeed, Konnor Baratolli was not the sort of lad that frequented the locality of North Wales. His tanned skin…obviously acquired from a youth spent on a surf board, along with his bleached blond curls, were not atypical of the Snowdonian gene pool.

She tried not to show her obvious attraction to him as she replied, 'no worries, please take a seat and I will locate Mrs Kyfinn.'

She approached him with a tray of various drinks.

'Can I offer you something whilst you wait?'

Konnor availed himself of a much welcome Cognac then sat down by the log fire whilst he awaited his step-moms twin sister. The receptionist cast him an embarrassed sideward glance. For sure, there was a chemistry. It confused Konner. It was unexpected and not something he really cared to explore. He became cold and dismissive of the young girl; more so than was in his kindly nature. Tellingly more so. It was a deliberate avoidance technique - the downward casting of eyes that didn't want to behold a beauty within their vision. Eyes that dare not look for fear of what they would see.

His uncomfortable shuffling around on his seat and pretence of interest in a Welsh farming magazine was most welcomingly relieved by a collective of voices shouting his name. The high-pitched squeal of his grandmother Ella and the raspy smokers voice of his grandfather Chris, was soon followed by an intense double hug. Following a multitude of questions and kisses and yet more hugs- his grandparents moved their young handsome grandson away from the public reception area and into the family quarters.

As Konnor passed into the grand hallway, he dared to take one last look at the striking young receptionist. It was then that he caught his own reflection in an oversized mirror; a wall decoration that would not let anyone escape or pass by its often-cruel vision of reality. It most certainly captured the look on Konnor's face and replayed it back to him as it saw him to be. It caught the wanton look of lust. At that moment, he felt like a cheat and more than anything he did not want to be that to Clarah. He knew what Denny had done to her. He knew what his own brother Asher had done to her. He knew what life had done to her. He didn't want to be yet another statistic in a growing line of males that had betrayed her, he would not…he could not. He resolved to avoid the receptionist. She looked like Clarah, but she wasn't Clarah – end of.

The very thought was pushed from his mind as he was guided into the arms of his Aunt Ruby. Before long he was overwhelmed by his step-mother's relatives, who were all delighted by his visit. Even the ancient stone bricks of Darwydden seemed to glow with the warmness of this reunion. The long table in the grand hall had been set for a feast and like it or not, a party had been planned.

His Aunt Ruby took him to his room. She didn't ask too many questions. Somehow, she instinctively knew not to. She could see he looked distracted. The dark circles beneath the eyes of one so young had not gone unnoticed.

'Just take your time Konnor. You must be tired. I will come and wake you in a few hours. Get some sleep. We have quite a night planned for you and we need the guest of honour to be wide awake and shimmering with energy.'

Konnor simply nodded. She was right. He felt drained. It was as though the energy had been sapped from his pores. He laid on the 4-poster bed, wrapped himself up in the heavy tapestry quilt and sunk into the mattress. What was he going to do about Clarah? He sent her a text message and then his heavy eyes closed – he was gone. Clarah was the last image on his mind as a deep slumber engulfed him.

***

Clarah had never experienced pain like it before. It was as though she had been hit by a speeding train at 120 mph. She was thrown backwards onto the icy glass. As the electric shock still pulsed through her being, she lay flat out, almost punch drunk.

A leather-gloved hand pulled her into a sitting position. A well-dressed young gent squatted down beside her.

'Are you okay Clarah? You hit the dome with some force.'

'What dome, and how do you know my name? Who in hell are you?'

'In hell, I am known as Tobiah. As for you, every being in my realm knows of your name. You are a disembodied soul; Clarah the human outlier. So very unusual…quite rare one may say. You are famous, Clarah Lee.'

Clarah felt unnerved in the man's company. She didn't know what he was, but she knew he wasn't human. Somewhat alarmed she tried to jump to her feet, but then slipped on the frozen blades of grass. She fell back down to the ground with a bump.

'Take your time Clarah. I won't hurt you. I have hurt many, but not you…never you.'

Clarah took a few deep breaths and rubbed her eyes. She tried to determine where on earth she was, because for once she had ended up in a place she hadn't expected to be.

Konnor had texted her and asked her to join him. She had done exactly as he had asked. She had focused on Konnor's location and usually that was all it took. Whoosh - she could transport herself to any place, any person, any date, any time, with just a simple thought. But on this occasion, it didn't work. She rubbed her eyes again.

'Where the bugger am I?

Before her she could see rolling hills and clumps of pine trees. Glazed with frost, their spikey branches seemed to glisten in the last rays of winter sun. On the horizon was a magnificent mountain vista. It seemed to be tinted with a bluish hue, topped off with white caps of snow. Directing her gaze down into the valley, she saw the turrets of a castle. A meandering road led towards a drawbridge. Connected to the castle walls like a Siamese twin, was a large gothic mansion. She could see flickering lights from within its windows. It seemed to be warm and welcoming. It beckoned her inside and yet something wouldn't let her in. She had been blocked.

She turned to face the young man sitting beside her. His attire was that from a bygone age. His leather ankle-high shoes were buttoned up on the side. He wore tweed knee breeches with a distinct herringbone design. A hunting jacket matched his knickerbockers. A heavily starched Stanley collar was perfectly finished off with a silk neck scarf. His immaculate style was completed by a bowler hat and walking cane. He didn't look as though he came from this century.

'Who are you?'

'Dearest Clarah I have already introduced myself. I am Tobiah. Look closely. Do you recognise me now?'

Clarah scanned his face with x-ray precision and then gasped.

'The taxi driver. Bloody hell, you are the guy who picked me up from outside the camp and took me to Hades Hall. You are the same person… I think.'

'Not exactly a person, but yes I drove you to Hades. I also drove your confused soul from the hospital to your Baba May's house in Whitby. Your grandmother is quite some shuvihani. She was lonely and she didn't want your spirit stuck inside a comatose body, so she evoked me and commanded assistance. You have your Baba May to thank or to blame for your present situation. It depends if you see this separation from your body as a blessing or a curse.'

Clarah didn't want reminding of her present situation. The thought was too powerful and one she feared she could not control. She had spent two wonderful nights with Konnor, and her body had felt real enough when lying intertwined with his. All she wanted was to be with Konnor again - inside his room, inside his bed, inside the manor house down in the valley. Yet, something had kicked her out. What was it?

'What is this dome thing you mentioned? Is that what stopped me in my tracks?'

For once Tobiah was at a loss as to how he could explain the dome to Clarah. He stood up and threw a stick into the place he knew it to be. The air wobbled ever so slightly…so slightly that is was almost impossible to perceive with the naked eye.

'Did you see that?'

Clarah nodded her head to confirm she had.

'This is an ancient place Clarah Lee. You cannot see it from where you are sitting, but the castle sits on a small hill in the middle of a large valley. Once upon a time, long long ago…the valley was filled with water and the place where the castle now sits was an island. The locals called this place "Caer Sidi". This will be difficult for you to take in, but before humans populated Earth, an ancient civilisation from another planet inhabited this area. They came from an otherworld within the constellation of Corona Borealis. Eventually mankind gained a foothold on this planet, and then the Druids came to live in this area. Before the beings from the otherworld left, they taught the Druids some of their magic tricks. One of those tricks was how to create an invisible forcefield by bending the natural energy lines of the earth, and shaping them into a dome. The dome ascends miles up into the sky and also an equal distance under the ground.'

'I am confused Tobiah. I mean, I am gobsmacked by everything you had just said, but my interest is in this magic dome. What purpose does it serve?'

Tobiah replied, 'well of course the dome is invisible. Nobody can see it. However, as you saw before when I threw the stick, the air had a bit of a quaver before allowing it to pass through…similar to throwing a stick into water and seeing the ripples it makes. Normally that wouldn't happen with the dome. People pass through it all the time. It covers a hotel and guests come and go. It's only because it was me throwing the stick, and the stick had retained some of my energy. The dome will allow all material objects through its walls, and of course that includes flesh and blood and wedding guests. However, it will not allow spiritual energy through, unless of course the energy is totally pure. I am negative energy Clarah. I stand no chance. It exists to keep the likes of me away. The Druids did this to keep out the bogeymen.'

Clarah began to feel quite insulted by what she perceived to be Tobiah's subliminal suggestion.

'Okay, so I get it. Technically I do not have a body as such, but I would hardly have described myself as negative energy.'

Tobiah started to laugh.

'Miss Clarah Lee, you have just twisted my words. You would make a great demon if you ever want to swap sides, but hey…I never said you were negative. I simply made the suggestion that you were less than pure. Only an angel is pure Clarah, and I doubt even you would pretend to be one of those.'

Clarah understood. She looked down upon herself. She saw herself as real. She could feel the icy chill from the ground beneath her. She shivered and the hairs on her arms appeared to stand on end. Yet, when she breathed out into the bitterly cold air, no steam came from her mouth. She now knew that it was her own grandmother who caused this to happen to her...her meddling witch of a granny - Baba May. The aging Romany woman who tinkered around in an occult world she should have left well alone.

'You seem to know a lot about me Tobiah. So, if you know so much, who was it that put my body in a coma? I have been eavesdropping at the hospital. I overheard a doctor talking about me. He called the police. Someone or something did this to me. Do you know who, why or what?'

Tobiah knelt over her and whispered into her ear. Clarah was silent... horrified and saddened by what she had been told. Part of her wanted to cry, but part of her was too angry to cry. She had been reminded of something she had forgotten and the remembrance was painful.

'I need to speak with Konnor. I need to talk to him urgently. How do I do this Tobiah? I am new at all of this paranormal thingie me-job.'

Tobiah laughed again. He quite liked Clarah's naivety. There was a freshness about her matter of fact-ness. He pointed to her mobile phone.

'You are residing in the 21st century Clarah. There is a lovely little ye-olde pub around the corner. Get him to meet you there. Your fingers are capable of tapping in a number or a few lines of text...or so I presume.

Clarah shot the demon a look of disdain. She had little time for sarcasm. She picked up her phone and began to tap on the keys, but then…just at that moment, she looked out to the valley and squinted, as though trying to focus on a distant image.

'Can you see what I can see Tobiah?'

Tobiah shrugged, 'I can see three people on horses riding through the valley. Is that what you refer to?'

'Well,' she replied, 'more like a knight in armour chasing another knight and then a woman in medieval dress following on behind.'

'This is a strange valley Clarah. It has a mystical vibe. It is steeped in many years of history. Witnessing a playback of a past event is not unusual. Probably a couple of guys fighting over the hand of a fair maiden. If I was you I would forget about what you have seen and do as I have advised.'

Tobiah stood up and pointed over to the church.

'Don't walk through the cemetery or you will hit your head on the dome again. Walk around the church, onto the High St and there you will find a pub called the Royal Oak. It may seem a bit of an old-fashioned way of getting around…with all this walking and texting malarkey, but it's how humans tend to move about and meet up. You were a mortal once, you must remember the way it works.'

He smiled and winked at her.

'Good luck Clarah. Stay in touch.'

'Dearest Tobiah…as if I would stay in touch with a demon.'

She walked quickly away…

***

Roserie stood by his bedside. She was about to wake him, but the young man was in the deepest of slumbers. She gently stroked his forehead. She still saw him as the lost little boy from Miami; a child growing up without a mother and left with a father who was never at home. His was a father away from home out of choice, not for a need to earn yet more money. Reed Baratolli had already gathered enough numbers to the left of a decimal point. What was the point in having more? She didn't understand Reeds addiction to wealth.

Roserie had been delighted when Eenayah entered Reeds life. His new wife excelled at being a step mother. Yet for Roserie his new bride was just another child to look after. The longest saddest sigh left her mouth, as Eenayah came to mind. Hers had been a deeply tragic life and one that had ended too soon. Blighted by the ancient prophesy of Tamar, Eenayah had given birth to twin boys and then died without even holding them in her arms. Now cherub faced toddlers - they would possibly never know who their mother was.

Lost in her memories, Roserie was swiftly brought back to reality by a series of bleeps on Konnor's phone. So deep was his sleep, that even the sirens call failed to rouse him. Roserie read the text. Should she delete it or leave it well alone? It was a difficult decision. Roserie was an earth-bound angel and she had the ultimate powers of foresight. She already knew that Clarah's time on earth was limited. She knew that another destiny awaited Konnor, a fate that involved a living woman – one who could give him a family and a future. The Clarah as she was right now, could not be that person.

It was not for Roserie to interfere with this process, and yet that was what she did...all the time. Shifting paths of destiny came with her job description. She kissed the already sun kissed brow of the young man, and wished a few more hours sleep upon his weary frame. She left the text on the phone. Depending on her next conversation, it was possible the words would delete themselves anyway. In her reality, the past could undo itself.

Walking out of the large castle doors, the young receptionist called out her name.

'Bye-bye Roserie...have a drink for me. I still have an hour left at work, but I may join you when I finish. Leave a tab open.'

The young receptionist waved her goodbye. Her eyes sparkled with life and her cheeks shone with blood...real blood being pumped from a real heart.

The situation evolving was a rare time paradox. As an outlier Clarah had created an inconsistency loop. Normally the past dictates the future, but because of Clarah's unusual ability to go backwards and forwards in time – even at the same time, all logical sequence had been redefined. There was no order anymore. The universe conducted itself by a succession of events, and so Clarah was a threat. The complexity being, that Clarah could visit the future and reshape the past. In all of this coming and going, it was even possible that Clarah could even meet up with herself from another existence. She had done it once before...when she had stopped her former self disfiguring her wrists with a knife. Roserie would have to do something about this bizarre situation. It was Aura's job to police such matters and yet Aura was nowhere to be seen.

***

Clarah sat at the bar at the "Royal Oak" and patiently waited. It may not have been a feminine trait to hang around at bars, but Clarah didn't care. Years of being grabbed by impassioned tinker boys had hardened her. She was immune to judgmental stares and casually dismissed disapproving gawks with the contempt they probably deserved.

The Royal Oak was a typical old-man's pub. It sat on the corner of a T-junction, facing the church and next to the undertakers. It had played host to many a wedding, christening and funeral wake – most likely within the same local families and in that precise order. It was also the place where the off-duty staff from Darwydden Castle Manor Hotel frequented. Unbeknown to Clarah, it was also the place where Konnor's aunt and uncle had first met.

Ruby and her best friend Becky had been on a mid-term break at Llandanwg Caravan Park near Harlech. They were trying to navigate their way home through the vast Snowdonia national park, when they got lost. The weary friends had called into the Royal Oak for supper and directions. Owyn was stood at the self-same bar where Clarah was now sat. Ruby asked him for help and he kindly obliged.

Their meeting seemed to be a happy coincidence – and yet is wasn't. It was anything but. It had all been a contrived and well-thought out Ledonite plan…one executed with military precision by Ruby's best friend-Becky. It was a plan that had been dictated thousands of years earlier from a place very far away.

This was information Clarah couldn't possibly know. She drank her chilled lager and lime in complete ignorance of the past. The winds of time had blown dust over many old footprints.

Clarah had caught the attention of the barman Gareth, who kept giving her peculiar looks. She was a stranger in a remote village and she was alone. She guessed that this must be the root cause of his idle curiosity. Gareth cautiously approached the stranger at his bar.

In his sing-song Welsh voice he asked, 'would you like another drink while you wait for your sister?'

It was an innocent enough question, but it hit a raw nerve. Clarah snapped back, bluntly stating, 'not really, she is dead.'

Gareth's reaction came as a surprise. With gaping mouth and shocked open eyes, he dropped the pint he was serving on the floor and trampling over broken glass, went running out of the pub.

He didn't come back. It bewildered Clarah. She considered him to be mard or perhaps mentally troubled. How could the bartender possibly know her sister Nina? It made no sense. She ignored his odd reaction and moved over to the window. She wanted to watch Konnor's floppy yellow hair waft in the wind as he came swaggering up the path. She was looking forward to seeing him again. She felt happy.

Clarah liked the Royal Oak. Aside from the nervous barman, it had a pleasant welcoming atmosphere. Nothing too fancy – a bit of an old bloke's domain with a much-pierced dart board. The table was engrained with many years' worth of circular glass stains. The carpet was slightly sticky from a decade of dribbled booze. It had an old pub smell – a mixture of cigarettes, beer and yesterday's lamb casserole. It was a sweet place, in an aging and much used sort of way.

She waited and waited. She hoped he had picked up her text message. She checked her phone- no reply. She was starting to worry. He was taking his time. He didn't come.

An older lady tapped her on the shoulder. Clarah spun around…she knew the face, she had seen it before. It was a kindly face. The woman almost exuded an inner glow. Clarah didn't know anybody in this town – or in Wales for that matter…yet she had seen this woman before.

Clarah stuttered, 'erm…err…erm…do I know you?'

The woman said nothing. Her face was radiated by the brightest of smiles. Without the need for further words or complex explanations,

Clarah understood. She wasn't sure what it was she understood- she just did.

'I have met you, before haven't I? You rescued me from the cemetery. It was a very dramatic exit. You sort of held onto my arm and whooshed me away. You are Roserie, or at least I think that's what you called yourself. What exactly are you? I am sorry if that question sounds rude, but I live in the strangest of worlds these days. I don't know if people are people anymore…even if they look like people.'

Roserie sat down beside her.

'Yes, I am called Roserie and don't worry about being rude; the quest for truth is often impolite and honesty has no need for apologises. I am here to tell you that your boyfriend can't make it – not yet anyway. Konnor is in a deep sleep. He hasn't seen your text message, but I did. I wanted to come here and meet with you. You see dearest Clarah, I was his step-mothers house keeper. I have raised Konnor from a young age. He is important to me.'

'Well, good for you and yes, he told me about you. However, he is important to me as well. Look…I don't want to seem ungrateful. I am eternally thankful that you pulled me from that weird situation back in the cemetery, but I asked you what you are. What are you Roserie? My life…if indeed I am living, is fairly screwed up right now, so please grace me with a factual answer.'

Roserie looked over to the landlord Alan and shouted, 'allwch chi ddod â mi dros wydraid o win coch a phaced o gnau.'

She then noted the look of surprise on Clarah's face and laughed at her bemusement.

'I am a celestial being Clarah and before you ask, yes I can speak Welsh plus every other language on earth. It comes in useful sometimes.'

'Are you an angel?

'Well. I guess…sort of. There are many different types of angels and we are assigned to many different planets and species. Your earth is just one of many and angels can be as diverse and various as there are types and species of life.'

'So, how do you differ from Aura? She confuses the crap out of me.'

'Aura is a deva. She is interplanetary. Her territorial responsibilities cover the entire universe, whereas I am only allocated humans on this earthly domain. Also, the toil of a deva is quite different to an angelic assignment. They monitor and protect physical aspects of the universe, like water, air, fire, gravity, light and so on. Angels are more concerned with the well-being of living creatures and the spirits within. Angels and devas are like chalk and cheese. A deva will govern specific laws of nature. They create orders and rules, whilst angels delight in breaking them. It is the reason why some of my kind have fallen and become what you will know as demons. Talking of which, I know you have just conversed with Tobiah, so you are aware of such entities.'

Clarah simply nodded.

'You may not know this Clarah, but an angel is always at risk of falling. It is our nature. We often skate close to the edge of what is permittable…a little like you do Clarah. You are a maverick. You would suit angelism. You have an attitude which fits with the duplicity of our ethos.'

'A chap in a nice suit recently told me I suit demonism. I must present the universe with an ethical conundrum.'

Roserie's laughed at her witty comment, as her glass of red wine and packet of nuts were dutifully delivered by landlord Alan. Roserie winked at him in a cheeky devilish way. Clarah was beginning to understand what Roserie meant when she said they skated close to the edge.

Clarah continued with her questioning.

'So, is that why Aura came into my life...because I broke some universal rule?'

Roserie took a swig of wine and almost chocked as a laugh redirected the fluid into her windpipe.

After a short coughing fit she replied, 'indeed – you are now beginning to understand Clarah. You have broken not just one, but so many universal rules. So much so that the Devic Kingdom is in a bit of a spin. Humans are not supposed to time travel, and yet you can. Humans are not supposed to mind travel, and yet you can. You can go anywhere with just a thought, as you have already found out and have been practicing daily. Trust me, many have been watching. A spirit is not supposed to escape its body until its body has died, yet yours has. Neither should a spirit be able to materialise a new body, yet you can and not just that, but create a body that appears as real as any other. Humans should not be able to become invisible, yet you have mastered the art of concealment and revelation better than my son Soul...and he is a professional magician.

You are unusual Clarah. You have fallen outside of the expected and to be honest with you, you worry the universe. You could potentially create chaos if not guided along the right path. Hence why both myself and Aura have acquainted ourselves with you. Aura just wants to put you back where you belong, because as boring as it sounds...a deva is the keeper of nature's commandments. Whilst I want to put you back on a path that is right for you and one that is right for the future of all. I am the keeper of man's destiny. Just different agendas – that's all. Humans also have different agenda's. We are more alike than you think. You need to understand that this isn't just about you Clarah. There are others I need to consider.'

Clarah's head slumped forward. She covered her eyes with her hands. Her people didn't show tears. In her community, such wet dribbles were a sign of watery weakness. She finally composed herself.

'This is a bit mind blowing Roserie. I think I need another drink. I am just a young traveller girl and this is all a bit too much to take in. Konnor was the last bit of reality I remember. Maybe that's why I can't let go. After Konnor and Bali, my life became a world of ghosts and demons and deva's and angels and heaven only know what else is waiting in the shadows to say boo. My agenda is simple - I just want to be with Konnor.'

'What about Asher?'

'Oh – you know about that?'

'I know everything about you Clarah, and so where does Denny figure in all of this?'

'He cheated on me…many times with many people, but doing it with my sister…aye, that took the biscuit. Denny doesn't even enter my mind. I threw his engagement ring away and that's the end of that.'

'You mean a demon through your engagement ring away.'

'Oh no, please don't tell me that Océane was a demon?'

'Yes Clarah – Océane is a demon and Hades Hall is the demons earthly lair. Do you not recall Tobiah telling you that he drove you there from the campsite?'

'I am surrounded. I am living in a Halloween circus.'

'You are interesting to us Clarah. You will attract all sorts of strange entities. I am sorry but this is your new reality. You are straddling between realms and at the risk of sounding like Aura, you need to be in one or another. I would say take your pick. Angles often push mortals to make decisions, but in this case, I am not sure the decision is yours to make.'

Clarah huffed and puffed. She had been quite enjoying her paranormal adventures to date. The sheer power of being anywhere at any time, had been a roller coaster ride. Yet she knew that with every day that passed, her comatose body was dying. Sometimes she could feel it dying. Occasionally she would float above it, and that was how she knew.

'I am aware that I am changing the subject here but I am also curious. Do you have a body Roserie? I mean…I know you have because I can see it, but is it a pretend body like mine?'

Roserie could see the sadness in Clarah eyes as she asked the question, but as an angel she was bound by honesty.

'This is maybe not what you hoped to hear, but I am real. I am an angel in a human body. I was born and I grow and I die and then I will be born again. I have been doing this same thing since mankind walked on earth. It is good for some of us to be mortal. Earth angels are enlisted to help humans, so some of us need to move around as one of you. Not all of us – just the lucky ones. I like my job. However, I can mind travel just as you can. I am not allowed to time travel…buy hey, I can speak fluent Welsh. Beat that one.'

Clarah laughed, perhaps a little too loudly…stating, 'wow that's cool Roserie. You are the ultimate divine undercover agent. Respect - I like that. High five to you and your kind. Can I get some of that whole multilingual thing?'

'You can get anything you want Clarah. That's exactly what makes you so worrying to the universe. Just think upon it and it will be yours…not always, but mostly.'

Clarah had become slightly tipsy and was becoming louder by the minute. She liked the angels last comment. It made her feel omnipotent. In her trampled-upon life she had never felt important before and now she was important…on a mega universal level of supreme importance. She giggled to herself as she tried to contain the thought – she could speak Welsh. Never had anything made her so happy in a long time. However, Roserie was conscious of the other people in the bar and gestured that Clarah should lower her voice as she practiced her new language.

'Shush – these people know me Clarah. The staff from the hotel frequent this place.'

'Okay, okay – I will speak English again. So – next steps Roserie. Do you have a plan?'

Clarah had more than a sprinkling of Yorkshire nouse and knew that Roserie had met her for a reason.

'I am guessing that angels don't often visit folks just to pass the time of day.'

'You can go back and forth in time Clarah, and I know you have been using your new skills….so don't tell me that you haven't visited your own death? Surely that would be the one big question piercing a hole in your mind?'

Clarah raised her empty glass to the landlord Alan; now working alone since his only barman had taken flight. With no words spoken, he refreshed her glass. She had always been able to command the attention of people, even before her newly discovered universal importance.

'Yes, I did. It's not something anyone ever wants to see – but I was curious.'

'How long have you got?' Roserie's question was blunt in its execution.

Clarah shrugged impassively.

'Visiting the future is weird. I have discovered that it isn't set in stone. As I go forward, I only see the things that will happen if today stays the same. However, if something changes the events of today, the future will change with it. The future is like bulrushes moving in the breeze, changing direction according to where the wind blows. It is inconclusive, but then again…you know all of this already Roserie.'

'You didn't answer my question Clarah.'

'As it stands right now…just months. As the wind changes direction, maybe weeks. My body is deteriorating fast. It wasn't a pleasant thing to watch. Nobody should ever have to see themselves die, although I did feel oddly unemotional and detached. I honestly don't know what to do. I don't know if there is anything I can do. From what Aura told me, I only exist if my body lives. When it goes, I guess I go…or maybe I join the ghost club. My Baba May has collected a fair number of members.'

Clarah tried to make light of the situation, but her eyes were filled with sorrow. She tried to act brave, but she was fully aware of her own forthcoming demise.

Roserie leaned forward and held Clarah's hand. She felt the young girl's confusion.

She began, 'Konnor is young and he is very much alive. When he is older he wants a family. His mother died when he was a child and until Eenayah came along, all else that was left was an absent father. People like this…people with an empty childhood, people left wanting, people raised without love, people just like Konnor – they need to surround themselves with a family. They crave to create what they never had. He has an empty void that needs to be filled. Filled with the laughter of children on Christmas morning, as they tear open their presents. You cannot give him that…ever. You can do many things Clarah, but you cannot give him the family he craves. Sometimes Clarah, when you love somebody, you have to let them go. Konnor Baratolli does love you, but you do know this won't work. You do know that…don't you?'

Clarah's head was hanging low. She was counting the beer stains on the pubs thread worn carpet. She avoided Roserie's eyes, the eyes of truth. She did not want to look into those eyes and see the message they delivered.

'Yes…sadly I do. I know you are right. So…where do I go from here Roserie?'

'There is a reason for you being what you are Clarah. First you must go back and find out where you came from. You have an unusual birthright and there are things you need to know about your past – a past which was shaped long before you were born. There are many questions that need answers. Only you can travel back in time to solve some ancient riddles. Do you understand?'

'No, I haven't a clue what you are talking about, but do carry on.'

Roserie continued, 'it is also your destiny to rescue somebody. I need you to rescue my son and for that you need to go into the future. It is important, and like you - he is also important. There are things that will happen, things that only you and you alone can alter. Once you have changed the future…if it is what you desire, you can go back and change the past. By that I mean, you can change your past. Clarah, you can become a normal human being again. You needn't be that girl in a coma who is dying little by little, day by day. All of this is within your power. Remember, you are an outlier - no rules, no boundaries. You really do not understand your own abilities my child, but you alone can alter your own destiny.'

'Will you show me what to do?'

Roserie smiled in a motherly, caring way.

'Not yet. First you must rest. I communicate in whispers. That's how angels operate. We tap on the door of your unconscious with silent instructions. I will visit you and you will just know what to do. We tend to be subtle, but we always get the message across.'

Already the words of Clarah's text message was disappearing from Konnor's phone. – letter by letter. The message was erasing itself as he slept.

She could have rejected Roserie's request. Konnor would have awoken, seen her message and come to meet her at the pub. Life would have seemed normal, but Clarah would have known that her pretence of normality was just that – pretence.

She had already decided not to tell Konnor the full truth about Asher. She would withhold the fact that he had dosed her with a drug that would cause her pregnancy to abort. This was what Tobiah had told her on the hillside. Asher had added pharmaceutical poison to her drink. It was a cruel concoction that would make her blood thicken… so much so that it would clot. That was what the drug did to her twin embryo's. That was how it killed them both. It built a clot around them so they would expire. A clot that would perish the growing placenta so it could not deliver much-needed maternal blood and oxygen. It was an illegal medication, one that should never have been given prior to a long-haul flight. Medication that would cause a deep vein thrombosis at altitude - a condition that would result in a heart attack and then a coma and then Clarah's hybrid half-life of existence.

No, she should not tell Konnor that it was his brother that put her in a coma. Once upon a time, she had pointed a finger and delivered similar news to her father Mick. As a result of this, he had beaten up the boys he believed had assaulted his daughter Nina. Clarah had told her father it was Peters brothers. One of them later died because of his injuries. It was like a stack of dominoes…one fell and so fell the rest. It ended with her father trying to hang himself. One tragedy just led to another. Clarah had learned the lesson of consequence. The life changing double act of cause and effect, had been etched into her psyche.

No, she would never tell Konnor what his brother Asher had done to her. She may be able to fix the past and then fix the future, but she had no intention of screwing up the present. She would do as Roserie asked. She would go home to her house of ghosts, walk along the beach, take some rests and then listen for the whispers.

She gave Roserie a hug and a knowing smile and then walked out of the door.

Roserie watched from the pubs bay window, but there was no sign of her young friend on the pathway. She had gone already. In fact, she was probably already back in Whitby.

It was a pity that her disappearance just happened to coincide with Gareth's decision to return to work. Seeing the young woman vanish into thin air before him, was just about more than the young barman could take in one day. Yet again, he fled. It amused Roserie.

A young woman then entered the pub. She was invisible to all but Roserie.

'Well done, good job,' uttered Aura.

'Being the bearer of bad news is always a very sad job, but necessary. Keep an eye on her won't you.'

'Of course, Roserie. It is always good to work with an angel as eminent as yourself. I will watch over her.'

Not that anyone in the pub could see it, but Aura knelt on the floor in front of Roserie, bowed her head and kissed the angel's feet. To the mortal world, Roserie was just a house-keeper and a part-time nanny. To her children she was just a mother. However, to the rest of a mystical unseen otherworld, she was an entity to be revered. One who had righted many wrongs. Not that anyone in this quaint Welsh pub would ever know what had just happened under their noses – although Gareth may have had a clue.

CHAPTER 24

Thursday 18th February 2016
INTO THE LAND OF CANAAN

Clarah was back home in Whitby, idly looking out of the large bay windows and watching the seagulls as they hovered in the air. They were noisy this morning, much noisier than usual. She enjoyed watching them squabble over a few crumbs of bread. They could be quite assertive, even aggressive. She concluded that hunger could bring out the fighter in even the meekest of creatures. She had also scrabbled for food many times in her young life. She understood the ravenous desires of the seagulls. Yet there was a part of her that longed to be back in that place. Battling for life made her feel alive. There was an energy that came from perseverance, tenacity and the desire to survive. And now...now she watched seagulls.

She then spotted a beautiful rainbow just beyond the end of the garden. In fact, it was a double rainbow, with a pink, lemon and lilac halo. As a little girl, Clarah had often tried to chase them...forever trying to find the pot of gold hidden in the ground. Ironically, she had already found the pot of gold, only to discover its treasure was worthless. She had a wad of cash gathering dust in her bank account, and it meant nothing. Should she desire to wear the most exquisite attire and be draped in the most priceless of trinkets, she could do so without spending any of her money. Anything and everything was a mere thought away. It had become too easy. By default, she had acquired a gift no other human possessed, yet Miss Clarah Lee was bored.

Baba May came into the lounge with a large mug of her cuckoo tea. Ah yes – the herbal concoction that solved everything. Clarah was grateful for the rejuvenating infusion. Her spiritual essence required high levels of energy to go on its many adventures. For some reason, cuckoo tea was the best pick-me-up brew she knew. As she gulped down the strange tasting beverage, she noted a strange expression on her grandmother's face. It was only then that Clarah realised how quiet the house had become.

'Where is everybody,' she asked.

'By that,' replied Baba May, 'I take it you mean your parents and your aunt and your brother and sister?'

'Unless you have been summoning up more ghosts from the local cemetery then yes…those are the familial spirits I refer to.'

Her grandmother wore a serious expression. She sat down at the small round table near the bay window, and started to lay out a deck of Tarot cards. This amused Clarah.

'Baba May, I have always been impressed by your psychic abilities, but for once in my life, I do believe I can foresee the future better than you can.'

Her grandmother ignored the sarcastic jibe and continued to deal the cards so they made a Celtic cross. Knowing her grandmother as well as she did, Clarah recognised that this was her typical aversion technique. Clarah repeated the question.

'Baba May, where is everyone? You can sit and play at being a Romany fortune teller all day long if you like, but at some point, you will need to tell me why this house is so empty.'

Baba May turned over the card at the centre of the Celtic cross, and as if to add dramatic effect, it was the death card. She looked over at her granddaughter as she sipped her tea. It was a deeply austere look.

'Clarah, we both know that your next of kin are dead…spare myself and your sister Katalyn. They are no longer here because they should not be here. It was wrong of me to imprison them in this house. So very wrong. I was just a lonely old woman, but I was selfish. I kept them for companionship and I have been scolded. I was ordered to release them.'

Her grandmother's hands started to shake as she continued to deal yet more cards upon cards. Her hands never shook. Clarah moved to her side and gave her grandmother a huge hug.

'You did what you did for love, Baba. Don't punish yourself. I would have been trapped in a sleeping body for a long time, had you not pulled me from out of it. You have given me a chance to live another life, and to make a difference. How can that be so wrong?'

Baba May moved the hair away from Clarah's damp eyes and kissing her forehead she said, 'then dear child – go and make a difference.' She turned over two more of her Tarot cards. It was the Empress and the moon card.

'The Empress is Tamar. She is our great-grandmother many times over. You and I are both replicas of her. Of course, even identical twins are not completely alike, but you remind me so much of a younger version of me.'

'So, what is Tamar to me, aside from the fact that I am a copy of someone who lived a very long time ago?'

'We are part of her legacy, Clarah. Throughout time, there have been many replicas and yet time itself was just waiting for the special ones. In the old language, we would call such a person – Időutazó . Clarah you are that person. Tamar has a message that she needs to bring forward to our modern times. You need to find her. You are the only one who can.'

Clarah was naturally quite taken aback. She moved away from her grandmother and focussed on the seagulls outside of the window. She wished she could be with them right now, hovering high above the cliffs of Whitby without caution or care. Oh for the freedom of a bird in flight. She then recalled Aura's warning – she had to guard her thoughts. If she wasn't careful, she would be souring above the sea as part of the flock. Eventually she turned to face her grandmother again, shutting out all imaginings of flying with the seagulls. It took a bit of practice, but now she was quite effectual in locking away idle daydreams.

'I am not sure Baba. Up until now I have only played at mind transportation and it has been a bit of a game. To go so far back in time and so far away – it worries me.'

'Neither time nor miles should matter to you. Be brave child. Go to your room, sit quietly and focus on Tamar. The moon card indicates that she is pregnant and her waters are about to brake. The moon pulls on water. Focus on her and her braking waters – here, take the Empress and the moon with you. Look upon them and utter her name.'

***

Clarah lay upon her bed, held the cards to her heart and created the thought. As she did she heard a whisper from the angels, 'make a difference Clarah – make a difference.'

The first thing that hit her senses was the smell. Clarah had never experienced anything like it in her 21st century Yorkshire life. Neither pleasant or unpleasant, it was confusing. On the one hand, it was like stale sweat and bread dough, mixed up with fish smoked over hot coals.

On the other hand, it was a blend of the most exquisite spices and incense. Combined, it was a sickly sweet primeval aroma. It connected her to something from a very long time ago. She liked its ancient earthy essence.

Clarah had always wanted to do this – to travel back in time in a bubble; unseen and yet able to observe. Despite her presumed bubble, the searing desert heat scorched her forehead. Of course, she had no skin to scorch, but just the thought of being out in the blistering mid-day sun, turned the thought into a reality. She remembered Aura's warning – she had to learn to control her thoughts. Looking at the blackened leathery faces of the locals, she realised that her English rose solar-deprived face could not cope with a middle-eastern climate. She immediately thought of herself as cool, and she was. It was that simple.

She found herself in what she presumed to be a market. It was noisy and farm like. Chickens, cows, donkeys, goats, camels seemed to be everywhere. There was at least a creature for every human, and both made as much of a racket as one another.

Gliding along a narrow street of stalls, the general direction of travel seemed to lead to a great wall. The wall was made from huge yellow boulders, held together by sandy mud. She noticed it had an archway in its centre. It was tall and as she looked up she saw men looking down from the top. Other men holding daggers and spears stood on either side of the arch. She presumed them to be guards. This must surely be a place of importance. She knew she had to go through the arch, yet she feared it. What was behind the walls?

Roserie had whispered that she should think about Tamar, yet such a person was nowhere to be seen. Clarah began to doubt her own abilities. She usually had no problem connecting to people by name, date or location. She had become quite an expert in mind teletransportation. As a seasoned traveller from birth, Clarah had no reason to doubt her abilities; yet so far, she had drawn a blank. She had no idea where she was or even when she was. Where and when?

By the Arabic dress she assumed the middle east, and by the lack of folks talking on mobile phones, she could only assume pre-1980. Clarah's knowledge of historical timelines was divided by the invention of the internet and wireless communication. Historians used BC and AD, whilst her generation used pre-internet and post-internet.

She tried to understand the local dialect. Maybe it was ancient Hebrew? She stood silently and concentrated on their foreign tones and throaty syllables. They spoke quickly, and some almost spat as they talked. She then tried to focus on a positive thought to make the magic work. Had she not recently conquered the Welsh language? If she could do that, then she could do this. She thought it – and so it became.

With immediate effect, she could understand them. Clarah gave herself a self-gratifying pat on her illusory thigh, followed by a dab salute. She considered that if only someone had taken her to one side in her childhood and explained to her the power of thoughts, how better life could have been? She wondered how the plump teenage Clarah would have defied the bullies with just a smidgeon of self-belief and confidence. Ah well – resigned to her present fate she shrugged her shoulders. Maybe she could go back in time and give herself a lecture in thought control. But then, a different Clarah would have lived a different life and heck...she wouldn't be here now. The complexities of consequence often tied her in mental knots. She now understood how simple life was if all one had to contend with was the here and now.

For a moment, she was lost in her own thoughts, but then something pulled her back into the moment. A general rumbling of hushed voices was passing covert messages down the grapevine.

'She is here. Who is here? She is here.'

Clarah asked herself, 'who the bloody hell is she?'

She, whoever she was…was divinely exquisite. She stood out from the crowd like a diamond in a dust pile. The woman had a small posse of guards surrounding her. Even without the protection squad, Clarah could have guessed that this was a lady of high social standing. She wore a tunic woven with the most vibrant bold colours. Deep reds, bright blues, rich purples, and all interwoven with tiny golden threads. The gold sparkled in the fierce sunlight as her courtiers carried her through the archway.

Her face was notably clean in comparison with the common folk who surrounded her. In fact, her skin had been scrubbed so clean, that it shone in the mottled light of the tunnel.

Clarah finally knew who the woman was. She had found Tamar. In that moment Clarah also knew who she was. She recognised the same facial features from old photographs of her mother Violet. The same applied to Baba May and astonishingly the same applied to her.

Tamar saw Clarah amongst the crowds. Making direct eye contact the woman subtly gestured that she should follow. Clarah wondered how that could be possible. Had she not made herself invisible? It confused her, yet without any resistance Clarah did as she was told. After all, this was her mission.

Tamar entered a place that resembled a palace. By modern standards, it was crude and simplistic, and yet it boasted an opulence not seen in the world outside the walled archway. Finally shedding her entourage,

Tamar indicated that Clarah should follow her into a small room. With just the smallest of windows at ceiling level, the air was stale and the light was dim. Yet even through the darkness Clarah could see that the woman was heavily pregnant.

She spoke, 'can you understand my language?'

Clarah replied, 'I have no idea what language you speak, but yes I can understand you.'

'Do you know who I am?'

'I believe you are Tamar.'

The woman took Clarah's hand and guided it towards her protruding belly.

'Yes, I am Tamar, and one of my unborn daughters will be you, and your mother and her mother before that. Generations and generations of women that will be born and will die will come through me, until we get to you. It is a strange thought, don't you think?'

Clarah quickly pulled her hand away from Tamar's tummy. What Tamar had just told her, was something just too bizarre for her to process. Yes indeed, it was a very strange thought. Tamar seemed to find Clarah's reaction amusing.

'Where am I?'

Clarah looked up, down, around and about. Even though she knew she could be back in her own time with just the blinking of an eye, her expression grew fearful. This leap into another world felt too strange, too far away, too long ago.

Tamar replied, 'I call this Kiriath-arbathe, but you may know it as Hebron in the land of Canaan.'

Clarah knew no such thing, but she nodded as though she understood.

'Ah yes, Hebron in Canaan. Now I understand,' she lied.

'Kings will be born here, anointed here and then will be killed here. Beyond that window is the pool of the Sultan, and one day it will run red with the blood of the innocent. That will be then, but this is now and for now, the people of Hebron are kind and protective of me and my unborn children. This small palace is crude and basic. It does not have the comforts I am accustomed to, but it is safe. I will raise my daughters here and they will be safeguarded. It is sad, but in less than 500 years this palace will crumble into the ground and be but a few stones scattered outside the cave of Machpelah. You can travel through time Clarah. If you are curious, go forward and see the spot where you are now stood. You will see nothing but dust and air.'

'What time period have I travelled to?'

'Time is the most unreliable of measurements, 'replied Tamar. 'It can slow down, quicken up and even go around in a loop. I cannot tell you how far back in time you have travelled Clarah, I can only say that for you to go back to your own time would be a journey of many thousands of years.'

Tamar then walked over to the wall with the window and agitated a stone until it came loose from the rest of the brickwork. The stone had been cleverly cut into a façade, and behind it was a small compartment. From within the hidden chamber Tamar removed a copper coloured scroll.

Tamar continued to speak. She spoke like one who had some inner wisdom and was the keeper of some great secret.

'I am a wealthy woman Clarah. Some would call me a queen, whilst others would call me a far more shameful name. No matter - whatever people may think or say, my sons and their sons will be heirs to many kingdoms – both earthly and heavenly.'

Tamar placed the copper scroll in Clarah's hands saying. 'so, you may find it odd that despite all I am and all I have, I can neither read or write. However, I do have other powers. Powers given to me by ancestors who were not born of this earth. I can see the future as an oracle would. Despite this, I live in a place and an era when powerful woman are seen as a threat. A woman is supposed to be weak…supposed to be inferior. She should know her place. I have to be careful. Many fear me because they know of me, but do not really know me. Do you understand?'

Clarah nodded. She understood only too well the coffin nails of prejudice, judgement and the whole daisy chain of intolerance. It didn't take a mystical woman from a bygone time, to explain to her the unfairness and inequality of life.

I have a prophesy to deliver to mankind. I asked a royal scribe to carve my words into a scroll so they could be preserved and delivered into the future.'

Clarah looked down upon the copper rolls cradled in her palms and asked, 'are these your words?'

Tamar looked down upon the precious scroll and replied, 'yes, these are my scrolls, but they were not the words that will be taken forward in time. The scribe made a copy and changed what I commanded him to write. I heard him talking with another scribe. They were whispering and plotting. I believe that on the command of King Judah, that the replica was to be taken to the Qumran caves near the Dead Sea. However, the replica scroll will be found sooner than intended and people will worship my words. However, the text has been distorted and the prophesy is incomplete. Their worship will be misdirected. The bogus scroll will tell part of the story, but not all of it. I have been waiting for you to come back and visit me Clarah. Part of my prophesy is that a granddaughter of mine from thousands of years in the future, would have the ability to move through time. I even knew your name, although for your own protection I did not disclose this in the prophesy. I am pleased that you made it back to me Clarah.'

Clarah was frozen to the spot. She gazed upon the copper scrolls in awe. She stuttered the words, 'I don't know what to do. What do I do now?'

Tamar replaced the stone back in the wall from whence it came. With the hem of her sleeves, she crouched down and wafted any tell-tale dust from the ground below the secret hiding place. Heavily pregnant, she struggled to get back to her feet. Clarah ran over to help her. Now close up to her face she gasped, as she saw her own eyes in Tamar's eyes. In that instant, she knew this wasn't some wild dream. It was true. All Tamar had said was madly wildly true. Clarah realised that she was entrapped within some destiny set thousands of years BC. A destiny set in what became known as the Holy Lands. She shook her head in disbelief.

'I am just a humble Gypsy girl. My kind are pushed to the bottom of the pile and taunted as beggars and thieves. I am not that wise or intelligent. I was born in a caravan parked in a junk yard. How can I carry so much responsibility? What if I get it wrong?'

Tamar wiped the girls perspiring brow.

'Fret not Clarah. You will know what to do with my scroll. Take it back to your own time and deliver it to its new owners. They need to read the real words. They need to understand the prophesy as it was meant to be written. They are confused and their good intentions are misdirected. You will know who they are. Providence will guide you.'

With those words, a sharp pain stabbed into Tamar's stomach and a trickle of water made its way down her leg.

'You must go now Clarah. Return to your own time and take the scroll with you. My daughters are getting ready to be born and I must go for help.'

She gasped as another contraction contorted her face with agony.

'Go, go now...take the scroll. Go quickly. I am not sure if we will ever meet again...fate will decide. If we don't, just know how important you are and how great this task.'

Clarah closed her eyes tightly as she thought about her bedroom back in Whitby...imagining it just as she left it. She saw it in her mind's eye. Outside the open window she heard the seagulls and the distant crash of waves on the rocks. She could taste the salt on the wind, as a gentle breeze blew her curtains inwards. She thought, she felt, she tasted, she saw, she savoured – she was home.

Away from the heat of the Middle East and back in the chill winter of Yorkshire, Clarah inhaled the briny sea air. Her new home could not have been further away from where she had just been - in culture, time and distance.

Perplexed and desperately needing to clear her mind, a walk along North Yorkshire's windswept cliffs would have helped...but alas her energy had been sapped of all its verve. Her body, whatever it is she believed it to be, was exhausted. She could hardly move one foot in front of another, and certainly didn't have the will or ability to mind-transport.

Clarah was starting to realise who she was, but the revelations were happening just a little too quickly.

She looked down at the scroll, and without even readings its ancient text, she knew what it foretold. The ancient prophesy of Tamar had revealed itself to Clarah. She and she alone knew its sacred story. She quickly hid it, almost afraid to gaze upon it a second longer.

It may not have been a secret hole in the wall, but the back of her underwear drawer was as safe a place as she knew. So, amongst her bras and thongs, lay a 3776-year-old copper scroll written in ancient Aramaic, and for now that is where the future of mankind would reside – in Whitby, in a young woman's underwear drawer.

As for Clarah - she collapsed onto her bed in a heap. She struggled to breathe. She knew she was connecting to her comatose body. As it's cells and organs were slowly dying…it was pulling her close…calling her back.

She didn't want to go back. She didn't want to be contained within a failing carcass, but she lacked the strength to fight it. Her eyes closed and like "Sleeping Beauty" she fell into a deep slumber. Back inside her own body. She slept for a long time.

CHAPTER 25

Friday 3rd June 2016
CHEATING DEATH

'I need to do what?'

It was a confused yell and nothing less than a scream from the soul. Clarah sat bolt upright from her sweat soaked bed. A nightmare had been interrupted by the repetitive pitter patter of raindrops. It had jolted her back into relative consciousness, whatever that was to one like her. Then the rain became heavier; driving its wetness down until a torrential downpour finally descended from the heavens in a liquid sheet. The storm raged, whipping up the sea into a frenzied whisk of liquid turmoil.

For some reason Clarah felt afraid. It was an alien emotion. Few things could incite that response in one so brave and so bold. She was confused by her own fear.

It was 3am and still dark, yet blasts of lightening illuminated her bedroom with splinters of electricity. The transient light was soon followed by a crunch of thunder. As a child, Baba May had told her that this was God moving his furniture around. At the time, she had believed her grandmothers fairy tale. It was reassuring. What else could create such rumblings in the heavens? She clung onto her bedsheets and uttered a prayer. She whispered to herself, 'just God moving furniture.'

The noise of the thunder was deep, dark and primeval. It wasn't anything like the shooting flame of a firework or even the blast of a bomb. It was something far more profound, like nature stamping its authority on a world mankind presumes to rule. Clarah understood the mastery of its roar. She was beginning to listen in a way she had never heard before.

In the shadows, her room looked different. Maybe it was due to the highly charged atmosphere? The ether was tangibly sinister. Dark forces were at large…she could sense them.

A black cat was sat on her window ledge like a conjuring sphinx. But they didn't have a black cat. Where had it come from? Romany folk were not overtly keen on feline creatures. It made no sense. Clarah looked down and stroked her tingling fingers. They were blue. How could they be blue? She was spirit, not body. She had no such thing as a circulation…not anymore. Something wasn't right. The world outside her window was a noisy cocktail of extreme weather, and yet somehow, someway…this mix of pandemonium had transported something else into Clarah's half-life. It was a new entity and one about to materialise very soon.

She held onto her blankets with all the naivety of a child, yet knowing that a simple piece of linen could not protect her. Something was coming to get her. The torrid heat of a summer storm had blown in pure evil. A demonic entity now stood upon the shores of Whitby and it was coming to find her.

Baba May heard her yell and came rushing up to her bedroom as best as her creaking joints could move. Upon seeing her granddaughter, she wrapped her up in her arms. 'You are back with me Clarah. Thank God, you are back home.'

'Where have I been Baba?'

'You went on a long journey my child. I think it must have drained all your energy, because you went back into your body again. Your body has not been very well. You have had pneumonia. At one point, I thought you were going to die. The doctors had to give you lots of those new-fangled anti-bionics.'

Baba May started to sob. As Clarah held onto the shaking frame of her grandmother, she began to realise that she was just a lonely old lady. Damned by the curse of begrudgery, she had lost all but her entire family. Now here she was clinging onto the one remnant of love she had left. Poor Baba had collected her ghosts because they were all she had to cling on to. Now that they had been banished into the afterlife, the big old house had become empty and meaningless. Clarah pulled herself away from her gran. She held her so she could look deep into her eyes.

'Baba May, I have to go on another journey. There is something very important that I need to deliver.'

'But…you have only just come back. Another long journey could kill you Clarah. These trips of yours, they sap you of your strength. When your spirit losses energy, you become ill.'

Clarah held up her grandmothers face, so to return her downward gaze back into her eyes. She loved her Baba May, but now she needed to be forceful and direct.

'Baba, something very nasty and horrible is making its way towards me. I know what it wants. On my travels. I went all the way back to the Old Testament. I met with Tamar and she gave me a prophesy to deliver. I don't have much time. I don't know how long I have been hibernating. but it was winter when I fell asleep and judging by the stickiness of the heat, I am guessing that we are now in summer.'

'June…we are in June, and it was February when you left me.'

'My God, 'pronounced Clarah, 'is that what it feels like being dead? Do we just shut our eyes, close down our brains and fall into a forever sleep? Is death just blackness, darkness, emptiness…nothingness? I remember nothing…just zilch.'

'Without thoughts and pain and all the worries of the world, surely comes peace. Death is peace, 'replied her grandmother. It was a strange form of assurance and not in the least comforting.

For a moment Clarah felt quite disturbed. She knew that her own life hung precariously in the balance. Time was not on her side. She knew that time was on no man's side, but hers was a clock ticking faster than most.

'I am so hungry…and thirsty. I have never known thirst like this before. I need to eat. I need to drink. I need to inject some power into this weak spirit of mine. I am off to the kitchen. I need to practice how to use these legs again.'

Baba May followed her as a flash of sheet lightening lit up the staircase.

'Where will you go to my child?'

'For some reason, I believe I have to take the prophesy to Darwydden. I have no idea how I am going to get into the place Baba May. Its protected by some invisible force-field that keeps spirits like me out – but somehow, I have to get inside. I need to deliver the scroll to someone who resides within. This could be a challenge.'

'Have you forgotten Clarah? You are able to materialise yourself. You can appear in the physical form any time you like. Why don't you travel on the spirit wind to the parameters of Darwydden, and then just walk in as a normal person. Surely a hotel cannot chase away its guests?'

'Hmm, I didn't think about that. You have a good point Baba. I will just walk in. Sometimes the simple solutions are the best. I overthink things these days.'

As Clarah looked around the darkened kitchen in the half light of dawn, she realised that no matter how beautiful the bricks and mortar of this house was, it could never be home. In her Gypsy soul, the road was her home and despite her new-found wealth, (money that she no longer needed) ...she missed her old life. Her grandmother noted the melancholy in her eyes and picked up on her thoughts.

'Are you wondering about Denny?'

'Oddly enough Baba, he rarely enters my mind. It's odd, 2 years ago I was getting ready to wed him. 2 years...where has the time gone to? Tell me, is he still a shepherd in Scarborough?'

Baba May shook her head to indicate a yes.

'Hmm, is he married now?'

Again, her grandmother nodded a yes.

'Is he happy and more to the point...is he faithful?'

'That's a yes and a yes, so am I told. But with men like Denny, there is always a risk. If his wife is smart, she will keep him busy with his flock.'

'Then I guess I wasn't his destiny. It simply wasn't meant to be. I did love him once upon a time, and maybe a part of me always will...but, if he could cheat on me with my own sister, then I guess his alleged love for me was just a sham. If someone is truly in love, they wouldn't have betrayal in their heart. But I am pleased he found happiness. I don't begrudge him that. I know what begrudgery can do to a person. It's best to just let go and move on.'

Clarah went to mix herself some eggs for an omelette. As she whisked the yellow yokes up into a froth, she sang to herself....

Are you going to Scarborough fair?
Parsley, Sage, Rosemary and Thyme.
Remember me to one who lives there.
For he once was a true love of mine.

Baba rubbed her granddaughters back as the poignancy of the words struck a chord. Clarah turned to face her.

'What about Konnor? Does he know what happened to me?'

'Konnor went back to America. When you didn't go to Wales to visit him, he took that as a rejection. He did come here to find you and we sat down at this very table and had a serious chat. He is a nice boy and he does love you, but I had to be honest with him. I hope you don't mind Clarah. Konnor is a young man with a future, and quite frankly, that is an asset you are missing Clarah.'

Nobody had put it quite so bluntly before. The words hit home. Her grandmother had delivered a killer blow. Indeed, she had no future.

'I am sorry child. Have I spoken out of turn? Should I not have said what I said to Konnor?'

Clarah sat down to eat her omelette. She looked desolate.

'It's okay Baba May. You just told him the truth and how can the truth be wrong? I have no time for men in my half-life anyway. There are important things I have to do in the time I have left. My body is perishing and when it goes, I go. The fuse has been lit.'

'Has it not occurred to you Clarah, that you do have the ability to change the past and maybe, just maybe…by doing so you can alter your future.'

'How?'

'By stopping the curse of begrudgery. I asked you to go to the post office and play my usual numbers. I gave you the money to buy a ticket. I know full well that you suspected I had used witchcraft to conjure up the winning numbers, and I also know that you purchased a ticket of your own, and used the very same numbers. Do I speak the truth?'

'Well…yes. I was too ashamed to confess as much, but yes. I was the one with the 2nd winning ticket. So, what? Did you use witchcraft?'

'I am a Romany witch. Surely that must come in useful for something? My daughter was in pain and my grandchildren needed help. I did it for a pure reason.'

'So, go on Baba. How can preventing you…I mean us…from winning millions on the lottery, possibly change anything?'

'Kane was a heavy drinker. You cannot change that about him. But he was never a drug user. He didn't have the cash in his pocket for hard drugs. Had it not been for the money in his bank account, he wouldn't have associated himself with those drug dealers. However, the lottery money introduced him to another world. He tried to negotiate with them…maybe to undercut them, or do them out of their takings. Kane was always up for a deal and for cheating folks out of what he owed. They strung Nina up onto the tree to show Kane that they were in charge. During the trial, I heard that they didn't mean to hurt her. It was just a threat…a game that went wrong.'

'Are you saying, that without the lottery win, that both Kane and Nina would be alive today?'

'Aye lass, I am saying just that. Not only that, but without Nina being strung up on a tree, your Da would not have gone after Peters brothers and attacked them as he did?'

'So, Baba, if I read you correctly, you are also saying that my Da wouldn't have gone to prison, probably wouldn't have hung himself and Patrick would still be alive and the other boys saved from months in hospital?'

'Aye yes. I cannot say that your Ma wouldn't have not got cancer, however stress is often associated with the disease – so who knows?' As for your Aunt Mary, if she hadn't moved to this big old house, she wouldn't have tumbled down the stairs and died.'

'I am guessing Baba, that you are also implying that without all of that crap happening on the night of the blood moon, that maybe just maybe, I would not have run away? But what about Denny? He was still unfaithful to me with Katalyn and that's why I ran away. It was everything else that went on as well…but mostly seeing Denny with my sister. That was what caused me to bolt.'

'Do you not find it coincidental that Denny proposed to you the day after we won a fortune. Even if had still proposed, before the lottery win you didn't have a bean between you. You would have delayed the wedding to save up, and you wouldn't have booked a hen night on the blood moon. Think upon it - Katalyn's husband Peter was away taking your friends to your hen night. You didn't go because you had a heavy period. Without the lottery win, Peter would have been at home with his wife. Fine…Denny may have lusted after her. She is a fine-looking woman, so many a man probably has indecent thoughts when they glance upon her. But with a husband and 2 kiddies in the caravan, Denny wouldn't have been able to get anywhere near her knickers. Sorry to be so blunt, but it is true.'

'So, you are saying that Denny wouldn't have had the opportunity to cheat on me, and I wouldn't have seen what I saw. I wouldn't have run off around the world nor would I have had the money to do so, even if I had wanted to.'

'Correct dear child. All would remain the same as it always had been. You wouldn't have met Konnor Baratolli and of course, that means you wouldn't have met Asher. I know what Asher did to you. My crystal ball sees more than you think.'

For a moment, Clarah was shocked. She thought such things were fairground gimmicks…but how else would her grandmother know all of this.

'So…I wouldn't have been raped and then fallen pregnant. Asher wouldn't have tried to dose me with some illegal medication to cause an abortion and I wouldn't have developed a blood clot on the flight home. In brief, I wouldn't be in a coma now. I wouldn't be dying.'

'Neither would we be living in this big old house. I hate this place. There are no stairs in a caravan, none to kill my daughter Mary. When we won that money Clarah, we should have done the right thing and shared it with the rest of the vitsa. We didn't do that, and the green-eyed monster caught sight of us. We brought upon ourselves the evil eye. Tis the curse of begrudgery and see how it has punished us.'

It may have been early morning, but Clarah had to grab herself a brandy from the cupboard. She was in shock. Shaking and visibly disturbed, she even had to sit down as she took it all in. Too many "what if'" and "if only" debates where dashing around inside her head. Eventually she broke her silence…

'So, I think what you may be saying Baba is…if I can go back in time and change the numbers I put on the lottery ticket, we could avoid the curse of begrudgery. My Aunt Mary, Kane, Nina, Patrick, my Da and maybe even my Ma, may all be alive right now.'

Clarah stared to get excited as the possibilities opened up.

'Sure, so what. I never get to go on my faraway travels and I never get to meet Konnor. Maybe I would still marry Denny eventually, and perhaps I will be the one he settles down with on some Scarborough farm. I would just be a normal girl and a wife…maybe a mother. I would never know that any of this had happened. I could untie all the knots. Is it possible? Could I go back in time and cheat death? I don't want to die – not now, not so young.'

Baba May shrugged her shoulders and went to heat up some cuckoo tea on the stove.

'You should drink this instead of Brandy. It's too early in the day for spirits.'

Baba May laughed at her own joke, but Clarah was obviously deep in thought.

'What do you think Baba? What do you believe in?'

'I believe in lots of things the gaje would pour scorn upon. I don't know what your destiny would be without the win. I can't tell you what would have happened if you had turned a different corner on another road. However, you say this scroll is important and you had to go back to bring it to our modern times. Who else could have done that but you Clarah? You had to half die, in order to become a time traveller. You should complete the job you were fated to do. Once you have done that –

think long and hard about your life. Nobody can promise you that a life with Denny would be any happier or any longer. Maybe most of your family still die anyway, but perhaps they just do it in a different way. Who knows how these things work. Just be aware that you have a choice. You can go back, alter the numbers I pick and stop the curse of begrudgery from ever having the wings to fly. Lots to think about.'

Indeed, lots to think about. Clarah would go to Darwydden tomorrow. In the meantime, she had a day to restore her strength. This would all be over soon. At long last, she knew what she should do.

CHAPTER 26

Saturday 4th June 2016
THE DRUID KEEPER OF SECRETS

Darwydden Castle Manor had been immersed into a hive of frenzied activity. Even from a distance, the clitter clatter of commotion was audible.

Preparations were being made for the wedding of Nico the resident chef and actress Tia Lembugo. These were high profile nuptials and with a selection of wealthy guests, the staff were naturally nervous. Security around Darwydden was now more than just an invisible blue dome, but also included a line of illuminous yellow jackets - humans with ear pieces and 2-way radios.

The occasional glint of a camera lens could be noted in the surrounding foliage, as undercover paparazzi lay camouflaged in the undergrowth. Gaining entrance into the wedding venue would be near impossible.

Clarah sat on a hill just outside the parameters and made a daisy chain from the wild flowers that grew besides her. Even from a distance, she could catch the perfume of the pastel garlands that lined the driveway to the drawbridge.

The sky was clear blue with just a few dappled clouds. It was a typical summers day in the Welsh mountains; cold when the sun went behind the occasional cloud and wonderfully warm when it escaped from behind its captor.

As Clarah sat on the embankment, she concluded that it was a perfect day for a wedding and for a few moments was lost in the musings of what her own wedding would have been like. She shrugged away the thought as she sucked on the purple tips of a clover, enjoying the subtle sweetness of its nectar as her teeth crunched its flowers. She was here to do business, yet had no idea what to do, who to see and how to even begin.

She looked down at the copper scroll as it shimmered in the Welsh green green grass of home. The song from Tom Jones had just popped into her mind, and she started to hum it as she idled away the time. She hoped the ancient text would talk to her as she stroked its jagged edges, but for now it lay in silence.

'A penny for them?'

'What?'

Clarah jumped to her feet. She had presumed she was alone on the hill and was pleased to look up and see a familiar face.

'A penny for your thoughts,' repeated Roserie. Clarah gave the angel a hug. Her entire body was filled with a supernatural warmth as she did and her nerve endings tingled.

'Oh, nothing much. Just watching the hullaballoo down in the valley.'

'It's a hive of activity in the manor today,' stated Roserie. 'Nico is much loved by all of the staff, so everyone wants everything to be perfect.'

Clarah put her hand to her brow to shelter her eyes from the sun as she focussed.

'I keep seeing an image of three people on horseback – a woman galloping after two knights. They seem to be chasing each other. I suspect that they are just mirages from a former time, unless they are part of the show that is…but every time I come here I see them. A damsel in distress and two guys in shining armour, just galloping along an old cart track. Do you know who they are?'

'Yes, I do know of them,' responded Roserie. 'I am not a time traveller in the same sense as you Clarah. I am earth bound and so I walk through the centuries by being re-born. However, I have heard about these people. They are caught in a love triangle.'

'Ye olde gossip,' sniggered Clarah. 'Do tell…'

'Back in the 14th century, the woman was a wealthy heiress. She was betrothed to marry an English knight. Anyway, the afore-mentioned knight disappeared off the scene. Some believe he went to fight in the crusades, whilst others say he was outlawed for taking part in some local revolution. Some even say he was the mythical Robin Hood. Whatever the rhyme or reason, let's just say that he was gone for a long time. So, whilst the cat was away, the mouse came out to play.'

'So, she cheated on him?'

'Well…not exactly. She thought her betrothed was dead, and so she found herself a Welsh knight – Sir Osmund Neville. As far as she knew she was doing no wrong. The other guy was history.'

'I am guessing that the English bloke wasn't dead, is that right?'

'Indeed, you are correct Clarah. After many years of absence, he came in search of his bride. The ghosts of the past you have been watching, are indeed one knight chasing the other one away.'

'So why is the rich heiress riding after them? I bet she could have any knight she wanted.'

'I guess that at different times in her life, she probably loved them both …maybe in different ways and for different reasons. I suspect she didn't want them to kill each other, so she gave chase.'

'What happened?'

'Her horse's leg hit a boulder. In pain, it reared its forelegs and threw her from its back. She died at the scene.'

'That's such a tragic story Roserie, but I am confused …why does it keep replaying itself? Is the valley haunted?'

'Maybe for some reason, you are just tuned into that time period. Or maybe, their energy has just been held within the area like a tape recording on the landscape. If my son Soul was here, that would be his explanation. Or perhaps, it's because the true story was never really told. Sometimes, over the years the truth becomes distorted. Some say that Sir Osmund died in a skirmish at Newton Park. The spot is marked by the "Bloody Stone". Some say that the dame in distress didn't die, and actually had to do penance for her adultery, by walking miles barefoot every day. Lots of stories told by lots of wagging tongues and in the end, history hides the truth. Perhaps these ghosts of the past are no different to Tamar and the scroll she wanted you to have. It is possible that history is attracted to a time traveller such as yourself. Perhaps it reveals itself to one who can tell it as it really was.'

Clarah looked down upon the scroll as a random sunray just happened to illuminate the copper.

'So, I am the messenger of truth it would appear. Who do I deliver this to?'

'Inside the manor house is a wedding guest called Dylan. He is a Wærloga,' replied Roserie. 'You need to find him and deliver its message. You can understand the ancient text Clarah, so read it to him.'

'He is a what? A Wærloga? That sounds like some sort of hobgoblin.'

Roserie laughed at Clarah's childlike humour.

'Dylan is a powerful sorcerer and one of the high priests within the secretive Ledanite society. It is told that he is a direct descendent of the powerful druid, Mug Ruith. He is the one who energises the blue dome. You need to mingle with the wedding guests and find him. Just think upon his name and your instincts will lead you to him…oh and dress appropriately. Get that imagination of yours channelled into the Stella McCartney wedding guest collection.'

Roserie was looking down upon Clarah's torn jeans and baggy tee-shirt as she spoke.

Clarah shuddered. She still recalled the searing pain as she bounced off the blue dome. Roserie could read her thoughts.

'Throw a stick at it,' commanded Roserie.

She did as she was told. The air wobbled around the stick, and it started to smoulder as it fell upon the ground.

'No way. That bloody barrier or whatever the hell it is, just set that stick on fire.'

'That's because the stick isn't real. I asked you to find one and conveniently, one just happened to be lying by your side. You imagined it into being. The dome only lets in material objects. It keeps out the world of spirits and fantasy to protect those inside. Now make yourself visible and real to the world, then hunt around for an actual object, one that actually exists. Go on Clarah – try it again.'

This time she threw a stone in the direction of the dome. It was a genuine stone, not a contrived illusion. It made its way through the invisible barrier intact.

'There you go, 'pronounced Roserie with a victorious smile, 'just believe and be real.'

Her angelic visitor then dusted the buttercup pollen from her dress.

'The ceremony will be starting soon and people will be wondering where I am. I act as a nanny to the young children of the house – Harry, Angelo and Alessandro. Their mothers, Ruby and Becky will be running around like headless chickens and wondering where I am. Time to bring in the cavalry.'

Clarah gave her divine mentor a warm hug.

'Will I ever see you again, Roserie?'

'I am sure our paths will cross. You walk many paths in my alternative destinies Clarah, and so do I. The chances are that we will meet again, in one lifetime or another.'

Roserie then hesitated, 'can I ask you a favour please?'

An angel wanted to ask a poor Gypsy girl a favour. Clarah beamed at the compliment.

'Yes of course, what is it?'

'My son is a magician, and by that, I mean a stage entertainer. His name is Soul. It is possible you may have heard of him.'

'Soul – no way. Yes, I watched him on TV when I was in India. He is your son? Wow- he is really talented, but…I didn't know angels could have children.'

'Earth angels are flesh and blood Clarah. I have a son and a daughter Eve. Anyway, that is by the by…this is about Soul. He is talented, but he is starting to use illusions and trickery because he doubts his own natural magic. I wondered if you could help to inspire and encourage him.'

'Sure – if I can. What do you need me to do?'

'When you are inside the manor, could you make yourself invisible and go down into the cavern. The wedding party will be there and my son will be on stage doing his usual tricks and sleights of hand. Can you whisper a thought inside his ear? Make it something to get him to believe in himself…after all Clarah, you must now be the mistress of self-belief.'

'That sounds like fun. Yes sure, I will think of something. It will be my pleasure. It has been a privilege knowing you Roserie.'

As Roserie turned to walk down the hill, she cast one last glance at her Gypsy friend. Now suitably dressed for the occasion, her raven locks were tied up into a braided updo. A thick plait crowned her head and thin snaking cornrows dangled onto the nape of her neck. She wore a cream Margot crepe de chine dress and as yet barefoot, held the matching shoes in her hand. Inside of her cream Burberry handbag lay something quite special. A gift that had travelled through time. She was ready – it was now or never.

Roserie picked up the discarded daisy chain from the ground. She placed it upon the young girl's head.

'Now you are a true princess - my dear lady Clarah, wear your crown.'

Roserie winked at her mischievously, then walked away – vanishing as she walked. Soon she was gone.

Clarah stood in front of the dome, and gazed down into the grassy valley. Her eyes followed the line of the cart track as they led towards the twin turrets of Darwydden. With its ghosts of star-crossed lovers, bloody battles and druid chants… she closed her eyes and walked in a straight line. She walked and she walked. She wished herself real, as she felt the cold tickle of the meadow grass beneath her feet. When she opened her eyes, she could see that she was through the dome. A huge sigh of relief escaped from her mouth.

As she turned to walk down the pasture, she suddenly thought she could hear a laugh. It wasn't a happy-go-lucky laugh, but more of a wicked sneer.

She turned to look up towards the hillside from whence she had just come. A woman was watching her. She was dressed in a long red robe with a caped hood. Her hair fell below her waist. It was laser straight and the palest shade of blonde. The woman in red said nothing – she just looked down upon her as though she was an ant beneath her feet. It was a cruel icy stare. Clarah instinctively disliked the woman. She wasn't human and the dome had locked her out.

Clarah didn't know who she was or why she was there, but her intuition sensed an abundance of evil. It was a juvenile thing to do and Clarah should have shown more maturity, but she removed the scroll from her handbag, wiggled it in the air high about her head and pulled out her tongue.

'You have come for this I take it, 'she yelled towards the demoness. 'Too late – bad timing ol girl.'

Emmanuelle turned into the true monster she truly was. Standing 8ft tall, with a lizard face and long tongue, she growled and spat out fire.

'Hmm, some new Welsh dragons in hood,' uttered Clarah nonchalantly. Nothing phased her anymore. She was well past being shocked.

With that she continued her journey towards the castle entrance of Darwydden. She wasn't quite sure how she would find Dylan, but she knew she would. She didn't know how she would enhance Souls magic tricks, but she knew she would. She wasn't sure when her body would die, but she knew it would. She knew she didn't have long, but she also knew she was meant to do this.

Lady Clarah…she liked that title. After all, she was special and she wore a crown of daisies to prove it. A messenger who could travel through time, yet she a humble Romany girl. Who would have thought?

***

Still invisible, she moved towards the noise. She felt like a tiny fish hooked at the end of a line, yet being pulled into a net by a hidden force. It drew her down steep granite steps into the voluminous cavern hidden beneath the foundations of Darwydden. Despite knowing she was immortal in spiritual form, she still walked gingerly down into the submerged arena. She was afraid. There was something about the place that felt hallowed and ancient, despite the fact it had now been converted into some sort of entertainment venue.

The caves and myriad of tunnels beneath the manor house and its adjoining castle, still cast out a magical vibration. It felt sanctified, revered and oddly enough…almost holy.

The wedding party were giddy and loud. They clapped and cheered as the magician before them performed impossible feats of illusion. The performer was a young man, with a blonde ponytail and an ankle length coat which appeared to be on fire. Defying gravity he levitated into the air. Clarah presumed he must be the son Roserie had mentioned to her. The lighting had been subdued for his final act, yet studying his facial features in more detail, she recognised that indeed it was Soul.

As cloned holographic images flew around the room, the real Soul eventually materialised on stage to enthusiastic applause. She watched him with interest, as he made his exit speech.

Soul took a bow before his appreciative audience and then announced, 'Thank you for participating in my little games. I trust that you have all located your jewellery and all handwriting has now returned to normal. The music show starts outside at 6 p.m. with DJ Izy Starker, who has just flown in from Ibiza, so for those of you who want to dance the night away – enjoy. Micah and his band will be on stage at 8pm and I am going to be doing something dangerously insane from the top of the castle battlements at midnight. In the meantime, I would like to welcome the comedian Eddie Bayn to the stage, who will entertain you for the next 40 minutes. Of course, I cannot leave without a toast, so can we all raise a glass to the beautiful bride and her fortunate groom… "Tia and Nico".

Clarah decided to intervene with the moment, recalling the request of her favourite angel. She approached Soul and whispered into his ear. 'Tell them to stand and leave their drinks on the table. Just trust me with this one Soul. Believe in your powers and the glasses will raise into the hands of their owners.' She hoped the angelic whispering trick would work.

Soul continued with his speech, then adding, 'actually, why waste valuable energy. Everybody please stand, leave your drinks on the table and simply hold out your drinking hand.'

Clarah dashed around the room and unseen by any of the guests, she elevated each champagne flute into a thirsty waiting hand. As the crystal rose through the air, everybody gasped at the pure, fantastical magic which defied all explanation and the law of gravity. Even Soul looked confused by what had just happened. He passed it off as his own genius moment of trickery, but Clarah could tell he was hiding his disbelief behind a well-rehearsed veneer.

Cloud of smoke – massive blast – and Souls clothes were left crumpled on the floor. As exits go – it was impressive.

Clarah felt pleased with her act of hocus-pocus, but then remembered she was here for a reason. The copper scroll was invisible as long as she held it in her hand, but despite that it was as precious thing of antiquity and it needed to be delivered to its new owner. Its message needed to be conveyed.

She refocused and felt inexplicably drawn towards a man who sat quietly in the shadows. All around him flitted crazy manic flashing lights, loud music and tropical holographic images, yet he was sat alone in a dark quiet corner. It was a place of peace and solitude amidst the madness. The man seemed to shun the party that reeled around him. Dylan Neville - she didn't know how she knew his name, she just did.

Clarah sensed that he was in harmony with some far greater power. He was not what she expected. She didn't know exactly what she had envisaged, but it was probably more akin to an old man with a long white beard. Possibly a wise old wizard who had taken centuries to master the order of Bard and Ovate. Yet what actually met with her eyes was the frame of a young man in his mid to late twenties.

He was partially dressed for a wedding. His upper half was donned in a crisp white cotton Gucci shirt, and yet from the waist down came the shock of torn black jeans. His shirt arms had been rolled up, revealing taut tanned muscles, covered in a variety of tattoos. He had the tattoo of a noose around his neck. It was an unpleasant image.

He looked directly at her – she was sure of it, and yet she was invisible to all mortals. His hair was wavy, shoulder length and jet black. His eyes were every bit as black as his hair. He sat silently smouldering in the shadows; like a fire that was not raging, but with ashes that held a secret heat. It was a heat that could not be contained.

Clarah felt ashamed as an injection of hormones filled her virtual bloodstream with pure desire. She didn't want to believe it was true, yet it was true. She felt an instant attraction to him. She knew the man to be Dylan, the direct descendent of the alien Mug; the very being that flew around on his silver disc and befriended Simon Magnus in biblical times. Mug Ruith- the druid king; the one who beheaded John the Baptist. Here before her was a man from his bloodline. She despised, hated and lusted after him, all at the same time.

'I don't know who you are, but I can see you. Make yourself known.'

She was in shock. If he could see her then maybe he could also read her mind, and quite frankly…that would be embarrassing.'

'I have come in search of Dylan.'

'Then you have hit the bullseye. I am Dylan. Who are you?'

'Clarah. My name is Clarah. How can you see me?'

'I can see all spirits Clarah. How did you get through the dome?'

'I can materialise myself. Your magic dome only shields you from energy forms. I can turn myself into matter, so I just walked through it like every other guest.

'Wow, that is impressive and yet worrying. We have a chink in our armour. So Clarah, you are a ghost that can actually become flesh and blood. Neat! I have not heard of that before. I didn't think that was possible. What species are you? What planet are you from?'

'I am human. I am from earth.'

'When did you die?'

'I haven't… not yet, but I don't think I have long.'

'Well you are unusual, I grant you that. Look erm…Clarah, it's a bit noisy in here and I am starting to get some odd looks. Folks think I am talking to myself and at best they have already classified me as some weirdo. If you can follow me, I will take you to somewhere private, somewhere quiet where we can talk. I have been waiting for you Clarah. I have waited a long time.'

Dylan rose from his seat and walking away from the wedding party, moved towards a cave entrance which was illuminated by a deep crimson light.

He joked, 'we call this the mouth to hell. It isn't really. We just say that to keep the kids out. People have been lost down here…lost and never found. However, there is a labyrinth of tunnels that lead to somewhere special. It's dark and tricky underfoot. I can only see your outline so I don't know if you are floating along or if you have to actually walk, but if you are doing the whole contact of foot with floor thing, please look where you are going.'

'Take a look behind you,' instructed Clarah.

Dylan stopped in his tracks and did as he was told. Clarah had completely materialised, still wearing her cream wedding suit, holding the scroll in one hand and her shoes in her other. She looked down upon her attire.

'I am not dressed appropriately for this situation. Give me a moment Dylan.'

She closed her eyes tightly and almost instantaneously she was wearing hiking boots and a navy-blue jump suit.'

Dylan was speechless.

'My wardrobe is only limited by my imagination, and sadly I am not that inventive when it comes to clothes. This will do for now I guess.'

Dylan was truly stuck for words. He turned the light on from his mobile. He studied her face carefully, teasing some hair away from her face and tucking it behind her left ear. It was a gesture that was unexpectedly and unnervingly intimate.

'I was told you were a clone. We could never keep track of you though. You were not like the others. You moved around within your closeted Gypsy community and we could never get close enough to you. Strange…I had presumed that all clones were identical, but you have a different look to you Clarah.'

He looked deep into her eyes and stroked her cheek.

'Your look is wild and untamed; like a feral kitten. Nobody can control you. I like that about you Clarah. Now take my hand and follow.'

Clarah muttered to herself, thinking that he could have used a better comparison.

'Bloody feral kitten,' she hissed to herself. Only her Baba May referred to her as that and she always took it as an insult.

As they descended deeper into the cave system, they came to the tunnel which was directly below the old castle dungeons. The floor was level and padded down with rushes and herbs. They trod upon a lavender carpet. It had been pitched upon the stony ground many centuries ago, yet still secreted a vague aroma from its purple flowers.

The smell of candle tallow lay heavy in the stale air. Combined with the herbs and perfumed carpet, the medieval pathway emitted a sweet sickly and musty fragrance. Clarah noted that rush lights had been impaled on vertical spikes driven into the stone walls. In places deemed to be dangerous underfoot, larger flares hung from iron rings in the granite. It may have been medieval, but this was still a well-used walkway.

The myriad of tunnels finally opened up to reveal another huge cavern. A hole in the cave roof illuminated the entire area with a shaft of brilliant sunlight from above. Trickles of rain water dripped down from the top and echoed around the eerie chambers.

This was no ordinary cave. Odd carvings of spirals and circles had been engraved upon the granite walls. They were caveman like in appearance. Clarah gained the immediate impression that she had walked into somewhere almost prehistoric, and certainly ritualistic. Incense hung in the air and gave this sacred space a ceremonial atmosphere. A large rectangular alter had been carved from out of the stone. Sprinklings of Malachite gave the alter a dark green hue. Large 3ft brown candles had been placed on each corner. Clarah shivered as she saw them. Brown was her least favoured colour.

Dylan noticed her shiver. 'What's the matter?'

She shrugged off the question. 'Oh nothing.'

He persisted. 'No really, please tell me. Something has made you feel uneasy.'

'My Grandmother is a shuvihani. That is our word for a witch. She meddles in the dark side and that makes me feel uneasy. I blame her for my present situation Dylan. She uses brown candles. I noticed them on your alter. I don't like the colour.'

Dylan put a comforting arm around her shoulder.

'Truly there is nothing to fear Clarah. We do not practice witchcraft in this place. All this is, is nothing more than an ancient druid's grotto.

We are not a religion. We simply respect all aspects of nature. When we burn a brown candle, we are simply sending a message to the universe to state that we respect the dignity and solemnity of mother Earth and that we acknowledge the delicate balance of all things living upon this Earth. We come in peace.'

Clarah understood. She could sense that about Dylan. He was young, and yet his wisdom was as old as the hills that contained these caverns.

'I just don't like the colour brown Dylan. It reminds me of a place I once went to in my dreams. I think it was just at the point I went into my coma. I guess I haven't explained that bit to you, have I? You see – my real body is lying in some hospital bed attached to drips and a ventilator. Somehow my soul escaped. I think my Baba May…that's my meddlesome grandmother, cast some spell upon me and hey...here I am.'

Dylan looked genuinely sad.

'I am sorry Clarah, but I am glad you are here and pleased to have met you. I would thank your Baba May for that much. So…this place you went to…it wasn't the brown mountain, was it?'

Clarah gasped.

'My lord – yes. Everything was a shade of brown. I was just walking around this bloody mountain, getting nowhere. Going around and around in circles with a weight upon my back. Do you know of this place?'

Dylan indeed knew of this place, but only through the myths and legends that had followed the prophesy of Tamar down through the centuries.

'Sheol. Some may call it Limbo, but that isn't what it is. It is worse than Limbo. Your Baba May did you a favour Clarah. She pulled you away from that terrible place.'

'Sheol…why does that name sound familiar to me Dylan?'

'It is because it was the name of one of Tamar's twin daughters.'

'I do not know this story. Tell me more.'

'Tamar was a woman who lived thousands of years ago and we believe she came from Palestine. She was not totally of this earth. It is our belief that a collective of ancient civilisations from beyond the furthest stars, visited earth and some bred with a chosen few. Tamar was one of those offspring. To being with, she had twin boys – Zarah and Pharez. They were the sons of King Judah. Then she had twin girls. The first born was named Leda and it is from her that the Ledanites get their name. She was an exact clone of her mother. It was destined that each clone would bear twin girls, of which only one would be a clone. This pattern would continue until Zarah and Pharez could be born again. The cloning was to protect Tamar's pool of unusual genes throughout the passage of time. Tamar knew that otherwise; her genetic inheritance would be diluted. The youngest of Tamar's female twins was Sheol. Although not a clone, Sheol was bestowed with supernatural powers so that she, and all her descendants, would have the magical ability to protect the line of clones throughout history. Many renowned soothsayers, psychics and magicians are alleged to have descended from Sheol. Unlike Leda's mostly female line, the line of Sheol could produce both male and female in equal numbers. However, it is told that Sheol had two sides to her character. Although being given the role of protector, she also had a tendency to misuse her powers. It is said that she created a place within the celestial realm, a place where she could collect and keep souls. Think of it as a holding bay, not heaven and not hell…but a place of lost souls.'

'Are you talking about a place for the outliers?'

'Indeed Clarah. I am told it has the appearance of a brown mountain. If you were neither dead or alive, then it is possible your soul was lost and for a short time was held captive in Sheol. Legend has it that she named the mountain after herself. Maybe this is just mythology, but it is what some believe.'

Clarah went quiet. Dylan had stunned her into silence.

She removed the copper scroll from her backpack. She had created the thought to place it there when she had transformed into her other more robust outfit. Now it was Dylan's turn to be stunned into silence. She placed it in his hands.

'This is yours I believe. I was told to give it to you.'

'But…it looks new. The copper scroll we have looks exactly the same as this. It is the scroll that contains the prophesy of Tamar and it is very old. We have tried to protect it from the elements, but it has partially corroded and is now covered by a flaky orange -green outer layer. I don't understand Clarah. The copper on this scroll looks brand new. How can this be? Have you made a copy?'

'I am afraid Dylan that your corroded scroll is the actual copy. What I have just given you is the genuine article. You see, I am not just a lost soul or a wild feral kitten for that matter. I can also travel through time, both backwards and forwards. I visited Tamar as she was about to give birth to Sheol and Leda. I was told to bring this with me – to bring it into the future and deliver it to the one who would know how to use it?'

Dylan had to sit down upon a nearby rock. It was the rock directly below the shaft of light that came from the cave roof. He held the scroll in both outstretched palms. The light illuminated it so it almost appeared to be on fire. He had no reason to doubt Clarah's story. He could sense the magic that came from the ancient text.

'Why, I mean why would someone create a copy of this?'

Clarah had no idea why she knew the answer to his question, only that she did.

'Tamar lived in a dangerous era. People viewed her with suspicion, especially after she tricked King Judah into impregnating her. When both her former husbands died, this only made life more difficult. They were brothers and they died young and without any trace of illness. There are those who thought she was a witch. She was feared. This was also a time when womankind was deemed as inferior to men. One could argue that this archaic attitude still exists today, especially in my community. But no matter...Tamar was special, better, different – and it was this difference that those around her feared the most. You see Dylan, she knew the future. She knew what mankind would have to go through, but she was illiterate and couldn't write it down. So, she commissioned a scribe. The scribe was one of King Judah's men and he was nervous about the situation. What Tamar told him to write, sounded like heresy to his male ears. So, he omitted parts of the text and changed other parts.'

'You know this for sure?'

A deeply serious look was etched within the worry lines on Dylan's brow.

'I take it you can read the scroll.'

'Whilst my body is lying in the deepest of depths of the unconscious, I have this floating brain that can just think about something and make it happen. So yes, I can both read and understand old Aramaic, and for that matter...Welsh.'

'If you know so much Clarah, then I take it that you know I am one of four chieftains of the Ledonites. We are a peaceful following…multi-racial and we belong to no single religion exclusively. We exist to adhere to a prophesy we have always believed to be true. We protect each clone as much as can. We knew about you and your sister Nina, but we couldn't get close to you. You moved around too much and your community was too protective and closeted. If you are about to tell me that all we have believed in for centuries, was from a fake copy of the prophesy…falsified by some scribe of the king, then I don't know what to say. I don't know how to share this with the others. We are a global society. The news will not be taken kindly.'

'The truth isn't like a badly fitting shoe Dylan, whereby no matter how much it hurts, you can push it and force it until you make it fit. The truth isn't up for negotiation, or interpretation. Quite simply – it is. Once you utter the truth, you can fall no further. Nobody can catch you out, because there are no lies to catch. No matter how ugly or how painful, truth is always the better option. To tell a lie is to insult he who listens – but to tell the truth is to respect he who listens. You know what you should do Dylan. You know what is the right thing.'

'For a young girl, you seem wise beyond your years.'

'Trust me, this wisdom stuff is all very new to me as well, and it takes some getting used to. I don't know where it come from sometimes. I think it could be an angel whispering in my ear. They do that, you know. Manipulators…every one of them.'

Dylan laughed. He enjoyed the company of his unexpected visitor. She had a dry sense of humour and he liked that about her. He also found her deeply attractive…these were feelings that confused and unnerved him.

'So, then Clarah – I will take this scroll to be transcribed by an expert and of course I promise that this will be done. You have my word. However, in the meantime, can you give me a brief about what it says…I know that you know?'

This time it was Clarah's turn to giggle. It was a flirtish response and totally inappropriate. She found the Celtic Druid chief, charming and attractive. She tried to wash her mind clean by thinking about Konnor - the young American boy who had recently captivated her heart. Yet try as she may, Dylan possessed an allure which was both extraordinary and alarmingly enthralling.

'The scribe found a couple of things in the prophesy that didn't fit in with the Middle Eastern way of thinking. This was way back in the day when ignorance and obedience would keep one's head on one's neck. So, he cut out what he considered to be controversial and maybe even treacherous. You see, folk back then believed in the sanctity of bloodlines. It's the whole biblical she begot, he begot family tree stuff. Royalty assumed they were special and somehow directly related to God. Tamar didn't agree with that. Only she and she alone carried some magical spark of DNA. Sure – she wanted it to continue undiluted into the 21st century, but in general she thought the royal bloodlines and inter-breeding of cousins and so on, was stupid, unnecessary and even dangerous. She understood the concept of genetics, way before anyone else. In her prophesy, she said those of mixed blood would eventually become the strongest humans on earth. That those with a large mixed genetical pool would gain domination. The thing is Dylan and this is what makes this scroll controversial… when she spoke of mixed blood she wasn't just referring to mixing races of humans. She was referring to other life forms…aliens from other planets. I mean this was full on ET science fiction stuff back in a time when the movement of the planets still freaked people out. Nobody even understood deoxyribonucleic acid back then, and please don't make me repeat that as I can't say it without spitting. The scribe thought she was crazy and would be condemned as a mad woman. Some of what he omitted was actually done to protect her.'

'What else? I sense there is more Clarah.'

'Well yes – it's the whole gender thing and men being better than woman. She did foretell that she would produce a line of clones and that one who lived a similar life to her would have male twins. Indeed, she did state that these twins would become great and powerful men. However, she also foretold that it was in fact a woman who would bring order to the earth. A powerful female born from human and alien mixed with evil and goodness, would become the supreme blend of all races universally. She would be so exceptionally skilled, that she even had the power to stop the moon in its orbit. These words were to be written back in an era when woman was considered to be just mothers, wives or concubines and nothing greater than this. More so, this remarkable woman of the future would marry one of the male twins, and their offspring would be yet more females and so – the meek would inherit the earth. You can see why this prophesy could be considered heretical, profane and what other big word do you want me to throw at this – perhaps blasphemous?'

'Shite, I don't mean to say that Tamar's prophesy is shite …I mean to say, shite what am I going to do now? So much has been omitted from the version we have been following.'

'That's three shite's in one sentence Dylan and that's money for the swear jar. I take it that all this has come as a shock.'

'Shock – well yes, that about sums it up. Out of idle interest – does the new leader of our earth have a name?'

'Erm. Candy.'

'You are joking with me surely. So, the new leader of earth has been named after American sweets or toffees or whatever?'

'Not quite Dylan – she will be named after Moses's wife Queen Candace. Slightly more regal and when I say she will be, I mean she hasn't been born yet. Where are we now? What is the date? I lose track of time in my timeless world?'

'June 2016.'

'Really? Wow, the weeks have flown. It was September 2015 when I came back from Bali. My God, I have been in a coma for 9 months…just like a gestation period. It all seems like yesterday to me. Anyway, according to Tamar's prophesy, Candace won't be born until Christmas 2017. So, she hasn't even been conceived as yet. Bit of a weird thought.'

Dylan had stopped listening to these remarkable revelations. They were almost too much for him to take in. He now focussed on the beautiful lady stood before him, with her hiking boots, overhauls and infantile daisy-chain crown.

'Will I ever see you again, Clarah?'

'If all goes to plan Dylan, you will remember everything I have told you about the scroll, but you will forget ever meeting me. That was the deal I struck with the devic kingdom.'

'The …what kingdom?'

'Hey, just google it.'

Dylan then looked on Clarah with some concern. She looked pale and drained. Her light was fading. His logical mind kept reminding him that she was just a spirit who appeared to be real and yet wasn't.

'Are you okay Clarah? I can see the alter behind you. It's like I can see through you. You are fading…I am losing you.'

'I am pure energy Dylan. I have to eat and sleep to stay strong. Aura highly recommends eggs and my Baba May fills me with cuckoo tea. These visits take a lot of energy from me. They drain my body of its life force and make me ill. My long-haul flight to visit Tamar …it almost killed me. Pardon me for being rude…but I have to…I have to go to….to my room...to rest…I need to…

Before he could ask who, Aura was…she was gone. She had simply vanished before his eyes, but the daisy chains were still on the floor. Dylan looked at the copper scroll and felt sad.

For the short time, he was in her company, he had connected with the beautiful Gypsy clone. He knew they would not meet again and he also recognised the enormous sacrifice she had made in recovering the original scroll from Tamar.

Yet he was a powerful Druid warlock, and also a descendent of an alien being – the mighty Mug. He too, was of mixed universal race. The unborn Candy did not hold all the cards on that claim. Could he not cast a spell of his own? Maybe he could divert the course of destiny and meet Clarah again – somewhere else…sometime else? He would think upon it.

He picked the daisies up from the floor and swore that they would meet her again…it was destiny.

Sheila Mughal

CHAPTER 27

Monday 14ᵗʰ June 2016

THE INTENSIVE CARE UNIT - WYTHENSHAWE

Dr Forshaw had broken a few rules, but given the circumstances, he didn't know what else to do. Simon De Vede was the nephew of his good friend Mercy and he could trust Mercy. Even though she had once masked the identity of his patient, falsified her own ID, forged legal documents, told lie after lie after lie and been implicated in a kidnap. Putting all that aside, she was indeed a trustworthy friend. He hoped her nephew had been cut from the same cloth.

Simon, along with his newest employee Sam Drummond, sat nervously in Tomas Forshaw's office. Sam kept tapping his pencil on the coffee mug the Dr's PA had given him. It irritated the hell out of Simon, but in a strange way he welcomed the distraction. The chemical smell of disinfectant irritated his nose, causing him to sneeze relentlessly. Sam was equally unimpressed by the harsh smelling floor cleaner. It reminded him of the luminous green stuff used to wash down the prison shower cubicles. He didn't welcome any memory remotely connected to his former career.

Tomas Forshaw eventually walked in, apologising profusely for his late arrival. Simon stood up to greet him.

'So, pleased to meet you at long last Dr Forshaw. My aunt speaks well of you.'

'Please just call me Tomas, and how is that amazing aunt of yours these days?'

'Still officially dead I am told.'

Both men smiled in a knowing way. The private joke left Sam totally confused.

'So, to business. I guess you are wondering why I gave your detective agency a call?'

The earlier laughter had now been brushed aside, as the young consultant wore a more sombre expression.

'I was curious Tomas. I sort of presumed it had something to do with my Aunt Mercy.'

'Not really,' Tomas responded. 'More to do with a young Gypsy girl you were hired to find. I understood that you were the chap that packed her bags for home and put her on a plane in Bali. Is that true?'

'We are talking about Clarah Lee I presume? I am so sorry. My aunt gave me quite a ticking off about that whole situation. I should have gone with her, I know that now. How is she? Is she recovering? My aunt told me she had some sort of blood clot.'

Dr Forshaw stood and gestured that the two detectives should follow him. The visitors stood in silence around Clarah Lee's bed.

The sight of a once healthy girl, looking so withered and lifeless quite stunned them both. The monitors, the equipment, the tubes, the alarms…collectively they were all so overwhelming. Although both Sam and Simon had met Clarah face to face, be it in different circumstances, - the person in the bed bore little resemblance to either of their respective memories. Her youthful bonny face with tanned skin and rosy cheeks, now appeared gaunt and sallow. Do Forshaw guessed what they were both thinking. It was his job and he was used to the technology of an intensive care unit, but he recognised that it was often frightening and overwhelming for visitors.

'Will she survive this? I am guessing that is the question you want to ask, yet dare not. Well gents, it would take nothing less than a miracle. Every day her body becomes weaker. She has the occasional good day when she has a few limb movements. It's a bit like watching a sleeping dog who moves its hindlegs when it dreams of running for a ball. Maybe she is dreaming…who knows? We suspect she has sustained fairly severe brain damage, so we cannot tell for sure.'

Sam bit his lip. To say anything otherwise would make him seem foolish. But he knew. He knew that Clarah was doing something far more remarkable than simply dreaming.

'I am sorry about Clarah Lee,' pronounced Simon. 'I really wish I had got on the plane with her, but I don't see how I could have prevented her blood clot.'

'Her blood clot was not an accident Simon. Someone deliberately and with intent, gave her unlicensed medication. It was a drug that induces abortion and it isn't licenced for use because it also causes blood clots. Combined with high altitude, this was almost a fatal cocktail for poor Miss Lee.'

'Wow. I wasn't expecting you to say that. Do you know who did it?'

'The police are about to make an arrest, so I can't say anything more. Come into my office. We need to talk in private.'

Both men followed Dr Forshaw back into his office, each in a state of muted shock.

'Can I get you some tea/coffee?'

'No, no…thank you but it's okay. What can we do for you Tomas?'

The young consultant poured himself a glass of chilled water then sat facing the detectives.

He began, 'Clarah Lee has an elderly grandmother who visits her almost every day. She hasn't been here in over a week and I am concerned. I am aware that you know the family. Mercy told me that they hired you to chase Clarah around the world. Can you please go to her grandmother's house and check that she is okay? I would have called the police, but I don't want the guys in blue bursting through the door if she is just resting up. Plus, I assume you know where May Loveridge lives, whereas it would take the police longer to track her down. I will pay for your services…personally.'

Simon De Vede shook his head, 'no… you don't need to pay. I was partially responsible for this mess and besides that, you are a friend of my aunt and she would kill me if I charged you.'

Tomas smiled, 'she really would kill you, wouldn't she?'

Simon recognised that they both knew Mercy's persona very well, indeed her infamy proceeded her.

'Leave it with me Tomas. We will drive over tomorrow afternoon and check that the old lady is okay. She lives over in Whitby, so we should be there before nightfall.'

Tomas stood up and shook their hands, pleased that they had agreed to the task in hand.

'One more thing guys… just in case things take a turn for the worse, can you also track down another next of kin. I am thinking about the grandmother's condition, but also…'

He looked over in Clarah's direction before he could finish the sentence.

He continued, 'I don't know how long Clarah has left, but we could be talking days rather than weeks. I know she has other family and a sister somewhere. The travelling community are hard to pin down, but just in case…we need a phone number. Do you understand what I am saying?'

They did….

***

On his way back to the hospital car park, Simon made a hurried phone call. Even though his Aunt Mercy was in hiding… aka retired…aka deceased, he knew that she was still close to Dr Tomas Forshaw and conversations would have been had. He also suspected that his aunt was still well connected with New Scotland Yard and her pals at the Met. If anyone knew who was responsible for Clarah Lee's demise, then surely it must be the omnipotent Mercy De Vede. He couldn't help but smile inwardly as he thought of his aunt.

Detective extraordinaire …Miss De Vede, the ultimate all-seeing eye. She knew far more than she was letting on…he was certain of it.

CHAPTER 28

Tuesday 15th June 2016
BABA MAY

Clarah woke up slowly, stirring little by little. Her awakening spirit could hear the sound of the flagpole outside, as the loose halyard rope made a clanging sound against the metal shaft. Baba May had been horrified that her father (Mick Lee) had erected an Irish flag in their driveway. It was his act of rebellion – Tinker versus Roma. Clarah had been told that her mother Violet was opposed to the flag; concerned it may attract the wrong sort of attention. Yet despite the internal family feuding and cultural begrudgery, the white, green and orange still wafted in the North Sea breeze.

The dawn chorus almost drowned out the clink of the hoist as it swung in the troubled air. As consciousness returned to her slumbering soul, Clarah started to count the clanking of rope against metal. It was a rhythmic sound - three short bursts of noise, followed by three drawn-out clangs and then another three quick beats. A shaft of sunlight burst through an opening in the curtains, causing her eyelids to open. Now fully awake, she counted the beats on her fingers. The sudden realisation hit her like a car crash. This was no random beating of a halyard on a flag pole...this was some sort of intelligent communication. She was receiving a message. She couldn't be sure, but she thought it could be Morse code and she believed the message to be an "SOS" – and yet...how?

She jumped up from her bed and looked at her wrist watch. Her arms were thin and blue, yet she was in spirit form. Her arms were only what she believed them to be, somewhat akin to phantom limbs. Yet they had changed. Clarah knew she was still connected to her body. It was as though there was an invisible umbilical cord that held them together and occasionally she felt what her body felt and vice versa…separated and yet still as one.

The blue arms were not a good sign. What day is it? Her mobile was still charging on the side of the bed. These days she only used it to tell the time, for who else would a spirit call?

She cried out, 'shit it's the 15th - I have slept for 11 days.' This was not a good sign. Her visit to Darwydden must have stripped her soul of energy, and in so doing had also compromised her body.

She knew was slowly fading into nothingness. Eggs and cuckoo tea – that would do the trick. She needed to revive her depleted spirit. There was yet more work to do before she exited this mortal coil.

As she slowly made her way down the old creaking staircase, her assumed joints creaked almost as much as the old steps. She knew she had to think herself healthy, but the tremendous amount of energy required just to generate that powerful vision, was something that eluded her.

The fragranced trajectory of a cooked breakfast pulled her towards the kitchen door. She expected Baba May to be standing at the oven flipping a pancake, but no, it wasn't her Grandmother. She rushed towards the Devic cook, almost leaping into her arms.

'Aura, I thought you had deserted me.'

Aura was taken aback by her young outlier's enthusiasm.

'Well…it's good to know you have missed me. For the record, I have missed you as well. Take a seat Clarah, you are looking weak. I have made a special omelette just for you. You really are my favourite spiritual maverick.'

Clarah's voice was barely audible as she asked, 'where have you been?'

'I have an entire universe to cover dearest. It's a big territory. Anyway, you have been in the safe hands of an earth angel so I wasn't overly worried about you.'

'You mean Roserie?'

'Yes, the very same awesome seraph. She has been reporting back to me on a fairly regular basis. I understand you have been on some interesting adventures.'

Clarah didn't have the energy to reply. She could hardly lift the fork to her mouth, and once accomplished – then struggled to chew. She could tell that Aura was trying to mask her shock, yet was unable to hide her facial expressions. Clarah caught sight of herself in the Edwardian mirror backed sideboard. The mirror was in need of a good clean, yet even with a subtle layer of dust it still reflected a frail vulnerable frame.

'I look crap,' she declared.

'You have done too much too quickly,' responded Aura. 'I have come to mend all that has been broken. You have other big journeys to take, journeys that are immensely important. But not right now. I need you to take time out to rest, to eat, to drink, to relax, to lie on the beach and feel the sun on your face. For now, just do nothing.'

Clarah laughed to herself with what little strength she could muster.

'You know, there was a time when the thought of doing nothing and being bored seemed like the worst thing in the whole world…but now I would give anything to have boredom as my only concern.'

Aura shrugged.

'Feeling blessed by hindsight is a common thought process for an outlier. You see Clarah, everything in mortal life is just a matter of perspective. Are you on the bottom of the ladder looking up, or are you standing on the top steps looking down? The truth is, that the ladder doesn't really exist. You are exactly where you believe yourself to be, and a poor man can feel more blessed than a rich one. Once human beings start to understand that the ladder is a thing of their own invention, and stop comparing themselves with each another, then they will be free.'

'That will never happen,' replied Clarah.

'My Grandmother used to say that we are all infected with the curse of begrudgery. People are just naturally jealous and they cannot help themselves. They look at someone who has bigger and better, and they think - why them, why not me?'

'What happens then?

'Often without them realising it, they unintentionally curse you. We call it the evil eye. My gran would tie red string around my bed, make me do the mano-cornuto hand gesture every morning and wear a jet amulet. My community are very suspicious. Yet how can trinkets prevent the curse of envy when you win millions on the lottery?'

'Is that what you think happened to you Clarah?'

'I know it is. I know it for sure. I have thought about it a lot. If I could only go back in time and make it that we didn't win all that money, then I would change my destiny back to what it should have been. Maybe right now at this very moment, I would be sat in a caravan watching the rain drops slide down the window like slippery eels…betting on which one would win the race. Sure, I would be bored, most likely complaining that the day was too darn long. But I would be young and alive. Shite, at least I would have a bloody body. I could be engaged or even married to Denny, but I wouldn't know that he was a two-timing rat because I would not have found him in bed with my sister. If I was poor, maybe he wouldn't have proposed. No wedding meant no hen night and Peter wouldn't have taken all the girls to Newcastle. Peter wouldn't have left his Katalyn alone on the site. Denny wouldn't have then screwed Peters wife. Sure – I may never have known what a shite Denny was, but ignorance is bliss…is that right? What you don't know cannot hurt you. Isn't that what folks claim?'

Aura smiled, but this time it was a sympathetic gesture and one tinged with sorrow. She put a comforting arm around Clarah's skinny back.

'The universe had a greater purpose for you Clarah. You had to become what you became, so you could bring back the real scroll with the true words of Tamar's prophesy. This was required so you could stop the Ledanite from their zealous pursuit of a belief based on misinformation.'

'Well, now I have ticked that box, can I just be a simple Gypsy girl again?'

'I am sorry Clarah, but there are just two more tasks for you to do, before…'

'Before I die – isn't that what you were going to say?'

'I am sorry Clarah. It is unavoidable.'

'Sure, my body will die. Everybody dies. Nobody can control that inevitable fate, but maybe I can control when it happens. You say I have two more missions to complete…well what if I say "no". Every time I do stuff, the journey seems to bring me closer to death. So, tell me Aura, why the hell should I go on these so-called missions?'

'Because mankind needs you to complete these final assignments. This is your calling. This was one of the reasons Tamar made herself into a clone. Yes, there were other reasons, but the main one was you…it was so you could exist. You have no idea how important you are.'

Clarah huffed and puffed. She walked over to the patio windows; stirring outside as though she was seeing the world through new eyes.

She drunk in the beginnings of a beautiful summers day. The coastal vista was wild and untamed. It reminded her of herself. She had never really noticed how green the grass was, how blue the sky, how white the clouds. Clarah Lee, had walked through the world with her eyes shut. She had often looked, but never really seen. Only now…in her final days, had she chosen to remove the blindfold.

Aura gently touched her shoulder and asked, 'what's running through that feisty little mind of yours?'

Feisty! Clarah liked that adjective. It reminded her of who she once was – Mick Lee's daughter. She spun around to face the mystical entity who was trying to entice her with softly spoken words.

'I am thinking that we never really appreciate something until it is about to be taken away from us. I don't want to die young and I am not ready to vacate this planet. People have looked down upon me and spit at me all of my life. I don't owe mankind any favours. I am going to go back in time and change all of this. You can't stop me Aura – I fell out of the shipping lane so I operate without rules…you taught me that.'

'Clarah, if you do go back and change destiny then you will undo all you have done. The universe will not allow that. It will make you go through this all over again and then again and then again, until you get it right. You cannot escape your calling.'

As Aura spoke, the vision of the brown mountain came to mind. Clarah didn't want to be stuck on an endless path for all of eternity. She had been to the place of Sheol and she didn't want to go back.

'What are my two missions? What is it that you need me to do?'

'Do you recall the young magician - the one you saw at Darwydden?'

'Yes – his name is Soul. He is Roserie's son.'

'Soul is a very good person. He has a kind heart. Heck his mother is an angel so he isn't exactly going to be one of the bad guys, is he? Anyway, this is a bit of a strange story, but in about nine months from now he will be asked to rescue beings from another planet.'

'What? Like aliens?'

'Don't sound so surprised my little outlier. You stepped off the path of normality into the realm of weirdo-land a long time ago. Anyway, I am technically an alien as well, so what's the big deal?'

'Okay, I get the point. So, Soul the nice guy will rescue aliens sometime next year - am I correct thus far?'

'You are correct Clarah. These alien entities are trapped underground. There are many of them and they exist all over this planet of yours. Ancient civilisations have spoken of them throughout history, but for some reason modern humans have disregarded their stories as fictional.'

'So why Soul? How does he get involved in all of this?'

'These aliens are much like you, in that they don't possess a physical body…well they do on their own planet, but on earth they are just pure energy.'

'Oh, I see where this is going. They are outliers just like me. That's why their predicament concerns you. You are the deva of lost souls – the one that gathers together the disembodied.'

'They are not as powerful as you Clarah. They cannot walk through walls or travel through time. They are mostly trapped in deep caves and the subterranean cities of Sudan. Some of them have adapted to wear the frames of humans no longer in need of their bodies.'

'By that, I am guessing you mean dead people. Ugh…that is simply gross.'

'Survival is a strong instinct and one that all life forms possess. If you were in the same situation, you would wear a dead man's skin if that was your only choice.'

'Okay Aura, let's move on – why Soul?'

'Soul has a rare ability. He can connect with all forms of energy. He can see it, hear it, touch it and read it like a book. He will be asked to rescue some of the trapped aliens and as he can connect with their energy, he has the ability to help them.'

'That all sounds well and good, but…I am sensing a "but" is coming up.'

'You are spot on Clarah…as always. Soul will put his own life in jeopardy to complete the rescue. There will be one last alien who will be too afraid to go with him, but Soul being the person he is…nice guy, son of an angel and so on…cannot desert the one remaining creature. During this rescue attempt he will get sucked up into their realm and his spirit then becomes trapped on their planet.'

'So – another outlier outside of the shipping lane.'

'Indeed Clarah.'

'So, you need me to do what?'

'Find him and bring him back.'

Clarah knew the answer before she had even asked the question. She was also beginning to understand Aura – who she was, what she did and why she was interested in her. Aura was the deva who gathered together outliers – those who were not technically dead, but who had somehow escaped their own bodies. She also recognised that she had abilities beyond the other outliers, and that made her important to Aura. Those abilities also shortened the life span of her estranged body, but Aura didn't care about that. She would use her for as long as she had a use. Clarah decided that devas could be mean.

As the daughter of a scrap-dealer, Clarah understood the rules of negotiation and it was all about power. She had watched her own Da barter with junk yards on enough occasions. The game of haggling was all about who had the bigger bargaining tools, and right now, it seemed that the balance of power was in Clarah's favour. She tried to think what her Da would say to her if he was in the room right now. Maybe it was his whisper in her ear that said, 'not to give anything away for free', or maybe she knew him so well that she simply imagined what he would say.

Then… at that very moment she heard the clanging of the flagpole outside. It was Mick Lee's flag pole, standing proudly aloft in the driveway, with the darn Irish flag that he was so proud of. Why hadn't she figured it out before? Of course, it was her Da that had awakened her from her deep sleep. He was with her. It wasn't her imagination. With his immense skill of wheeling and dealing guiding her, Aura would be outnumbered and outmanoeuvred.

Clarah asked, 'so, you said there were two tasks required, in which case what is the second one?'

Aura sensed a change of tone in Clarah's voice, which was now more assertive and commanding. The change made her nervous.

'Just a final trip into the future. You don't have to do this if you don't want to Clarah, but there is a girl who has yet to be born. She has powers beyond yours, powers beyond any human who has ever lived and beyond any alien life form I have encountered. She will rule the world and worlds beyond. There is an important message you need to take to her. You don't have the message yet, but when you meet her you will know what to say.'

'Hmm…and if I don't do any of this…what?'

'The earth will continue to spin, humans will continue to breed and the grass, and the clouds and the sky will all remain the same colour…but, it will be a badder, sadder and darker place. You will be long gone Clarah, but the legacy you will have left behind will not be a good one.'

She shrugged, 'so no pressure then.'

'I am sorry to ask this of you. It is a big sacrifice, I understand that.'

'You have misjudged me Aura. You see…I am not some sacrificial lamb. I may be dying, but I am not a martyr. Unlike Soul, my mother was no angel. You can see what one trip to bloody Wales did to me. Look at my arms…they are blue. If my spirit is only a 20% reflection of what my body looks like, then I must look like a bag of shit right now. I slept for 11 days after visiting Wales, and that was in my own time zone. So how long will I sleep after a visit to another solar system and a little jaunt into the future to meet the new Queen of planet Earth? Give me an answer Aura… how long will I sleep?'

'You will not sleep.'

'So, I will die then, is that what you are saying?'

Aura hung her head low; ashamed for even requesting such an enormous favour. For once the beautiful alluring smile which was always favouring her face, was absent.

She replied, 'I am sorry.'

'Don't be sorry Aura. Don't be sorry at all, because it isn't happening. The chain of events that brought me to this very time and place can all be changed with a few numbers on a lottery ticket. I am going back to 2014 to reclaim my life.'

'Please don't do that Clarah. You will alter destiny. The prophesy of Tamar will remain but a sham of the truth. Soul will be forever lost in a distant galaxy. You will never meet the girl from the future and tell her what must be told. It will all be undone.'

'That's not exactly true Aura. Baba May can read the Tarot cards and see into a crystal ball. She understands destiny. I once asked her how it was that God gave us the mental capacity of free will, if in fact we had no free will at all, say if our lives were fated from birth. That would surely make us prisoners of some greater providence. I mean, why give us a blasted brain at all if we couldn't be in control of our own decisions?'

'So, what is your point?'

'Baba May told me that life was a mixture of both free will and fate. For example, it could be my destiny to say…travel to Leeds in June, but how I got there, who I met along the way and on what time and date I arrived, would be my decision. Only the destination is fated, not the journey. So, if that's the case, my decision is to change my journey. If I am destined to achieve the things you say I am fated to do, then they will happen anyway, even if I take another route. I refuse to believe it is my destiny to die so young and I won't let it happen.'

Aura shrugged, surrendering to a battle she knew she could not win. She hadn't realised that Clarah was as smart as she was unique.

'I will need to ask for some special dispensation, to allow the events to remain the same, even though you intend to alter the future to become someone very different. I am sure this exemption to the normal rules will be accepted, as long as they don't twist time in a way which will disrupt the universe. I can but ask.'

'Well you need to call your superior, whoever that is - because my mind has been made up. I just want to be normal again and that is non-negotiable.'

'So, you will do as I ask?'

'Yes Aura, but there is another condition. You need to get some energy for me. I don't know where you can bottle up the stuff, but I need more than cuckoo tea to get me though this. If I slept 11 days after a simple jaunt to Wales, I will sleep forever after some inter-galactic journey to planet Zod. Worse still, I may never wake up at all. Forget omelettes, I need some real energy injecting into both my spirit and my body. I will visit my body to check up on this and if I don't see an immediate improvement in my physical condition – the deal is off.'

'Life energy is precious …its sacred. I can't just buy it from the supermarket Clarah.'

'In the words of my Da - Mick Lee, make it happen or the deal is off.'

Aura looked disturbed, but it wasn't her outlier's tough negotiation talk putting her on her guard, something else was happening.

'We are both invisible...right?'

'Err yes. What's wrong Aura?'

'I sense that someone is walking up the path. Two men, strangers, or at least strangers to me.'

Clarah suddenly thought about her grandmother. The combination of exhaustion and complex conversations with a deva, had caused her to forget that Baba May should be somewhere in the house. With that sudden thought came the searing realisation that she hadn't seen her grandmother in a long time.

'Baba May,' she yelled out.

Silence! No reply.

'Shush,' implored Aura. I can hear them at the door.

***

The two men looked up at the big white house. The windows were covered in condensation and looked dark against the pale rendering.

'I take it you have been her before Simon?'

'Yes, about two years back. It was when Clarah went missing and the family hired me to find her.'

Sam Drummond knocked on the door, and then spotting a door bell – rang it. They both sensed that neither noise would receive an answer.

Simon asked, 'I take it that you stayed at the village pub last night? Did any of the locals have anything to say about the family?'

'Only that they kept themselves to themselves. The locals seemed to have figured out that they were the Gypsies who had the big lottery win.

Of course, everyone claims that the house is haunted and always has been. Some say a pirate once lived here, and it is said that a secret staircase leads down to the coves below. Sounds intriguing. If I lived here I would have been down there looking for buried treasure.'

Simon made no comment. He had sensed the house was haunted from the moment he first met the family. He couldn't put his finger on what it was…just a sort of eerie feel about the place.

'It looks like nobody is at home, 'stated Simon, 'as the brother of ex SAS superman JD, I am presuming you know how to pick a lock?'

Sam knelt down and removed a door key from beneath the flower pot.

'JD also taught me to check for the simplest solutions first.'

The two detectives walked nervously into the hallway, looking around and yet not knowing what they were looking for.

'I feel I am being watched.'

'Yeh – me too.'

The air was cold. They could see their own breath in front of their faces, even though outside it was a mild summers day. They walked into the kitchen, which felt much warmer than the rest of the house. Simon picked up a pan which had been sat on the aga. It had a layer of oil coating the bottom.

'This pan is still warm. Someone has recently used this. The old lady must be okay.'

'Then we should take care not to give her a heart attack. I mean, technically this is breaking an entry isn't it?'

Simon ignored the remark and called out, 'Baba May, Baba May – Mrs Loveridge, its Simon De Vede. Are you at home?'

Both men stood silently, awaiting a reply that didn't arrive.

'Sam, this kettle is still warm and so is a pan of some noxious solution left on the stove.'

He sniffed it and then sneezed, as the strong spices in the cuckoo tea irritated his nostrils.

Sam laughed, 'yes, the locals also claimed that Mrs Loveridge was a witch and her herbal portions were well known in the village. Try some Simon, it may do something to help with your…err defective love life.'

Simon hit his young employee with a knitted pillow he found on the chair. It was Clarah's favourite pillow and one that her mother had made for her when she was a baby. She did not take kindly to it being used as a weapon, and so the pillow made its way back towards Simon's head.

'Ouch – chill out Sam. I was only playing with you. No need to get into a pillow fight.'

'I didn't throw it.'

'You so did.'

'Honestly mate – I really didn't.'

'So, if you didn't, who did?'

Both men looked around the kitchen. Sam was already uneasy, having encountered Clarah back at Pathways Prison.

Sam asked nervously, 'can we leave here soon? This place gives me the creeps.'

'Me too, but we have a job to do first. Let's check all the rooms and if we don't find anything, lets scarper.'

Clarah went to follow them but Aura held her back.

'I am sorry Clarah, but I forgot to tell you something and there are some things you should not see.'

Clarah looked deep into Aura's eyes. They were deadly serious and she could see the glint of a sympathy tear. She knew…she just knew. Her worst fears were soon confirmed by the loud bellow of a man's voice. She heard the alarm in his vocal cords as he yelled out, 'Simon – get in here. I have found her.'

Clarah went to rush towards her grandmother's bedroom, but Aura blocked the door.

'Don't Clarah. She passed away over a week ago. It's best not to go to her room. Let the detectives take care of everything.'

'Whilst I was sleeping? My gran died while I was sleeping and I wasn't there to hold her hand. I need to go back in time and be with her when she passes. I can do that much for her. Why the hell didn't you tell me?'

'I am sorry Clarah. We had to have a serious conversation and if I had told you earlier, then our conversation wouldn't have happened.'

Clarah shot Aura a look of pure contempt. Indeed, the deva was devious.

Simon and Sam walked back into the kitchen. Simon was already on the phone to the GP as they sat back down on the table. Still shaking, Sam put on the kettle.

Finally finishing the call, Simon uttered 'Poor family, they have been beset with tragedy. 6 deaths in just 2 years, and judging by the way Clarah looked yesterday, it could be 7 very soon. They have literary been wiped out.'

'Did the police ever find out who put her in a come?'

'Well yes, but they weren't ever going to tell me. However, my Aunt Mercy knows just about everything about everything.'

'So?'

'According to my aunt, it was her boyfriend's brother - Asher Baratolli. Seems he had administered the medicine without Clarah's knowledge. She had just found out that she was pregnant, and there was no way it could have been the boyfriends, as he had gone back to the States several weeks earlier. I guess she must have had an affair behind the boyfriends back and big brother didn't want to be found out. My aunt knew his father Reed, and uttered a few expletives about bad blood and the son being cut from the same cloth…that sort of stuff. God, she hated Reed Baratolli.'

Clarah shouted out, 'I didn't have an affair. The bastard raped me,' but of course, nobody heard her words. She was but a spirit…listening in, but not visible or audible.

'Wasn't it an illegal or unlicensed substance? Did the police ever trace where it came from?'

'Good question Sam, but this is a hot potato so please keep this to yourself. If the tabloids got hold of this one, they would have a field day.'

'Yeh – sure. Won't say a word.'

'My aunt says it was from the Siberian Beselovaya plant, which it seems is co-owned by the Lezemel dynasty.'

'Shit! But hang on, how the hell would Asher Baratolli get his hands on an unlicensed drug from some Siberian factory. Seems like an unlikely longshot?'

'Not when you realise that Asher was a close pal of Ze'ev Lezemel. He was at university with Ze'ev, and in fact it was Asher who introduced him to his sister Armarni. Ze'ev and Armarni are now engaged. My aunt says that calls were made from Bali to Colorado and to Ze'ev's number.

Then calls were made from Ze'ev's cell phone to the Siberian plant. The package was flown over via private jet, it wasn't even put in the normal post. There is an audit trail for all the calls and transactions.'

'Bloody hell fire – that is big news. So, has Ze'ev Lezemel been arrested?'

'Oh yes, and when Clarah dies…which doctors believe will be quite soon, then the famous billionaire playboy could be an accessory to murder.'

'My God Simon. This will be all over the tabloids. Why does the name Beselovaya sound so familiar then? I have heard that name before.'

'You probably have Sam. Sergei Beselovaya is a well-known oligarch. His daughter Katya was one of my aunt's closest friends. Katya Beselovaya was murdered in Atlanta back in July 2013. It was a professional job. And…get this Sam, there was also a Baratolli connection with this murder, accept that this time it was the father Reed. It seems that Katya had been trying to blackmail Reed in some way. He had sexually molested her at a party once, so she had some shit on him.'

'I am shocked. So now I understand your aunts comment about like father like son. Was Reed accused of Katya's murder?'

'He was – but they could never find any evidence of his involvement. They found the hitman…some Russian ex KGB bloke, but they never found out who paid him and I believe he was paid with rare red diamonds. Diamonds that were never licenced or reported stolen – so he gets to own them and walks from prison a rich man when he finally gets out.'

'But... if they were so rare, could they not trace the mine they came from?'

'Oh yes, they found the diamond mine. It is owned by some highly secretive organisation called the Ouroboros. I am told that they denied ownership. I guess the blood red diamonds were also blood money – so they didn't want any involvement. It was all a bit of a mystery and my aunt thinks it will never really be solved. I find it odd how it's all so interconnected. There is another world out there Sam. An underworld of crime and money and riddles. It's a world which is unbeknown to us. I wish I understood it – but I don't. It's like one big secret, and those in the know aren't going to tell. Maybe one day, mere peasants like ourselves will finally understand.'

At that moment, the GP walked in through the open door. Sam and Simon went to greet him and then showed him towards Baba May's bedroom.

Clarah sat in shock. Aura looked down upon her pale silent outline. She didn't know what to do or say to comfort her.

Clarah finally spoke.

'When I die, and the detectives think this will be soon…it will go to a murder trail wont it? Due to Asher's connections and these so called Lezemel big-wigs, it will be all over the news. I will be disgraced posthumously. My entire community will hear how I ran away from my husband-to-be and how this happened on my hen night. Nobody will be able to tell them it was because I caught him in bed with my sister, because aside from Denny and Katalyn, who else knows any of this? Nobody still living- that's for sure. Then the press will tell them that I then found myself a new boyfriend within months, and then cheated on him by sleeping with his brother. Nobody will be able to tell them that actually I was raped. My vitsa will believe that I have brought disgrace and shame upon them. Our family name will be mud, and they will be happy for it to be mud because we were the arrogant greedy scum who didn't share our winnings. Their jealousy has created all of this, but who can tell our side of the story? Nobody. They will think I caused my father to hang himself. They will even think I caused my mother's cancer. They will believe my brothers drug habit is what caused my sister to die, and that part of it will be true. It will all come out in public wont it, and yet none of us will be around to defend ourselves. Asher Baratolli, son of a famous musician and Ze'ev Lezemel playboy billionaire – this will be all over the TV and the papers. I will be publicly named and shamed.'

What could Aura do but listen in silence.? She knew Clarah was speaking the truth. She also knew that there would be no negotiation on Clarah's terms and conditions. After these revelations, her young outlier would be keener than ever, to wipe the past and alter her destiny. She wasn't sure how she could do it, but somehow this collector of lost souls would have to find a precious slice of the most valuable type of energy – life force itself.

Clarah turned to face her.

'I am going back to be with my grandmother as she passes. One should not be alone in death.'

With those words, she faded away. Shortly afterwards Aura also vanished.

The funeral director arrived at the house, and once again the house was empty. Yet those who were sensitive to such things, knew there was something else…something they could not see. It was a house that was never really empty.

CHAPTER 29

Tuesday 22nd June 2016
OUT OF THIS WORLD

Since being a tiny lass, Clarah had been a rebellious little mare. From the minute, she could walk and talk, her parents would yell at her, 'do as you are told,' but Clarah never did as she was told. Her defiant Romany spirit would stamp her feet and kick dust into the weary eyes of those who tried to tame her. That was… until now. Right here and right now, she had to obey precise instructions. The gravity of her mission and the importance of getting it absolutely right, had placed her in a serious mood.

As the negotiations with Aura had unfolded over the past week, it became clear to Clarah that she held less aces up her sleeve than she had first assumed. The balance of power was not in her favour.

Aura was a deva of the spirit world. Clarah had assumed that this was some highfalutin title that didn't really mean anything. However, Aura had flexed her wraithlike muscles and demonstrated exactly what it meant. The faerie mistress controlled the movement of souls between worlds, and in Clarah's case, between places and time. Aura could click her divine little fingers and stop Clarah's teletransportational jaunts within a zeptosecond. Clarah had been merely allowed to manipulate the laws of physics by way of a temporary measure. The permission to distort time and destiny, could be taken away as easily as it was granted.

The devic kingdom was in control. If Clarah wanted to go back to being a poor traveller girl sat in a caravan on a Yorkshire lay-by, she would have to do as she was told. Exactly as she was told.

Aura had taught her how to cleanse her mind of all other thoughts, and so after a period of intense meditation, she concentrated on the date.

This journey was a trip into the near future. She was going forward in time to an up and coming equinox, on the 20th March 2017. She was told that she could focus on any time after 10.30am and so she chose 12 midday. Her grandmother had taught her that magic was at its strongest at high noon, at the time when the Sun was highest in the sky. Baba May sometimes chanted lines from the bible as she lit incense, and so Clarah copied *(making a few bespoke alterations)*.

Holding a white feather, she whispered a prayer. She had absolutely no idea if she had said the right words or not, she only knew that what she was about to do felt dangerous.

Her journey through time and the vastness of space was immediate. In all of her earthly travels, she had never experienced floating before, yet now she floated. She could fly. She had never flown before. Yet now she could just think of a direction and simply be there.

Was this the effect of zero gravity? She couldn't be sure, but the feeling was pure exhilaration.

When she was twelve years old, Kane dropped some acid into her food by way of a joke. Shortly afterwards she experienced a mind-blowing trip, which she could only recall as crazy multi-coloured euphoria.

Kane was grounded for weeks after that, but the memory of the sensation had never left her. Yet now she was living it over again. She was losing her sense of self…blending with the surrounding environment as though she was part of it and not a separate entity. It was as though she was returning to the universe that had created her…. like a river running back into the sea. Salt water and rain water connecting to make a vast ocean.

She was nothing, yet everything, nowhere yet everywhere. Clarah was being eaten…consumed by a greater existence. She came to her senses. She couldn't let this happen. At that moment, she fully understood the process of death. Dust by dust, molecule by molecule, surrendering one's life force back from whence it came. Being one with the universe and its creator. Death was losing one's self….and that was what she was doing. She was dying.

She then felt a sharp electrical shock run through her being and she knew that her body back on earth was being resuscitated. Defibrillator paddles were begging the return of a normal sinus rhythm. Her heart had stopped, and at that very moment she actually wanted to die. Her earthly chest had been surgically opened, and someone was holding her heart in his hands. It was a man, one of many a man who had held her heart. However, on this occasion he was a doctor and he was performing manual cardiac massage. Tomas – she knew his name. She heard someone call it out. Part of her was in a hospital bed, and yet another part of her was somewhere else…some other galaxy, some other solar system, somewhere very far away.

She didn't care. What was a body anyway? Just meat, and meat that stinks when it rots. She felt no attachment to her physical self. The umbilical cord was about to snap. The feeling of total peace, total warmth, total calm was immense. Even her LSD experience could not emulate this beautiful altered state of self. She had no words. Nothing could describe it.

Clarah Lee had a job to do. She had to wake up and shake herself out of this trance like condition. She wasn't ready to join the universe quite yet, but she would always remember what it felt like to pass over. From now on, death would not be feared. It wasn't an ending, or even a beginning…but simply a returning. She knew that now.

Clarah was being shaken. She couldn't work out if it was her earthly body or inner spirit being agitated, but something or someone was being fairly assertive and heavy handed. She turned and saw her grandmother.

'Child; snap out of it. You have been drifting. You must refocus. There is a man down on that planet; a human who shouldn't be there. You are here to rescue him. You are not here to die. Clarah…wake up, wake up.'

Her eyes opened and she glanced down to the sphere below her. It was a brown globe with a yellowish haze. She then went to hug her grandmother, but her arms passed through her.

'We are both in spirit form Clarah. We can't actually touch, but I feel your love. Touch is not a sensation we require in the afterlife. We don't have those nerve ending thingies.'

Clarah smiled and then cried.

'I guess I am not supposed to have tears either?'

'You just think they are tears, but if you wipe your eyes I think you will find that they are not wet.'

'What should I do now Baba May?'

'You should do down there and focus on Soul. Think about him and you will find him.'

'I don't like the look of that planet. Earth is blue with fluffy bits, whilst that planet looks like cow dung. Why is it that colour?'

Baba May smiled reassuringly.

'The yellow smoke is Fluorine gas. This planet doesn't have air on its surface as Earth does. Its atmosphere is highly toxic, but don't worry Clarah as you are not really breathing. You may think you are, but these are just thoughts.'

'I am afraid.'

'You will be fine lass. When you get closer to the surface you will find jagged rocks of Iodine crystals...some reaching as high as a mountain. They give off an amazing purple cloud, but it can make it hard to see. Just trust your instincts more than your eyes.'

'How do you know all of this Baba May?'

'Ah well now, when I was a teenager, my cousin Babik and I used to go out on his scooter to do a recce of the nearby area. When I say scooter, it was actually more of a scrambling bike, but it was fit for purpose. We could ride over hills and ditches and through woodland. We were on the lookout for places to set up camp. Once we had found somewhere suitable, we would go back and tell the rest of the vitsa where to head. Ah...those were the days. We had a lot of fun.'

Clarah laughed, 'are you telling me that you went onto this planet to do a recce for me?'

'It was interesting – more of an exploration...mind stretching.'

'So, what else should I look out for Baba May?'

'There's a big mountain. You can't miss it. Awful big brown thing, there's a hole in the side that leads to their underworld. You need to head for that opening, as the creatures that live here, exist under the ground. They even have air down there. It's not as fresh as earth air ...mixed with a tiny bit of methane and sulphur but hey... they seem to like it. As a word of warning Clarah, I think the mountain could be technically classified as a volcano. I have seen it spew out molten silicone, which then cools off and rains down as glass. Scared the bejesus out of me when I first saw it, but nothing for you to worry about.'

'What? You mean it actually rains glass on that planet?'

'Glass as sharp as a surgeon's knife...so now you know why they live underground.'

'Anything else I should know?'

'Oh yes, it has two Suns. You don't see them both at once, accept on the odd occasion and boy oh boy does it get hot then. There is a lake of mercury and you can actually see it boil. Quite hypnotic...little silver bubbles pop up on the surface and then burst like a steaming metallic geezer. Fascinating to watch.'

'What about the aliens?'

'There are two species Clarah. From what I can tell, they live in harmony with each other. If only Earth folks could learn a bit more tolerance, we might be as happy as they seem to be. They seem equally as gentle and as intelligent. They both live deep below the mountain. One type lives in the water. They have a body like ours, but their skin is transparent. They look a bit like jellyfish. They communicate by changing colour. They have colours that we have never even seen before, Clarah. Colours we can't even imagine...I mean how can anyone ever imagine a new colour anyway? I think they are the most beautiful beings that I have ever seen.'

'What about the other species.'

'They live above the water, but they do have a tendency to self-combust from time to time. Their inner souls are like a furnace, and so they live in cool dark places. I suppose that's to keep their temperature down. I am only guessing, but that's my theory anyway. Aside from that, not too different from humans. Smaller than us, white hair...which probably gets singed from time to time.'

Her grandmother then laughed at her own humorous quip.

'What about the magician – Soul. Where is he? Is he okay?'

'He rescued some of the fiery ones, and in doing so, his spirit was set alight. He is unconscious and lying somewhere inside the mountain. He is like you Clarah – an outlier separated from his body. An alien from the Ouroboros will take residence in his corpse to keep it alive...unless you can get to him first. However, Soul's spirit will perish if he stays here. I didn't know that spirits could expire, but it seems it can. Their energy can ebb and subside, like everything else in this fluctuating cosmos. His spirit cannot remain asleep forever. You need to return him to his body.'

'How do I do that?'

'If you think of him, you will find him. Just hold his hand, close your eyes, think of the equinox and imagine yourself to be wherever his body is on earth. Then let go of his hand. His spirit will naturally jump back into his body, like a turtle's neck moves back into its shell. It is an instinct.'

'What about the alien residing in his body? I mean, it's going to get mega pissed off with him gate-crashing back in.'

'Oh, don't you worry about that. ET won't mind sharing until it's time to phone home. It will all work out in the end. However, if you can use your time travelling skills to get back a bit sooner, who knows…maybe you can prevent the alien intruder from claiming squatters rights.'

Clarah looked back at her grandmother. Her face looked so serene. She seemed happy. She had a golden halo, which she wore around her head like a crown. Whatever…she looked like an angel.

'Grandmother – thank you for doing all of this for me. For looking after me for a lifetime, and continuing to watch over me in the afterlife.'

'Granddaughter – thank you for coming back to hold my hand whilst I gasped my last breath. I was frightened, and you made my passing easier.'

'Are you sure these tears aren't real? They sure feel wet to me. Will I ever get to see you again Baba May?'

'Yes, one-day child, but you are here to make sure that day is a long time in the future, and not any day soon. Now is not the time for sentiment. You are a strong arse-kicking Gypsy girl. You are my little feral kitten with a mind of your own. Now go do what you came here to do.'

With that, her Baba May seemed to dissipate into the darkness – particle by particle, dust by dust. The universe had swallowed her, and she it…

***

Soul lay huddled up on the cave floor like a foetus; naked and curled up into a ball. A jelly like substance had been thrown onto him, presumably to reduce the heat emanating from his core. He was completely bald; his long yellow mane having been scorched from the image of his human self. His spirit was charred and his energy levels so low, that he almost didn't exist.

A spirit is meant to have an eternal life force, but sometimes and on very rare occasions, it could be so badly damaged that even it could die. Souls life force was but a flickering candle and perilously close to extermination.

Clarah found him, exactly as her Baba May had said she would. What next? She squatted on the floor and touched his near-invisible frame. She immediately moved her hand away. The warmth of his spirit shocked her. It was far hotter than she had anticipated. He kept fading in and out of sight. She was sure that this wasn't a good sign.

She then heard a strangle splashing sound in the distance; almost like water but heavier. It made more of a plod-plod noise as something hit the surface of the shimmering pink lake. Glancing over to her left, she saw a mercury waterfall cascade its silvery contents into the lake. She would have liked to have spent longer looking at her bizarre surroundings, but she knew time was against her.

As she was about to take Soul's hand, she heard something talking to her. It wasn't talking with a voice, or even with some telepathic thought – it was communicating with feelings. It liked her, it was thanking her. She turned to see one of the transparent water beings rise out of the lake. She mumbled to herself, 'my God Baba May, you are right. This is the most beautiful creature in the universe.' Clarah was mesmerised. It wore flashing colours of a palette she had never seen before. Exquisite hues flowed through its veins like a piece of art. Silvers and golds illuminated the aliens beating hearts, of which she could count two …maybe even three. It had no facial features to speak of, yet she knew it was smiling. Conversation seemed to be conducted by both visual and emotional perception.

It was trying to communicate. She struggled to understand and again mumbled to herself, 'come on Clarah. If you can understand Welsh, you can understand jellyfish.'

She felt it laugh. In her mind she replied, 'bloody hell, you have a sense of humour. How can I not see your face or hear your voice, yet I can feel your laughter?'

The being stepped out of the water and came towards her. She understood. It was telling her how great she was. She had never been called great before, and so this compliment quite chuffed her. It told her that Soul must go back to earth, as he would rescue more of their kind. They had sisters, brothers, mother and fathers – all trapped within planet Earth. Because she was here to rescue him, indirectly she was also helping them. Her name would go down in history as the one that saved their civilisation. The being knew her name and asked her to confirm she was who it thought she was.

She stood proudly and replied, 'Yes - I am Clarah. Well, actually my full name is Clarah Jayne Lee …in case you need to reference me…for prosperity and all that.'

The alien being put a vision inside her head. She was told to seek out the woman who could stop the moon. She would find the answers she needed from such a person. The name she should call upon was Candace, the date was the 20th March 2034 and the time and place was the Sudan at the exact moment of the solar eclipse. She had been given her next mission, but not as expected.

The creature handed her a glowing crystal. It was solid and yet not, levitating a few inches above the alien's hand. She understood that this was to give her additional life force energy for her next journey. She said a silent, "thank you" to Aura. So her deva friend had listened.

Looking down at the fading frame of the magician, she asked why the energy had not been given to him instead. Surely, he needed it more than she did? Yet before she could mentally ask the question, she knew it had been offered to him and he had refused… saying it was for Clarah.

She then understood the compassionate nature of the man she knew to be Soul – a kindly man who had sacrificed his own life for others, and even in his crumbling desperate state, continued to put others first.

'Time to take you home,' she uttered, then kneeling down to touch his hand.

***

Clarah found herself in the strangest of rooms. It was white and clinical like a hospital, yet perfumed with roses. She was still knelt down, just as she had been on the yellow/brown planet.

Soul as his spirit self, was still unconscious on the floor.

She saw his lifeless body in the far corner of the room. He had virtually no colour in his cheeks and his lips were tinged with a deathly shade of blue. The room was full of people – strangers she had never met. They were yelling at each other. She could sense their panic.

Silenced alarms had not alerted anyone in the room to the flat, green line being pushed across the screen. A strange looking woman moved into action and tried her best to resuscitate Soul's body. Another woman attended to an unconscious woman lying motionless on a leather massage bed. She was shaking her and trying to wake her.

She called her name. Clarah heard her shout 'Eve' and then the woman suddenly sat bolt upright. She was quavering and appeared to be in shock. The room was in turmoil. Clarah was confused. She didn't know what was happening.

The woman they called Eve, got up from the massage table and slowly walked over to Soul's table. The strange looking thin woman was still pumping his heart and filling his lungs with her breath.

The woman called Eve said, 'it's too late - you can stop now. My brother isn't in there.'

Clarah whispered to herself, 'My God, so Eve must be Soul's sister. Poor thing, she looks torn in half.'

The thin woman stopped her CPR efforts and looked back upon Eve - a twisted, confused look etched upon her face. Eve was totally composed as she continued, 'Soul has been sucked up into the channel with the three aliens. Wherever their planet is – he is there right now. There was nothing I could do to stop him. He didn't want to leave one of them behind.'

As though the reality of the situation had suddenly sunk in, Eve collapsed on the floor. Her tired body was shaking with exhaustion. Her eyes wide open, staring into nothingness. Pupils dilated, eyelids motionless with disbelief. Time seemed to freeze.

Clarah tried to pull Soul off the floor so she could push him back towards his body. Baba May said it would happen naturally, like a turtle's neck popping back into its shell. So why was he so heavy. Clarah had never considered the notion that energy may have a weight. She then recalled a documentary about dark energy, and how it had puzzled scientist because it also seemed to have a weight. She cursed the weight of nothingness as she struggled to drag Soul's spirit across the floor, totally invisible to all around them. Except maybe Eve.

Was she a psychic or something? She was looking in their direction as though she couldn't actually see them but could sense they were there. Now was not the time for all these random chaotic thoughts. Soul's body didn't have a heart beat and she didn't have much time. Plan b – she would have to try and wake his spirit.

Before she had time to yell in his vanishing earlobe, a man walked into the room. He was a tall man, with an even bigger presence than height. She heard someone call him George and someone else addressed him as Mr Smith. What was he doing? He was leaning over Soul's body. Surely not? Was he going to leap into his body as her grandmother had predicted?

Clarah shouted out, 'no – you can't do that. We got here first.' Nobody heard her. This must be the alien Baba May told her about.

She instructed herself to be strong.

'Think strong and be strong.'

She was- it worked. She lifted Soul up and threw him towards his own carcass. It was an almighty throw.

'Where is that bloody turtle neck of yours Soul? Wake up. This was supposed to be instinctive and easy, but it doesn't crappin well feel that way.'

Disaster; Mr Smith did the same at the exact same time. She got a glimpse of him as he abandoned his own body, which immediately crumbled on the ground as a powdery skeleton. She recognised Mr Smith. He was one of them…one of the fiery aliens. He must have been one of those lost on Earth, and now he was inside Souls body alongside Soul.

'Cosy – real cosy,' she thought to herself.

She thought about her sister Nina and her alleged "dissociative identity disorder" and she pondered over the idea that maybe the same thing had happened to her twin. Perhaps these multiple personalities could be cosy spirits all crammed into the one person? It was a strange thought to have at such a time.

She caught her breath and then gasped. Everyone else in the room did the same thing. Soul was alive. The monitor was making zigzag lines across the screen. His heart was beating.

Clarah had done her job, although she conceded her timing could have been better.

'Just wait until they find out that there is two of them in there,' she uttered.

Eve approached her. Surely, she couldn't see her. Clarah knew she was invisible.

'You are right, I cannot see you,' said Eve, 'but I think I should thank you. I don't know who you are or how you did it, but thanks anyway.'

Clarah stirred directly into her eyes. Eve had stunning blue eyes, just like her brothers...but she was ill. The woman had cancer. Clarah could see it. Her Baba May told her that the eyes were a reflection of the soul, and if that was the case, Eve's eyes had lost all their sparkle.

With that thought, Clarah grew tired. The lethargy descended upon her like a sudden fog. She thought of her comfortable snug bed back in Whitby...and she was there.

CHAPTER 30

Monday 28th June 2016
MEETING CANDACE

Clarah woke up six days later. It was the day before she was due to die. Of course, she didn't know this at the time, but she had sensed that time was running out.

She took the biggest and longest yawn. Clarah had become accustomed to these long sleeps. The little sphere of energy she had been given by the alien jellyfish men, was hovering a few inches above her head. It provided sudden visual evidence of the fact that she hadn't been dreaming. This was for real. Clarah was actually jumping through time and space and it wasn't an hallucination or weird acid trip. She had entered the realm of the bizarre.

Finally, alone in a big house, all the ghosts had finally gone. She then wondered when Baba May's funeral would be. She presumed that Katalyn and Peter would be making all the arrangements. She also wondered how soon they would be moving in. All the other next of kin had died themselves, so who else was left? She hated the thought of sharing a house with Katalyn, but then again…it may not come to that.

As she opened the bedroom curtains, her questions were soon answered. She saw the "for sale" sign at the end of the driveway. Katalyn and Peter hadn't waited long. It was time to leave. There was nothing else and nobody else left here for Clarah.

She walked down the stairs and into the kitchen. Aura wasn't there. She was disappointed. On occasions, Aura could be a mischievous and manipulative little sprite, but in general she had a warm positive energy. Clarah enjoyed her company, and her cooking.

There was no cuckoo tea warming on the stove, no omelettes in the pan and no homemade bread baking in the oven. Sterile, cold, empty...Clarah hated this scrap of an existence.

How sweet, the sphere had followed her downstairs. For now, it was her only companion. She should give it a name. "Fred", that would be its name.

She thought about the rugged cliffs over Whitby, and she was there. She sat for a while in the long grass. She watched the seagulls as they ducked and dived through the waves, trying to catch fish. She then lay back and enjoyed the heat of the sun on her face. She listened to the calming clap of the surf on the rocks below, and inhaled the crisp salty air. Clarah had started to drift into a state of perfect tranquillity. It was too perfect. She recognised this feeling. She was becoming one with her surroundings. This was not good. This was a bad sign.

She thought of her body and she was there. She hadn't seen herself in a long time, and what she saw came as a tremendous shock. Her spiritual hair was long, dark and luscious, but her real hair on her real self, was peroxide yellow with black six-inch roots. She looked a mess...and she looked ill. She looked very ill. Her chest was bruised and there was a long line of stiches on her breast bone.

If she was going to do this...going to alter her fate, then she would have to do it quick. Time to say her goodbyes.

She hadn't wanted to see Denny again; after all he had betrayed her with her own sister. However, once upon a time he was one of the men who had held her heart in his hand. She should go to see him. It was a chapter that had to be closed…a final ending that was long overdue.

She saw him. Of course, he looked older, but he also looked happier. He was riding his tractor through some field on some hillside somewhere in Scarborough. He had bags of grain on the back of his vehicle, and she presumed he was off to feed his flock. She looked around at his small-holding. He had sheep and dogs and hens and Shire horses and…he had a wife – a lovely wife.

So, Denny finally got to live the dream. She hoped he would be faithful to his wife. Can a leopard change it spots? She wasn't sure. Of course, she knew he couldn't hear her, but maybe in a moment of quiet reflection, perhaps he would feel the emotions. Sadness, regret…a longing for what could have been, but never was. The jellyfish men had taught her how to talk with emotions instead of words. A mouth can tell lies, but the heart tells the truth.

Maybe he would hear the words one day.

Fred, the spherical orb had shrunk ever so slightly. She wished it had come with an instruction manual, but despite not knowing how it worked, she figured that she was depleting it of its energy with every journey she took. It would have been lovely to go back and visit all her family whilst they were still alive – her father Mick and mother Violet, Aunt Mary, Nina and Kane. Lovely yes, but possible no. Time was running out. She rang her mother's phone one last time. Of course, the line was dead. What had she expected? It was a silly thing to do.

***

The year is 2034.

Clarah was sat on a sand dune in the middle of the Sudanese desert. She looked out towards the pyramids of Meroë, completely transfixed by a gush of light shooting towards space. The beam was radiating from the centre of the pyramids and the lilac light was bathed in an exquisite golden glow. Pearls of pure energy seemed to be emitting their radiance from within the beam. It was an awesome sight.

She knew how to speak their language. She understood what was in the middle of the light. She felt their exhilaration at finally going home. The excitement, the relief, the laughter, the anticipation– it was intense.

It was in the midst of an eclipse, and the moon was still hanging over the sun…its orbit detained by some formidable force. The moon had stopped moving.

The silhouette of a female appeared. The feminine outline was totally engulfed in a radioactive-type glow. This was power. Magnificent raw power in its purest form.

A small crowd ran towards her, surrounding her and bombarding her with questions. Clarah sat quietly to one side, waiting for them to leave her be.

She recognised Soul, his sister Eve and his mother Roserie. She also thought she saw the gaggle of demons crouched behind a dune – Océane, Arabella, Tobiah and the one she later discovered to be Emmanuelle. Those long red talons on the ends of her fingers, still made her want to vomit. Memories of them stuck in her brother's skull, was an image she simply couldn't erase. That aside, all the other folk were just the faces of strangers.

Eventually the crowd fell silent. Clarah had overheard part of the conversation, especially the part about Candace being part demon, part angel, part human and part alien – in brief, the perfect eclectic mix.

The crowd were stunned. Nobody knew how to react. Eve looked at her watch and then at the moon.

'I hear what you are saying, dear niece; however, you have held the moon still for ten minutes and that could affect our calendar system or the tides or whatever. Any chance you could return it back to its orbit?'

'So,' thought Clarah, 'the young lady is Eve's niece, and that must make her Soul's daughter.' She smiled. She was pleased that Soul had a daughter.

The crowd stood back as heat started to emerge from Candace's body. A lime glow consumed her entire being. She raised both her hands towards the moon as though cradling it between her palms. It took less than a minute for the moon to continue along its path, casting a shadow upon the Earth as its journey continued.

Lunar experts, astrologers and other prominent scientists would debate this for many years to come. None would know the answer to this scientific conundrum aside from a select few. Yet under their noses, a young female with a perfect spiritual, racial and cosmic mix was gaining dominance.

Clarah wondered if she actually knew her own destiny, and if past, present and future had maybe all merged into one. The queen of an ancient Kushite kingdom had returned to the Garden of Eden. Princess Candace, wife of Moses, had returned yet few had even noticed.

Once the crowds had dispersed, Clarah approached Soul's daughter. She clapped loudly as her bare feet sunk into the dunes.

'Hi Candy, nice to meet you at long last. Well done on the moon thing.'

Candace looked through her, as though her eyes were an MRI scanner…thus examining every cell and organ in her body.

'You are of a similar age as me,' Candance stated. 'Yet you are older. How can that be? Have you have travelled from the past to meet me?'

Clarah smiled as she replied, 'of course I have Candace. I wouldn't have missed this spectacle for anything in the world, or the moon for that matter. That was impressive.'

Candace was divinely powerful and exceptionally gifted, even when compared to universal standards of phenomenal brilliance, but she was not alone. Clarah was also gifted, the only difference being that she wanted to shed her gift.

'So, you are a time traveller – interesting. Why have you come here?'

'I am not sure why I came here. I have travelled from 2016 to 2034 to see you. I was told I had some sort of message to deliver, but I don't think that is entirely true. A deva tricked me. They do things like that sometimes. I believe it is possible that I have come to ask for a favour.

Candace had already read her mind.

'Really? You really just want to be normal again? You are a time traveller and you want to give all of that up?'

'It is that or I die, and I choose life. Let's just say that I have left a body behind and right now it is in a coma. My body isn't looking too good.'

'Oh, I get it now. You are an outlier.'

Clarah sat back down on the dune, picked up a handful of sand and watched as it fell through her fingers.

'My time is running our Candace. Every action has a cause and an effect. Every action has a consequence. Sometimes even the most inconsequential routine event can change a person's entire destiny.'

Candace was beginning to understand.

'I see, so you want to undo whatever put you into a coma.'

'Yes, I do – but Huston, we have a problem.'

'What is your problem?'

'Many years ago, before you were born, your father was zapped up into one of those lilac lights and zoomed up to another planet. I was the one who rescued him and returned him into his body. It didn't go exactly to plan…'

'Shit – no it certainly didn't. Is that your fault. I mean, well done for rescuing him and all that, but I grew up with two fathers – George Smith the Ouroborous alien and my Dad Soul. It was worse for my mother, she had to sleep with 2 men. So, it was you – you who did that? What is your name?'

'Clarah, and for the record, George Smith was not my doing. The timing was just bad and he jumped into your father's body at the same time as I pushed Soul back. It was an accident. Hey…you could try thanking me. It was a tough assignment. Seems just like yesterday, and in my reality – it was.'

'I am sorry. Thank you Clarah. So, re the Huston problem…your point is?'

'My coma leads to my death. To prevent the chain of events that led to me going into the coma, I have to stop my family winning the lottery. Yes, I know it sounds trivial and stupid and its a long, long story, but just believe me. I either screw up the numbers or lose the ticket – but I just need to go back into my past and alter my future.'

'Sounds like an ideal solution Clarah, but I still don't see what your problem is.'

'If I don't go into a coma, I don't become an outlier and I don't get to travel through time and space and so I won't be able to rescue your father. You will grow up with George Smith, and if he went back home with the other...erm aliens, then right now your Dads body would be a skeleton lying on the sand. That is how I change your future Candace.'

'Holy crap – I haven't thought this through have I?'

'Also, I had to bring an ancient copper scroll back from biblical times, because some cult following had the wrong copy and so have been believing in all the wrong things...thus screwing up lots of people's lives over the centuries. So, it's not all about you Candace.'

'You have done some important work as an outlier Clarah. You should not undo any of this. It would be wrong of you to reverse this.'

'It also feels wrong of me to die. Look at me Candace. You are only a few years younger than me. Would you choose death?'

'I am sorry, can I do anything to help Clarah?'

Clarah didn't know what to say next. She looked around for clues. There was a reason she was told to come and visit Candace. She mumbled to herself, 'think, think Clarah. What is your reason?' She then caught sight of the moon as it hung in the sky, pale and distant against the blue of the daylight. She jumped to her feet as though she had found her eureka moment.

'I get it now. I understand Candace. Aura wanted me to come here, and please don't ask who she is. The thing is, if you can stop the moon in its orbit, then perhaps you can freeze frame just 2 moments of time, so that even if I do change my destiny, I don't unravel the important things I have achieved. I still need to rescue your father and I still need to deliver the scroll, but I want to be normal again. Can you undo my past, aside from these 2 events?'

Candace thought long and hard.

Eventually she concluded, 'well I am powerful, and I guess if I know the exact dates and times, I could freeze them. It would mean creating a mini causal loop. For these specific periods of time, you will exist as two people in different places. One of these will be the woman in a coma with her spirit wandering free as an outlier, and the other will be you – the normal humdrum person who doesn't have a clue that you ever existed at the same time somewhere else. It's a strange consistency paradox, I have read about such things.'

'Can it be done Candace?'

'It can be done, but care must be taken that these parallel existences never collide. The Clarah in the coma isn't going anywhere, so she is safe. However, the Clarah reinvented should never meet Clarah the outlier. I am not sure what the consequences of this would be. Have you ever had any experiences whereby you think that you have met yourself coming backwards?'

'No – I don't think so.'

'Well, we could give it a go. But it is a risk. I cannot guarantee that you won't end up in a coma again. For all I know, that is your fate and if it is, the same situations will keep happening again and again to put you back were you were meant to be. History may well repeat itself.'

'I am determined not to die Candace. I will go back and change my destiny. I know that sounds selfish, but I really don't do sacrifice. I am not like your father. He really is somebody very special, but I am not. I am selfish and as common as muck, and I like it that way.'

Candace knew that she had little choice in the matter. Clarah's mind was made up.

'Okay. Let's give it a go. I need you to tell me as many details as you can remember, and then let's get to work. I will see if I can isolate the specific time periods and hold them for the future, no matter how it changes. Follow me…this could be a long night.'

CHAPTER 31

Saturday July 12th 2014

BACK IN THE GYSPY CAMP – SCARBOROUGH 2014

The air had a toxic smoky flavour. Somebody had been burning damp logs and thrown both paraffin and plastics onto the offensive flames. The resulting alchemy covered Northway Road with a noxious cloud.

There was a commotion on the corner. Some travellers had pitched their vans on a rectangular strip of common land. It was a well-known beauty spot and some of the local folk were protesting. The police were on site. It had all gotten out of hand.

Eve walked quickly past the angry crowd; head lowered so as not to make eye contact. She hated confrontation.

Eve felt quite sorry for them. The Gypsies seemed to be doing no harm. They were simply using what the town's folk had made redundant. None the less, the clock was ticking and it wouldn't be long before someone accused them of breaching the peace. Freedom of the road was always a double-edged sword in the traveller world, and the police or bailiffs were only ever a heartbeat away.

It was a full blood moon. Eve was superstitious about such things. Tonight, was not a night for a woman with a heavy suitcase to be trundling the streets alone. She quickened her step.

She hoped she was in time for the 18.50 from Scarborough to Llandudno Junction. She glanced at her watch and sighed a breath of relief– she was in plenty of time; no need to panic. None the less, it was a long journey, so not something she was looking forward to.

Sitting quietly on platform 3, she couldn't help but notice a young woman. The girl was holding her head in her hands; fingers hiding her eyes as though trying to mask a tear stained face.

Eve was a gifted psychic. She didn't use her abilities professionally, and she tried not to use them personally or accidentally, but every so often her suppressed clairvoyance would ambush her. Right now, on platform 3... was such an occasion.

The girl seemed distraught. It wouldn't take a psychic to figure that one out. Her mascara was smudged, her hair looked a mess, and worse still...poor lass, her period had started and the girl hadn't even noticed. Eve felt mortified on her behalf. She should say something to her. She had some tampons in her handbag. She should offer her some.

Eve was not naturally a sociable person, but her desire to help overcame any feelings of shyness. She approached her cautiously.

'Hello, I am Eve.'

'Hello.'

The girl was cold and abrupt. She hadn't intended to make friends whilst contemplating her meaningless hollow life.

'Sorry,' said Eve, 'but I thought someone should tell you – woman to woman and all that.'

She discretely passed the girl a box of tampons.

'Shit,' the girl was deeply embarrassed. She jumped up and ran to the toilets. Eve ran after her. When she came out of the cubicle, Eve was waiting outside. She handed her a spare pair of her jeans.

'You look about the same size as me. I have packed too many clothes anyway, so please take these. I don't think you should carry on wearing those pants.'

The girl looked down at her blood-stained crotch and couldn't help but agree. After changing her trousers, she re-emerged from the cubicle.

'That really was very kind of you. I am sorry if I was so curt before. I have had a crap day. My name is Clarah by the way.'

Eve could read the girl like a book. Clarah didn't need to say a word. Eve could see all the jumbled suicidal thoughts racing around inside her head. Eve looked at her watch. It was 25 minutes before her train arrived. Surely, she could spare the girl a bit of time.

'Can I buy you a drink Clarah? You look like you could do with some company.'

The girl had the most striking green eyes, but they were eyes that were hiding some deeper sadness.

Clarah was a tinkers daughter and she didn't normally mix with the gaje, but this lady seemed nice. She followed her into the bar.

Eve was direct. 25 minutes to save a life wasn't a whole lot of time.

'You are running away, aren't you? I don't mean to be nosey Clarah, but I am a psychic and whether I like it or not, I can see this about you.'

Clarah shrugged, 'then lady, you are a very gifted psychic. My grandmother is the same. She can read the Tarot guards and see the future inside a crystal ball. She is a Romany. Such gifts are in our genes.'

'Wow, you are a Romany Gypsy. Fascinating. Are you with the people who have camped near to the park. I saw all the commotion on my way into the station. Is that why you are running away? No – of course it isn't. It's to do with that ring on your finger, isn't it?'

'You are good Eve. I will give you that, you are very good. Yes, it is to do with this ring. I was considering tossing it onto the train line. Either throwing it or throwing myself. Neither of us seem to have any value.'

'Is his name Dan or Dennis?'

'You are close. Hi name is Denny and he is a low life piece of scum. I was engaged to be married, but no more. I have had enough.'

Eve felt deeply sorry for the young woman. She could feel her pain.

'What did he do to you to make you want to run away?'

Clarah smiled. It was the first time Eve had seen her face lighten up. It was good to see.

'You are a gifted psychic Eve. You very nearly got his name right, so I am darned sure that you already know exactly what he has done.'

Eve did. She was being polite.

'He cheated on you.'

'Oh yes. I think he has cheated on me many times to be fair, but tonight I caught him red-handed…with my best friend. Shit, she was going to be my bridesmaid. I don't get it Eve. I don't understand men. We have been saving up for bloody ages and now he does this to me a couple of months before our wedding. He is a shite.'

Clarah removed the engagement ring from her left hand.

'Do me a favour Eve. Just chuck this somewhere for me, somewhere I can never find it. I don't want to be tempted into forgiving him. So that is why I have to get away.'

She pressed the ring into Eve's palm, refusing to take no for an answer. As Eve made contact with the ring, more images came into her mind.

'What's all this about numbers Clarah? Why have your family fallen out with you? Why does everyone keep talking about numbers?'

Clarah knocked back her bottle of Bud before replying.

'You must be talking about the numbers 4,5,7,11,13,15. They are the various birthdays of the folk in my family. My gran, I call her Baba May, always puts the same numbers on the lottery every week. Anyway, she had flu so she asked me to call at the post office and do it for her. I did as she asked. I even bought myself a ticket. I know those bloody numbers off by heart. I don't know what happened. I put down the wrong numbers. How could I have made such a stupid mistake? I don't understand.'

'Don't tell me,' replied Eve, 'your Baba May's numbers won. Am I right?'

Clarah just nodded her head to indicate a yes. A single tear fell to the floor.

Nobody will let me forget. Everybody has ganged up on me. They all keep reminding me how much the money would have changed our lives for the better. My Aunt Mary has bad arthritis and living in a damp caravan is making her ill. They keep saying how they could have bought a nice warm house where she could be kept warm. My twin sister has brain problems, and that's supposed to be all my fault as well. She was a breach and I pushed her out of the way to be born first. She went short on Oxygen and it seems I am to blame. The win would have been millions Eve, and I mean many millions. Nina would have gotton proper medical treatment…maybe even private treatment. But now she is screwed and I am to blame. Everybody hates me.'

'Where are you going to go to? I assume you are going to catch a train to somewhere or the other.'

Clarah pulled £75 out of her pocket. It was the grubbiest pile of notes that Eve had ever seen.

'I will go to wherever this money will buy me a ticket to.'

'How will you eat.'

'I will beg, borrow or steal. I can always catch a rabbit. To our kind, the hedgerows are like a supermarket shelf. It's tasteless, but it fills a gap.'

Eve looked closely at the girl. She recognised her desperation. Eve's train was due in the station anytime soon, but how could she leave the young woman alone in such a terrible state. She feared for the girl's life.

'Come with me, 'Eve asked.

'What?'

'You heard me, come with me. It's okay, I will buy you a ticket.'

'Is your husband rich?'

'Well, he isn't that rich, but he is a doctor so he is a caring chap.'

'Erm, well…okay. Seems I have limited options. You are a very kind woman Eve. Where are you going?'

'North Wales. It's a long journey Clarah and we won't get there until late. Are you okay with that?'

'Where will I sleep? Do you have enough rooms?'

Eve laughed.

'We will be staying at a hotel Clarah. My mother is a nanny. She looks after the owner's children. It's a very big place. You will love it. There are plenty of rooms to choose from. It is a bit in the middle of nowhere, but maybe that's just the kind of breathing space you need. It will give you time to think about your future.'

'What is this place called?'

'Darwydden.'

'That sounds very Welsh. I can't speak Welsh.'

'Neither do I Clarah, but it's okay, they all speak English as well.'

'How will I pay for my keep? I don't want anyone to resent me.'

'I happen to know they are looking for a receptionist. Do you think that is a job you can do? You are well spoken and a very pretty girl. I bet you scrub up well.'

Clarah felt an enormous sense of relief. It seemed that destiny had come to her rescue and given her another chance, perhaps another shot at normality and happiness.

'I don't know how to thank you Eve. Are you sure it will be okay?'

'I am sure it will be fine.'

'Okay,' replied Clarah.

'As long as I can get my hair cut short. I don't want to look like a Gypsy any more. I need to move on and leave my old life behind.'

Eve stroked the girl's hair.

'Well, it's a shame as you have the most beautiful luscious long locks, but if getting your hair cut makes you feel better, then just leave it with me. I will get it sorted. I think that a short pixie style and a splash of auburn would suit you. Does that sound like a plan?'

With that, she touched the girls cold hand to comfort her.

CHAPTER 32

Tuesday 16th February 2016
THE NEW BEGINNING

19 months had passed and Clarah had changed beyond all description. She now wore a sharp auburn bob, had lost two stone in weight, and was now a much-loved member of staff at Darwydden Castle Manor Hotel.

As the life and soul of every social occasion, the local Welsh boys adored her, and more to the point – so did Dylan. She was certainly never short of admirers.

Denny was but a distant memory and she never did ask Eve for her engagement ring back. To this day, she still didn't know if Eve had kept it or not. The woman who had rescued her was an infrequent visitor to the hotel, and Clarah was happy not to see Eve too often. It wasn't that she wasn't grateful, just that she wanted no reminders of her old life.

As for her family; she made the occasional phone call on various anniversaries, but nothing more than that. They didn't know where she lived and she had no idea what piece of scrub land they were camped on. They struggled to forgive her for the numerical errors on a lottery card, totally oblivious to the fact that the correct numbers would have cost them their lives. Slowly and over a period of time, all contact with her past life was lost. It was for the best.

The folks at Darwydden had taken her under their wings. They were her new family now. People even thought that she was the sister of the proprietor 'Ruby Kyfinn'. They did look similar, and Clarah was pleased that folks thought Ruby was her elder sibling. She was a more caring sister than Katalyn could ever be, so the sibling exchange was openly welcomed.

***

A young American boy walked into the hotel reception. She hadn't noticed him as first, as the huge vase of valentine roses Dylan had sent her seemed to block all views of incoming guests.

Clarah had been told to expect Ruby's nephew, and had been pre-warned that he was a tall, tanned, blonde hunk. She thought that Ruby had been exaggerating about her young relative, so was pleasantly surprised to find he was exactly as promised.

The boy seemed lost in some sort of nostalgic mental wanderings of his youth, when his thoughts were suddenly disturbed by the voice of the young receptionist.

'Hello, I am Clarah. Can I help you sir? Have you a reservation?'

Of course, she knew exactly who he was, but was desperately trying to play it cool.

Konnor had almost forgotten that what was once a family home, was now a business. A business with guests, and bookings and profit to be made. The grand hallway now housed computers, an ATM and credit card machines. His aunt and uncles home was a commercial entity – yes of course it was. He turned to look at the receptionist. The young woman quite took his breath away. She was very attractive and he immediately became overwhelmed with guilt. Had he not just professed his love for his girlfriend back home in LA?

'I am Konnor Baratolli,' he announced. 'I am Mrs Kyfinn,s nephew. Is she around? If not, maybe my uncle Owyn is available?'

Clarah blushed. She knew to expect a young American male, but she didn't expect him to be this attractive. She felt her pale skin redden as that thought played havoc with her hormones. Indeed, Konnor was not the sort of lad that frequented the local area. His tanned skin; obviously acquired from a youth spent on a surf board, along with his bleached blond curls, were not atypical of the North Wales gene pool. She tried not to show her obvious attraction to him as she replied, 'no worries, please take a seat and I will locate Mrs Kyfinn.'

She approached him with a tray of various drinks.

'Can I offer you something whilst you wait?'

Konnor availed himself of a cognac. He then sat down by the log fire whilst he awaited his step-mom's sister.

Clarah cast him an embarrassed sideward' s glance. For sure, there was a chemistry. It confused her. She had just become engaged to Dylan. Dylan was dark, tattooed, gothic, exciting, forbidden, mysterious and to top it all off, he even had the title of a Druid prince.

Ruby's American nephew was a college student studying law in UCLA, and he even wore a cardigan. He had the appearance of a surfer dude, with whiter than white teeth and a deep tan that could only be attained by years spent on a beach. With clear blue eyes and kiddie freckles, he was a boy…whereas Dylan was all man.

Yet, her reaction to the young visitor was unexpected and not something she really cared to explore. They both had a sense of dejevu. Had they met somewhere before? It was unlikely, but there was certainly some sort of connection.

Konnor became tellingly cold and dismissive of the receptionist…more so than was in his usual friendly nature. Significantly more so. It was a deliberate avoidance technique - the downward casting of eyes that didn't want to behold a beauty within their vision. Eyes that dare not look for fear of what they would see. Eyes averting temptation.

His uncomfortable shuffling around on his seat and pretence of interest in a Welsh farming magazine was most welcomingly relieved by a collective of voices shouting his name.

The high-pitched squeal of his grandmother Ella and the raspy smokers voice of his grandfather Chris, was soon followed by an intense double hug. Following a multitude of questions and kisses and yet more hugs- his grandparents moved their young handsome grandson away from the public reception area and into the family quarters. As Konnor passed into the grand hallway he dared to take one last look at the striking young receptionist.

It was then that he caught his own reflection in an oversized mirror; a wall decoration that would not let anyone escape or pass by its often-cruel vision of reality. It most certainly captured the look on Konnor's face and replayed it back to him as it saw him to be. It caught the wanton look of lust.

At that moment, he felt like a cheat and more than anything he did not want to be a cheat. He had a girlfriend back in LA, and he was not the kind of guy to mistreat a lady. The very thought was pushed from his mind as he was guided into the arms of his Aunt Ruby. Before long he was overwhelmed by his step-mother's relatives, all of whom were all delighted by his visit.

After half an hour or so, his Aunt Ruby noticed he was visibly wilting in front of her eyes, so took Konnor up to his room. She didn't ask too many questions. Her nephew was tired – he needed his rest. His eyes were heavy, and yet his mind raced as the beautiful green-eyed receptionist invaded his mind. Wild and untamed like the North Sea, she was haunting his heart like some ghost from an unknown past.

"Clarah" – he couldn't get her name out of his head….

***

Clarah remained totally unaware of her former life.

It had been an alternative existence, changed by amending six numbers on a piece of paper. She had undone what the universe deemed could not be undone. She had broken rules, pushed boundaries and swam well outside of the shipping lane. She had been an outlier.

The new Clarah remained completely ignorant of her former achievements; a triumph of not just making our world a better place, but also saving beings from other worlds beyond. She was now enjoying life as a hotel receptionist in the Welsh valleys, and that life was good. It was simple and uncomplicated. She would never know the truth, and it was better that way. The truth was far too bizarre to even contemplate.

Roserie kept a watchful eye on her, but Clarah only knew her as a nanny. They were work colleagues, and nothing more.

Yet there was another life she also didn't know about.

The two knights that chased each other across the valley in a jealous tryst, were also the shadows of her former lovers. Maybe they were Denny or Konnor or Dylan or even Gareth…the nervous barman from the local pub.

A woman like Clarah would always capture hearts and souls, and so even with the passage of time through history, many a medieval knight would fight for her affection.

Yet her ultimate fate could not be avoided, even though she had made different decisions. A simple act of changing numbers on a lottery draw may have changed some things, but it couldn't change everything. Sometimes the destination is fated, even though the journey one takes to get there can vary.

Candace had given Clarah no guarantee's and made no promises. She had warned Clarah about the causal loop...the pre-destination paradox that screws up the fabric of time travel. It is a strange mythical phenomenon, whereby the future dictates the past, rather than the other way around.

Candace had also warned her that some bullets could not be dodged. She had explained that if something is fated to be, then no matter what one does to elude it...it will pull at your coat tails until it makes itself happen.

It is possible that even if Eve hadn't have brought Clarah to Wales, that something else would have occurred to take Clarah to America. For whatever reason, she had to meet and fall in love with Konnor Baratolli. It was a fateful meeting, and one beset with tragedy.

Would history repeat itself?

Would modern day knights chase each other across the valley in a jealous tryst? Would a 21st century fair lady be thrown from her horse yet again? Time would tell it story when the time was right.

Llandudno News 2nd July 2016

A double fatality occurred outside the internationally renowned Darywyyden Castle Manor Hotel on the night of Tuesday 29th June, as three motorbikes collided on the corner of Lower Castle Lane. A third person has been described as being critical.

Konnor Baratolli, son of the famous New York musician and music producer Reed Baratolli, died at the scene. Dylan Neville was rushed to Glan Clwyd hospital by air ambulance, but was pronounced dead on arrival.

Clarah Lee, (who worked as a receptionist at the hotel), remains in a critical condition. The hospital spokesperson confirmed that she is in a coma and has life- threatening injuries.

It has been reported that an argument broke out at a party, and Miss Lee went in pursuit of the men in order to calm the situation. Witnesses at the scene say that Miss Lee's vehicle hit a pothole, causing her to be thrown from her motorbike and causing her vehicle to then crash into the other two vehicles.

The police have requested that Miss Lee's next of kin get in touch. It is understood that they are from the Yorkshire area and are part of the Gypsy travelling community. If anyone has any information as regards the whereabouts of Miss Lee's family, please call North Wales Police using the 101 line.

***

Living the life she lived before, the 29th June 2016 would have been the date of Clarah's death. Living a different life, she escaped that fate…but only for the moment. Clarah Lee was back in a coma. Unfortunately she lost the twins she had been expecting. Clarah was 9 weeks pregnant at the time of the accident.

None of her family came forward, despite national public appeals. They never did forgive her for betting on the wrong numbers. So one way or another, it seems that Clarah was always fated to lose her family. Destination the same – just a different path.

It was a risk Clarah had been willing to take. The original copper scroll remained safe in the hands of the Ledonites, who now preach the true meaning of the prophesy as Tamar intended.

Soul the magician remains rescued, although for many years to come he did share his body with an alien visitor known as George. An interesting story to tell at a dinner party…

As for Clarah, she would have done anything to get off the brown mountain, but now she was back on it, walking around and around in circles until…who knows what, who knows when and who knows where. She remains an outlier.

In the words of Albert Einstein – 'Everything is determined, the beginning as well as the end, by forces over which we have no control. It is determined for the insect, as well as for the star. Human beings, vegetables, or cosmic dust, we all dance to a mysterious tune, intoned in the distance by an invisible piper.'

The End

Are you going to Scarborough fair? Parsley, Sage, Rosemary and Thyme. Remember me to one who lives there.
For he once was a true love of mine.

Other quotes to ponder …

- "It is not in the stars to hold our destiny but in ourselves." - *William Shakespeare*

- "There's nowhere you can be that isn't where you're meant to be..." - *John Lennon*

- "Destiny is not a matter of chance; it is a matter of choice. It is not a thing to be waited for, it is a thing to be achieved." - *William Jennings Bryan*

- "Does the walker choose the path, or the path the walker?" - *Garth Nix, Sabriel*

- "I am the sum total of everything that went before me, of all I have been seen done, of everything done-to-me. I am everyone everything whose being-in-the-world affected was affected by mine. I am anything that happens after I'm gone which would not have happened if I had not come." - *Salman Rushdie*

- I feel like I've dreamed half of my life that hasn't happened yet, so a lot of times I'm going along, and I do stuff, and I know that I've done it. I have deja vus more than I have regular experiences. If half of your day is a deja vu, then you start to wonder, 'What is real and what isn't?' - *Marilyn Manson*

ABOUT THE AUTHOR

I was born in the Lancashire mining town of Leigh, back in the days of black & white TV and when children played out, climbed trees, scuffed their knees and made dens. Enid Blyton was my heroine, and I have often aspired to write an adult version of "the secret seven". Some of us never really grow up…

My father died when I was a baby, and so as a child I was raised by my Grandmother Florrie Gibbons. She lived in Howe Bridge near Atherton and was a loving intelligent lady. She was also an avid reader, who went through about 5 books a week. Every night she read to me, and so by the time I started school at 4 years old, I could already read and write. It didn't give me any advantages over the other kids at Pennington school, but none the less, I thank her. With her encouragement, I have been writing books from about the age of 6. These were for my own entertainment and not for public consumption.

It has taken me a long time, *(and life has a way of creating other priorities to distract us), but* eventually I decided I should publish.

With a love of history, mythology, theology, genealogy, the paranormal, gothic mansions and anything that involves secret tunnels – I was destined to be a science fiction writer. I like to add authenticity to my books, by using well researched chronicles, and then scattering a thimble full of fairy dust to magic the facts into a story.

I hope you enjoyed CLARAH – book 3 of the Tamar prophesy series.

Thank you

Please don't forget to leave a review if you like what you have read – your appraisal means everything.

www.ingramcontent.com/pod-product-compliance
Lightning Source LLC
Chambersburg PA
CBHW071002280626
47160CB00014B/11